Praise for *The Human Body*

"*The Human Body* is a great novel of life in wartime: A chronicle of war's multifarious crimes against the body and soul, and a heartfelt meditation on how men, together and collectively, repair the burdens of their fate." —Joshua Ferris, author of *To Rise Again at a Decent Hour*

"Paolo Giordano's new novel, like his last, is full of sensitivity and intelligence. *The Human Body* is a brilliant addition to the literature of our modern wars."   —Kevin Powers, author of *The Yellow Birds*

"With an extraordinarily keen eye and a pitch-perfect ear, Giordano has magnificently captured the surreal existence of the modern soldier. By turns poignant and gripping—when not downright hilarious—every page of *The Human Body* rings with an authenticity and appreciation of the absurd that very few novelists writing about men stumbling about the business of war have achieved. Very few indeed; think of O'Brien's *Going After Cacciato* or Heller's *Catch-22*, because Giordano is just that good."   —Scott Anderson, author of *Lawrence in Arabia*

"Paolo Giordano has written his generation's war novel. Tender, cruel, beautiful, heartless, a brilliant story of desire and youth and death in Afghanistan. Readers of Kevin Powers have been searching for another modern classic, and *The Human Body* is it."
—Andrew Sean Greer, author of *The Impossible Lives of Greta Wells*

"Giordano follows *The Solitude of Prime Numbers* with a stunning exploration of war. Giordano makes the tedium of combat fascinating with his well-drawn characters . . . and the beauty, texture, and acuity with which he captures the day-to-day routines of the soldiers and their efforts to make sense of their lives." —*Publishers Weekly* (starred review)

PENGUIN BOOKS

THE HUMAN BODY

Paolo Giordano is the author of the critically acclaimed international bestseller *The Solitude of Prime Numbers*, which has been translated into more than forty languages and praised by the *New York Times* as "mesmerizing . . . An exquisite rendering of what one might call feelings at the subatomic level." His third novel, *Like Family,* is being published by Pamela Dorman Books/Viking. Giordano has a PhD in particle physics and is now a full-time writer.

THE
HUMAN
BODY

Paolo Giordano

English Translation by
Anne Milano Appel

PENGUIN BOOKS

PENGUIN BOOKS
An imprint of Penguin Random House LLC
375 Hudson Street
New York, New York 10014
penguin.com

First published in the United States of America by Viking Penguin,
a member of Penguin Group (USA) LLC, 2014
Published in Penguin Books 2015

A Pamela Dorman / Penguin Book

Originally published in Italian as *Il corpo umano* by Arnoldo Mondadori Editore S.p.A., Milano.

THE LIBRARY OF CONGRESS HAS CATALOGED THE HARDCOVER EDITION AS FOLLOWS:
Giordano, Paolo, 1982–
[Corpo umano. English]
The human body / Paolo Giordano ; English translation by Anne Milano Appel.
pages cm
ISBN 978-0-670-01564-1 (hc.)
ISBN 978-0-14-312773-4 (pbk.)
1. Afghan War, 2001—Fiction. 2. Soldiers—Fiction. 3. Italians—Afghanistan—Fiction.
4. War stories. I. Appel, Anne Milano, translator. II. Title.
PQ4907.I57C6713 2014
853'.92—dc 3   2014006927

Printed in the United States of America
1 3 5 7 9 10 8 6 4 2

To the tumultuous years at La Cascina

And even if these scenes from
our youth were given back to us
we would hardly know what to do.

—Erich Maria Remarque, *All Quiet on the Western Front*
A. W. Wheen, translator

Cast of Characters

EGITTO FAMILY

Lieutenant Alessandro Egitto, an orthopedic specialist assigned to
    the Alpine brigade
Marianna Egitto, his older sister
Ernesto Egitto, his father
Nini, his mother

OFFICERS OF THE SEVENTH ALPINE REGIMENT STATIONED
IN BELLUNO

Colonel Giacomo Ballesio
Captain Filippo Masiero

THIRD PLATOON OF THE SIXTY-SIXTH COMPANY OF THE SEVENTH
ALPINE REGIMENT (CHARLIE COMPANY)

Marshal Antonio René
Senior Corporal Major Francesco Cederna
Senior Corporal Major Salvatore Camporesi
Senior Corporal Major Arturo Simoncelli
Senior Corporal Major Michele Pecone
First Corporal Major Cesare Mattioli
First Corporal Major Angelo Torsu
Corporal Major Roberto Ietri
Corporal Major Giulia Zampieri, the only female in the platoon

Corporal Major Vincenzo Mitrano
Corporal Major Enrico Di Salvo
Corporal Major Passalacqua
Corporal Major Michelozzi
Corporal Major Rovere

DARI-ENGLISH INTERPRETER AT THE FOB

Abib

OTHER CHARACTERS

Irene Sammartino, Egitto's former girlfriend
Rosanna Vitale, one of René's clients
Flavia Magnasco, Salvatore Camporesi's wife
Gabriele Camporesi, Salvatore and Flavia's 4-year-old son
Agnese, Cederna's girlfriend
Tersicore89, Torsu's girlfriend
Dorothy Byrne, Marianna's piano teacher
Roberto Ietri's mother
Oxana, the masseuse at the base in Delaram
Colonel Matteo Caracciolo, commander of the Alpine brigade
Lieutenant Commander Finizio, military psychologist

Contents

The

Human

Body

Prologue

In the years following the mission, each of the guys set out to make his life unrecognizable, until the memories of that other life, that earlier existence, were bathed in a false, artificial light and they themselves became convinced that none of what took place had actually happened, or at least not to them.

Lieutenant Egitto, like the others, has done his best to forget. He moved to another city, transferred to a new regiment, changed his beard length and his eating habits, redefined some old personal conflicts, and learned to ignore others that didn't concern him—a difference he had by no means been aware of before. He's not sure whether the transformation is following some plan or is the result of an unsystematic process, nor does he care. The main thing for him, from the beginning, has been to dig a trench between past and present: a safe haven that not even memory would be able to breach.

And yet, missing from the list of things he's managed to rid himself of is the one thing that most vividly takes him back to the days spent in the valley: thirteen months after the conclusion of the mission, Egitto is still wearing his officer's uniform. The two embroidered stars are displayed at the center of his chest, in precise correspondence to the heart. Several times the lieutenant has toyed with the idea of retreating to the ranks of civilians, but the military uniform has adhered to every inch of his body, sweat has discolored the fabric's pattern and tinted the skin beneath. He's sure that if he were to take it off now, the epidermis would peel away as well and he, who feels uncomfortable even when simply naked, would find himself more exposed than he could stand. Besides, what good would it do? A soldier will never cease being a soldier. At age thirty-one, the lieutenant has given in and accepted the uniform as an unavoidable accident, a chronic disease of fate, conspicuous but not painful. The most significant contradiction of his life has finally been transformed into the sole element of continuity.

It's a clear morning in early April; the rounded leather boot tops of the soldiers marching in review gleam with every step. Egitto isn't yet accustomed to the clarity, full of promise, that Belluno's sky flaunts on days like this. The wind that rolls down from the Alps carries with it the arctic cold of glaciers, but when it subsides and stops whipping the banners around, you realize that it's unusually warm for that time of year. In the barracks there was a big debate about whether or not to wear their scarves and in the end it was decided not to; the word was shouted out from corridor to corridor and from one floor to another. The civilians, however, are undecided about what to do with their jackets, whether to wear them over their shoulders or carry them over their arms.

Egitto lifts his hat and runs his fingers through his damp, sweaty hair. Colonel Ballesio, standing to his left, turns to him and says, "That's disgusting, Lieutenant! Dust off your jacket. It's full of those flakes again." Then, as if Egitto weren't capable of doing it himself, the colonel brushes off his back with his hand. "What a mess," he mutters.

There's a break. Those, like Egitto and Ballesio, who have a seat in the stands, can sit down. Egitto can finally roll down his socks at the ankles. The itching subsides, but only for a few seconds.

"Listen to this," Ballesio starts off. "The other day my little daughter started marching around the living room. 'Look, Daddy,' she said, 'look at me, I'm a colonel too.' She'd dressed up in her school smock and a beret. Well, you know what I did?"

"No, sir. What?"

"I gave her a good spanking. I'm not kidding. Then I yelled at her and said I never wanted to see her mimicking a soldier again. And that no one would enlist her anyway because of her flat feet. She started to cry, the poor thing. I couldn't even explain to her why I got so angry. But I was beside myself, believe me. Tell the truth, Lieutenant: in your opinion, am I a bit burned-out?"

Egitto has learned to be wary of the colonel's requests to be frank. He replies: "Maybe you were just trying to protect her."

Ballesio makes a face, as if Egitto has said something stupid. "Could be. So much the better. These days I'm afraid I may not be all there, if you know what I mean." He stretches his legs, then unashamedly adjusts the waistband of his undershorts through his pants. "You hear about those guys who overnight end up with their brains fucked up. Do you think I should get one of those neurological checkups, Lieutenant? Like an EKG or something?"

"I don't see any reason to, sir."

"Maybe you could check me over. Examine my pupils and so on."

"I'm an orthopedist, Colonel."

"But still, they must have taught you something!"

"I can suggest the name of a colleague, if you'd like."

Ballesio grunts. He has two deep grooves around his lips that inscribe his face like the snout of a fish. When Egitto first met him he wasn't so worn-out.

"Your fastidiousness is catching, Lieutenant, did I ever tell you? That must be why you're in the state you're in. Just relax for once, take things as they come. Or find a hobby. Have you ever thought about having kids?"

"Excuse me?"

"Kids, Lieutenant. *Kids.*"

"No, sir."

"Well, I don't know what you're waiting for. A kid would cleanse your head of certain thoughts. I see you, you know? Always there brooding. Just look how ready and willing these troops are, such eager beavers!"

Egitto follows Ballesio's line of sight, to the military band and beyond, where the lawn begins. A man standing in the crowd catches his attention. He's carrying a child on his shoulders and standing stiffly, chest out, in a strangely military posture. A familiar face always makes itself known to the lieutenant through a vague fear, and all of a sudden Egitto feels uneasy. When the man raises a fist to his mouth to cough, he recognizes Marshal René. "That guy over there, isn't he . . . ?" He stops.

"Who? What?" the colonel says.

"Nothing. Sorry."

Antonio René. On the last day, at the airport, they took their leave with a formal handshake and since then Egitto hasn't thought of him, at least not specifically. His memories of the mission mostly assume a collective quality.

He loses interest in the parade and applies himself to observing the marshal from afar. René hasn't made his way deep enough through the crowd to reach the front rows; most likely there's not much to see from where he is. From where he sits on his father's shoulders, the child points to the soldiers, the banners, the men with the instruments, clutching René's hair like reins. The hair, that's what's changed. In the valley the marshal's head was closely shaven; now his brown, slightly wavy hair nearly covers his ears. René is another fugitive from his past. He too has altered his looks so he won't recognize himself.

Ballesio is saying something about a tachycardia that he surely doesn't have. Egitto replies absently, "Stop by to see me in the afternoon. I'll prescribe something for the anxiety."

"Are you completely out of your mind? That stuff makes your cock limp!"

Three unarmed fighter-bombers whiz by, low, over the parade ground, then soar sharply, leaving colorful streaks in the sky. They turn onto their backs and cross paths. The child on René's shoulders is awestruck. Like his, hundreds of heads turn upward, all except those of the soldiers in formation, who go on staring firmly at something that only they can see.

At the end of the ceremony Egitto makes his way back through the crowd. Families linger in the square and he has to sidestep them. He gives a perfunctory handshake to those who try to stop him, and he keeps an eye on the marshal. For a moment Egitto thought he was about to turn and leave, but he's still there. Egitto joins him and takes off his hat once he's standing in front of him. "René," he says.

"Hello, Doc."

The marshal sets the child down on the ground. A woman comes up and takes him by the hand. Egitto nods at her, but she doesn't nod back; she tightens her lips and backs away. René nervously rummages in his jacket pocket, pulls out a pack of cigarettes and lights one. That's one thing that hasn't changed: he still smokes the same slender white cigarettes, a woman's cigarettes.

"How are you, Marshal?"

"Good, good," René responds quickly. Then he repeats it, but with less confidence: "Good. Trying to scrape along."

"That's right. We have to carry on."

"And you, Doc?"

Egitto smiles. "Me too, getting by."

"So they didn't give you too much trouble over that incident?" It's as if pronouncing those words costs him a great deal of effort. He doesn't seem to care much about the answer, in fact.

"A disciplinary action. Four months' suspension from the service and some inconclusive hearings. Those were the real punishment. You know how that goes."

"Good for you."

"Good for me, right. You decided to quit instead."

He could have said it differently, used another word instead of *quit*: change jobs, resign. *Quit* meant giving up. René doesn't seem to be bothered, though.

"I work in a restaurant. Down in Oderzo. I'm the maître d'."

"Still in command, then."

René sighs. "In command. Right."

"And the other guys?"

René's foot scrapes at a tuft of grass in a crack in the pavement. "I haven't seen them in a while."

The woman is now gripping his arm, as if wanting to drag him away, rescue him from Egitto's uniform and the memories they have in common. She shoots quick, resentful glances at the lieutenant. René, however, avoids looking at him, though for an instant his eyes focus on the quivering black plume attached to his hat and Egitto seems to glimpse a trace of nostalgia in him.

A cloud covers the sun and the light suddenly grows dim. The lieutenant and the ex-marshal fall silent. They shared the most important moment of their lives, the two of them, standing as they are now, but in the middle of a desert and a circle of armored tanks. Can it be they have nothing left to say to each other?

"Let's go home," the woman whispers in René's ear.

"Of course. I don't want to keep you. Good luck, Marshal."

The child holds out his arms to René, asking to be put back on his shoulders. He's whimpering, but it's as if his father doesn't see him.

"You can come and find me at the restaurant," he says. "It's a good place. Fairly good."

"Only if you give me special treatment."

"It's a good place," René repeats absently.

"I'll be sure to come," Egitto pledges. But it's clear to both of them that it's one of those countless promises that are never kept.

Part One

EXPERIENCES

IN THE DESERT

Three Promises

First came the talks. A series of preparatory lectures by Captain Masiero: thirty-six hours of groundwork in which the troops received a smattering of Middle Eastern history and technical briefings on the strategic complexities of the conflict, during which western Afghanistan's endless expanses of marijuana were also talked about, with no avoiding the obvious jokes. Or the stories of soldiers who had already served in the area and now, with a certain condescension, were quick to dispense advice to those about to set off.

Head down on the incline bench where he has just completed a fourth set of crunches, Corporal Major Roberto Ietri listens with growing interest to the conversation between two veterans. They're talking about a certain Marica stationed at the base in Herat. He finally gives in to his curiosity and interrupts: "Are there really a lot of girls there?"

The guys exchange a look of tacit complicity; they'd been waiting for that. "As many as you want, buddy," says one. "And they're not the kind we're used to here."

"That's for sure. Over there they don't give a shit."

"They're far from home and so bored they're willing to do anything."

"Anything—believe me."

"There's no goddamn summer camp where you fuck as much as on a mission."

"And then there are the Americans."

"Oooh, the Americans!"

They start telling him about a colonel's secretary who brought three NCOs into her tent and threw them out at dawn, worn to a frazzle. "No, not us—I wish! Some guys from another company, but everyone at the base knew about it."

Ietri's eyes dart from one to the other, while the blood flows from his feet to his head, making him dizzy. When he leaves the gym, in the velvety air of a summer evening, his mind is full of wild fantasies.

It was Ietri himself, in all probability, who started certain rumors among the guys in the Third Platoon, rumors that filter back to him after making a lengthy circuit, and that he ends up believing with greater certainty than anyone. Mingled with a mild fear of death is a longing for adventure that gains the upper hand. Ietri fantasizes about the women he'll encounter in Afghanistan, the naughty smiles during morning muster, the exotic way they'll pronounce his name.

Even during Captain Masiero's lectures all he does is undress and dress them, over and over again.

"Corporal Ietri!"

In his head he calls them all Jennifer and has no idea where that name came from. *Jennifer, oooh Jennifer* . . .

"Corporal Ietri!"

"Sir!"

"Would you be so kind as to repeat what I've been saying?"

"Of course, Captain. You were talking about . . . the tribes . . . I think."

"Do you perhaps mean the ethnic groups?"

"Yes, sir."

"And which ethnic group was I talking about, exactly?"

"I think the . . . I don't know, sir."

"Corporal, leave this classroom immediately."

The embarrassing truth is that Ietri has never been with a woman, not in the sense that he considers *complete*. No one in the platoon knows this and it would be a disaster if they were to find out. The only one who knows is Cederna; he told him about it himself one evening at the pub when they were both smashed and in the mood for confiding.

"Complete? You mean to say you've never fucked?"

"Well, not . . . fully."

"A goddamn little virgin! Hey, I have a new name for you: *verginella*. Do you like that? That's what I'm gonna call you from now on."

"Don't shout!"

"You're in bad shape, buddy. Really bad. Shit!"

"I know."

"How old are you?"

"Twenty."

"Damn. So you've already wasted the best years. Listen up now— it's important. The tool down there is like a rifle. A 5.56, with a metal stock and laser sighting." Cederna shoulders an invisible weapon and aims it at his friend. "If you don't remember to oil the barrel from time to time, it will end up jamming."

Ietri looks down at his mug of beer. He takes too big a swig, begins to cough. Jammed. He's a guy who's jammed.

"Even Mitrano manages to shoot his wad every now and then," Cederna says.

"He pays."

"You could do it too."

Ietri shakes his head. He doesn't like the idea of paying a woman.

"So, let's go over it," Cederna imitates Captain Masiero's voice. "It's not all that difficult, Corporal. Follow me closely. You meet a girl you like, you weigh the size of her tits and ass—I personally, for example, like them both big, but there are some perverts who prefer their women skinny as a toothpick—then you go up to her, spout some bullshit, and finally ask her politely if she'd like to go someplace private with you."

"If she'd like to go someplace private with me?"

"Well, maybe not those words exactly. It depends on the situation."

"Look, I know how it's done. It's just that I haven't found the right one."

Cederna bangs his fist on the table. The forks clink in the empty plates where they've eaten French fries, attracting attention from the other tables. "That's the point! There is no right one. They're *all* right. Because they *all* have a——" He specifies the part by forming a diamond with his fingers. "Anyway, once you start, you'll see how easy it is."

Cederna's tone annoys him a little. He doesn't want to be pitied, but his friend's words are also reassuring. He wavers between irritation and gratitude. He'd like to ask him how old he was when he started, but he's afraid to hear the answer: Cederna is too cool, and also too good looking, with that high forehead and a smile full of white teeth and mischief.

"You're as tall as a giant and you let women scare you. It's nuts."

"Don't shout!"

"If you ask me, it's your mother's fault."

"What does my mother have to do with it?" Ietri balls up the napkin in his fist. An unnoticed packet of mayonnaise explodes in his hand.

Cederna pipes up in falsetto: *"Mommy, Mommy, what do all these naughty girls want from me?"*

"Stop it—they can all hear you." He doesn't dare ask his friend for his napkin. He wipes his hand on the edge of the chair. His finger brushes something stuck underneath.

Cederna crosses his arms, satisfied, while Ietri grows more and more gloomy. He makes circles on the table with the damp bottom of the glass.

"Don't put on that face now."

"What face?"

"You'll see. You'll find some twit who will spread her legs for you. Sooner or later."

"I don't much care."

"We're going on a mission soon. They say there's no better place. The Americans are wild . . ."

The guys are given a weekend's leave before the reassignment and almost all of them spend it with their respective girlfriends. The girls have come up with some outlandish ideas, like a picnic by the lake or a marathon of romantic movies, when all the soldiers want to do is tank up on sex for the upcoming months of abstinence.

Ietri's mother takes the night train from Torremaggiore to Belluno. Together they run some errands in the center, then go to the barracks, where he sleeps in a hot, messy dormitory with seven other men. She doesn't fail to comment on it: "All the fault of the vocation you've chosen. With everything you could have done, intelligent as you are."

On edge, the corporal is compelled to get away. He invents an excuse and retreats to a corner of the square to smoke. When he comes back, he finds his mother holding the photograph of his induction oath tight to her chest.

"Look, I'm not dead yet," he says.

The woman's eyes widen. She gives him a sound slap on the cheek. "Don't say such things. Idiot."

She insists on packing his bags no matter what ("Mama knows you'll forget everything otherwise"). Ietri dozes off as he watches her devotedly lay out his clothes on the bed. Occasionally he gets distracted and his mind wanders back to the Americans. He lets himself drift into an exciting half sleep, drool trickling onto the pillow.

"There's moisturizer and soaps in the side pocket, one lavender and one unscented. Use the unscented one on your face—you have sensitive skin. I also put in some chewing gum for when you can't brush your teeth."

That night they share a double bed in a deserted small hotel and Ietri is surprised that he isn't embarrassed to sleep with his mother, even now that he's a man and has been away from home for so long. He doesn't even find it strange when she pulls his head to her soft bosom and holds him there, listening to the strong beat of her heart beneath her nightgown, until she falls asleep.

The room is lit intermittently by the storm that broke out after supper and his mother's body jerks each time the thunder claps; it's as if it scares her in her dreams. It's past eleven when Ietri slips out of bed. In the dark, he empties the pocket of the backpack and throws everything into the trash basket, way down at the bottom so she won't see it. Then he fills the pocket with condoms of various kinds, which he'd hidden in his jacket and in his spare boots, enough to last his platoon for a month of nonstop orgies.

Back in bed, he has second thoughts. He gets up again, sticks his hands in the trash, and gropes around for the chewing gum: you never know, it might come in handy if he were to find himself close to the eager mouth of an American without having brushed his teeth.

Jennifer, oooh Jennifer!

Cederna and his girlfriend are back in the apartment they've been sharing for almost a year. The storm caught them on the way home, but they were so high they didn't even look for cover. They went on staggering along under the downpour, stopping from time to time to exchange lingering kisses, tongues probing.

The evening has taken an excellent turn, though it didn't start out that well. For some time now, Agnese has become obsessed with ethnic restaurants and just tonight when Cederna wanted only to have a good time, Agnese decided to celebrate his departure with a proper dinner by settling on a Japanese restaurant where her university friends had gone. "It'll be special," she said.

But Cederna didn't feel like anything special. "I don't like that Asian stuff."

"But you've never even tasted it."

"Sure I tasted it. Once."

"That's not true. You're acting like a child."

"Hey, watch your mouth."

When he realized they were headed for a serious fight he gave up and said, "Okay, let's go to the damn sushi bar."

Except he didn't eat a thing at the restaurant and spent the time making fun of the waitress, who bowed continually and wore terry socks with her Japanese tatami sandals. Agnese tried to explain to him how to hold the chopsticks and it was clear she loved playing teacher. He made only one attempt, then stuck the tips of the chopsticks up his nostrils and started talking like a retard.

"Can't you at least *try*?" Agnese burst out.

"Try what?"

"To be a civilized person."

Cederna leaned toward her: "I *am* civilized. It's these people who are in the wrong place. Look outside—take a look. Does this seem like Japan to you?"

They didn't say a word to each other for the rest of the meal—a dinner at which he stubbornly refused to taste a thing, not even the batter-fried tempura vegetables that didn't look too bad, while Agnese forced herself to finish it all, just to show him how much braver and more emancipated she was. But the worst moment came later, with the bill. "I'm going to raise hell," Cederna said, his eyes popping.

"I'll pay. Just stop making a scene."

Cederna shot her down coldly: "I don't let my woman pay for my dinner." He threw the credit card at the waitress, who bowed for the umpteenth time as she picked it up.

"What a shitty place!" he said when they were finally outside. "You ruined my last night of freedom, thank you very much."

Agnese started crying softly, her hand pressed over her eyes. Seeing her like that made Cederna feel ashamed. He tried to hug her; she pushed him away.

"You're an animal—that's what you are."

"Come on, baby. Don't be like that."

"Don't touch me!" she yelled, hysterical.

She didn't hold out for long, though. In the end he nibbled her ear and whispered, "What the hell do they call that stuff—yadori? *Yu-dori?*" Finally she laughed a little and admitted: "It was really disgusting. I'm sorry, sweetheart. I'm so sorry."

"Yuuudori! Yuuuuuudori!"

They started laughing and didn't stop even in the pouring rain.

Now they're both sitting on the floor in the small foyer, sopping wet, and they're still chuckling, though less enthusiastically. Cederna is beginning to feel that dissociating sense of emptiness and dejection that comes after laughing so hard. And there's a lump in his throat, because he won't see her again for many long weeks.

Agnese collapses on him and rests her head on his legs. "Don't die over there, okay?"

"I'll do my best."

"Don't get wounded either. Not seriously, at least. No amputations or conspicuous scars."

"Only superficial wounds, I promise."

"And don't cheat on me."

"No."

"If you cheat on me, I'll wound you myself."

"Ooh!"

"Never mind ooh. I'm serious."

"Uh-oh!"

"So will you come back for my graduation?"

"I'll be back, I told you. René promised me leave. But it means that afterward we won't see each other for a long time."

"I'll be a young unemployed graduate waiting for her husband's return from the front."

"I'm not your husband."

"I'm just saying."

"What was it, some kind of proposal?"

"Could be."

"The important thing is that the unemployed young lady not console herself with someone else in the meantime."

"I'll be inconsolable."

"There, that's better."

"Inconsolable. I swear."

In a larger apartment, with a sliding glass door overlooking a parking lot, Marshal René is awake, looking out at the night. The storm has released the heat from the asphalt and the city smells like rotten eggs.

When it comes to picking a woman to spend his last night in friendly territory with, the marshal has a wealth of choices, but the truth is he doesn't feel much like any of them. After all, they're clients. He's sure they wouldn't want to listen to his concerns twelve hours before the flight. When he talks too much, women feel the urge to turn their backs and do something, like light a cigarette or get dressed or take a shower. He can't blame them. None of them knows what it means to be in command; nobody knows what it takes to hold the fate of twenty-seven men in your hands. None of them is in love with him.

He takes off his T-shirt and absently runs his fingers over his chest: the line between his pecs, the dog tag with his date of birth and blood type (A-positive), three well-defined abdominal bands. Maybe when he returns from Afghanistan he'll stop taking gigs. Not that he dislikes the activity, and the extra money comes in handy (last month he was able to buy saddlebags for his Honda, which he's now watching proudly from the window, wrapped in its tarpaulin). It's more a moral issue. Though the stripteasing was a necessity when he'd first moved to Belluno, now that he's career military he could afford to give it up, focus

on a more mature plan. He doesn't yet know what, however. It's difficult to imagine a new version of yourself.

By midnight indecision has also eliminated the possibility of a
proper dinner: he's munched on two packets of crackers and is now no
longer hungry. A little miserable as a celebration. He would have been
better off letting his parents come from Senigallia to see him. Suddenly
he feels sad. The TV is unplugged, covered with a white sheet to keep
off dust. He's shut off the central gas valve and collected the garbage
in a bag. The house is ready to be deserted.

He lies down on the couch and is already dozing when he gets
Rosanna Vitale's message: "Were you going to leave without saying
good-bye? Come on over. I need to talk to you." A few seconds later
there's another one: "Bring something to drink."

René takes his time. In the shower he shaves and masturbates
slowly, to make himself immune to pleasure. He picks up some spumante at the Autogrill on the highway. As soon as he steps out the
door, he turns around and goes back in to add a bottle of vodka and
two bars of chocolate. He feels a certain gratitude to Rosanna for sav-
ing him from a monotonous last night and he plans to reward her as
she deserves. Usually he goes to bed with younger women, mostly girls
who want to create a bold memory before embracing the life of a judi-
cious wife. Rosanna, on the other hand, is over forty, but there's something about her that he likes. She's an expert at sex and is extraordinarily
open-minded. Sometimes, after they're done, René stays for dinner or
to watch a movie—he on the couch, she in a chair nearby—and maybe
they make love again, in which case the second round is on the house.
If he wants to leave, though, she doesn't keep him.

"Did you get lost?" Rosanna is standing in the doorway, waiting for
him.

René comes up beside her, kisses her on the cheek. He notices a
different perfume than usual, or maybe it's a different smell beneath
the usual perfume, but he doesn't say anything.

The woman checks out the bottles. She puts the spumante in the refrigerator and opens the other bottle. The glasses are already set out on the table. "Would you like a little music? The silence is getting on my nerves tonight."

René doesn't mind. Like other distractions, music doesn't matter to him. He sits at the kitchen table. He's been sent off before—Lebanon twice, Kosovo—so he knows how difficult it is for civilians to come to terms with it.

"So you're leaving tomorrow."

"Yeah."

"And how long is this mission?"

"Six months. More or less."

Rosanna nods. She's already finished her first glass. She pours herself another. René, on the other hand, sips slowly, in control of himself.

"And are you glad?"

"It's not a pleasure trip."

"Sure. But are you glad?"

René drums his fingers on the wood. "Yeah, I think so."

"Good. That's the important thing."

The music forces them to speak more loudly than necessary. René is annoyed. If Rosanna would lower the volume, they'd be more comfortable. People don't notice many of the things that he does; this has always disappointed him in a way. Tonight, moreover, Rosanna seems distracted and determined to drink herself into a stupor before they end up in bed. Drunk women are limp, their movements repetitive, and then it's up to him to make an ungodly effort to make them come. Pointing to her glass, he doesn't hesitate to say: "Go easy on that."

She gives him a furious look. René isn't talking to one of his soldiers. Until proven otherwise, she's the one paying, so she can decide when enough is enough. Afterward, though, she hangs her head as if to apologize. René interprets her nerves as a sign she's worried about him, and this moves him. "I won't be in any danger," he says.

"I know."

"It's more a matter of defensive operations."

"Yes."

"If you look at the statistics, the death rate in this conflict is ridiculous. It's riskier crossing the street out there. I'm not kidding. For us Italians, at least. There are some who are really fighting and for them it's a different story. The Americans, for example, have—"

"I'm pregnant."

The room sways slightly around the shimmering liquor bottle. "What did you say?"

"You heard me."

René runs a hand over his face. He's not perspiring. "No. I don't think I heard you."

"I'm pregnant."

"Can you turn the music off, please? I can't focus."

Rosanna walks quickly to the stereo and turns it off. She comes back and sits down. There are other sounds now: the hum of the water heater, someone trying to play a guitar in the apartment above, vodka being poured into her glass for the third time, against his advice.

"You told me clearly that—" René says, trying hard to control himself.

"I know. It was impossible for it to happen. A chance in a million maybe."

"You're in menopause—you told me so." His tone isn't aggressive and he looks calm, just a little pale.

"I *am* in menopause, all right? But I got pregnant. That's what happened."

"You said it wasn't possible."

"It wasn't. It was a kind of miracle, okay?"

René wonders if he should make sure the child is really his, but apparently it's beside the point. He considers the word *miracle* and doesn't see the connection.

"The responsibility is mine—let's get that clear right now," she continues. "One hundred percent mine. So I guess it's up to you to decide. You're the one who's been screwed. I'll respect your decision. There's still time, a month and a half, a little less. You leave now, take your time and think it over, then let me know what you decide. I'll take care of the rest."

She blurts it all out in one breath, then brings the glass to her lips. Instead of drinking, she holds it there. She rubs her lip on the rim, lost in thought. She has permanent wrinkles at the corners of her eyes, but they don't look bad. In the course of his clandestine career René has learned that mature women bloom one last time before fading altogether and that at that stage they're more beautiful than ever. His own body feels inadequate now, a sensation that provokes a fit of anger: "If you're pregnant you shouldn't drink."

"A little vodka seems like the least of my worries right now."

"Still, you shouldn't."

They fall silent. René mentally retraces the conversation, step by step. *I'll take care of the rest.* He has a hard time seeing clearly beyond those words.

"Do you feel like doing it anyway?"

Rosanna asks him just like that, as if it were something they could do. She's pregnant, yet she's drinking and wants to sleep with him. René is disconcerted. He's about to shout to her face that she's crazy, then realizes that it would be a way of giving the evening a sense of closure: make love and go out the door with the impression of having done what was expected of him and nothing more. "Why shouldn't we?" he says.

They move into the bedroom and undress with their backs turned. They start out slowly, gently, then René allows himself to force Rosanna down on her stomach. To him it's like a small punishment. Rosanna comes liberally, he more discreetly. He pulls out a moment before, as if it makes any difference. She doesn't reproach him.

"You can stay and sleep here," she says instead. "I'm not working tomorrow morning. I'll take you to get your things and then to the airport."

"It's not necessary."

"We can have a few more hours together."

"I have to go."

Rosanna gets up and quickly covers herself with a robe. She rummages in her bag for her wallet and hands René the money.

He looks at the hand holding out the bills. He can't accept money from a woman who's pregnant with his child, but Rosanna doesn't move and doesn't say anything. A discount, maybe? No, that would be hypocritical. She's just a client, he thinks, a client like any other. If something unexpected happened, it's not his fault.

He grabs the money and in less than ten minutes he's ready to go.

"So then you'll let me know," Rosanna says at the door.

"Yeah, I'll let you know."

In the morning the heat is unbearable, the sky covered with a bright gray glaze that triggers a headache. Civilians hang around the airport terminal, drawn by the unusual concentration of soldiers. The ashtrays outside are overflowing with cigarette butts. Ietri and his mother have arrived by bus. He looks around for his buddies and some of them wave to him from across the way. Mitrano has the largest family and the only one in his group who isn't making a racket is his grandmother in her wheelchair: she has her back turned to her grandson and is staring straight ahead, as if seeing something horrible, though in all likelihood—Ietri thinks—she's just senile. Anfossi's parents check the clock repeatedly, Cederna is smooching with his girlfriend, his hands boldly on her ass, Zampieri is holding a child who is having fun yanking her hair and pulling her velcro insignia on and off. She lets him do it for a while, then abruptly puts him down and the child begins to whine. René is sitting down, talking on the phone, his head bowed.

Ietri feels someone grab his right hand. Before he has time to protest, his mother has already squeezed the tube of cream on the back of his hand.

"What are you doing?!"

"Be quiet. Look how chapped they are. And what about these?" She lifts up his fingers for him to see his nails.

"What's wrong with them?"

"Come to the bathroom and I'll cut them for you. Luckily I have my nail scissors with me."

"Mama!"

"If we don't cut them now, they'll be all black before evening."

After a lengthy negotiation, Ietri gives in, but at least he gets to do it himself. He goes off to the toilets, browbeaten.

He's just finished the first hand when a loud fart trumpets from one of the stalls.

"Gesundheit!" the corporal says. He's echoed by a grunt.

Shortly thereafter, Colonel Ballesio comes out of the stall. He goes to the mirror, buttoning his fly, followed by a foul stench.

Ietri snaps to attention and the colonel smiles at him complacently. He eyes the nail clippings in the sink and his expression changes. "Certain matters should be taken care of at home, soldier."

"You're right, Commander. I'm sorry, Commander."

Ietri turns on the tap. The nail clippings bunch around the drain and clog up there. He lifts the stopper and shoves them down with his finger. Ballesio observes him coldly. "First mission, soldier?"

"Yes, sir."

"When you get back, these toilets will seem different to you. Spotless as those in a hospital. And the faucet. When you see a faucet like this again, you'll feel like licking it."

Ietri nods. His heart is pounding like mad.

"But it won't last long. At first it all seems magical when you get back. Then it goes back to being what it is. Crap."

Ballesio tugs on the towel roll, but the dispenser is stuck. He swears, then rubs his wet palms on his pants. He nods his head toward the corporal. "I can't manage with scissors," he says. "My wife bought me a nail clipper. Only thing is, it leaves rough edges."

When Ietri returns to the airport terminal, he's furious. He looked like a fool in front of the colonel and it's all his mother's fault.

She stretches her neck to check his fingernails. "Why did you only cut them on one hand? I told you I should do it. Pigheaded—that's what you are! You can't do it with your left hand. Come on, let's go."

Ietri pushes her away. "Leave me alone."

The woman looks at him sternly, shakes her head, then starts rummaging in her handbag. "Here. Eat this—you have bad breath."

"Will you stop it? Shit!" the corporal hollers. He knocks her hand away. The candy falls to the floor and he stamps on it with his boot. The green sugar shatters. "Happy now?"

Di Salvo and his family turn to watch them, and out of the corner of his eye Ietri notes that even Cederna has turned around.

He doesn't know what's gotten into him.

Two teardrops well up in his mother's eyes. Her mouth is open, the upper lip trailing a resilient strand of saliva, and her lower lip is trembling a little. "I'm sorry," the woman whispers.

Before now she's never apologized to him. Ietri is torn between wanting to shout at her that she's a stupid imbecile and the urge to bend down and pick up the slivers of candy one by one and piece them back together. He feels his troop mates' eyes on him, judging him.

I'm a man now, and I'm going to war.

Later he won't remember if he actually said it or if he just thought it. He grabs his backpack and throws it over his shoulder. He kisses his mother briefly on the cheek, one side only. "I'll be back soon," he says.

The Security Bubble

Securely stored in Lieutenant Egitto's cabinet, though with the key handy in the lock, is a personal stockpile of medications, the only ones in the dispensary not recorded in the inventory register. Besides a few over-the-counter drugs for short-lived ailments and some totally ineffective ointments for flaking skin, there are three bottles of yellow-and-blue antianxiety capsules. The bottles are not labeled and one is just about empty. Egitto takes sixty milligrams of duloxetine in the evening before going to the mess hall, as he has for almost a year; it seemed to him that most of the unwanted side effects were worked off during sleep that way, starting with sleep itself, which hit him like a ton of bricks and rarely allowed him to stay up later than ten o'clock. When he first started taking the pills, he had experienced just about all the side effects mentioned in the explanatory leaflet for antidepressants, from acute headaches to loss of appetite, from intestinal bloating to intermittent nausea. The most bizarre of all was a severe numbness of the jaw, like when you yawn too wide. He's past all that, however. Just as he's past showing any trace of the shame he felt at the beginning, when he felt like a loser for taking the capsules, like a drug addict, the same shame that led him to slip the pills out of the blister packs and transfer them into unlabeled bottles. For some time now, Egitto has accepted his defeat. He's discovered that hidden within him is a vast, soothing amiability.

The serotonergic drug performs to perfection the task for which it was created, which is to keep any kind of anxiety and emotional in-volvement at bay. The turbulent angst of the period following his fa-ther's death—with all the psychosomatic reactions and dark, seductive thoughts that the leaflet generically described as "suicidal tendencies"—floats somewhere above it all, held in check the way a reservoir is by a retaining wall. The lieutenant is satisfied with his level of peacefulness. He wouldn't trade that serenity for anything. Sometimes his mouth gets parched and he still hears a sudden, high-pitched whistling in his ear, followed by a roar that's slow to fade. And there's that other little drawback, of course: he hasn't had a proper erection in months and the few times he did he wasn't able to make the most of it, even on his own. But what does he care about sex at a military base in the middle of the desert, populated almost exclusively by male specimens?

He's been in Afghanistan for 191 days and at Forward Operating Base Ice for almost four months; the FOB is at the northern entrance of the Gulistan Valley, not far from Helmand Province, where U.S. troops have been fighting every day to cleanse the villages of insur-gents. The marines consider their work in Gulistan concluded, after building a scant ten-acre outpost in a strategic area and reclaiming several surrounding villages, including Qal'a-i-Kuhna, where the ba-zaar is. In truth, like all operations since the start of the conflict, the mop-up operation in the area has been incomplete: the security bubble extends for a radius of just a few miles around the base. Inside there are still insidious pockets of guerrillas and outside is hell.

After a period in which the FOB was occupied by the Georgians, the territory came under Italian command. In mid-May, a convoy of ninety vehicles left Herat, following the Ring Road south, as far as Farah, and from there cut east, vainly pursuing some Taliban caught off guard. Lieutenant Egitto had participated in the mission as head of—and sole component of—the medical unit.

The base they'd found was in appalling condition: a few huts full of cracks, some deep holes in the ground of dubious utility, garbage, coils of barbed wire and vehicle parts scattered everywhere; showers—nylon bags riddled with holes and hanging from a hook—lined up out in the open, without partitions. There was no sign of toilets. The only structure in decent condition was the armory, which said a lot about their predecessors' order of priorities. Egitto's regiment chose it to house the command center. During the first weeks, efforts had focused on providing the camp with a minimum of basic amenities and strengthening the defense of the main entrance by building a long, zigzagged row of fortifications.

Egitto concentrated on setting up the infirmary, in a tent not far from the command center. In one half he arranged a gurney and a table, with two cabinets full of drugs and a small field refrigerator to store the perishable ones. Separated by a tarp with a mottled camouflage pattern is his personal area. The waiting room is a bench outside, fashioned out of bent wire mesh.

Once the tent became, in his opinion, sufficiently presentable, his efforts definitely slowed down. Now that he might make a number of improvements—hang some anatomical prints on the walls, see to it that patients who are waiting might enjoy a little shade, unpack the last cartons, and consider a more appropriate place for his surgical instruments—he doesn't feel like it. Instead, he wastes a lot of time reproaching himself. It doesn't matter much; by now he's about to go home. His six-month tour of duty is up and the rest of his brigade has abandoned the outpost. Some of them are already back in Italy, frantically enjoying their twenty-five days of leave and renewing intimate relationships, which at a distance had taken on the appearance of pure fantasy. The last to leave was Colonel Caracciolo, whose words, as he climbed into the helicopter and looked over the barren landscape, said it all: "Another shitty place I won't miss." Colonel Ballesio's confident, well-rested division took over the place and it will be a good number of days before the base is operating normally. Just in time for the new rotation.

Seated at his desk, Egitto is dozing—undoubtedly the work he's been best at for some time—when a soldier sticks his head into the infirmary.

"Doctor?"

Egitto jumps. "What is it?"

"The colonel informs you that the relief medic will arrive tomorrow. A helicopter will take you back to Herat."

The young man is still half in and half out, his face indistinct in the shadows.

"Has Sergeant Anselmo recovered?"

"Who?"

"Sergeant Anselmo. He's the one assigned to replace me."

As far as he'd been told, the sergeant had the flu with respiratory complications; until a few days ago he'd been in the field hospital in Herat with his nose and mouth squeezed into a soft oxygen mask.

The soldier raises his hands, intimidated. "I don't know, sir. They just told me to inform you that the relief medic will be here and that the helicopter—"

"Will take me to Herat. Right, I got it."

"Exactly, sir. The day after tomorrow."

"Thank you."

The soldier lingers in the doorway.

"Anything else?"

"Congratulations, Lieutenant."

"For what?"

"You're going home."

He disappears; the tent's flap swings back and forth a few seconds, alternately exposing and obscuring the harsh light outside. Egitto leans his forehead on his folded arms and tries to go back to sleep. Before the week is over, if all goes as it should, he'll be in Torino. Thinking about it, he experiences a sudden sense of suffocation.

His nap ruined, he decides to get up and go out. He walks along the east fence and across the fortified area of the corps of engineers, where the tents are placed so close together you have to hunch your shoulders to get through them. He climbs a ladder leaning against the fortification. The man stationed on guard duty salutes, then steps aside to make room for him.

"Are you the doc?"

"Yep, that's me."

Egitto puts a hand to his forehead to shade his eyes from the light.

"Want my binoculars?"

"No, that's okay."

"No, here—take my binoculars. You can see better." The soldier slips the glasses off his neck. He's very young and eager to be of service. "They have a manual focus. You have to turn the little wheel. Here, I'll do it."

Egitto lets him focus them; then he slowly explores the flat, open expanse that lies exposed to the early afternoon sun. In the distance the light creates mirages of small shimmering pools. The mountain is scorching hot and seems determined to display its innocence at all costs: hard to believe that it harbors a myriad of caves and ravines from which the enemy constantly watches the FOB, even at this very moment. But Egitto knows it too well to let himself be fooled or to forget.

He aims the binoculars in the direction of the Afghan truck drivers' encampment. He spots them sitting in the shade of the tarpaulins they've carelessly hung between the vehicles, crouched with their backs against the wheels, knees to their chests. They're capable of staying in that position for hours, sipping hot tea. They transported matériel from Herat to the FOB and now they don't dare head back for fear of reprisals. They're confined to that one area they consider safe: they can't leave but they can't stay there forever either. As far as the lieutenant knows, they've never washed. They survive on a few jerry cans of water a day, enough to quench their thirst. They accept the food offered to them from the mess hall without saying thanks, but not seeming to demand it either.

"Not much to see, huh, Doc?"

"A little boring," Egitto says, but he doesn't think so. The mountain changes shape every second; there are infinite nuances of the same yellow, but you have to be able to recognize them. It's a hostile landscape to which it was easy for him to grow attached.

"I didn't think it would be like this," the soldier says. He seems forlorn.

When Egitto climbs down from the fortification, he heads for the phones, even though there aren't many people he can call, no one he has—or wants—to tell about his return. He calls Marianna. He enters the code on the prepaid card; a recorded message informs him of the remaining credit and asks him to please hold.

"Hello?"

Marianna always sounds abrupt when answering the phone, as if she's been interrupted doing something that requires her utmost concentration. As soon as she recognizes his voice, though, she softens.

"It's Alessandro."

"Finally."

"How are you?"

"I have a headache that just won't quit. And you? Did they leave you all by yourself in the end?"

"The new regiment arrived. It's strange—they treat me like an old wise man."

"They don't know how wrong they are."

"Yeah. They'll soon find out."

There's a pause. Egitto listens to his sister's slightly labored breathing.

"I went back to the house yesterday."

The last time they were there they'd gone together. Ernesto had been dead a few days and they were already wandering through the rooms, their eyes choosing which pieces of furniture to keep. In front of the mirror in the foyer, his sister had said, Could I take this? Take whatever you want, he'd replied; I'm not interested. But Marianna had been furious: Why do you do it, huh? Why do you try to make me feel guilty by saying, Take whatever you want, as if I were a selfish pig?

"How was it?" he asks.

"How do you think? Empty, dusty. *Sad*. I can't believe I lived in such a place. Just think, I found the washing machine with a load of wash in it. They hadn't even looked. The clothes were pasted together. I got a trash bag and threw them out. Then I opened the wardrobe and threw out the rest as well. Everything I happened to get my hands on."

"You shouldn't have."

"Why shouldn't I have?"

Egitto doesn't know why. He knows it's something that shouldn't have been done, not yet. "They might have been useful," he says.

"Useful to whom? To you? That stuff is awful. And besides, I happen to be on my own here. You could at least have the decency not to tell me what I should or shouldn't do."

"You're right. I'm sorry."

"I contacted a couple of real estate agents. They say the house needs to be fixed up, we won't get much for it. The important thing is for us to get rid of it as soon as possible."

Egitto would like to tell Marianna that the sale can wait, but he remains silent.

She presses him: "So when are you coming back?"

"Soon. I think."

"Did they give you a *date*?"

"No. Not yet."

"Maybe I really should make that phone call. I'm sure someone would take an interest in the matter."

Marianna always shows a certain impetuosity toward his affairs, as if she claimed the right to preempt his decisions. Recently she's threatened several times to lodge a complaint with the Defense Administration no less. So far Egitto has managed to talk her out of it. "They'll get back at me. I've already explained it to you," he says.

"I don't know how you can live like that, not knowing where you'll be in a week, or a month. Always at the mercy of other people's whims."

"It's part of my job."

"It's a stupid job and you *know* it."

"Could be."

"Getting involved in a place that has nothing to do with you. *Zilch.* Hiding among a bunch of fanatics. And don't try to tell me they're not, because I know *exactly* how they are."

"Marianna . . ."

"There's a certain amount of stupidity in that."

"Marianna, I have to go now."

"Oh, *of course.* I thought so. Look, Alessandro, it's really urgent that we sell the house. The way prices are going in the area is appalling. Only *they* could have made the place seem idyllic. Ernesto was convinced he was an expert when it came to investments, remember? He was convinced he was an expert *in everything. In fact,* the apartment isn't worth anything anymore. I'm really worried."

"I'll take care of it, I told you."

"You have to do it *quickly,* Alessandro."

"All right. Ciao, Marianna."

Egitto isn't sure how much intelligence lies hidden behind Colonel Ballesio's meditative stance. Not much, he'd guess. What's certain is that the colonel harbors several idiosyncrasies. For example, he's hung a disproportionate number of tree-shaped air fresheners in the tent, which fill the space with the scent of bubble gum.

"Lieutenant Morocco! Come in."

"Egitto, Colonel, sir."

Ballesio leans forward to read the name on his jacket. "Oh, well, not much difference, right? At ease, Lieutenant, at ease. Have a seat over there. As you can see, this tent doesn't have many amenities. Caracciolo is a spartan type. Only because he's young, mind you. I, however, am beginning to appreciate comfort." He caresses his belly indulgently. "By the way, I'd like to get a refrigerator to keep a few beers here. I noticed you have one in your infirmary. Do you really need it?"

"The vaccines are in it. And the adrenaline."

"The adrenaline, right. That's important. I could keep it here, though. That way I'll have room for some beers. After all, my tent is open—everyone is welcome at any hour of the day or night. I don't have any secrets to hide. Besides, you're leaving soon, right?"

Egitto lowers his eyes.

"Anyway, think about it. Maybe it's not a good idea. I don't know about you, but I've always liked beer, even warm." The colonel squeezes his lips between his thumb and forefinger, nodding his head vacantly. "Well, okay, then," he murmurs. And again: "Okay, then."

On the desk there's a copy of *The Little Prince*. The two soldiers turn their eyes to the slim little boy drawn on the cover.

"My wife," Ballesio says, as if to justify himself. "She gave it to me. She says I need to get in touch with our kids. I'm not sure what she means. Have you read it?"

"A long time ago."

"If you ask me, it's for homos. I fell asleep twice."

Egitto nods, uncomfortable. He's not sure why he came to the colonel's tent. The Little Prince seems more out of his element than usual under the greenish light filtering through the canvas.

"Was there something in particular you wanted to tell me, Lieutenant?"

"I'd like to extend my stay, Colonel." The meaning of the phrase isn't fully clear to him until he's uttered it in its entirety.

Ballesio raises his eyebrows. "Are you serious?"

"Yes, sir."

"Here in Afghanistan or here in this Gulistan shithole?"

"At the FOB, Colonel."

"And to think, I'd already like to leave. Ski season starts in three months. Don't you want to go home and ski, Lieutenant? Don't tell me you're one of those southerners who've never put on a pair of skis."

"No. I ski."

"Good for you. Of course, I have nothing against southerners. Some of them are good people. But naturally, to call them Alpines is a different story. They're suited to these rotten deserts. They're used to it. Me, on the other hand, I'd give my right arm to go back to the mountains and ski all winter long. Ahhh! I tell myself each time, This year I'm devoting all my time to skiing, but then something always gets in the way. Last year my wife tripped on a curb and I found myself having to be her nurse. A depressing experience. From the windows I gazed at the Tofane Mountains with their white blanket of snow, and I would have climbed them on foot just to be able to ski back down. I would have come down on my ass. This year I won't even see the snow. A waste of time, a waste of life. Especially at your age. Anyway. Are you really sure you want to stay?"

"I'm sure, Colonel."

"I hope it's not because of some kind of missionary spirit. They told me about that kid you saved, you know. The opium smoker. Congratulations. A touching story." He mulls it over. "But we aren't missionaries, remember that. We're commandos. We like to play with guns, and preferably use them."

"It's for the money," Egitto lies.

The colonel rubs his jaw thoughtfully. "Money is always a good reason."

The Little Trees fresheners flutter crazily in front of the air conditioner's jet, giving off a cloying aroma. Egitto is beginning to feel nauseated.

Ballesio points to him. "That thing on your face. Will it go away?"

Egitto sits up straighter in his chair. He pictures the pattern of blotches on his face. It changes every day, like an atmospheric disturbance, and he keeps an eye on it as if he were a meteorologist. By now he knows how each area will behave: the cheeks heal quickly, the skin around the lips is painful, the scaly eyebrows disturb people, the ears are a disaster. "Sometimes it improves. A little. With the sun, for instance."

"It doesn't seem like it. It makes you look like a mess. No offense."

Egitto grabs onto his belt. All of a sudden he feels very hot.

"I have a problem too," Ballesio says. He loosens the collar of his uniform. "Here. Look at this. There are spots, right? They itch like hell. Does your stuff itch?"

Egitto goes around the desk to examine the colonel's neck. A slight rash follows the edge of the uniform. Red pustules, tiny as pencil marks. "It's just a rash. I have some calendula cream."

"Calendula? What the fuck is that? Don't you have any cortisone?"

"You don't need cortisone."

"It makes me feel better right away. Bring me the cortisone. You should try it up there as well, Lieutenant."

"Thanks for the advice, Colonel."

He returns to his seat, puts his hands on his knees. The colonel straightens his jacket.

"So, then, you'll be staying with us," he says. "If it were me, they'd have to pay me a ton of money to make me hang around here. Anyway. Your business. A real doctor will come in handy for us. Your colleague Anselmo can barely manage with stitches. I'll communicate your decision today, Lieutenant."

Egitto requests permission to leave.

"One more thing, Doctor."

"Sir."

"Is it true what they say about the roses?"

"What's that?"

"That in the spring the valley is filled with roses."

"I've never seen them, Colonel."

Ballesio sighs. "I thought so. Of course. Why should roses grow in such a horrible place?"

Sand

For Ietri everything is new and interesting. He studies the strange terrain from the helicopter, the rocky plains interrupted here and there by emerald green meadows. There's a lone camel standing halfway up a slope, or maybe it's a dromedary, he can never remember the thing about the humps. He didn't think that dromedaries existed in the wild, though: they're zoo animals. He'd like to point it out to Cederna, who is sitting beside him, but his friend doesn't seem to be interested in the landscape. He's staring at some point of the helicopter from behind his dark glasses, or else he's sleeping.

Ietri takes out his earbuds. The distorted, cavernous guitars of the Cradle of Filth are replaced by the very similar noise of the rotor blades. "Will there be a bar at the FOB?" he asks his friend. He's forced to shout.

"No."

"What about a gym?"

"Not even that."

"Ping-Pong at least?"

"You still don't get it. Where we're going there's not a goddamn thing."

He's right. There's nothing at Base Ice, only sand. Yellow, clinging sand—your boots sink in it up to your ankles. If you brush it off your uniform, it swirls in the air a bit and then comes back and lands in the same spot. The first night in Gulistan, when Ietri blows his nose, he leaves dark streaks on his handkerchief. The next day blood mixed with sand comes out, and so on for a week, then nothing. His body is already used to it; a young body can get used to anything.

The space assigned to the platoon is in the northwest zone, next to a concrete structure, one of the few on the base: it was left behind by the marines. It's a large bare room, plastered only at certain points. There's graffiti on the walls: a flag with stars and stripes, some lewd sketches, and a mean bulldog with a studded collar. The holes, dozens of them, are from bullets fired from within.

"What a lousy wreck," Simoncelli says when they enter the first time, thereby choosing the name with which to baptize their digs: the Wreck. It becomes their headquarters.

They soon discover that it's infested with cockroaches. They're heaped up in the corners and crevices, but occasionally an explorer crawls out onto the floor. They have shiny brown carapaces, which make a crackling noise when you crush them under your boot and spurt blood half a yard away.

Luckily Passalacqua has brought along some insect repellent and spreads the powder around the outside perimeter and in the corners. "You know how it works?" he asks, tapping the bottom of the can to discharge the last puffs of powder. If it isn't enough, they're fucked: they'll have to kill the critters one by one. "It releases a smell that excites the cockroaches. It's called a pheronome."

"Phero*m*one, you idiot," Cederna corrects him.

"Pheromone, whatever. It's the smell of their females in heat. The cockroaches get horny and go looking for them, and instead of the females they find the poison."

"Fantastic!"

"The ones who end up in the poison drop dead on the spot and give off a different odor that drives the other cockroaches crazy."

"Crazy?"

"Crazy. They devour each other."

Ietri imagines a cockroach scurrying out of the Wreck, slipping into the tent, climbing up the leg of the cot, and crawling over his face as he sleeps.

"Just imagine if the Taliban did that," Cederna says, "if they sprayed the smell of pussy on the base instead of hurling grenades. We'd start killing one another."

"We already have Zampieri giving off the pheromone," Rovere says.

"No, she only smells from her armpits."

They all laugh. Only Ietri is left frowning. "Do you think we're like cockroaches?" he asks.

"What?"

"You said that if the Taliban sprayed the smell of pussy we'd start killing each other. Like the cockroaches."

Cederna smiles faintly. "Maybe you'd be saved, *verginella*. You don't know that smell yet."

The first task assigned to the Third Platoon, Charlie Company (since the Sixty-sixth Company set foot on foreign soil, its designation was changed to its battle name), is the construction of a masonry structure to house the washing machines. The sand has already put two of them out of order, and they are now stacked in a corner of the camp along with other discarded materials, receptacles full of empty cans and scrap metal.

Ietri has been working for a couple of hours with Di Salvo and four masons from the village. In actuality, all the soldiers do is watch to see that the Afghans don't bungle it. It's not clear who among them has the most experience with construction. The plan they have to follow is sketchy and the design lacks the lateral dimensions, so they've marked out the perimeter roughly by counting the number of bricks in the drawing. It's just past noon and the sun is beating straight down on their naked shoulders.

"We could use a beer," Ietri says.

"Yeah, ice cold."

"With a lemon wedge stuck in the neck."

"I like to suck the lemon after the beer."

The wall they're building seems straight, at least to their eye, yet there's something odd about it. They're at the eighth row of bricks; soon they'll need a ladder and Ietri hopes he won't have to escort the Afghans to the storeroom to get it.

All of a sudden the Afghans stop what they're doing, drop their tools on the ground, and spread out some mats that had been piled aside, arranging them in the sole triangle of shade. They kneel down.

"What the fuck are they doing?"

"What do you think?"

"Do they have to pray right now?"

Di Salvo shrugs. "Muslims are always praying. They're fundamentalists."

Ietri fishes a glop of mortar out of the bucket and throws it on the wall. He flattens it with a trowel. What lunacy, he thinks, then turns to look at the Afghans again. They're doing a kind of gymnastics: they bend down to the ground, straighten up, then hunch over again, all the while intoning a mantra. For a moment he has the urge to imitate them.

"Fuck this," Di Salvo says.

"Yeah, fuck this," Ietri echoes him.

They drop their rifles. If the Afghans can take a break, they too can take a little rest. Di Salvo gropes around for the pack of cigarettes in the side pocket of his pants and offers him one. They lean against the wall, where the mortar is still fresh.

"They shipped us over here to build a laundry room," Ietri says. "Does that seem right?"

"No, not right at all."

It just doesn't sit well with him. They had promised him American women and there's not a trace of them here—they were pulling his leg. He'd gotten a glimpse of them in Herat, of course, during the few days he was there: soldiers with ponytails, firm breasts, and the look of a woman who will eat you alive in the sack, but then they shipped him to Gulistan to build a stupid wall. Or rather, to watch someone else build it. He can't imagine any place on earth farther removed from sexual temptation.

"To think our parents came here to smoke joints," Di Salvo says.

"Joints?"

"Sure, you know, the seventies. The hippie fuckers."

"Oh, sure," Ietri says. He doesn't know, actually. He thinks for a moment. "Anyway, my parents never came here. They never went anywhere." He's sure about his mother. For all he knows, his father might very well have come here, to Afghanistan; maybe he joined a group of Taliban and buries IEDs in the roads now. He always was an unpredictable type.

"I was just kidding. My parents never went anywhere either. But it was that generation. They did a lot of grass and then everyone fucked everyone, constantly."

"What a life," Ietri says.

"Yeah, what a life. Not like today. The girls nowadays are all no-I-don't-drink, no-I-don't-smoke, no-I-don't-put-out."

Ietri laughs. Di Salvo is right; girls today don't put out.

"You practically have to marry them before they'll go to bed. Although it depends on the location."

"What do you mean, the location?"

"The ones from the Veneto hop into bed right away, for instance." Di Salvo snaps his fingers. "Not in Belluno, though. You have to go farther south, where the students are. The students are little sluts. Once I was in Padua, I got three of them in bed in a week."

Ietri makes a mental note of the number and location. *Padua. Three.* You can be sure he'll go there, once he returns.

"The students shave it—did you know that?"

"Why?"

Di Salvo spits on the ground, then covers the spit with sand. "It's a fad. Plus it's more hygienic."

Ietri is dubious. He's never seen a female with shaved pubes, except in certain videos on the Internet, and little girls at the beach, of course. He's not sure he'd feel comfortable.

The Afghans stick their foreheads in the sand, as if they want to plant their heads in it. Again Ietri feels the urge to kneel down and join them, see how it feels. Di Salvo arches his back and swivels his neck around, yawning. The sun is roasting them. Ietri has some sunscreen in his backpack, but he doesn't know how to smear it on himself and he doesn't feel right about asking his buddy. A soldier doesn't rub cream on another soldier's back.

"Can you imagine? Coming here when there's no war and roaming around the country, free, with a girl beside you," Di Salvo muses. "Smoking marijuana leaves just picked off the plant."

"That would be cool."

"It would be awesome."

He moves closer to Ietri. "Do you smoke?"

Ietri, puzzled, looks at the cigarette he's holding between his fingers.

"I'm not talking about those, asshole. Grass."

Ietri nods. "I've tried it, once or twice."

Di Salvo puts an arm around Ietri's bare shoulders. His skin is surprisingly cool. "You know Abib?"

"The interpreter?"

"Yeah. He has grass to sell."

"How do you know?"

"Never mind that. You can come with me if you want. We'll each pay half. For ten euros he gives you a bag this big." Di Salvo uses his hands to show him.

"Are you nuts? If they catch us we're screwed."

"Who's going to catch us? Does Captain Masiero sniff your breath or something?"

"No," Ietri admits.

"This is different from the stuff you find at home. This stuff is natural, it's . . . *wow!*" Di Salvo tightens his grip around his neck and puts his mouth to his ear; his breath is just slightly hotter than the air. "Listen to this. Abib has a small wooden statue in his tent, one of those tribal statues, you know? With a big head and square body and enormous eyes. It's some old carving that his grandfather gave him. He told me the whole story, but I was smoking and I don't remember. Anyhow. The statue stares at you with those huge yellow eyes, and the last time, there I was smoking Abib's grass and looking at the statue while it was looking at me, and at a certain point, *bam!*—I was stoned and I realized that the statue was death. I was looking death right in the face!"

"Death?"

"Yeah, death. But it wasn't death like you imagine it. It wasn't angry. It was a peaceful death, not scary. It was like . . . indifferent. It couldn't care less about me. It looked at me and that's it."

"How did you know it was death? Did Abib tell you?"

"I just knew it, that's all. Actually, no, I realized it afterward, outside the tent. I was full of energy, an energy unlike any other. It wasn't anything like the usual sensation you get when you've smoked grass and feel wasted. I was extremely lucid, very focused. I had looked death in the face and I felt like a god. Then, listen to this, I pass by the flag, the one on the main tower, you know? It was fluttering because there was a little wind and I . . . I can't explain it. I *felt* the flag fluttering, okay? I don't mean I noticed the wind was making the flag flutter. I'm saying I really felt it. I was the wind, and I was the flag."

"You were the wind?"

Di Salvo drops his arm. "You think I'm talking like an asshole hippie?"

"No. No, I don't think that," Ietri says, but he's bewildered.

"Well, anyhow, happiness or sadness had nothing to do with it. I mean, those are . . . just pieces of it. They're incomplete. Whereas I was feeling *everything*, all at once. The flag and the wind, everything."

"I don't understand what the statue and death have to do with the flag."

"They're part of it, I'm telling you!" Di Salvo scratches his beard. "You're looking at me like I'm telling you a load of hippie crap."

"No. Finish the story."

"I'm done. That was it, get it? Something inside me opened up."

"A revelation," Ietri says.

"I don't know if it was a revelation."

"It was a revelation, I think."

"I'm telling you I don't know what the fuck it was. It is what it is. I'm just trying to explain to you that the stuff Abib gives you is different. It makes you feel different. It makes you feel things," he said, suddenly irritable. "So, you want to come?"

Ietri isn't much interested in drugs, but he doesn't want to disappoint his platoon mate. "Maybe."

Meanwhile, the Afghans have rolled up their mats and gone back to work. They rarely speak and when they do, it sounds to Ietri like they're arguing. He looks at his watch; it's twenty minutes to one. If he hurries, maybe he can beat the line at the mess hall.

Three days later, when it comes time to poke their nose out of the FOB, he doesn't get to go.

"Today we'll go take a look around," René says in the morning. "I want Cederna, Camporesi, Pecone, and Torsu with me."

The guys watch the chosen ones get dressed in front of their cots. They do it ceremoniously, like ancient heroes, although nothing more than a routine patrol at the village bazaar awaits them.

Cederna struts around the most, because he's also the fittest. If there were an Achilles, son of Peleus, in Third Platoon, Charlie, it would be him; that's why he had the first verse of the *Iliad* tattooed on his back just above the waist. It's written in Greek—the tattoo artist copied it, with some inaccuracies, from one of Agnese's high school books—and Cederna has her read and reread it in his ear when they're in bed.

In shorts and a T-shirt, he plants himself in front of Mitrano's cot; the corporal has already figured out what's in store for him and gets up reluctantly, his eyes sad.

"Did your parents have any children that lived?"

"SIR, YES, SIR!"

"I'll bet they regret that! You're so ugly you could be a modern art masterpiece! What's your name, fatbody?"

"SIR, VINCENZO MITRANO, SIR!"

"That name sounds like royalty! Are you royalty?"

"SIR, NO, SIR!"

"Do you suck dicks?"

"SIR, NO, SIR!"

"*Bullshit!* I'll bet you could suck a golf ball through a garden hose!"

"SIR, NO, SIR!"

"I don't like the name Mitrano! Only faggots and sailors are called Mitrano! From now on you're *Fatbody*!"

"SIR, YES, SIR!"

"Do you think I'm cute, Fatbody? Do you think I'm funny?"

"SIR, NO, SIR!"

"Then wipe that disgusting grin off your face!"

And on and on, until Mitrano kneels down and offers his neck to Cederna, who pretends to strangle him—and actually does choke him a little, enough to make his face turn a bit purple. Mattioli urges him not to quit; the others laugh like madmen, even though they've seen the performance dozens of times. Cederna is able to quote the first forty minutes of *Full Metal Jacket* from memory, line by line: Mitrano is his Private Gomer Pyle, his designated victim, and like the soldier in the film, he's not enjoying it one bit. When they're done, he climbs back on the cot and curls up, minding his own business. If he doesn't go along with the game, Cederna slaps the back of his neck so many times it gives him a crick.

Now that Cederna has everyone's attention he can continue getting dressed. The senior corporal major's equipment includes: a TRU-SPEC combat shirt, an eggplant-colored Defcon 5 armor carrier vest with coordinated accoutrements, a Kevlar helmet, an ESS Profile TurboFan mask, a pair of Vertx pants with a gusseted crotch and articulated knee (they're the most expensive and fit decidedly better than any other tactical pants), Quechua socks and briefs, a Nite MX10 quartz watch with GTLS whose dial and hands are illuminated fluorescent green even during the day, a pair of Otte Gear waterproof gloves, a keffiyeh, a pair of 12×25 binoculars, a Condor T&T belt, elbow and knee pads of the same brand, an ONTOS Extrema Ratio knife with a 165-millimeter steel blade, a GLX grenade launcher, a CamelBak canteen, a Beretta 92FS tucked into a thigh holster, a Beretta SC70/90 assault rifle, Lowa Zephyr GTX HI TF task force desert boots, monocular night vision goggles with IR illuminator, and seven magazines with appropriate ammunition. Aside from the firearms and the helmet, the items have all been ordered via the Internet. In the inside pocket of his jacket there is also a photo, a selfie that Agnese slipped into his backpack as a surprise, a three-quarters shot in which she's wearing a thong and barely covering her breasts with one arm, enough to make your eyes pop out of their sockets. Sixteen kilos and two thousand euros' worth of equipment: when he has his weapons on him Cederna feels different, more clearheaded, more alert. More fit. More cocky.

"I'll buy you some peanuts," he says to his buddies on his way out. He goes by the cot where Ietri is still lying in his skivvies, green with envy (though his nose, ears, and shoulders are red from the severe sunburn he got), slaps him sharply on the thigh. "Be a good girl, *vergi-nella*." Ietri raises his middle finger.

Cederna sits up front in the Lince, on the right, and sees to commu-nications. Camporesi drives. In back are Pecone and René, with Torsu in the middle, standing on the turret. The convoy of three armored vehicles is commanded by Captain Masiero. There's bad blood between Masiero and Marshal René—Cederna knows it and he sometimes likes to tease René about it.

He's not afraid. Not at all. Instead, he's excited. If they were to be ambushed, he knows that his reaction time to load the rifle or draw the pistol and take aim at the target would be less than two seconds; he also knows that less than two seconds might be too long, but that thought is a waste of time, so he sets it aside and focuses on the positive.

Nothing happens. The patrol rolls along without a hitch. They park the vehicles near the Afghan police barracks, which controls the road to the market. The soldiers take a guided tour inside to familiarize them-selves with the place, since starting the following week they'll have to go there every day to train the Mau Maus. From the way the Afghan policemen hold their weapons, it's clear to Cederna that they're hopeless: he's ready to bet that if the politicos decide to withdraw the troops and turn the war over to them, Afghanistan will fall back into the hands of the Taliban immediately. Cederna hates politicians; all they think about is lining their own pockets and that's it.

Once they've left the blockhouse the atmosphere relaxes and the patrol allows itself a walk along the road. The armored vehicles follow the soldiers, who are on foot like tame animals. From their shoddy holes-in-the-wall, the Afghans watch the soldiers parade by. Cederna frames them one at a time in the SC70/90's sight, imagines hitting them in the head, the heart, the knees. In a specialization course he learned to breathe with his belly, so that the shoulder his rifle butt rests on remains still—it's a technique used by commandos, just what Cederna wants to become. At the end of the mission he'll submit his application to enter the special forces.

For the time being his job is anything but that of assault: Captain Masiero has distributed handfuls of candy to the soldiers and children buzz around them like wasps. René tries to disperse them, flailing his arms.

"Don't worry, Marshal. They won't hurt you, you'll see," Masiero makes fun of him.

"We shouldn't let too many of them come near us at one time," René snaps back. He's citing the regulations.

"Are you expecting a bomb on a beautiful day like this? If you act like that, I won't allow you out anymore. You're scaring all my little friends." The captain bends down to one of the children and ruffles his hair. "It seems to me you still haven't understood a thing about our mission, Marshal."

Cederna watches his leader take his lumps. He can't stand Masiero either—he'd gladly knee him in the stomach. He gives René a consoling clap on the shoulder instead, and he too starts handing out candy.

A little boy, smaller than the others and wearing a tattered smock, is about to end up crushed. Cederna lifts him up and the child lets him carry him, staring at him with wide, rheumy eyes, his nose caked with dried snot.

"Doesn't your mother ever give you a bath, kid?"

The answer is a kind of gap-toothed smile.

"You don't understand a word I'm saying, huh? No, you don't understand a word. I can say whatever I want, then. That you're lousy with fleas, for instance. Filthy. Smelly. That makes you laugh? Really? Smelly, smelly. You stink. Look at you laughing! All you want is your candy, like all the others, right? Here you are. Uh-oh, slow down. Promise me, though, that when you grow up you won't become a Taliban, okay? Otherwise I'll have to put a bullet from this in your little head." He waves the rifle in front of him; the boy follows it with his eyes. "Torsu—hey, Torsu, come over here."

His cohort approaches at a slow jog, followed by his swarm of kids.

"Take my picture. Come on."

With one arm Cederna holds the child—who after trying unsuccessfully to unwrap the candy has popped it into his mouth, wrapper and all—and with the other raises the rifle in the air, holding it by the stock. It's a brazen pose, and he'll use it to beef up his online profile.

"Did I come out okay? Take another one—one more."

He sets the boy down on the ground, takes the last of the candy from his pocket, and tosses it far away, in the dust. "There. Go get it."

Food Supplies

Replenishments come by air, without much notice or regularity. Although requests sent from the FOB are always detailed, the bureaucrats in Herat send whatever they want, taking advantage of excess inventory: toilet paper instead of ammunition, juice when the soldiers have no water. For six days the helicopters haven't flown over the area because of the haze. Any longer and the soldiers will be forced to eat K rations. Fortunately, the meteorological situation has improved in the past few hours, the sky is once again a blazing blue and the guys from Charlie are grouped on the flat open space in front of the base, waiting for an airdrop.

The helicopter appears in the notch between the hill and the mountain, silent and tiny as an insect. The guys' eyes, all shielded by reflective lenses, turn toward the little black dot, but no one takes a step forward or unfolds his crossed arms. The aircraft descends and they can now make out the incorporeal circles described by the whirling rotor blades. No matter how many times you've seen a C-130 approach with its rear cargo hatch open, no matter how many bone-stiffening hours you've spent traveling in it, you can't help thinking how much it resembles a bird with its ass wide open.

The pallets are dropped in rapid succession; the cords of the parachutes—about a dozen in all—grow taut in the air and the white nylon canopies bloom against the cobalt sky. The aircraft makes a turn and disappears in a few seconds. The parachuted containers dangle in the air like abnormal jellyfish. Something goes wrong, though. A burst of wind slams into a parachute, which tilts over and nudges the cord of the one beside it, as if looking for company. It wraps itself around it and the beleaguered cord in turn goes into a spin. The spiral they form picks up speed, and the cords get snarled up all the way to the top, strangling the canopies. The Siamese parachutes knock into two of the ones below them, and together they form a tangled knot.

The soldiers hold their breath, some instinctively cover their face with their hands, while the cargo containers, intertwined and now lacking air support, plummet to the ground in free fall, the unprecedented speed dragging the heavy load down.

The crash raises a cloud of dust that takes several seconds to clear. The guys aren't sure what to do. They step forward a few at a time, their keffiyehs pressed against their noses.

"What a fucking mess," Torsu says.

"All because of those air force dickheads," Simoncelli says.

They surround the crater carved out by the cargo pallets.

Food, that's what was in them. About a hundred boxes of canned tomatoes have exploded, spraying red liquid all around, but there are also crushed packages of frozen turkey meat—pinkish shreds scattered in the sand, shimmering in the sun—canned mashed potatoes, and milk streaming out of plastic containers in several places.

Di Salvo picks up a handful of crumbled cookies. "Breakfast anyone? You can even dunk the cookies in the milk."

"What a fucking mess," Torsu says again.

"Yeah, a big fucking mess," Mitrano repeats.

The pool of milk spreads around the pile, skims the soldiers' boots, and mingles with the tomato purée. The birds of prey, which have already started wheeling about in ever tighter circles, mistake it for an inviting puddle of blood. The parched soil quenches its thirst by quickly soaking up the red liquid; it stays dark for a few seconds, then forgets it was ever moist.

Very little of the meat supply is salvageable. The slices of turkey recovered from the dust are barely enough for a quarter of the men and the cooks refuse to cut them into smaller pieces because they'd end up with children's portions. What with delays and glitches, the soldiers haven't eaten meat in over a week, and when they see trays of pasta with vegetable oil again, a riot almost breaks out in the mess hall. To calm things down (and because he himself has a great desire for steak), Colonel Ballesio agrees to the first breach of regulations, authorizing an expedition of two vehicles to go to the village bazaar and buy meat from the Afghans. The soldiers chosen for the mission show up at the FOB three hours later, triumphantly greeted by whistles and applause, with a cow stretched out on its side tied to the roof.

The animal is butchered on a nylon tarp spread out on the ground behind the dormitories of the 131st, hung out overnight at ambient temperature, and roasted for lunch. Due to adverse winds, the smoke from the grill fills the mess hall, but instead of bothering the soldiers, the stench of burning meat fuels their excitement and their appetite. They shout that they want the meat cooked rare and the cooks are happy to oblige. The thick steaks come to the table nice and pink inside: planting a fork in them releases trickles of pale blood that pools on the bottom of the plastic dishes. The meat is tough and not too flavorful, but still more appetizing than the thawed turkey, which is now rotting in the garbage bins. The guys eat until they're bursting. A spontaneous ovation erupts for Colonel Ballesio, who stands on the bench, raises his glass, and recites a phrase that, given what happens later on, is destined to become famous in its way: "I tell you with a colonel's certainty that this is the best meal you'll find anywhere in all of shitty Afghanistan."

After lunch, the guys of the Third return to their tents to rest. Torsu and a few others head for the Wreck. They've done their best to make it habitable: there are now folding tables with Ethernet cables hanging overhead, along with sticky rolls of flypaper full of dead sand flies. Michelozzi, who knows something about woodworking because of his father's trade, has built a bar counter by nailing together the boards of some walkways. It's all it takes for the Wreck to attract people from the other tents, especially at night, even though there are almost never enough drinks to restock it.

Like most of his companions, First Corporal Major Angelo Torsu also keeps hard-copy pornographic material in the double bottom of his backpack, but he hasn't yet used it: since he's been spending time with his virtual girlfriend he has something better available. It's because of her that he's subscribed to a satellite connection that costs him a small fortune and attracts the envy of his fellow soldiers. But man, it's worth it, since it means he can talk to her whenever he feels like it.

He sits down in a corner of the room and inserts the modem key. He waits for the signal light next to the name of Tersicore89 in his list of contacts to go from red to green.

THOR_SARDEGNA: r u there?

TERSICORE89: ciao my love

That's one of the fantastic things about his new girlfriend: she greets him in certain ways that make the skin on the back of his neck tingle.

THOR_SARDEGNA: what were you doing?

TERSICORE89: i'm in bed . . .

THOR_SARDEGNA: but it's at least ten thirty in the morning there!

TERSICORE89: it's saturday! and i was out late last night

A twinge of jealousy clenches Torsu's belly. He literally feels something shift inside.

THOR_SARDEGNA: who were you out with?

TERSICORE89: none of your business

He feels like closing the laptop screen, slamming it down. He doesn't like playing games. "Bitch," he writes.

TERSICORE89: movie with a girlfriend + a glass of wine. satisfied?

THOR_SARDEGNA: who cares

TERSICORE89: come on, stop it. how's your mission going, soldier? i miss you like crazy. i looked up the place you're at on google earth and printed the map. i hung it over the bed

With Tersicore89, Torsu has discovered that pure imagination has some indisputable advantages. First: when done at the computer, sex lasts as long as he wants, provided he restrains his hands as needed. Delaying ejaculation enables him to reach unprecedented and almost painful levels of arousal—often he feels like he's about to explode. Second: he's able to picture a woman who is exceedingly gorgeous, sexy, and tall, much more gorgeous-sexy-and-tall than he thinks he deserves (not that he's tried to construct a complete portrait of Tersicore89; for the time being it's easier to think of her as individual body parts, details). Third: the medium of the Net helps him confess certain intimate things that he wouldn't otherwise dare say out loud. Having a woman's body close by, its reality and urgency, has always inhibited him a little.

Nevertheless, for some time now he's had an urge to see Tersicore89. Not exactly in the flesh, not yet, but at least framed half-length by the webcam. It's a desire that arose in him with the approach of the mission. She excludes the possibility, but he keeps insisting, even now.

THOR_SARDEGNA: let me see you

TERSICORE89: stop it

THOR_SARDEGNA: just for a minute

TERSICORE89: it's not the right time yet. you know it

THOR_SARDEGNA: but it's been four months already!

TERSICORE89: we're just getting to know each other

THOR_SARDEGNA: i know more about you than about that bastard Cederna who sleeps in the cot next to me . . .

TERSICORE89: if i let you see me, you won't listen to a thing I say anymore, all you'll think about is whether i'm pretty enough and about my body and my breasts, which maybe you'd like to be bigger. you wouldn't even see who's inside anymore. you men are all like that and i've already been through it, thanks

THOR_SARDEGNA: i'm not like that

He's lying—he knows it and she can tell. His most recent relationship, with Sabrina Canton, had ended in part because of a raised mole she had on her chin. Torsu couldn't take his eyes off that dark growth. In the final weeks the mole had become gigantic, a chasm that had swallowed her whole.

TERSICORE89: you men are obsessed with looks

THOR_SARDEGNA: how about i let you see me?

TERSICORE89: don't you dare!

THOR_SARDEGNA: then you're the one obsessed with looks. are you afraid i'm not good-looking enough?

TERSICORE89: no. that's not it. you'd put me in a situation of being manipulated. showing yourself would be like saying, look, i have nothing to hide, and that would imply that i, on the other hand, since i won't let you see me, do have something to hide, and that's manipulation

THOR_SARDEGNA: would imply??? you talk too complicated!

Actually, it's precisely her way of talking—that is, of writing—that fascinates him. He never would have imagined that something like that could interest him in a woman. It's true, Torsu likes chatting with Tersicore89. In a few months they've each confided more secrets to each other than they've ever shared with anyone. For example, she's the only one who knows about his mother's recent stroke, and how now she drools a little whenever she eats. And Torsu, at least according to what she swears, is the only one who's read the poems she writes at night in a leather-covered notebook. Not that he understood much, but certain phrases really moved him.

TERSICORE89: when you come back from your mission . . . maybe . . .

THOR_SARDEGNA: they might kill me this very day

TERSICORE89: don't even say that as a joke

THOR_SARDEGNA: they could launch a rocket right here in the place where i'm writing to you and rip my arms and legs to shreds. my brain would squirt out of my ears and eyes, and smear up the screen and i wouldn't be able to write to you anymore

TERSICORE89: stop it

THOR_SARDEGNA: never again

TERSICORE89: stop or i'll log off!

THOR_SARDEGNA: okay okay. your tits aren't really small though, are they?

TERSICORE89: no. they're big and firm

THOR_SARDEGNA: describe them better

TERSICORE89: what do you want to know?

THOR_SARDEGNA: everything, how they look. how y—

"If you ask me, she's a he."

The voice is very close to Torsu's ear. Frightened, he gives a little yelp and snaps the lid shut. Zampieri is standing behind him.

"What the fuck do you want? How long have you been standing there?"

"Are you sure she's not a guy?"

"Get the hell away!"

"Tersicore is a man's name."

"She's not a guy!"

"How do you know that?"

Zampieri leans her behind on the edge of the table and crosses her arms, as if wanting to get into a long discussion. Torsu has the beginning of an erection in his pants and Tersicore89 waiting for him inside the computer. "Would you please leave?" he says, controlling himself.

She ignores him. "The Internet is full of people who pretend to be what they're not for their own smutty purposes. Men who pretend to be women, for instance."

"Do you mind telling me what the fuck you want from me?"

"I'm just trying to protect you. You're a friend of mine."

"I don't need anyone to protect me."

Zampieri tilts her head. She studies her nails, chooses one, and starts biting it.

Torsu says: "Anyway, a man wouldn't write certain things." He has no idea why he's now trying to convince her.

"I'd be able to write like a man if I wanted to," Zampieri replies, skeptical.

"No one had any doubts about that."

"Besides, if she doesn't want to be seen, it means there's something wrong."

"Fuck, you actually read all of it?"

"Some. Big, firm tits. Mmm . . ."

"Shut up! Anyway, I don't want to see her either."

"How come?"

"Just because."

Zampieri strokes his hair and the back of his neck, making him shiver. "Torsu, Torsu . . . what's the matter? Do real women scare you?"

He shoves her hand away forcefully and she bursts out laughing. "Give my regards to your little boyfriend," she says, then walks away. She'll probably go straight to the others and blurt it all out. Who the hell cares. Torsu opens the computer lid again.

TERSICORE89: r u still there?

THOR_SARDEGNA: i'm here. sorry, i lost the connection

Awkwardly they pick up where they'd left off. The conversation quickly degenerates into a rapid exchange of you-do-this-to-me-I-do-this-to-you, but the first corporal major's mood has been ruined. He's constantly turning around to make sure no one is watching him. From time to time the image of a young male adolescent sitting in place of Tersicore89 crosses his mind, disconcerting him. A severe fit of nausea rises up as he writes and reads, and he has stomach cramps. The malady worsens until he can no longer stand it. He's obliged to sign off in a hurry. He promises Tersicore89 he'll be right back.

Walking briskly through the base, he forces himself not to make eye contact with the other soldiers or be distracted by the small hawks wheeling around the watch tower. He wants to keep what's left of his arousal alive until he reaches the latrines.

Halfway there the first wave of wooziness hits him. The unsteadiness quickly passes from his head to his body, a quaking that he feels in the lower part of his abdomen. Within seconds, the pangs intensify to a point that makes him start running.

He reaches the chemical toilets, turns the first handle but the door is locked; he opens the second cubicle and finds a gruesome spectacle there; he enters the third and barely has time to latch it and pull his pants down, then he crouches over the aluminum squat toilet and releases his bowels in a single surge.

Slowly he exhales, his heart pounding in his ears. Another discharge takes him by surprise, coming suddenly and even more violently than the first, accompanied by acute stabbing pains. His digestive tract is in complete revolt. Torsu squeezes his eyes shut and grips the handle; he has the feeling he's being sucked into the hole. He tries not to look at the splatter of liquid shit on his bare thighs and the edge of his pants.

When the sharp pangs subside, he rests his head on his outstretched arm and remains like that another minute, exhausted and appalled by the gravity of what's happened to him. A feeling of relief spreads through his entire body along with a powerful drowsiness. For a few seconds he dozes off in that unnatural position.

Angelo Torsu is the first to show symptoms of food poisoning, maybe because he overdid it, filling his plate with cow meat three times, or because he's never had a strong stomach. Nevertheless, while he's still cowering inside the cramped toilet, two soldiers hole up in the adjoining latrines and he recognizes the sounds of an emergency similar to his own. Within a few hours *Staphylococcus aureus* has invaded the FOB and the base is in chaos. There are eighteen toilets available and at least a hundred men affected, with attacks hitting them twenty minutes apart.

By four in the afternoon the latrine area is overrun by a pack of trembling soldiers with greenish faces. They're gripping rolls of toilet paper and shouting to those inside the stalls to hurry it up, damn it.

There are four people ahead of Corporal Major Enrico Di Salvo, among them Cederna. Di Salvo is considering asking his buddy to switch places with him, because he's afraid he won't make it, but he's sure he'll say no. Cederna is a top-notch soldier, funny when he wants to be, but he's also a real bastard.

Di Salvo tries to remember when he's ever felt this bad in the past.

When he was thirteen he was operated on for appendicitis, and in the months prior to that he'd wake up at night with cramps that prevented him from walking upright to his parents' room. His mother was mistrustful of drugs and his father wary of specialists' fees, so they treated him with *limonata*. The pain didn't go away and at some point his mother would return to bed, upset with him: "I told you to drink it while it was hot and you insisted on waiting. So it didn't do any good." When the ambulance came to take him, the inflammation had worsened into peritonitis. But not even the pain at that time may have been as intense as what he's now feeling. "Cederna, let me go ahead of you," he says.

"Forget it."

"Please, I can't hold it anymore."

"Get a bag and do it in there, then."

"I don't like shitting in bags. Plus I can't make it to the tent."

"Your fucking problem. We're all in the same boat."

Di Salvo doesn't think that's true, though. Cederna isn't at all pale and he has yet to let out a moan or make a grimace. The other guys are gasping with pain. The first in line has started jerking the handle of a toilet that's been closed for too long. He receives an insult in return and kicks the metal door.

No, he's definitely never felt this bad. He has knives planted in his spleen and liver, he's got the chills, and he's dizzy. If he doesn't get to the toilet in a few minutes, he'll have to throw up, or worse. He might even faint. That stuff they ate was poison.

As if that weren't enough, after lunch he'd made a brief visit to Abib's tent and they smoked some hash together, just one gram, crumbled into the tobacco of a cigarette. Abib has a strange way of preparing the mixture; instead of heating it with a lighter, he rubs it between his fingers for a long time and then lets his saliva drip over it. You're disgusting, Di Salvo told him the first time. *What?* You're disgusting. Abib looked at him with that sly smile of his. After months at the base with the Italians he could speak a few words of Italian but instead he always spoke English: *Italians no know smoke,* he'd replied.

Maybe it's because of Abib's saliva that he now feels worse than the others. Who knows what disgusting infection he's passed on to him. He lives in the tent with the other two interpreters, on those carpets that stink of feet. An incredible odor, like sticking your nose in a sweaty sock. At first Di Salvo didn't want to sit down, but now he's gotten used to it. He just tries not to put his head down, even when he feels light-headed.

Now he's disoriented and miserable. He has cold sweats. Shortness of breath. He won't go to Abib anymore. For the whole rest of the mission he won't touch a pipe ever again. He mentally utters a vow to God: *If you let me make it to the toilet, if you save me from this stuff, I swear I won't go to Abib's to smoke anymore.* He's about to go further, to promise that he won't smoke even once he's back home, but then he remembers the pleasure of sitting on the terrace in Ricadi, with his feet on the railing, slowly inhaling a joint as he contemplates the oily sea, and he thinks twice about it. Six months without drugs may be enough of a commitment.

Another violent cramp makes him cough and lean forward. For a moment Di Salvo loses control of his sphincter; he feels it dilate suddenly. He's soiled himself, he's almost certain of it. He taps Cederna on the shoulder. "I'll give you ten euros if you let me go ahead."

The senior corporal major turns his head slightly. "Fifty."

"You're a bastard, Cederna! So it's true you're not as bad off."

"Fifty euros."

"Up yours. I'll give you twenty."

"Forty and that's as far as I'll go."

"Thirty. You're a bastard."

"I said I won't take less than forty."

Di Salvo feels the animal in his bowels rebelling. He has rhythmic, involuntary contractions in his anus. There's something alive in there, with its own beating heart. "Okay, I'll give you forty—forty," he says. "Now get the fuck out of the way."

Cederna gestures with his arm as if to say, By all means, go ahead. He snickers. He's probably not sick at all; he's just there to annoy the others. The first guy in line has gone in, so now there are only two more ahead of Di Salvo. It won't take much longer. He stares at his wristwatch as three minutes go by, excruciatingly slow, second by second; then the door of a toilet opens for him, like an invitation to paradise.

There are steps on both sides to enter the walkway with the latrines. Di Salvo rushes forward, but before he can get into the toilet an officer from the engineer corps comes up on the other side and beats him to it.

"Get out of there!" Di Salvo yells.

The second lieutenant points to the stripes on his jacket, but Di Salvo has forgotten all about rank. He waited all that time on line and gave forty euros to that scumbag Cederna and no one is going to swipe his place now, not even General Petraeus himself.

"Get out of there!" he repeats. "We're all sick here."

The second lieutenant doesn't appear threatening; rather he has an imploring look, as if he too has just shit his pants a little. He's a guy with a square head, not very tall but more solidly built than Di Salvo. The name on his insignia says Puglisi. Di Salvo instinctively notices those details. He takes in the parameters that a fighter must consider before confronting an opponent: height, circumference of the biceps, bulk. His brain informs the muscles that he should fight.

"Please," the engineer begs, pulling the door toward him so he can close it. Di Salvo sticks his foot against the jamb and forces the door open.

"Not on your life. It's my turn." He drags the second lieutenant out by his jacket collar.

"Hands off me, soldier!"

"Or what?"

"Don't tick me off. I'm from Catania, you know," the officer says, as if it meant anything.

"Oh, yeah? And I'm from Lamezia and I'm gonna shit all over you!" Before you know it, Puglisi delivers a not very forceful but well-aimed punch to his jaw, which goes *cra-a-a-ck*. Di Salvo is stunned.

A few seconds later they're scuffling on the walkway, little more than a foot wide, blocking the entrance and access to two of the toilets. Amid the shouts of the guys on line—a line that, at this point, has turned riotous—Di Salvo ends up on the ground with his face pressed against a grate; under it flows a liquid whose origin he doesn't want to know. He's wiped out. He ineffectively knees the second lieutenant's calf; he can't move otherwise because the guy is straddling him and immobilizing his free arm. His other arm is pinned under his own body. Puglisi keeps pummeling his ribs, weak but steadily repeated punches, always in the same spot, like an expert boxer.

As he's being beaten, it slowly dawns on Di Salvo that he's just assaulted an officer. Or was he the one who was assaulted? It's irrelevant. He's fighting with a superior—that's what matters. There are serious consequences for such behavior. Solitary. Expulsion. Court martial. Prison.

A blow to the head, unexpected, makes him spit something out. He's afraid it's a tooth. He's short of breath. That toilet belonged to him. He forked over forty euros to that greedy asshole Cederna, who is now yelling things at him that he can't understand because one ear is squashed against the grate and the other is under Puglisi's hand. The cramps have backed off or else they've merged with the agony of the punches. He absolutely has to get out of that hold. He's wheezing. With a forceful lunge he manages to arch his spine and free his arm from under his back. He lands a blow on the engineer's face. "Now you'll change your tune, you ugly bastard!"

He's all worked up, ready to give it back to him with interest, but the lieutenant stands up and takes his hands off him. He steps back. Di Salvo, stunned, looks up at him. "Coward!" he yells, outraged. He's pleased to see that he's at least managed to give him a bloody nose and cut his eyebrow. "Get back here!"

But his opponent is looking away. In fact, all the soldiers have turned their attention elsewhere. Di Salvo follows their gaze and sees Colonel Ballesio making his way through the crowd, clutching his belly.

"Come on, move—let me through!"

Just before losing consciousness, Di Salvo sees the commander's stubby legs step over him as he closes himself inside the contested toilet. He just has time to hear an animal gasp from inside the cubicle, then nothing.

It's in that state of distress that Egitto meets the guys from Third Platoon, Charlie, for the first time. The food poisoning has kept him busy all afternoon, administering Imodium tablets two at a time and massive doses of intestinal antibiotics; supplies are now starting to run low, so he's had to cut the dosage in half. He's repeatedly inspected the condition of the toilets, which minute by minute testified to the worsening of the situation: at the moment, three toilets are unusable for hygienic reasons, one is stopped up by a wad of wet wipes, and another by a flashlight stuck in the waste pipe (miraculously it's remained lit, projecting intermittent flashes of light on the metallic walls and on the washbasin).

Inside the Third Platoon's tent, the air is hot and smelly, but the lieutenant pays no attention, just as he pays no attention to the eerie silence. Going in there is no different from going into any of the tents he's already visited: the camps all look alike, the soldiers too, they're trained to look alike, and now they're suffering from the same spasms and the same dehydration. Nothing suggests to Lieutenant Egitto that his fate will soon be bound to that platoon in a special way. Looking back, later on, he will find that indifference ominous.

"Who's in charge here?" he asks.

A shirtless soldier, drenched in sweat, struggles to a seated position on his cot. "Marshal René. Sir!"

"As you were," Egitto orders. He asks those who are experiencing the staph symptoms to raise their hands, and counts them. Then he turns to the only man not affected: "Your name?"

"Salvatore Camporesi."

"You didn't eat the meat?"

Camporesi shrugs: "You bet I ate it. Two nice big helpings."

The lieutenant orders him to go to the command center and cover the guards' night shifts.

"But I was on guard duty yesterday," Camporesi protests.

The lieutenant shrugs in turn. "What can I tell you? It's an emergency."

"Have a good night, Campo," a soldier mouths off. "If you see a shooting star make a wish for me, honeybunch."

Camporesi expresses aloud the wish that his colleague drown in his own excrement, then pulls on his boots and struts to the door while the others target him with balled-up T-shirts, dirty tissues, and plastic spoons.

Egitto prepares the syringes and the guys get in position, lying on their side, undershorts lowered halfway down their butts. A fart escapes, or maybe someone did it on purpose; in any case it's applauded. Complete freedom, almost obscene, reigns among them; for each of them the other soldiers' bodies are no less familiar than their own, even for the only female in the group, who displays her bare hip indifferently.

One of the soldiers is in particularly critical condition. Egitto records the name in the notebook he will refer to later to make a report to the commander, Angelo Torsu, first corporal major. The young man's teeth are chattering inside the sleeping bag, under four layers of blankets. Egitto takes his temperature: 102.

"Earlier it was 104," René puts in.

Egitto notices the marshal's eyes on him. He's a concerned, caring platoon leader; you can see it in his face. He set up his cot in the middle of the tent so he could keep an eye on them all.

"He can't walk anymore. The last time he had to do his business in here."

There's no reproach in the way he says it and the others don't comment. That body that's so sick belongs to them as well and they treat it with respect. Egitto thinks about the fact that someone took the trouble to help the soldier with the bag, then sealed it and threw it in the garbage. When it was up to him to do the same for his father, he'd preferred to call a nurse. What kind of doctor feels disgust for a man who's suffering? What child refuses to care for his father's body?

"How many times?" he asks the soldier.

Torsu looks at the lieutenant from behind a veil of confusion and prostration. "Huh?" he murmurs.

"How many times did you empty your bowels?"

"I don't know . . . ten. Or more." His breath is rancid; his parched lips stick to each other. "What have I got, Doctor?" Egitto measures the pulse at his throat; the beats are weak but not alarmingly so. "It's nothing serious," he reassures him.

"They're all looking down at me from heaven, Doc," Torsu says, then rolls his eyes back.

"What?"

"He's delirious," René says.

Egitto gives the marshal some medication to be administered to the soldier and bottles of milk enzymes to dispense to the others. He directs him to keep Torsu's mouth moist with a wet sponge, to take his temperature every hour, and to notify him if his condition worsens. He promises to return in the morning, the same promise he made to each of the units, though he certainly won't be able to see them all.

"Doc, could I talk to you for a second?" René says.

"Of course."

"Privately."

Egitto closes up his medical kit, follows the marshal outside. René lights a cigarette and for half a second his face is illuminated by the lighter's flame. "It's about one of my boys," he says. "He screwed up." His voice trembles a little, because of the cold, the cramps, or something else. "With a woman, you know."

"A disease?" The lieutenant takes a guess.

"No. That other thing."

"An infection?"

"He got her pregnant. But it's not his fault either."

"How do you mean, if I may ask?"

"The woman is of a certain age. In theory, it wasn't supposed to happen to her anymore."

The tip of René's cigarette glows. Egitto follows that one luminous spot because there's nothing else to look at. He thinks that voices in the dark have more character, that he won't easily forget the marshal's. In fact, he won't. "I see," he says. "There are remedies, as you probably know."

"That's what I told him myself. That there are remedies. But he wants to know exactly what they do to it. To the baby, that is."

"You mean when a pregnancy is terminated?"

"An abortion."

"Normally, the fetus is sucked out through a very thin catheter."

"And then?"

"And then it's over."

René takes a long drag. "Where do they put it?"

"It's . . . disposed of, I think. We're talking about something minuscule, which practically doesn't exist."

"Doesn't exist?"

"It's very tiny. Like a mosquito." He is telling him only part of the truth.

"Do you think they're aware of it?"

"The mother or the fetus?"

"The baby."

"I don't think so."

"You don't think so or you're sure of it?"

Egitto's patience is running out. "I'm sure," he says, just to cut it short.

"I'm a Catholic, Doc," René confesses. He doesn't even notice that he's given himself away.

"That can complicate things. Or make them a lot simpler."

"Not one of those Catholics who go to church. I believe in God, sure, but in my own way. I have my own faith. I mean, priests are people like you and me, right? They can't know everything."

"No, I don't think they can."

"Everyone believes in what he feels, if you ask me."

"Marshal, I'm not the right person to talk to about this. Maybe you'd be better off talking to the chaplain."

René's cigarette has burned down only halfway, but he crushes it out between his fingers. The ember falls to the ground and lies there smoldering. The glow slowly fades and turns black like everything around it. René throws the butt in the dumpster. He's a man who cares about order, Egitto thinks, a proper soldier.

"How long does it take?"

"For what, Marshal?"

"To suck the baby out through the tube."

"It's not a baby yet, at that point."

"But still, how long does it take?"

"Not long. Five minutes. Not even."

"Anyway, he doesn't suffer."

"I don't think so."

Even in the dark Egitto can tell that the marshal would like to ask him again if he's really sure. How do you make certain decisions if you don't know the terms of the operation, the logistical details, the coordinates? A soldier demands clarity, a soldier likes to plan things out.

"What would you do if you were that guy, Doctor?"

"I don't know, Marshal. I'm sorry."

Later, as he crosses the square by himself, with the flashlight's bluish beam lighting the way, Egitto wonders whether he shouldn't have allowed himself to influence the marshal, to direct him toward the right choice. But how does he know what the right choice is? He's not in the habit of interfering with the course of other people's lives. What Alessandro Egitto does best is stand on the sidelines.

There are people prone to action, inclined to play leading roles—he's just a cautious, meticulous observer: forevermore a second born.

Un Sospiro

She had always been their favorite. I realized it very early on, when I was still little enough for our parents to think that putting on a good act was all it took to disguise their biased feelings. Their gazes instinctively focused on Marianna, and only afterward, as though suddenly remembering they'd passed over me, would they turn to yours truly, making up for it with a broader smile than necessary.

It wasn't blind obedience on their part to the order that nature had imposed when we came into the world, much less apathy or inattention. Nor was it true that they noticed Marianna first because she was *taller*, as I told myself for a time. It was her girlish presence that beguiled them, whether sitting at the table with her hair held back by a headband, or in the tub hidden by foamy bubble bath, or bent over her desk doing homework; it was as though it caught them by surprise, time and time again. Their eyes widened simultaneously and a bright flash of satisfaction and awe exploded in the center of the pupils, the same spark that must have flared when they tremulously witnessed the miracle of her birth. "There she is!" they exclaimed in unison when she appeared, dropping to their knees to offset the matter of height. Then, noticing me, they added: ". . . and Alessandro," their voices fading on the last syllable. The only thing in store for me, having arrived three years later via an emergency Caesarean section—Nini asleep and Ernesto overseeing his colleague's performance in the operating room—was a stale, halfhearted rerun of the attentions my sister had received.

For instance: I knew that for her my father's car had a name—*La Musona*, "Snout"—and that it spoke to her as it took her to school every morning. In the traffic along the riverside boulevard, as the mottled trunks of the plane trees regularly interrupted the eight a.m. light, La Musona came to life and took on animal features: the side mirrors were transformed into ears, the steering wheel into a navel, the wheels into hefty paws. Ernesto disguised his voice, chirping in falsetto with a distinct nasal twang. He hid his mouth behind the collar of his coat and uttered pompous phrases: "Where may I take you today, signorina?"

"To school, thank you," Marianna replied with a queenly air.

"What do you say we go to the amusement park instead?"

"No, no, Musona. I have to go to school!"

"Oh, school—how boring!"

Years later, I found myself garnering clues to the radiant past that had preceded me in the episodes often evoked by Ernesto in order to regain, for a moment or two, his daughter's affection, at one time manifest and now latent. The nostalgia that he betrayed on those occasions led me to imagine a brimming, matchless bliss, which mysteriously vanished after my arrival. At other times, I thought it was just one of the countless ways in which our father vaunted his flamboyant imagination: he seemed more concerned, in fact, with commemorating his actions as a parent than with reawakening my sister's dormant joy.

"Let's see if Marianna still remembers the name of the Croma," he'd say.

"La Musona." Marianna drew out the vowels and slowly lowered her eyelids, because that game had bored her for some time.

"La Musona!" Ernesto exclaimed contentedly.

"That's right, La Musona." Nini echoed him softly, smiling innocently.

To become wholly convinced that Marianna held a special place in our parents' hearts, all you'd have to do is take a look in the closet of our old apartment, turn on the dim bulb that Ernesto never got around to fixing (it still dangles unsteadily from the electrical wires), count the cartons with "Marianna" written on the side and right after that the other boxes, marked "Alessandro," mine. Seven to three. Seven cartons overflowing with my older sister's glorious childhood—notebooks, tempera and watercolor paintings, school exams with astounding grades, collections of nursery rhymes that she could still recite today—and on the bottom shelf just the other three, full of all my junk, stupid talismans and battered toys that I stubbornly refused to throw away when the time came. Seven to three. That was roughly the proportion of affection unwittingly established in the Egitto household.

I didn't complain, though. I learned to accept my parents' biased love as an inevitable, even just, disadvantage. And if at times I gave in to secret bouts of self-pity—inanimate objects had never wanted to talk to me—I soon shrugged off that jealousy, because I too, like my parents, had a special fondness for Marianna and worshiped her above all else.

To begin with, she was beautiful, with narrow shoulders, nose crinkled up in a mischievous grin, blond hair that would later darken a bit, and a host of delightful freckles that peppered her face from May to September. Kneeling in her room in the middle of the carpet, surrounded by outfits for Ballerina Barbie and World Peace Ambassador Barbie and three My Little Ponies with colorful manes—each element positioned exactly where she wanted it—she seemed to be mistress not only of herself, but of everything that belonged to her. Watching her, I learned to care for small objects in a way I wouldn't have otherwise: the way she looked at them, the way she attributed personality and import to one or the other just by touching them, all that intoxicating pink surrounding her, convinced me that the feminine world was more fascinating, luxuriant, and fulfilling than ours. That, for sure, made me burn with envy.

Then, too, Marianna was incredible. She was a slender yet tenacious reed in her ballet classes, before Ernesto insisted that she stop because of the disastrous consequences that dancing en pointe could have on her feet, among them arthritis, seriously debilitating tendonitis, and various other osteopathic conditions; she was a brilliant conversationalist who delighted my parents' cultured friends (Ernesto's chief surgeon complimented her at a communal dinner for using the term *blandishments* properly); but above all, she was a scholastic prodigy. Nini's greatest source of concern in middle school was trying to avoid the compliments that rained down on her from all sides, from teachers, from other envious parents, even from unexpected acquaintances who had heard of her daughter's impressive results. There was no subject in which Marianna did not demonstrate a proclivity, and her approach to each discipline was always the same: compliant, serious, and strictly devoid of passion.

She also played the piano. On Tuesdays and Thursdays at five her instructor Dorothy arrived at our house. An imposing woman, with bulging breasts and belly and an old-fashioned taste in dress, apparently aimed at drawing attention at all costs to her British origins on her father's side. I was required to be in the entrance hall to welcome her, and again to say good-bye to her, an hour and a half later: "Good afternoon, Miss Dorothy."

"Dorothy is more than enough, sweetheart."

And later: "Good-bye, Dorothy."

"See you soon, dear."

She was the first victim of Marianna's secret wrath. The alliance with my sister, which for a long time (wrongly so) I considered unshakable, was founded on cruel mockery the afternoon when, waiting for the music teacher, Marianna said: "Did you know that Dorothy has a daughter who stutters?"

"What does that mean?"

"It means she t-t-t-t-talks like th-this. And she can't say words that begin with *m*. When she calls my name she says Mmm-mmm-mm-arianna."

She twisted her little face and began mooing loudly. It was a monstrous and irresistible imitation, hilariously naughty. Nini would find it reprehensible: she spent much of her time worrying about unseen ways in which our behavior could hurt others, and carefully avoided any reference to her children in conversations lest she might give the— wrong, totally wrong—idea that she was bragging or making comparisons. If Marianna, talking about a classmate, said, "She does much worse than me, her grades are all so-so," she immediately seemed alarmed: "Marianna! We mustn't make comparisons." Just imagine if she caught her mimicking Dorothy Byrne's stuttering daughter, with her mouth all screwed up and her eyes crossed!

For this reason, since at eight years old my most immediate reactions always emulated those I presumed would be my mother's, I was initially taken aback by Marianna's lowing as she stammered out the consonants. Then, little by little, I felt my lips widening. To my horror, I realized that I was smiling. More accurately, I was now laughing outright, with gusto, as if I had suddenly discovered the kind of thing that was really funny. Marianna let out another bellow, *m-m-moo*, before she too burst out laughing.

"A-a-and then . . . take a look at Dorothy's underarms . . . She has dark stains . . . they stink to high heaven!"

We couldn't stop: the laughter of one of us set off the other. And as soon as she gave signs of stopping, Marianna would twist her mouth to one side and we'd begin all over again.

Before that day we hadn't shared anything. Any possible closeness, or even just complicity, was swept away by the difference in the years that separated us and by the disdainful resignation with which Marianna seemed to tolerate me. The wicked imitation of Dorothy's daughter was our first direct bond, our first secret. At supper, when Ernesto was detained at the hospital and Nini turned her back to give the unappetizing mashed potatoes one last stir, Marianna would distort her face and I'd nearly swallow my food the wrong way. It would become a habit: picking on certain people we knew, discovering absurd aspects of our regimented lives, and laughing until we collapsed, setting each other off in turn until we no longer had any idea of what had been so funny.

That afternoon, when Dorothy appeared at the door in a long, dark teal dress with pleated sleeves, we had tears in our eyes. I immediately noticed the rings under the armpits, and though even then I could display a certain restraint when called for, I could not manage to say "Good afternoon, Dorothy" without laughing and spraying her with spittle.

"It's a pleasure to find you both so cheerful," the teacher remarked, somewhat annoyed. She dropped her handbag on the couch and walked purposefully toward the piano stool.

At that point I left them alone, as usual. Making sure that a carafe of water and two glasses were available on the glass-topped table, I then closed the door to the hallway and went back to my room. After a few moments of silence, I heard the ticking of the metronome begin.

A good half hour was devoted to warming up: chromaticisms, triplets and quadruplets, sight-reading, Pozzoli exercises and the tendon-breaking ones by Hanon. Then they started on the repertoire. There were a few pieces I particularly liked: Debussy's *Doctor Gradus ad Parnassum*, Beethoven's Moonlight Sonata, a Bach minuet whose ritornello is all I remember, and Chopin's *Prelude Op. 28, No. 4*, whose first part with its soft descending chords filled me with a piercing melancholy. But the one that became my favorite was unquestionably *Un sospiro* by Franz Liszt, with which Marianna reached the height of her virtuosity and the most evident interpretative intensity. She had already turned fourteen and was preparing for a presentation, her first real performance as a musician after an eternity of solitary study. Dorothy had arranged a student recital in a small Baroque church in the city center.

Marianna practiced the étude ad nauseam, since the piece involved several technical intricacies, including crossing the arms in the complicated opening arpeggio: the left hand, after skimming over two octaves, passed rapidly over the right to complete the melody on the high notes. It was a piece that was almost more beautiful to see than to hear and sometimes, while Marianna practiced, I opened the door a crack and watched her fingers moving gracefully, caressing the keyboard, closely monitored by her constantly shifting pupils. The movement was so swift that you couldn't believe she was really touching the keys, her right pinky extended so that it stood out from her palm.

But the critical passage came further on when, approaching the languendo, the score launched into a dizzying descending scale. Marianna stumbled at that point; the tiny muscles of her fingers couldn't sustain the speed and she would stop, letting the sharp clacks of the metronome tick on. Undeterred, she would resume playing from a few bars back and tackle it again, once, twice, ten times, until she thought she had acquired the correct fluidity. Often, however, she'd stumble again the following day and then she'd get angry and slam her hands on the keyboard, leaving behind a mournful rumbling.

Nevertheless, by a week before the recital she had achieved complete mastery, and it was time to worry about what she would wear. Nini took her to a shop under the arcades and together they chose a sleeveless sheath with matching pumps. For me, a pair of navy blue pants and a salmon shirt—a color that dominated my wardrobe before disappearing entirely to avoid inopportune reminders of my psoriasis-inflamed neck and face. Meanwhile, on tiptoe, I tried to see as much as possible of my figure in the bathroom mirror. I was at least as excited as my sister, probably even more, or so I tell myself today.

The church was cold and the audience members, about fifty in all, did not take off their coats, making the event seem somewhat temporary, as though everyone might rush out at any moment. Dorothy was dressed at her most elegant and was greeted by warm applause, despite the fact that as of September she had increased the cost of her private lessons by nearly twenty percent. Her daughter sat in the front row, a little to one side, her deformed mouth tightly sealed.

Marianna was scheduled among the final players, since she was one of the proficient students. I curbed my impatience by focusing on the music. I recognized many of the pieces played by the little girls who preceded her, because Marianna, too, had studied them in the past. None of them seemed to be on her level, or at least as precocious as she had been. Each time a girl took the stage, I held my breath, afraid I might find that she was more talented than Marianna or that she might perform a more impressive piece. But there was no one as gifted as my sister, nor a piece more impressive than Franz Liszt's *Un sospiro*.

Nini was sitting next to me; each time she took my hand and squeezed it. She too was nervous. Silently she studied what the other young pianists were wearing, gauging if by chance she had overdone it with Marianna. She responded politely to the smiles of other mothers seeking complicity, but as though to say: Wonderful, of course, but I can't wait for it to be over. She'd much rather her daughter's music practice take place in the living room as usual, in a safe place, because being there that night required a display of emotions well above what she could stand. I was dying to tell her Marianna was the most talented, but I knew what I would have to face. Nini would look all around, terrified, before admonishing me: *Alessandro, for the love of God! We mustn't make comparisons!*

One seat over, much of Ernesto's face was covered by a scarf. He also wore a raw-wool hat with earmuffs and various layers under his coat. It was the second day of his Absolute Fast (nothing but quarts and quarts of water at room temperature), a self-imposed purification that would free him from a series of mysterious toxins present in every type of food. During the Absolute Fasts, which would last for three years and occurred at six-month intervals, Ernesto took time off from the hospital and spent whole days lying on the couch, surrounded by half-empty plastic bottles, wheezing in distress. On the third and final day he would rave deliriously, asking whoever was around what time it was (the Fast ended at ten p.m.) while Nini kept dabbing his forehead with moist cloths. On the evening of the recital he was still in his right mind, but in that drafty church he felt colder than all the others. Before leaving home Nini had beseeched him to have at least a few tablespoons of broth: "It's just water, Ernesto. It will make you feel better."

"Oh, sure, water laced with animal fats. And salt. You have a strange concept of 'just water.'"

If he were to pass out in front of everyone, collapsing over the seats in front of them, Nini would be quick to explain it by citing his numerous night shifts as the cause: Sometimes six or seven a month, truly too many, but when someone asks him for a favor he just can't say no.

Ernesto did not faint, however, and sat through the evening with his arms crossed, his breathing labored under the scarf from the lack of nourishment. When Marianna stood up from the front row and approached the piano, he was the first to clap his hands to encourage her. He straightened his shoulders and cleared his throat, as if to underscore, That's my daughter, the beautiful young girl up on the dais, my daughter. I thought of the descending scale that had entangled Marianna during the lengthy preparation period, and repeated to myself in silence, Don't let her stumble, don't let her stumble.

My wish was granted. Marianna did not stumble over the scale. It went much worse. Her performance was a disaster from the first cluster of notes. It wasn't that the sequence was inaccurate—I'd have noticed any false note, that's how well I knew the piece—but the execution was heavy-handed, wooden, to the point of being irritating, especially in the initial arpeggio, which required suppleness and spontaneity. Marianna's fingers had suddenly stiffened and were producing staccato-like sounds disconnected from one another, like fitful sobs. Her tenseness made her contract her shoulders and she was hunched over the piano, almost as if she were fighting it, almost as if it hurt her wrists to play it. Nini and Ernesto didn't move a muscle, they were holding their breath like I was, and now there were three of us who hoped it would all be over as quickly as possible. The Sigh, *Un sospiro*, had become a Heartache.

When she had finished, Marianna stood up, red-faced, made a slight bow, and returned to her seat. I saw Dorothy go over and whisper something in her ear, rubbing her back, while the applause around us was already dwindling uncertainly. I could barely contain myself from standing up and shouting, *Wait! That wasn't how she was supposed to play it—I swear she can do much better, I've listened to her every afternoon and that piece is breathtaking, believe me, it was the stress, let her try again, let her try just one more time . . .* But another girl had already taken her place at the piano and was beginning a Brahms rhapsody with shameless audacity.

On the way home, we spoke little. Ernesto said a few kind words, complimenting the evening as a whole rather than my sister's performance, and Nini concluded by saying: "Oh, how exhausting! But now we'll go home to our nice warm house and tomorrow everything will be back to normal."

Marianna continued the private piano lessons every Tuesday and Thursday for a total of thirteen years, with waning dedication, until she failed the entrance examination for her seventh year at the conservatory, a disappointment that was passed over in silence in our house and soon forgotten. By then Nini and Ernesto had bitterly opened their eyes to how greatly their daughter's true inclinations differed from what they had earlier imagined for her. After that, Marianna never again raised the lid of the Schimmel grand, not even once; when walking through the living room she stayed away from it, as if the beast had tormented her far too long and, even though now dormant, was able to arouse fear and loathing in her. The piano is still there, silent and gleaming. On the inside, the steel strings are no longer taut and have lost their pitch.

Strong Wind, Blackout

"How long have we been here?"

"Twenty-five days."

"What the hell! A lot longer than that."

"Twenty-five, I'm telling you."

"Still, it seems like an eternity."

On the twenty-fifth day after the Alpines' arrival in Gulistan, the thirty-sixth day since they'd landed in Afghanistan, FOB Ice is attacked for the first time.

A sandstorm has been raging since nightfall, the air is thick with particles, and a dense orange fog obscures the sky. To go the few dozen yards to reach the mess hall or the toilets, the soldiers have to walk with their head down, eyes narrowed and mouth closed, while their exposed cheeks are scraped raw. The tents quake like shivering animals and wind gusts shriek with a frightening *whooosh*. The grains of sand whirling crazily in the squall at top speed have electrically charged every obstacle in their path—it's as if the entire base were suspended over a low-voltage pylon. The molecules' frenzy has even permeated the mood of the soldiers, who seem more garrulous than usual. Inside the Wreck, the guys of the Third Platoon are talking loudly, over one another. From time to time someone gets up from the benches to approach the only window in the place and contemplate the churning cloud of sand and the twisters writhing in the square outside, like ghosts. "Look at that," he mutters, or maybe, "Shit."

The shouting is especially annoying to Marshal René, who is struggling to write an e-mail to Rosanna Vitale that he can't seem to find a way to formulate. In his head he's organized his thoughts systematically, as he usually does, but as soon as he transfers them to words, the logic that holds them together suddenly proves shaky, equivocal. He had begun with a long account of his military venture—the exhausting trip from Italy, the inertia of the days in Herat, the transfer to the FOB—and he even allowed himself a detailed description, poetic in its way, of what he saw during the excursion to Qal'a-i-Kuhna and of the storm currently raging. Only afterward did he get around to the real reason for the message, in a paragraph that began, "I've thought a lot about what we talked about the last time," and continued with increasingly foolish verbal gymnastics just to avoid the word *baby* at all costs, replacing it with circumlocutions such as "what happened," "the accident," or even "you know what." Reading it over, however, he realized that the initial digression was somewhat offensive, the key issue relegated to just one of several topics, as if it were of little or no importance to him, whereas it *is* important to him, and he wants it to be clear, so he deleted everything and started over again. He's now on his fourth attempt and, despite his lexical efforts, despite the fact that he thinks he's tried every opening to approach what he's concerned about, he's failed to arrive at a solution. He's wondering if there really is a way to say what he wants to say without sounding brutal or vile, or both. In a fit of irritation, he composes the lapidary message:

Dear Rosanna,

I think you should have an abortion

and clicks the send button. The storm has slowed down the connection, however, and René has time to discard the e-mail before it's sent into cyberspace.

A small, smelly pile of cigarette butts and ashes has formed at his feet, the smoke hangs in the air in velvety layers, but René lights another cigarette. A child would ruin his life—at the very least it would mess it up considerably. Besides, what sense does it make to have one with a woman he barely knows, or rather whom he doesn't know at all, a woman fifteen years older than him who pays him for the pleasure of his body? A child is a serious matter, it's no joke, it requires certain conditions, it should be planned. The doc said it just takes a minute to get rid of it, that neither the mother nor the baby is aware of it . . . He has to stop using that word, *baby*, stop it! It's little more than a mosquito, that's what it is, it's sucked out through a tube and that's that. There's only one way to get out of this bad situation: Rosanna has to have an abortion, period. Unfortunately he can't be with her because he's tied up on the mission, and he's sorry about that, but when the time comes he'll have flowers sent to her in the hospital, or directly to her house. What kind of flowers are suitable for an abortion?

When he reaches this point, a doubt creeps into the marshal's thoughts: the suspicion that he's being selfish. What if he's wrong? What if what he's about to do is one of those crimes for which there is no forgiveness? Rosanna said it was her fault, one hundred percent hers, but what does René know about how the Almighty will assign blame when the time comes? He's riveted again, his vacant stare turned toward the window that's being buffeted by gusts of sand. René is unfamiliar with the treacherous spirals human reasoning can run up against; his brain is used to following a linear chain of logical steps. All of these back-and-forths, objections and counterobjections, are the most exhausting thing he's ever experienced.

"WAKE UP, MARSHAL!"

Passalacqua claps his hands under his nose. René flinches. Angry, he gives him a shove. Zampieri, from another table, comes to his defense: "Hey, leave him alone. Can't you see the marshal is writing a love letter?" She winks at him. René doesn't respond.

He shuts down the e-mail program and double clicks on the *War-Craft II* icon. Distraction, he needs a little distraction.

A few yards away, at a table kept from wobbling by half a roll of toilet paper flattened and wedged under one of its legs, Ietri, Camporesi, Cederna, and Mattioli are challenging one another at Risk. It's a typical game, showing Cederna to be the bullying braggart he is. He chose the black army and was defeated in multiple territories after less than an hour. Left with an army spottily deployed, he's decided to concentrate all his remaining forces in Brazil, doggedly taking aim at Ietri's soldiers entrenched in Venezuela. Each time it's his turn he renews the attack with maximum strength and Ietri is beginning to feel exasperated. He's sure his buddy's objective has nothing to do with the destruction of his army, nor with the conquest of the South American continent. Cederna's goal is pure and simple arrogance: he wants to irritate him, spoil his fun in the game because he's losing and can't stand the fact that things are going well for Ietri, who after conquering the North American continent is moving slowly southward.

"Brazil attacks Venezuela with three dice," Cederna crows. "You can kiss your tanks good-bye, *verginella.*"

"I don't know why you're always picking on me," Ietri whines, but he's immediately sorry. In fact, Mattioli smiles sarcastically.

Cederna mimics him: "*I don't know why you're always picking on me* . . . Because Venezuelans are shitty communists and have to be punished. That's why."

He rolls the dice on the board and clearly does it on purpose to scatter Ietri's troops, after he's taken the time to align them carefully. A five, a six, and a deuce. "*Booom!*"

Ietri reluctantly picks up the blue dice. His army, though great in number, now appears weak, caught up in a disorderly retreat. He throws the dice and scores lower with two out of three. Cederna is quick to remove the corresponding tanks, simulating the same number of explosions.

"Get your hands off. I'll do it."

Ietri has had enough. If he were in Cederna's shoes, he wouldn't act like that. He would team up instead, probably against Mattioli, who has that greedy, silent way of playing, like someone who isn't enjoying it because he takes the competition too seriously. There are twenty euros in the kitty—it's not much, but it's still something. Ietri's desire to win it is so heated, it scares him. At times, more and more often, his thoughts are swept by forces that he can't control.

"Another attack! On Venezuela. Death to the communists!"

"Hey! That's enough!" Ietri blurts out.

"I'll decide when it's enough, *verginella*."

Camporesi laughs. No one has the foggiest idea of how great Ietri's humiliation is at this point. He grips the dice in his fist.

This time he scores lower with all three—he's lost the territory. He doesn't get ruffled; he has many others left. He removes the tanks and puts them back in the box. If Cederna wants to act like a jerk, that's his problem. He certainly won't give him the satisfaction of getting upset.

It's Mattioli's turn now, and he's getting ready to apply one of the insidious strategies he's been hatching at length in silence, when they hear the first explosion. An ominous, reverberating thud, like an anvil striking the ground. The guys' hearing is trained to distinguish artillery sounds. But of them all, Marshal René is the first to utter the word *mortar*.

He says it quietly, to himself. Then he immediately yells: "Bunker!"

The boys spring to their feet and head for the door, swift and orderly. They know the evacuation plan—they've run through it a hundred times at least. For Senior Corporal Major Francesco Cederna, it's the first mortar strike he's heard outside of a training drill. He's amazed at how the sound is identical to the one he's familiar with, but, obviously, of course it is. He almost feels like thanking the enemy for interrupting his losing game of Risk.

Camporesi and Mattioli have lined up to go out. Cederna is left across from Ietri's suddenly pale face. He sweeps the tanks off the board with his forearm: "What a shame, *verginella*. You were doing so well." He grabs the euros and shoves them in his pocket. Ietri doesn't breathe a word. There's another explosion and this time they unmistakably feel the ground shudder under their feet. "Let's go. After you."

Cederna is the last to plunge into the sandstorm. He wants to appear offhand and give the impression that he has everything under control. Another shell explodes somewhere to his left. Closer this time. It may have landed inside the base, but visibility is reduced to a few yards—it's impossible to know for sure. The shrill wail of the siren and the collective shouts of the men produce a deafening cacophony in stereophonic sound. Commands intended for soldiers on duty mingle with instructions urging the others to take shelter. Cederna regrets the fact that his platoon is off duty today; they'll have to stay in the kennel like dogs frightened by fireworks. Fucking shitty.

He hears the engines of the armored vehicles start up. Where do they think they're going? With a storm like this they're likely to cause more damage than a hail of shrapnel. He opens his mouth to shout to his companions to get a move on, but a spray of sand smacks him right in the throat; he's forced to slow down, stop, and spit it out on the ground, swallowing the urge to retch. The detonations are closer together now, pumping adrenaline into his bloodstream. It's not unpleasant; it makes him feel jacked up. They're on a rampage, the bastards!

He reaches the bunker. His eyes burn, especially the right one, which has a grain of sand stuck in it; as he pictures it, it feels as big as a rock. The concrete tunnel is crammed with soldiers. "Make some room for me," he says.

The men try to shift, but the shelter is so packed and they're so jammed in that they don't free up even an inch. Cederna swears. "Squeeze in, damn it!"

René orders him to cut it out, to stay where he is; he can see for himself there's no room in the bunker.

"I'll go to the other bunker, then."

"Don't talk bullshit. Stay there—you're covered."

"I said I'm going to the other one. I'm not staying out here."

"Stay there. That's an order."

A HESCO Bastion wall made of sand protects his back, but the dirt-filled air filters into the passageway and lashes his face. Cederna's bravado dissolves and he starts feeling nervous. He begins shaking. If only he had his helmet and vest with him he could withdraw like a turtle, but he's exposed. His hair is caked with sand; it's seeped in everywhere—the collar of his jacket, inside his socks, in his nostrils. If a shell were to land close enough, a fragment could easily pierce his shoulder or, worse yet, his neck. He has no intention of taking a fragment—he's going on leave in a few days and he wants to get there all in one piece. Even that asshole Mitrano managed to make it into the bunker, at least halfway in; he's scraping the dried mud off the tip of his boot with his thumbnail.

Cederna has an idea. "Hey, Mitrano."

"What do you want?"

"I think I see something out there. It could be a man on the ground. Come and look."

Everyone turns around, suddenly tense. Cederna reassures them with a crafty look.

Mitrano remains on the defensive, however. "I don't believe it," he says. He's learned the hard way that Cederna is not to be trusted. It's his fault that he's become the laughingstock of the FOB, especially after Cederna welcomed a helicopter full of visiting officers with a sign reading "Take Mitrano Back." He teases him constantly; he steals food from his plate in the mess hall, chews it, and then spits it back in the dish, mashed to a pulp; he calls him a retard and a jerk-off. Just yesterday he took Mitrano's shaving foam, smeared it all over his waxed chest, and started running around the base half naked, raving deliriously.

"I'm telling you I see something, a dark shape. He might need help. Come on—take a look."

"Stop it, Cederna," Simoncelli speaks up. "You're not funny."

"Yeah, it's another one of your little tricks," Mitrano says.

"Forget it, then, chickenshit. I'll go by myself." He starts to get up.

"Are you serious?"

"Of course."

Mitrano hesitates a second; then he disentangles himself from Ruffinatti's legs, there in front of him, and crawls out of the bunker. Cederna points to a spot.

"I don't see a thing."

"Take a closer look."

As they'd all expected—all except Mitrano—Cederna elbows him aside and takes his place in the shelter. "Gotcha!"

"Hey, get out of there! I was sitting there."

"Oh, yeah? I don't see your name anywhere."

"It's not fair."

"*It's not fair it's not fair it's not fair*—what the hell are you, a girl?"

Cederna hunkers down, making room for his back against the concrete. The others don't take it well, though. They give him dirty looks. "What a shitty thing to do," Camporesi says. Zampieri roughly shifts her calf out from under his leg.

He doesn't understand why they're acting that way; they always enjoy it when he teases Mitrano and now all of a sudden they're quick to defend him. They're just a bunch of hypocrites, that's all, and he says so. But saying it doesn't make him feel much better and doesn't stop the shame that's spreading inside him, a slimy feeling that he's not used to. Even Ietri avoids looking at him, as if he were embarrassed by him. "You're a bunch of hypocrites," he repeats, softly.

Mitrano tugs at his sleeve. "I was sitting there," he whimpers.

Cederna grabs his arm and squeezes it until the corporal begs for mercy.

"Do you know how to play rummy, Lieutenant?"

"No, sir."

"Trump?"

"Not that either."

"You must at least know Three Sevens!"

"Colonel, do you really want to play cards . . . *now?*"

"You have a better idea? Don't suggest Queen of Hearts, though. It's a game for idiots." He cuts the deck in half, looks at the card that's revealed: a jack of hearts. "How boring, Lieutenant. Believe me. That's how we'll lose this war in the end. Those bastards will kill us with boredom."

The only things moving in the bunker are little hairy spiders with quivering legs, which also sought shelter from the sandstorm and from the bombs. They creep upside down along the only space the men have left free, the ceiling, which is crawling with them. The soldiers' eyes follow them, because there isn't much else to stare at. Mattioli reaches up, picks one off between his thumb and forefinger, watches it thrash about, then crushes it.

Marshal René is the first to break the silence—silence so to speak, since the mortars continue to drop. He says the words no one wants to hear in such a situation: "Where's Torsu?"

He did a head count of his men and realized that the Sardinian corporal was missing. It took him only a moment to know who wasn't there; over the years roll call has become instinctive. It wouldn't take him any longer to realize which finger of his hand was missing if one of them were cut off.

The soldiers remain silent, apprehensive. Then Allais says: "He's still in the tent." As a collective justification, he adds: "He's too sick. He can't get up."

In the past few days Torsu's fever has fluctuated wildly up and down, often approaching 104. In his worst moments he mumbles senseless gibberish that leaves his buddies in stitches. He can't manage to swallow anything solid, even his face is gaunt, his cheekbones protrude beneath his eyes, and despite not eating, the diarrhea hasn't subsided. At night René hears his teeth chattering from the cold and a couple of times he's had to resort to wax earplugs.

"We have to go get him," Zampieri urges, but her anxiety is somewhat too hysterical to convince them.

Some of the guys get to their knees, undecided, waiting for the marshal's go-ahead. When it doesn't come, they settle in again. René questions Cederna with his eyes: he's his most reliable man, the only one whose advice he feels the need to ask for.

"We can't bring him here," Cederna says. "He can't even sit up and there's no room to lay him out on the ground."

"You're being an asshole as usual." Zampieri jumps up.

"And you're being an idiot, as usual."

"Are you afraid Torsu will steal your place, by any chance?"

"No. I'm afraid someone will get killed."

"Since when did you become so altruistic? I thought the only thing that mattered was for *you* not to get killed."

"You don't know what you're talking about, Zampa."

"Oh, no? So how come Mitrano is out there now while you're here glued to my ass?"

"The only things glued to your ass are ticks."

"Stop it!" René breaks in. He needs silence, he has to think. Aside from the effort involved in carrying Torsu in those conditions, there's the problem of space. They could go to the command center, but it would mean crossing the square, unquestionably the most exposed area of the FOB. Should he seriously risk four or five men by being overly concerned about just one. Does it make sense?

Cederna is staring him in the eye, as if able to read his thoughts. He shakes his head.

There's another burst of explosions, followed by the return of machine-gun fire, wasting round after round. The marshal thinks he sees a purple flash, incoming fire, but maybe it's just an impression. Two spiders meet on the ceiling, they stop and study each other for a while, brush each other with their legs, then go off in different directions. Concentrate! René tells himself. One of his men has been left behind in the tent. He makes an effort to erase Torsu's pale, clammy face from his mind, along with the sound of his voice and the memory of their last climb together, when they came close to a deer, just the two of them. Depersonalize every man, every buddy, that's the trick, delete his features and tone of voice, even his smell, until you're able to treat him as a mere component. Maybe that's the course he should adopt to resolve that other issue as well. This is not the time to think about that. Mortars are exploding, now. Don't get distracted, Antonio. Don't listen to Zampieri's labored breathing. Keep the fear under control. Consider the facts, only the facts. There's a soldier in danger, but close enough to the outer fortification to have the benefit of some protection. On the other hand, think about five men on the move, exposed to enemy fire for at least three minutes, though most likely longer. Being a leader means considering the possibilities and René is a good leader; he's the right person for this role. When he communicates his decision, he's perfectly confident. "We stay here," he says. "We wait."

"What time is it?"

"Ten past midnight."

"We should go out and see what's up."

"Bravo, you go."

"I'm going."

But no one moves.

Cederna hasn't been thinking about Mitrano for some time, but his earlier thoughts have left him in something of a bad mood. He doesn't see any sense in sitting cooped up in here while the enemy intermittently bombards the base. They should get out there and waste them, every one of them, go ferret them out, drop cluster bombs on their stinking hidey-holes—that's what those who fight like cowards deserve. If only he were already in the special forces: awakened in the dead of night, parachuted from nearly ten thousand feet into the middle of a red zone to sift through a village, flush out the terrorists, put hoods on them, and tie their hands and feet. If a shot is fired by mistake and blows one of them away, so much the better.

It's hot in the bunker and his leg muscles are stiff. He thinks about his upcoming leave, about Agnese; he's going to snatch her away right after she graduates and take her to the shore, to San Vito. In October, with a little luck, you can still swim, but even if the weather is bad they'll have a great time just the same, having sex on his aunt's rickety bed, with the curtains open to let the neighbors peer in at them. The house in San Vito smells of his childhood, his vacations as a boy; even sex has a different pleasure when they do it there. The rusty aviary where his aunt kept her two tropical parrots still stands in the courtyard. The cage was too small and the birds constantly tormented each other with their wings and beaks. Cederna had given them names, but he doesn't remember them anymore—for the others in the family they were only "Zia Mariella's parrots." The birds had disappointed everyone because they never learned a single word; all they did was utter harsh shrieks. They spent their time fighting and littering the cage with excrement, yet he'd been fond of them and had cried when they died within a few days of each other. Cederna closes his eyes. He tries to remember.

The siren wails again at four in the morning. Three short bursts, spaced apart, to signal the all clear. At that point, many of the guys in the bunkers are asleep; they've lost touch with hunger and their countless joint pains. Their numbness makes the return to the tents slow and fretful.

For Lieutenant Egitto it's not over yet, however. He's awakened just when he's managed to get to sleep, or so it seems to him (actually he's slept for more than an hour).

"Doc, we need you."

"Yeah, okay." But he can't seem to get up and for a moment he drops off to sleep again.

A hand shakes him. "Doc!"

"Yeah."

"Come with me."

The soldier shoves him off the cot. Egitto isn't quick enough to make out his features or rank. He rubs his hands vigorously over his face, causing bits of skin to flake off. He grabs his pants from the chair. "What's happened?"

"One of our men doesn't want to leave the bunker, Doc."

"Is he hurt?"

"No."

"What's the matter with him?"

The soldier hesitates. "Nothing. But he doesn't want to come out."

Egitto pulls on a sock. It's full of sand; the gritty particles scratch his foot. "So why did you call me?"

"We didn't know who else to call."

"Which company are you in?"

"Charlie, sir."

"Let's go."

The storm is still going on, but its intensity has decreased; now it's little more than a grimy wind. They press ahead, heads bent forward, protecting their eyes with their hands.

The boy is huddled halfway down the bunker. Around him are a couple of soldiers and it's clear they're trying to talk him into something: when they see Egitto duck into the tunnel, they salute and hastily go out through the other side.

The young man looks like a rather limp rag doll, as if someone has pulled out the stuffing and sewn him back up again, empty. His shoulders are sagging, his head is slumped over his chest. Egitto sits down in front of him. When they left, the soldiers took their flashlights with them, so Egitto has to turn his own on. He leans it against the concrete wall. "What's wrong?"

The soldier remains silent.

"I asked you a question. Answer your superior. What's wrong?"

"Nothing, sir."

"You don't want to leave?"

The soldier shakes his head. Egitto reads the name on his insignia. "Your name is Mitrano?"

"Yes, sir."

"Full name?"

"Mitrano, Vincenzo, sir."

The boy is breathing through his mouth. He must have perspired a lot because his cheeks are flushed. Egitto imagines the bunker crammed full. A strong smell of sweat still lingers, mixed with another, less recognizable odor, the smell produced by lots of bodies pressed against one another. Vagal crisis, he thinks. Panic attack, hypoxemia. He asks the soldier if he's ever experienced anything like this before, but he doesn't say the word *panic*, or *attack*, better to use *claustrophobia*—it sounds more impersonal and doesn't suggest debility. The soldier says no, he doesn't have claustrophobia.

"Do you feel dizzy right now?"

"No."

"Are you nauseous, light-headed?"

"No."

A thought occurs to Egitto. "You haven't . . ." He points to the soldier's groin.

The boy stares at him, appalled. "No, sir!"

"There would be nothing to be ashamed of."

"I know."

"It can happen to anyone."

"It didn't happen to me!"

"All right."

Egitto finds himself in a quandary. He needs symptoms to work with. Medical history, diagnosis, treatment: that's how a doctor does his job; he doesn't know of any other reliable method. Maybe the soldier felt scared, that's all. He tries to reassure him: "They won't fire anymore tonight, Giuseppe."

"My name is Vincenzo."

"Vincenzo, sorry."

"I told you a minute ago. Vincenzo Mitrano."

"You're right. Vincenzo. Tonight they won't fire anymore."

"I know."

"We can go back out. It's safe."

The soldier hugs his knees to his chest. His pose is that of a child, but not his eyes. The eyes are those of an adult.

"Anyway, there wasn't any real danger," Egitto persists. "No mortars fell within the base."

"They came close."

"No, they didn't."

"I heard them. They were close."

Egitto is beginning to grow impatient. Consoling people is unknown territory for him; he lacks the proper words. Mitrano sighs. "They left me outside, Doc."

"*Who* left you outside?"

The soldier makes a vague gesture with his head, then closes his eyes. Soft murmuring can be heard a few steps from the bunker; his companions are waiting for him. Egitto makes out the words "a bit of a wimp" and is certain the boy heard them too. In fact, he says: "They're still out there."

"Want me to send them away?"

Mitrano looks toward the exit. He shakes his head. "It doesn't matter."

"I'm sure it was by accident."

"No. They left me outside. I was sitting there and they set a trap for me, to kick me out. They did it on purpose."

"You can talk to Captain Masiero about it. If you think you should."

"No. You mustn't tell anyone, Doc."

"All right."

"Swear?"

"Sure, I swear."

The silence lasts for three, maybe four minutes. An eternity in a situation like this, half asleep in a dark burrow.

"How old are you, Vincenzo?"

"Twenty-one, sir."

"Isn't there someone you'd like to talk to? A girl maybe? It would make you feel better."

"I don't have a girl."

"Your mother, then."

Mitrano clenches his fists. "Not now," he says shortly. After a moment he adds: "I have a dog, you know, Doc?"

Egitto reacts with excessive enthusiasm: "Oh, yeah? What kind of dog?"

"A pinscher."

"Are they the ones with the pug nose?"

"No, those are bulldogs. Pinschers have a long snout and pricked ears."

The lieutenant would like to milk the subject to distract the soldier, but he doesn't know a thing about dogs. He vaguely recalls having wished for a puppy at one point in his life, or maybe not, maybe it was Marianna who wanted one and he wished it for her—in any case nothing ever came of it. Ernesto viewed animals kept in apartments as carriers of deadly germs, and for Nini another presence would have meant adding complexity to an already demanding network of domestic relations. Egitto wonders whether he was deprived of something. Even if it were so, that deprivation hasn't mattered to him for some time.

"Doc?"

"Yeah."

"I'll come out of here. At some point I'll feel like leaving and I will."

"Not now, though."

"No, not now. If that's okay with you."

"It's okay with me."

"I'm sorry they made you come."

"No problem. Don't worry about it."

"I'm very sorry."

Egitto gets up, using his arms. He brushes the dirt off his pants. He's done there. His head grazes the top of the bunker.

"Doc?"

"Yeah?"

"Could you stay here one more minute?"

"Sure."

He sits back down, bumps the flashlight with his elbow. The beam of light ends up skimming the ground, revealing boot prints in the sand: each one partially erases the others, the fossil remains of a struggle. It's at that point that the soldier starts to cry, softly at first, then louder. "Fuck," he says through clenched teeth. Then he repeats: "Fuck fuck fuck fuck," as if the toxin he wants to release were lurking in that word.

Egitto doesn't try to stop him, but for some reason he chooses to turn his gaze to the chink of sky visible between the wall and the outer fortification—it's almost light. He listens to the boy's weeping; he breaks it down into its elements: the shuddering diaphragm, the nasal passages filling up with mucus, the breathing that accelerates to maximum intensity and then suddenly subsides. Mitrano is quiet again. Egitto hands him a tissue. "Feel better?"

"I think so."

"We're not in any hurry, though."

Actually, he's wiped out. He'd like to lie down on the ground right there and fall asleep. He closes his eyes for a moment, his head drops forward.

"Doc?"

A second is all it takes for him to find himself in a confused dream, in the middle of a firefight.

"Doc!"

"What is it?"

Women

The sandstorm is over. The morning's clarity holds no trace of the confusion of the strike. The men are still shaken, however, exhausted and nervous as one by one they drift over to breakfast. Despite the general anxiety, activities take place as on any other day: at exactly eight o'clock trainers arrive at the garrison where the Afghan police forces are stationed and teach them how to search a van and rough up the suspects on board; a patrol ventures out to an unexplored settlement near Maydan Jabha; others engage in domestic chores that under different circumstances would be considered unmanly—doing the laundry, sweeping sand out of the tents, washing down the latrines with buckets of water.

But a new awareness makes them tremble imperceptibly. The veterans, who are familiar with the feeling from other missions, accept it phlegmatically and respond to the recruits seeking reassurance: *Where the hell did you think you were, at summer camp?* Yet for the first time they, too—tough, experienced soldiers though they are—see the impregnable fortification they erected for what it really is: a sandpit exposed to danger.

At eleven o'clock the Third Platoon assembles at the foot of the west tower for firing practice. The soldiers are waiting with their butts resting on the table where the gleaming artillery stands ready for use, or with their backs against the HESCO Bastion, in the shade. They're doing their best to look relaxed, even bored. In reality they're exhausted and a little depressed; no one has anything left to say, after they spent the rest of the night in the tent with the bare bulbs lit, some with their eyes closed trying to futilely catch a few hours' sleep, some commenting over and over again on the dynamics of the attack (which no one really understood)—all of them, however, with their ears pricked, on the alert for any new explosions. Marshal René had racked his brains to come up with an encouraging speech for his men, but the words wouldn't come to him and in the end all he said was, "We're at war, we knew it," as if it had been their fault.

The rifle barrels glint in the sun and the two boxes of ammunition give more than one of the guys the urge to load his weapon, leave the base, and start shooting randomly at any Afghans who come within range. René knows that itch; he can feel it himself and it was predicted in the training courses ("a natural human reaction that must be kept under control"). Pecone somewhat awkwardly acts out how they all feel when he wields a rifle and points it toward the mountain and then at the sky, jerking around guardedly. "Come on out, you bastards! I'll pick you off one by one. Bam! Bam!"

"Put down the gun. Or you're more likely to knock off one of us," René says. It's a joke, but no one laughs.

When Captain Masiero appears at the edge of the square, the soldiers get to their feet and stand up straight. The colonel has ordered that the captain be in charge of the firing ranges during the stay at the FOB, though generally each platoon manages the matter internally. Needless to say René is not at all happy with the change; he feels passed over. He has a congenital dislike for Masiero, whom he bluntly considers an asshole and an ass licker of the worst kind. As far as he can see, the feeling is mutual.

By the time the captain reaches the tower, the guys have formed a line. "Is the weapon in position?" Masiero asks.

"Yes, sir."

"Then we'll begin. Let's go."

One at a time the soldiers clamber up the wooden ladder. René hands them a gold-plated ammo belt. Masiero stands behind each of them and repeats the same order in each one's ear: "You see the hill? There are three barrels. Aim at the red one in the center. Short bursts and push forward. The MG is a bitch who wants to turn cartwheels, remember that. You have to hold her down—got it? Down. Load up and fire when ready. Use the plugs, unless you want to burst your eardrums."

René shoots first and is flawless. When hit, the barrel jumps and then falls back into place. The shots that miss kick up clouds of dust among the rocks and low scrub. Masiero, however, can't resist a jab: "Pretty good, Marshal. Try to relax when you shoot. You'll enjoy it more—you'll see."

René imagines shoving his index and middle fingers up the man's nostrils and poking them out through his eyes.

He hates to admit it, but it's important to him that they look sharp in front of the captain. He hopes his men will make him look good, too.

It starts out promising. Most of the guys hit the target at least once. Camporesi, Biasco, Allais, and Rovere do extremely well; Cederna is complimented on the speed with which he loads and aims the weapon.

Corporal Ietri is the first to disappoint him a little. As usual, the ceiling of the watchtower is too low for him. He has to hunch over the machine gun. Maybe that's the reason—or maybe it's because the captain breathing down his neck makes him nervous—he holds the trigger down too long.

"Don't waste ammunition," Masiero chides him.

When Ietri passes René, looking grim, the marshal pats him on the shoulder. Ietri is still young; he takes offense at everything.

Zampieri steps up last. René involuntarily looks at her breasts as she climbs the ladder, but has no explicit sexual thoughts toward her. He never has thought of her that way, maybe because she's sort of a friend or because he's seen her belch loudly after knocking back a can of beer, and certain things don't go with his idea of femininity. He treats her like all the others, like a guy. Zampieri is a good soldier, she drives the Lince with full control and requisite boldness, she's dogged and never backs away, even when Torsu puts porn movies on in the barracks. She stays and watches them, arms folded, until the end. From certain looks he's caught, René would bet she's had the hots for Cederna for a long while, though no one suspects it. They all think she's a lesbian.

Zampieri listens to the captain's instructions, nodding. She fits the plugs in her ears and stretches her neck. She fumbles with the cover of the feed assembly to insert the cartridges, but her hand can't quite reach it. Each time she tries to place the belt, the lid snaps back on her fingers. The gun stock slips out of the hollow of her shoulder. "I can't reach it," she says, and tries again to no avail.

Masiero orders the men to bring a wooden footboard. Di Salvo finds one in the equipment shed and two of them hoist it up on the fortification. René arranges it on the platform and Zampieri climbs on it. "Better?" he asks warmly, to reassure her.

"Yeah."

"It would be even better if you turned the cartridge belt right side up," Masiero says sharply.

"Of course. Sorry, sir."

Zampieri goes on fumbling with the lid, but the machine gun keeps slipping and pitching forward, a recalcitrant animal. René is impatient. From below, the guys are watching their platoon mate with a mixture of sympathy and curiosity and glancing at René, as if asking him to intervene. The captain, leaning his forearms on the windowsill of the tower, wears a sarcastic grin. Zampieri finally manages to hold the weapon with her elbow and close the feed assembly. "Done."

"It's about time. Charge!"

The girl tries to pull the charger handle back, but it's too stiff. René himself felt a little resistance earlier. Now he's sure Zampieri won't make it. In fact, she tries again, but can't pull it all the way back.

"Maybe it's jammed," she says softly.

Masiero elbows her aside. "It's not jammed, damn it! It's you who's inept!" He loads the weapon with a violent jerk. "Now fire!"

Zampieri isn't trembling, but her cheeks are redder than usual, her neck rigid. René, too, can feel the blood pulsing everywhere, in his ears, hands. Zampieri hastily takes aim, the MG recoils, and the round winds up about twenty yards above the barrel. The captain swears, then stands behind the girl and shoves her forward with his pelvis, toward the butt of the machine gun. If they weren't appalled, the guys would certainly venture a few salacious remarks.

"Fire, damn it!"

The rounds land even farther away from the target. Zampieri gives a little cry: her breast is painfully pressed between the weapon and Masiero's sternum. He yanks her around and starts shaking her. "And you're supposed to be a gunner? Huh? A gunner? We're in Gulistan, goddamn it! Here they'll slaughter us thanks to people like you!"

The guys in the platoon have bowed their heads a little. René, on the contrary, is determined to stare the captain down till the end.

"What if you'd been on guard duty last night? You'd have gotten us all killed. This is a war and you don't know how to use a machine gun!"

Zampieri is rigid. She looks like she's surely going to break at any moment in Masiero's grip. The capillaries in her eyes have exploded into red.

"Captain," René speaks up.

Masiero turns around, furious. "What?"

"Maybe you're being too intimidating."

René remains at attention, expressionless, as Masiero slowly walks over to him, breathing through his mouth.

"I'm *intimidating* her?"

"The men have never used that weapon before today."

"Oh, darn. I'm sorry about that. Maybe I should have given the young lady a water pistol. Has she fired that yet?"

René remains silent. His expression doesn't change at all, nor does that of his men, speechless at the foot of the tower. They've been trained to be strictly impassive, to keep their worst thoughts well hidden behind their eyes, and Masiero was one of their instructors. The captain moves even closer to René, stops a few inches from his face. He looks at the stripes pinned to his jacket, as if he weren't perfectly familiar with them. "Marshal, tell me. Have you ever been involved in a firefight? A real firefight, I mean."

"No."

"Answer the way you respond to a superior, Marshal."

"No, sir."

"I see. Too bad. Oh, but don't let it worry you. This mission you'll have your turn. And you know why? Because over here they shoot. Here they hate us and want to kill us all. Did you hear those dazzling fireworks last night? Well, be aware that it wasn't a party and that they won't stop until they've razed this base to the ground and wiped out all the infidel dogs like you and me. You know what the Taliban do to prisoners, Marshal?"

"No, sir."

"They crucify them. Like Jesus Christ. Can you imagine a rusty nail planted in the nerves of your hand? You men down there, can you imagine that? Mademoiselle, can you imagine it? You starve to death, or bleed out. It can take up to three days. The fuckers moisten your lips to make you last longer. And you know what else they do, Marshal?"

"No."

"No, *what*?"

"No, sir."

"They bludgeon you with a club, for hours and hours, until you can no longer tell whether you still have clothes on. But they're careful not to kill you. Because afterward they lock you in a cell full of insects and let them finish the job. Or else . . . ask me, Or else what?, Marshal."

"Or else what, sir?"

"Or else they hang you upside down until all the blood flows into your brain and it bursts. *Pow!* Now do you understand why it's useful to know how to load an MG?"

"Yes, sir."

"And do you think the young lady with the blond curls back here has also understood?"

"Yes, sir."

"Because it would be a shame if those beautiful golden locks were to get smeared with blood, don't you think?"

"Yes, sir."

Masiero pauses. The silence is so absolute that René can hear his own breathing. "Well, then," the captain says finally, "we're done here."

Masiero climbs down the ladder. The soldiers stand at attention as he parades by them, not deigning to look at them. Up on the fortification, René smiles at Zampieri as if to tell her not to take it so hard— nothing serious, really.

Twilight is Lieutenant Egitto's favorite time of day. The air suddenly turns cooler, but it's not yet biting cold like at night. In the evening light, the FOB seems to shrink, and colors other than the usual ocher and green can finally be seen around the rock-strewn square as the soldiers go about in colorful robes and flip-flops. For a couple of hours, the mood is one of peaceful everyday life. Even the lieutenant's hardened apathy cracks and he experiences unexpected bursts of good humor.

Adjacent to the showers is a tent with a heater, used as a locker room, but Egitto doesn't like to undress in front of his colleagues— he'd rather do it inside the stall, even if the space is tight. He's perfected a way to take off his clothes and put them back on while balancing first on one leg and then the other, so that his feet don't make contact with the filthy floor without his flip-flops. Survival at the FOB requires skill in countless little things like that.

The water is lukewarm, not really hot, but after about ten seconds it feels pleasant enough. Someone left his body wash on the shelf. Egitto unscrews the cap and sniffs the contents: it has a strong aroma, pungent and inescapably male, the kind that often lingers in the locker rooms at the barracks. The guys like to swathe themselves in dense clouds of fragrance. They spray their chests, even their genitals, with powerful deodorants, which then stagnate in the muggy air—another difference between him and them: the lieutenant washes with alkaline soap from the dispensary.

He pours the liquid into his hand, rubs it onto his chest and shoulders. The scrubbing opens small, dark wounds at the spots that are in the worst shape, which then heal immediately. The lieutenant directs the stream of water to the shreds of dead skin scattered on the ground until they're sucked down the drain. Maybe the owner of the body wash is waiting outside the door. When Egitto passes him he'll recognize the scent of his shower gel and God only knows how he might react. The guys are unpredictable. In any case he'd be right: you don't steal a buddy's soap—it's one of those crimes that in an outpost in the middle of the desert takes on gigantic import. He pours out some more, spreads it over his groin and on his legs. Then he stands under the water with his eyes closed, until someone knocks on the door. He's used up his three minutes in the shower.

Back at the infirmary, he finds the tent zipper halfway open. "Anybody there?"

A female voice comes from the other side of the green canvas: "Alessandro? Is that you?"

The flap opens and a bare arm emerges followed by a shoulder, a strip of white towel, then the round face of Irene Sammartino, with her hair pinned up. Irene. The half-naked hologram of her is projected before the lieutenant from a distant universe, far off in time and space. Bewildered, Egitto takes a step back from the apparition.

The woman smiles at him. "I chose this cot. I didn't know where you slept. There's no sign of a living soul."

"What are you doing here?"

Irene tilts her head to one side, folds her bare arms across her breasts. Her breasts were never very large, though they weren't small either; Egitto roughly remembers how it felt to cup one of them in the palm of his hand.

"Is that any way to welcome an old friend? Come here. Let me give you a kiss."

Egitto approaches, reluctantly. Irene looks up to study him carefully, compensating for the slight difference in height that separates them; she seems to want to make sure that all his features are in place. "You're still pretty good looking," she says, satisfied.

The towel covers only part of her thighs and sways each time she moves. What's holding it closed at the collarbone isn't a knot, just a corner tucked under the edge, which could come loose at any moment, displaying her entire body. Egitto doesn't know why he's considering this possibility. Irene Sammartino is there, barefoot, in his tent, and he has no idea why—he doesn't know where she came from, whether she rained down from the sky or sprouted from the earth, what her intentions are. She plants two friendly kisses lightly on his cheeks. She's wearing a nice scent that doesn't arouse any memory in him. "Come on, Lieutenant, say something! You look like you've seen the devil himself!"

Half an hour later Egitto is asking Colonel Ballesio for an explanation, as the colonel meanwhile turns his attention to wiping out the bottom of a container of yogurt with his finger.

"Irene, right. She said you were friends. Lucky you. Nice piece of ass, no doubt about it. But she blabbers a mile a minute. Nonstop. And she makes jokes that frankly I don't get. Don't you think there's something pathetic about women who make jokes that aren't funny? My wife is that way. Never had the guts to tell her." Ballesio sticks his whole finger in his mouth, pulls it out, glistening with saliva. "Plus, she seems like one of those who have a tendency to put on weight. Her legs—I mean, have you looked at them? They're not *fat* but you can tell there's a good chance they will be. I had an overweight girl as an NCO and . . . phew! Those chubby ones have something about them . . . something swinish. Did she get settled in okay?"

"I let her have my cot."

"Good. I appreciate it. I would even have kept her here, but since you're already friends . . ." Did he just wink at him? Or was it only his impression? "Besides, I have this terrible snoring problem. It almost cost me a divorce. My wife and I have slept in separate rooms for fourteen years. Not that I mind, but sometimes I wake myself up because I'm snoring so loud. A buzz saw, that's me." He coughs. "No remedy for it, Doctor?"

"None, Colonel." Egitto is angrier than he lets on.

Ballesio inspects the bottom of the container, in case there might still be a trace of yogurt. He even scrupulously licked the foil lid, which is now lying on the table. He tosses the container into the trash can, but misses. The plastic cup bounces off the rim and rolls on the ground, at the lieutenant's feet. Egitto hopes he won't ask him to pick it up. "Of course. Because there is no cure. Patches, lozenges, sleeping on my side—I've tried everything. There is no solution. If a person snores, he snores, end of story. Anyway. Our Irene will be here a week, helicopters permitting."

"What is she doing here, Colonel?"

Ballesio looks at him sideways. "You're asking me, Lieutenant? How should I know? Afghanistan is full of these Irenes wandering around. They look into things, they investigate. It wouldn't surprise me if your friend were here to gather information about one of us. Who can tell? Today a soldier complains about some bullshit and they immediately pounce on you like vultures. She can be my guest, though. I have nothing to protect anymore. If they were to force me to retire tomorrow, I'd be more than happy. You, on the other hand. Watch your ass."

Egitto takes a breath. "Commander, I'd like to ask permission to sleep here. I won't bother you."

Ballesio's face darkens, then relaxes in a smile again. "Oh, no, I know that. Of course you wouldn't. If anything I'd be the one disturbing you. Tell me: what's the problem, Lieutenant?"

"I feel it's more appropriate for Irene to have her privacy."

"Don't tell me you're a faggot."

"No, sir."

"You know what my old man always used to say? My dear Giacomo, he'd say, *Se 'l te pias moll, ghe n'è fin che te vöret*—if you like them limp, there are as many as you want. That's just what he said, but in dialect, which sounds even worse." The colonel grips his jewels through his pants. "He was a pig. At eighty he would still get into bed with his caregiver. Poor thing, he died alone like a dog. I don't know if we understand each other, Lieutenant"—the wink again, this time obvious—"but as far as I'm concerned, you and your guest can do whatever you want. I have nothing against a little healthy promiscuity."

Egitto decides to completely ignore the gist of the colonel's allusions. How would Ballesio react if he knew the exact nature of his friendship with Irene Sammartino? He has no desire to reveal it. He repeats slowly: "If I won't disturb you, I'll move in here. Temporarily."

"Okay, okay, whatever you like," Ballesio says impatiently. "You know something, Egitto? You're the most boring officer I've met in thirty years of service."

That night, however, Egitto doesn't sleep at all. Ballesio really does snore like a buzz saw and the lieutenant spends his time fretting, imagining the commander's gluey uvula vibrating in his air passage, the glands suffused with blood, swollen, hypertrophic. He'd like to get up and shake him hard, but he doesn't dare, he'd like to go back to the infirmary and grab a packet of Ativan, but he doesn't dare do that either. Irene Sammartino is in there, sleeping. When he thinks about it, he's still dubious, wondering whether it may have been just a lengthy, detailed hallucination. The most he can do is tone down Ballesio by shushing him. The colonel quiets down for a few seconds, then starts in again, louder than before. Sometimes he goes into apnea and when he starts breathing again he produces monstrous sucking sounds.

Egitto's frustration leaves him vulnerable to the assault of memories. The protective shell of the duloxetine softens, and gradually he surrenders to the stream of thoughts. The lieutenant retraces the few, predictable episodes that he still recalls about his affair with Irene. How long had it lasted? Not long, a couple of months at most. They'd attended the same courses together at officers' training school. They'd become close because they were somewhat more casual than their very proper colleagues—she in that vehement way of hers and he with his caustic style, an unexpectedly valuable legacy of Ernesto's rants.

The attraction the lieutenant felt for Irene was on the cool side, but at times it suddenly flared up and blazed like a fire doused with gasoline. What he remembers best about the time he spent with her is having sex in the cramped dorm room, the sheets always a little damper than he would have liked. But Irene's emotional excesses had soon become a cause of anxiety, and when the erotic flare-ups had begun to occur less frequently, Egitto hadn't found a way to reignite them.

He has an image of the two of them lying on his single bed, awake and inert; it was a Sunday morning and they were listening to the guttural cooing of the pigeons on the windowsill. It sounded like the cries of wild human orgasms, a suggestion that Egitto chose to ignore: it was the precise moment when he realized that he no longer had any desire. He said so to Irene, in those same brutal terms, more or less.

But getting rid of Irene Sammartino hadn't proved to be so simple. A couple of weeks after the breakup there'd been an unpleasant aftermath: she summoned him to a café in the city center and with a devastated air confessed that she was six days late—it couldn't be a coincidence, no, her cycle was always right on time, infallible. Still, she hadn't wanted to take the test, not yet. They'd walked for hours under the arcades, not touching; in his mind Egitto considered various scenarios, barely keeping his nerves under control and occasionally trying to persuade her to make sure. It turned out to be a big mistake. In the months that followed, Irene would turn up when he least expected it. Their mutual friends, generally speaking, were more his than hers, but Irene never passed up a chance to run into him. She always arrived alone, smiling, and for a while she'd be implausibly animated. She'd talk to everyone, ignoring him, but when she could no longer keep up the role, she retreated into silence. She'd start looking around, fidgety as a cat, throwing frequent glances in his direction, and sooner or later in the course of the evening they would find themselves alone, asking each other how things were going, increasingly uncomfortable.

Then, overnight, Irene disappeared into thin air. The conjecture that spread among the school's students was that Intelligence had enrolled her in a special program abroad. Egitto wasn't surprised: she had always been sharp, skillful at communicating. He hadn't wondered too much about it, in any case. He felt relieved.

Colonel Ballesio's nose emits a high-pitched whistle, like the shriek of a rocket, which then ends in a sudden burst. Egitto tosses and turns on the cot for the millionth time. Irene Sammartino . . . How many years has it been? Eight? Nine? And after all those years she shows up right there, in Gulistan, in his tent, like a Trojan horse that fate has suddenly slipped into his protected haven. To disturb him, to bring him back. To what, he doesn't know. To the glittering world of the living? No, fate has nothing to do with it. Egitto is often tempted to give in to the lure of coincidence, but in this case Irene Sammartino has had a hand in it. If she came to the FOB, it's because she chose to come—she must have something in mind: he's not going to let himself be fooled. *Watch your ass, Lieutenant.*

————

Ietri and Zampieri climb the main tower for guard duty. The moon is a luminous crescent over the mountain and Ietri recalls a mnemonic verse he learned in elementary school: *The moon is a liar—when it forms a D it's* crescens, *waxing; when it forms a C it's* decrescens, *waning.* With D in the sky, his father would get up before dawn to plant sugar beets. With C he'd left the house one evening in May and never returned.

"There's a waning moon," he says to himself.

"Huh?"

"Nothing."

Zampieri sits on the ground, legs outstretched. She swings the tips of her boots back and forth. "It's cold," she says. "Shit, just think about January. We'll freeze to death."

Ietri pulls his gloves out of his pocket and offers them to her. She ignores him and goes on talking while studying the stripped skin around her right thumbnail. She bites it where it's pinkest. "The captain should come up here. To see how cold it is. Not a chance, though— he doesn't get his ass dirty."

"Who, Masiero?"

Zampieri stares at the tip of her boots, persistently gnawing at her finger. "Did you see how he treated me? He called me 'mademoiselle,' like I was some dumb fashion model."

"Is that what it means?"

Again she ignores him. "I know how to load an MG—take my word. I can load any weapon in the world. That machine gun was mounted too high. Masiero should see me shoot with my SC. I'd rip that barrel to shreds."

"You couldn't hit that far with an SC," Ietri contradicts her, but right away he gets the impression that it wasn't the right thing to say. Zampieri in fact looks at him confused, somewhat disgusted, before she continues. "That gun was jammed, I told him. It must have been Simoncelli who fired before me. He always fucks up the artillery."

She takes her thumb out of her mouth, rubs it with her forefinger. She loosens her ponytail and shakes her head. She's more beautiful with her hair like that, Ietri thinks, more feminine.

A moment later she's sobbing uncontrollably. "He called me 'young lady'! Sexist bastard! He doesn't act like that with you guys. Oh, no! It's only because I'm a girl. Stupid me. An idiot . . . when I chose . . . this . . . line of work."

Her shoulders heave as she weeps and Ietri has to suppress the urge to stroke her head.

"I'm . . . not . . . capable."

"Of course you're capable."

She jerks her head up suddenly and gives him a withering glance. "No, I'm not! What do you know, huh? Nothing. Not a damn thing!"

The outburst seems to calm her down. Ietri decides not to protest. Zampieri is still crying, but more softly, as if it were just a different way of breathing. Ietri doesn't know how to console a girl. He consoled his mother many times, especially during the tough time when his father disappeared in the fields, but that was different. He didn't have to do much, because she did it all: she held him tight enough to nearly smother him and repeated, *Mama is here with you, Mama is here with you.* "I think I'm incapable sometimes too," he says.

"But you always do everything right. Your cot is always in order, you're always on time for muster, you never complain or act like an asshole. There he is! Corporal Ietri, the perfect little soldier!"

Ietri doesn't like her tone. He applies himself to doing things right, it's true. He doesn't see that there's anything wrong with that. Still, he feels the need to defend himself. "Hey, look—I fuck up too sometimes!"

"Yeah, right."

"I'm serious."

"Oh, sure."

"The other night I dropped my flashlight in the toilet."

Zampieri turns to look at him, dumbfounded. "The flashlight that clogged up the toilet was yours?"

"I tried to fish it out, but it was pitch dark. I didn't want to stick my hands in there. It was disgusting—it turned my stomach."

The girl slaps her palms on her knees and bursts out laughing in that raucous way of hers. "You're a real asshole!"

"Stop it! You'll wake the whole base."

But Zampieri won't stop. "You really are an asshole!" she repeats. Then she falls over on her side, unconcerned about her face landing in the dirt.

"At least I can shoot," Ietri mutters, resentful.

She sits up again. Her cheek is a little grimy; she wipes it off with her forearm. "Okay, okay. Don't get pissed," she says, but then she starts laughing again.

The earthen square of the watchtower is littered with cartridge cases. Ietri picks one up, turns it around in his fingers. He wonders whether it belonged to a shell that killed someone or one that missed.

Zampieri snorts. "Hey, are you offended?"

"No."

"You sure? You look to me like you're mortally offended."

"I'm not offended."

"You're cute when you pout like that."

Ietri's jaw drops. "What?"

"I said you're cute."

"What do you mean?"

"*Nothing* in particular. You're cute, that's all. Didn't anyone ever tell you?"

"No."

"You should see yourself now. You're all red."

"How can you tell when we're practically in the dark?"

"You're so red it's obvious even in the dark. Hell, you're practically glowing."

She's probably right. Ietri *feels* flushed. He turns his back to Zampieri and pretends to look out the narrow opening. The mountain is a hulking animal barely darker than the sky; he can just make out its crouching silhouette. Zampieri told him he was cute. Should he believe her? She opens the zipper of her jacket and slips a hand into the inside pocket. She pulls out an aluminum flask, takes a sip, and offers it to him. "Here. It'll calm you down a bit."

"What is it?"

She shrugs.

"Are you nuts? If we get caught drinking on sentry duty we'll end up CB."

"What did I tell you, gentlemen? There you have it! Corporal Ietri, the perfect little soldier!"

She takes another sip and then chuckles to herself. Ietri is now mortified. "Give me that," he says.

Zampieri hands him the flask. He takes a sip. It's grappa and it's harsh. He gives it back. "How can you swallow that stuff?"

"I drink whatever there is. You want more?"

"Yeah."

They go on like that for a while, passing the flask back and forth. Ietri doesn't refuse it even when he doesn't want any more, because at each turn he manages to brush his comrade's fingers. "Were you scared last night?" he asks her.

"I'm never scared," she says. She toys with a strand of hair, twirling it. "You?"

"No, no," Ietri is quick to say. "Of course not."

Zampieri has left her jacket zipper open a bit, her green T-shirt stretched over her breasts. Ietri imagines her without clothes. He constructs her naked figure systematically, from her neck to her feet. She's torturing her thumb with her teeth again and seems distant, wrapped up in thoughts that have nothing to do with him. "I'll make the captain pay for it," she murmurs. "One day I'll make him pay, I swear."

They stop talking. The grappa is finished. And Ietri has an erection. He continues peeking into Zampieri's jacket, to conjure up her white breasts, until she sadly pulls the zipper closed again and curls up. In a minute she's asleep; he can tell from her breathing and from her head, which rhythmically snaps upward.

When it's time to trade places, two hours later, he doesn't wake her. He spends the whole shift on his feet even though his calves are twitching. He's watched her persistently, almost the entire time. He allows himself to fantasize about how he would make love with his duty partner, lying on the floor of the sentry box, how he would grip her thighs tightly and press his mouth on hers. But he also has more tender thoughts, where they kiss and caress each other's hands and he shows her the house in Torremaggiore and they have dinner together at his mother's, who prepares her special potato focaccia for the occasion. It's no less exciting a fantasy. Ietri knows only one way to release all that tension. He'll have to venture to the latrines when he finishes his shift. The problem—and it's not at all an insignificant problem—is that he's been left without a flashlight.

Look, Look, and Look Again

"An IED is a homemade bomb, remember that. Improvised explosive device. Anyone can build one. Take a jerry can of chemical fertilizer, a couple of copper wires and some clips, connect them all together. The simplest electrical circuit you can think of—even a child can do it. The instructions are on the Internet. There's nothing you can do about it. An IED costs about the same as a pizza and beer and the material can be found at any hardware store. It's a mousetrap, that's what it is. And we're the mice. It's because of IEDs that this war has become a shitty war like Iraq. You don't see the enemy anymore; he's not there. He buries his bomb and then hides behind a rock to enjoy the show. *Boom!* There's not a thing you can do about it, just watch out. You have to look at everything, all the time. Look, look, and then look again. A pile of garbage on the roadside? Suspected IED. A little boy standing on a roof, waving at you? Suspected IED. A clod of earth a little darker than the rest? Suspected IED. If the earth is lighter, it's also a suspected IED. Some stones lined up? An abandoned car? The rotting carcass of a camel? Suspected IED. We're the truffle dogs of this war. If there's any danger of an explosive device, stop and let the ACRT do his job. Don't rush him. If the ACRT hurries through it, you blow up. Bring him something to drink if he asks for a drink and even if he doesn't ask, because if the ACRT is thirsty and gets a headache and gets confused, you blow up. Remember that. It's a lousy war, the lousiest of all. You can't plant a bayonet in those Talibans' guts—get used to it. They go around in their pure white garments. They smile at you, they say *As-salaam alaikum* to you, and meanwhile they've placed their little gift less than a mile farther on. They're sons of bitches. It was better when you could plant a knife in their belly—at least you looked them in the eye. (*Murmur of approval.*) You won't know anything about the IEDs—ever. Remember that. Each IED is a story in itself. We have metal detectors and they build the pressure plates in ceramic. We send robots on ahead to reconnoiter and they place the charge a mile back from the pressure plate. We find the plate and happily lift it up to defuse it and it activates another one right there under us and the charge explodes up our ass. These Taliban fuckers know how to wage war. They've done nothing else for fifty years. (*A question.*) A Lince can withstand twenty-two pounds of explosives, maybe twenty-six. Here they make fifty-five-pound bombs. Even a Buffalo would go flying through the air with fifty-five pounds. A charge like that rips you in half like a lightning bolt plunging through your skull. It depends on where it explodes, of course. If it's in front, it may be that the two gun operators will be saved. If it explodes at midpoint, it's all over. If it explodes behind, the driver and radio specialist might make it, though without arms or legs, or both. The gunner is fucked in any case. Whoever is behind picks up the pieces. You know the drill. If an IED has exploded, it's exploded. If someone's dead, he's dead. You have to think about cleaning up. Remember that as well. Remember everything I've said. What you forget is what will get you killed. If an IED has exploded and a friend of yours has lost his life because the ACRT didn't see it and you're infuriated with him and feel like giving him a good kick in the ass, don't do it, because there could be another IED twenty yards away and an ACRT with a sore ass is a less efficient ACRT and you sure as hell don't want to blow up too. Wait until you're back at the base to waste him. (*Laughter.*) Whoever was killed is dead now and the ACRT can't do squat about it. No one can do squat about it. (*A question.*) ACRT stands for Advanced Combat Recognition Team. An

IED is an Improvised Explosive Device, as I said before. If you add a D at the end it becomes Improvised Explosive Device Disposal, which is a whole other thing. EOD, on the other hand, means Explosive Ordnance Disposal. A VBIED is an IED planted in a run-down vehicle. You need to know the abbreviations—they're important, all of them. If you don't know English, learn it. The right abbreviation at the right time will save your life. This is not a clean war. It's not an evenhanded war. You are the targets. You're mice in a piece of moldy cheese. There isn't one single friend of ours out there. Not even those kids with flies on their faces. Not even the Mau Maus. Nine times out of ten, a Mau Mau knows where an IED is buried and won't tell you. They're as corrupt as whores, those guys. Never go where a Mau Mau doesn't want to go. And never go where a Mau Mau tells you to go. (*A question.*) A Mau Mau is an Afghan policeman. Where the hell have you been till now? (*Laughter.*) We're in a country of filthy, corrupt people. There's nothing to improve here. When we've straightened a few things out and go home, everything will go back to being the same mess it was before. All you should care about is going home. Make it home and your mission will have been a success—the hell with Afghanistan. (*A question.*) Because we're soldiers, we do what has to be done. Don't waste my time with dumb-ass questions."

There's word of a tip-off. One person told another, who leaked it to yet another, who then reported it to the auto parts dealer at the bazaar (who thanks to a favor he received has become an informant of average reliability), that those responsible for the attack the other night are hiding in an area in the northern part of the village. In the last week there's been an unusual parade of motorcycles to and from that district. It's enough to organize a retaliatory action.

Naturally, Ietri knows nothing about any of this. Communication breaks up as it trickles down the chain of command. The only thing he and his companions hear from René are the name of a target and a departure time. They leave the FOB two hours before dawn. The idea is to surprise the Taliban by moving in stealthily, though it doesn't make much sense: forty tons of metal advancing at a crawl over rough terrain doesn't exactly create what might be called a surprise. Should the Taliban think of escaping, however, they'd find their passage barred, since the soldiers are converging on the district from five different directions, blocking the roads. The higher-ups in Herat have guaranteed aerial coverage with two fighter-bombers that will fly unseen over the area and can detect heat sources within a several-mile radius. Colonel Ballesio worked out that flawless strategy in less than no time, a few hours earlier.

Ietri is aboard the Lince driven by Zampieri. From the backseat, he'd rather look at her than at the flat terrain outside, as the horizon brightens with an orange glow. Zampieri greatly disturbs him or greatly soothes him, depending on the situation. It's a curious thing, which makes him think. The ACRT orders three stops for suspected explosive devices: a dead bird flattened at the side of the road, a few limp sacks abandoned in the middle of nowhere, a group of three rocks arranged in nearly a straight line. They're false alarms, but enough to intensify Ietri's apprehension. From a place where he'd been keeping it at bay, it spreads to every part of his body. He tightens his grip on the barrel of the automatic rifle, which he's holding straight up between his knees. He starts studying the possible geometries of the rocks, in case he might pick out a suspect one that's escaped the bomb tech. He can't make heads or tails of it, though; they're all regular or irregular depending on how you look at them. He can't understand how the sappers can do the job they do. Maybe they too just take a guess, and in fact every so often one of them is killed. "Are we almost there?" he can't help asking.

Nobody answers.

"Well, are we nearly there or not?"

"We're there when we get there," Zampieri replies coldly, without taking her eyes off the road.

By the time they get out of the Lince, the sun has risen. The soldiers cover about fifty yards at a run, turn a corner, and then another. René seems to know where they're headed. They line up against the wall of a house.

They communicate with arm, head, and finger gestures, prearranged coded signals that roughly mean: You guys move forward. Keep an eye out over there. You, bring up the rear. We'll go in that door. A final command is for Ietri: You go first. Cederna will cover you. Kick in the door and jump aside. René raises his right thumb, meaning: Do you understand? Ietri thinks so, but what if he's wrong? He rotates his forefinger to ask the commander to repeat it. René runs through the sequence again, more slowly.

Okay?

Okay.

Ietri moves to the head of the column, then lunges for the other side of the door. Cederna follows two steps away. Did he have to pick me? Ietri thinks. For some reason he's reminded of the cockroaches at the Wreck, the way they silently scurry across the room, looking for cover along the way.

A rooster crows loudly in the distance and calls him back. There's a narrow, empty track that runs between the houses and fades into the barren desert; part of the road is in the shadow of the house where they think the enemy is hiding. Seven of them, René in the lead, are standing in this shade, to the right of the wooden door. He and Cederna are the only ones on the other side of the door.

Ietri slides a hand inside his collar, feeling for the chain with the cross; he pulls it out, brings it to his lips, and realizes that his hands are shaking. His legs are too. And his knees. Fuck. He has only one chance to kick in the door. It looks pretty rotten, but there's a latch. Maybe they've bolted it on the inside with iron bars, in which case he's screwed. It's possible they'll finish him off in a second, that the Taliban in the house are aware of their arrival and are now waiting for them with their Kalashnikovs aimed at the door. They'll fire on the first one to appear, and that first one will be him. There was something he had to remember before he died; he had it on his mind until a moment ago. Was it his mother, maybe? The way she used to comb his hair into a pageboy when he was a little boy, using her fingers? He doesn't think it was that. Anyway, all he remembers about his mother now is the slap she gave him the day before he left and how she started crying at the airport. Ietri feels a surge of anger toward her.

"Go on, *verginella*, move," Cederna urges him from behind.

But Ietri's calves are as heavy as wet sandbags. He can't even think about raising his leg to kick. His boots might have fused with the ground, for all he knows. "I can't," he says.

"What do you mean, you can't?"

"I can't."

"Why can't you?"

"I feel dizzy."

Cederna is silent for a second; Ietri feels his hand on his shoulder. René is signaling him again to break down the door.

"Breathe, Roberto," Cederna says. "Do you hear me?"

He can't die, not as long as his mother is alive. She's already been through so much, poor woman. Roberto Ietri's life doesn't belong to Roberto Ietri, not entirely; a nice big chunk of it still belongs to his mother and he can't let himself take it away from her. It would be a crime, a sacrilege. He feels so light-headed. Sweat is running down his forehead and down his neck, under his armpits, pouring down inside his clothes.

"Take long, deep breaths, okay? Just do that. Breathe. It's the only thing you have to worry about. Everything will be fine. Count to five. Keep breathing. Kick down that fucking door, then jump aside. I'm here to cover you. You hear me, Roberto?"

Ietri nods. What about his final thought, though? And his mother? The hell with his mother.

"Breathe, Roberto."

One.

How does it go? Which comes first, the noise of the blast or the bullet? For sure the interval isn't enough to get out of the bullet's path. But maybe it's enough for the brain to understand, to tell the rest of the body it's on its way, you're dead.

Two.

He glimpses movement at the edge of his field of vision, to the left. He snaps his head around and sees a white flash of light.

Three.

It's just a stone reflecting the sun's rays. He looks in front of him. The door, the door, the door, kick down the door.

Four.

He shuts his eyes a minute, jumps to the side, and kicks with his right leg. The wood shudders, the door bursts open, springs back once, then stops halfway, still attached to its hinges.

Egitto returns to the infirmary with his sleeping bag rolled up under his arm and catches Irene snooping on his computer. Before he has a chance to say anything to her, like, how the hell did she discover his e-mail password and would she mind exiting his mailbox immediately, she defuses him with the most seraphic voice in the world: "I didn't know about the child you saved. The commander told me. That's wonderful, Alessandro. I was moved." With a smooth, swift gesture—not swift enough, however—she closes the mailbox and brings up another window, which contains a sterile list of folders. She turns to him. "You're kind of a hero, in fact."

Egitto, staggered by such nerve, finds nothing better to do than collapse in the chair across the table, like a customer in a travel agency, or one of his patients. He drops the sleeping bag. "I wouldn't say that," he snaps.

All right. If Irene is willing to pass over the reason he went to sleep in another tent last night and why he's now come back looking haggard, he, in return, won't ask her to account for her awkward intrusion into his private life. After all, there's nothing really that interesting in his e-mail. They seal that pact in silence, in a fraction of a second. A residue of accord still exists between them.

Irene frowns, gazes into the lieutenant's eyes with great tenderness. "I didn't get around to telling you yesterday, but I heard about your father. I'm so sorry, Alessandro. It's just awful."

This time Egitto isn't able to suppress his irritation. "And you came all the way here to give me your condolences?"

"You're so harsh. Always on the defensive." Then, suddenly cheery, she adds: "So, tell me, what have you been up to all this time? Are you married? Do you have a million kids?"

"I have the impression you're already in possession of that information."

Irene shakes her head. "You're the same as always. You haven't changed one iota." Is that meant to be a criticism? Or rather, a show of relief? Friendships fall into exactly two categories: those who'd like you to change and those who hope you'll always stay the same. Irene undoubtedly belongs in the second camp. "Anyway, no," she continues, "I'm not in possession of 'that information,' as you put it. Still, I admit to having noticed that your ring finger is still bare."

Hers is too, Egitto observes. "And you're in Gulistan for what? To investigate?"

"Let's say I'm making a tour of the bases in the south. Just to see how things are going."

"And how are they going?"

"Worse than they seem." She remains absorbed for a moment, withdrawn.

"Meaning?"

She turns back to him with an icy expression. "Forgive me, Alessandro. I can't discuss the details of my assignment with you. I have instructions that come . . . from above, you know." She flutters her hands vaguely.

"Of course. I didn't know you were involved in such a mission, that's all."

In fact, he's irritated by Irene's superior manner, as well as by being more curious than he'd like to be about the circumstances that brought her to Gulistan—and about her life. He's also remotely envious. All of a sudden there seems to be an implicit disparity between them: while Irene Sammartino has become someone who receives *instructions from above*, he has pursued the inconsequential career of a junior army officer.

"You've moved up. I get it," he says.

"Oh, no big deal," Irene replies, self-importantly. "I'm just staff, like all the others." Then she adds, as if offering him a small concession: "In recent years, however, I've learned Dari. It's a language that fascinates me. So ancient. It has convoluted and very elegant ways of saying the simplest things."

At one time, like many of his willing colleagues, Egitto had also attempted to learn Dari. He still has the manual somewhere in his footlocker. He didn't get beyond the greetings. Irene, however, must have taken the challenge seriously—she's a persistent woman. His brilliant classmate let the fruit of her awesome study ripen and is now waving it, succulent and sweet-smelling, under his nose. It doesn't work out that way for everyone, Egitto thinks; the tree of knowledge also produces fruit that is stunted and bitter. He remains silent.

Irene unplugs the power cord from the laptop, as if it were really her computer after all and he merely some annoying pain in the neck. "If you don't mind, I'll take it over there. I have an urgent report to finish. With us, it's a disaster—they're continually seizing our computers for security reasons, they always have to . . . *update* them. It's exasperating. I'll see you for lunch, if you want." Once again without asking his permission, with the impulsiveness that characterizes her, she picks up the laptop, blows him a kiss, and disappears around the canvas divider. Once again Lieutenant Egitto, as dismayed as if his lunch has just been snatched away, is unable to object.

Ietri's face is red, his lips scored by small, dark cracks with a blob of saliva clotted at each corner. He feels confused. He has the urge to vomit and he's more fatigued than he's ever been in his entire life. He dumps his helmet and backpack on the ground, grabs his canteen, drinks until he has to come up for air, then spits.

"Well? Did you get them?" Zampieri had stayed behind the whole time to guard the vehicles; she probably gnawed her fingers till they bled while she was waiting.

Ietri shakes his head, avoids looking at her.

"The bastards," she says.

He'd been afraid, scared shitless, and now all that fear can't find a way out. It's stuck in his throat. He's about to start crying, but he can't, he mustn't, because the men are around and Zampieri is right there. Is he a soldier or what? Isn't this what he wanted? Isn't this the reason that he trained, the reason he marched for dozens of hours up and down the mountains? If Zampieri doesn't quit staring at him that way, he really might burst into tears. He leans against the hood of the Lince. It's sizzling hot, but he doesn't move. He'd stayed outside, frozen against the wall of the house, while the others scoured the interior. When they came out escorting the family, he tagged after them, like the last of the seven dwarves, the dopey one whose tunic is too long.

Cederna surprises him from behind. He pounces on him, grabs him by the collar of his camouflage vest, and knocks him to the ground.

"Were you trying to get yourself killed, *verginella*? Huh? Did you want them to put a hole in your belly, you son of a bitch? Right here? Did you want a fucking hole right here?"

He presses his knee into Ietri's stomach, against the lead plate of his bulletproof vest. Ietri protects his face with his hands. "I'm sorry," he gasps.

"Sorry? *Sorry?* Sorry doesn't fucking cut it, *verginella*! Tell God Almighty you're sorry. He's the one who saved you."

Cederna slaps him once, then a second time. Quick smacks that take Ietri by surprise and cloud his vision. Cederna picks up a handful of dirt and throws it at his buddy's face—maybe he'd like to stuff it in his mouth, suffocate him, but he doesn't. Ietri doesn't defend himself; Cederna is right. He feels like his chest might cave in at any moment. The dirt gets in his nose, his eyes.

It's Zampieri who comes to his aid. "Leave him alone," she says, but Cederna shoves her away.

"Why didn't you move? Huh? Why didn't you move, you ugly piece of shit?" His eyes are red, possessed. He knees him again, cutting off his breath. "Fuck it!" Cederna swears, then lets go of him and quickly walks off, swearing at the Virgin Mary.

Ietri coughs for a long time, writhing, unable to stop. After he'd kicked in the door he'd stood there, rooted to the spot, until Cederna covered him. If there'd been a gun in there, he'd be in the arms of the Creator now. His first taste of action was a total failure, and everyone witnessed it. His head abandoned him almost immediately and instinct did not take over. Not even the worst, the most inexperienced soldier in the world would have behaved that way. Surely René thinks so too: when he'd slapped him lightly on the butt and said "Good job" earlier, he didn't really mean it; it was just to encourage him, and in fact he'd quickly turned on his heels.

Zampieri kneels beside him. "Look what he did to you," she says. She slips the keffiyeh from around her neck. She pours some water from the canteen on it and wrings it out. She pats his face, first his forehead, then his cheeks.

"What are you doing?"

"Ssshh. Close your eyes."

She wets the keffiyeh again and wipes his neck. When it goes behind his ears, Ietri feels an intense pleasure. He shivers. "I don't know why he acts like such an asshole sometimes," he says.

She smiles at him. "He cares about you. That's all."

But it's not true. Cederna didn't beat him up because he cares about him, he beat him up because his own life could have been at stake. Ietri had put every one of them in danger. He tries to get up, but the girl holds him down. "Wait."

She passes the cloth under his nose to wipe away the encrusted snot.

"Doesn't it disgust you?"

"Disgust me? No. Not even a little."

Symbols and Surprises

Torsu's illness is never-ending. The food poisoning led to dysentery, the dysentery to a fever. To bring it down he took antibiotics, which caused a gingival abscess and another fever, which kept him in bed so long that he developed hemorrhoids. The shooting pains make him cry like a baby. If that weren't enough, now that his temperature is at least under control, he feels really depressed. His platoon mates treat him with a lack of concern, or open hostility. When they bring him his meals in the tent, the food is cold and even more disgusting than usual. No one is eager to stop and keep him company during the afternoon, and all those hours alone in bed have a crushing effect on him. At the beginning it wasn't like that—they took care of him—but his lingering infirmity quickly irritated them. This morning Cederna, going past his cot, taunted him with a resounding gibe: "Another day of jacking off, honeybunch?"

"I'm sick."

"Right, you're yellow as piss. If you ask me you're going to die, Sardinian."

There's more. He's just made a disturbing discovery. If he lines his toes up on the sleeping bag, he can clearly see that his right leg is longer than the other. He'd never noticed it—it must have been the illness that made him asymmetrical: the affliction modified his body. Just to be sure, he does a few tests. He lies down nice and straight on the cot, arms down along his sides, flexes the arches of his feet as far as he can, then raises his head slightly to look: there's no doubt about it—the right leg is longer than the left, the tip of the big toe extends much farther out. The thought drives him wild. He imagines half of his body expanding. There was a guy in his village who wore corrective shoes, with a black wedge under one of his feet to balance him out, but even so he walked like a cripple and was plainly avoided by everyone. Overwrought, Torsu writes to his virtual girlfriend, the only person he can confide in. It takes a great deal of courage to explain what's happened to him, but she appears indifferent, skeptical.

> THOR_SARDEGNA: i wasn't like that before, don't you see?

> TERSICORE89: it's just your impression. you must be tired, try to sleep on it

> THOR_SARDEGNA: that's all you tell me these days, that I should sleep. hell, that's all i do. i've had enough of sleeping. and if i tell you that my right leg has gotten longer you should believe me, but no, because you always know everything

> TERSICORE89: i don't like you talking to me in that tone

> THOR_SARDEGNA: i'll talk to you any way i like

For nearly half an hour Torsu stares at the screen of the laptop that's resting on his belly (besides being the only place possible, it warms his stomach pleasantly). He doesn't write anything and Tersicore89 doesn't either. Every now and then he takes a peek at his feet; now it seems like his right leg is growing longer by the minute. He's becoming a monster! Tersicore89 is still online, mute. *Come on, say something!* In the end, he's the one who gives in.

THOR_SARDEGNA: would you still love me if i were different than i am?

TERSICORE89: i've never even seen you! . . . i love you for what's expressed in the words you write, nitwit. i don't care how long your legs are. and you?

THOR_SARDEGNA: me, what?

TERSICORE89: would you love me even if you found out i'm different than you imagine?

Torsu stiffens. He plumps up the pillow to straighten his back. What does she mean? Different how? Zampieri's words run through his head: *If you ask me, she's a he.*

THOR_SARDEGNA: different how?

TERSICORE89: who knows . . .

THOR_SARDEGNA: stop teasing me!!! different how?

TERSICORE89: look, i really don't like the way you're talking to me today. you're abusive and aggressive. i think you need to get some rest. we'll talk when you're feeling calmer.

THOR_SARDEGNA: I ASKED YOU DIFFERENT HOW! ANSWER ME!

TERSICORE89: hey i don't take orders from you. i'm not a serviceman

THOR_SARDEGNA: why did you write serviceman?

TERSICORE89: ???

THOR_SARDEGNA: you wrote SERVICEMAN

TERSICORE89: so?

THOR_SARDEGNA: you should have written SERVICEWOMAN, not SERVICEMAN

TERSICORE89: i don't know what you're talking about

THOR_SARDEGNA: oh no? you don't know? i think you know very well

TERSICORE89: you should get some sleep

What a fiasco! Torsu feels his temperature rising quickly, clenching his temples. His sweaty fingers slip on the keyboard. A man! For months he's had a relationship with *a man*, a fucking pervert. He feels like throwing up. He writes the question and deletes it, then rewrites it, looks at it for a while, and finally presses the send key.

THOR_SARDEGNA: are you a guy?

His virtual girlfriend—or his boyfriend, at this point he has no idea anymore—takes her time thinking about it. It's not a question that requires reflection: either you're a man or you're not; few issues are that simple in the world. If she's hedging, it's because she's considering how to get around the truth. From time to time, Torsu continues to monitor the state of his lower limbs. Very soon he'll end up deformed, and alone.

TERSICORE89: you're pathetic. good-bye.

She disconnects immediately. Torsu figures it's probably over between them and, at the moment, he doesn't feel any great regret.

In the afternoon, however, as he crosses the square (with the impression of limping, as if his pelvis were now off kilter), he automatically thinks, Now I'll go write to Tersicore89, and the recoil from that thought chills him. What the hell was he thinking? Tersicore89 can't possibly be a man, not after all the wonderful, intimate things they wrote to each other. It must have been extreme exhaustion that made him imagine something so absurd. And that meddlesome Zampieri. The problem is he's not sure how to put things right now, he's not too experienced in apologizing. But what is he worrying about? He'll find a way for sure.

For a few moments optimism even alleviates the nagging concern about his legs. In fact, when he'd revealed his discovery to the doc a little while ago—better they know it right away; if they had to kick him out they might as well do it as soon as possible—the lieutenant had merely shaken his head skeptically: "Bones don't grow after you've developed." In return, he'd listed a number of absurd maladies that should be considered, given the ineffective response to the drugs: cholera, typhoid, some amoebic infestation, and others he can't remember now.

He was a little put out by the doc's failure to show concern for his problem. Lieutenant Egitto is a decent enough sort. Torsu has seen him regularly, he hasn't skipped even one injection, but the doc has a brusque way about him all the time; he never says one word more than necessary. Who the hell cares. Now Torsu knows the leg isn't serious, he's had to run to the latrines only once since this morning, and soon he'll have Tersicore89 all to himself again. Feeling confident, he hurries to the tent.

The spark of terror that runs through his body at the sight of the snake coiled up near his foot gives him instant, unexpected vigor, proof that his body, if it wants to, is fully capable of reacting. Torsu jumps backward, then takes a few more steps back, stumbles, and gets up again, never once taking his eyes off the reptile.

"Fuck!" he cries. His face feels all tingly from the fright.

The snake's triangular head swings slowly from side to side, as though dazed. The skin is glossy, pale blue, marked with bands of a lighter color. Torsu feels dizzy, for a moment the fever flares up again, clouding his mind, and he regards the reptile with the detachment of a delirious vision. Then the snake makes a 180-degree turn, languidly unwinds to its full length, and begins to move away from where Torsu is standing. The first corporal major is fascinated. He glances around, looking for something. Finally he bends down and cautiously grabs one of the large bricks piled around the tent stake. "Stay still," he whispers.

He knows quite well that snakes are fast. He saw a documentary once about constrictors and he recalls how quickly they can pounce. He wonders if this snake is the kind that constricts or if it has poison in its glands. There's no way of knowing: snakes all look somewhat alike. He raises the brick with both hands. He holds his breath and hurls it down.

The snake's head explodes, splattering bluish blood around; the brick teeters for a moment, then tips over on the battered head again. Deprived of its brain, the reptile's long tail begins thrashing wildly; it wheels around, waving its dripping extremity. Torsu slowly moves closer, mesmerized. Seized with a violent spasm, the decapitated snake grazes his calf, as if trying to sink its fangs into it though it no longer has any. Torsu lets out a scream.

Then the slimy creature grows quiet. It continues pulsating on the sand for a few seconds, then expires completely. The soldier is forced to close his eyes the instant the creature dies.

"Wow!" he yells. "Holy shit! Wowww!" His heart is pounding with excitement. In their first days in Gulistan the guys set up a kind of locker area outside the tent where they could hang their towels: simple

S-hooks affixed to the iron mesh of the HESCO Bastion wall. Torsu removes his stuff, hangs it on a buddy's hook, then slips his hook off the wall. He walks back to the dead snake, bends down, and plants the iron S-hook in its tail, raising the decapitated reptile off the ground and above his hip. It seems a bit slender to be able to strangle a man, but Torsu knows that nature is full of paradoxes—you never can tell. In any case it's a respectable prize.

He hangs the carcass in the Wreck, in the middle of the clothesline. Then, suddenly exhausted, he flops down on a chair and sits there admiring it for a long time. He's never seen anything so repulsive and attractive at the same time. As a child he fished for crabs and, sure, sometimes he happened to come upon an eel or a river snake, but they were small and scary, nothing to do with the creature that now dangles limply before his eyes in the lethargy of early afternoon. It's majestic, that's what. In his region, he recalls, they say that every snake guards a treasure.

Cederna and Ietri are working out on a bench in full sun. They've lifted makeshift dumbbells and are now grinding out mixed abdominals: normal, twisting, and reverse crunches, so as to involve all the muscles. The body must be sculpted piece by piece, methodically, although many people don't know it. There are some who always repeat the same three or four exercises at the gym. They have no idea what they're doing.

The two soldiers take turns holding each other's ankles down and now it's Cederna's chance to catch his breath. When Ietri rolls up toward his knees, he can smell his buddy's pungent odor: sweat mixed with the "keto" breath you get during physical exercise. It's not unpleasant, not too much.

"You're not pumping much, *verginella*. You look like a sack of potatoes. What's up?"

Ietri grimaces with fatigue. He's in a bad mood. Since they scoured the village, he's felt out of sorts. At night he's had distressing dreams that he can't shake off by day. "I don't know," he says. "I just don't feel like being here anymore. Maybe."

"If that's it, I'll let you in on a little secret: *no one* wants to be here."

"You're going on leave in a week."

Ietri loosens the fingers laced behind his head to help push himself up. At eighty crunches he stops with his back flat on the bench. His stomach is pulsing rapidly. The acute pain in his lower back tells him he did well. "Cederna?"

"Yeah?"

"Remember the house we swept yesterday?"

"You call that a house? It was a shitty pigsty."

"Maybe it wasn't right to burst in that way. We broke down their door, those poor people."

"No, *you* broke down the door."

"Well, okay, that's not the point."

"And anyway, who the hell cares about the door?"

"It was just a family."

"What the fuck are you saying? How do you know? Those Taliban bastards disguise themselves. Maybe the guy had a stick of dynamite hidden up his ass and we weren't even aware of it."

"Mattioli dragged him by the hair. There was no reason to."

"He wouldn't move."

"He was scared."

"Hey, what the hell's got into you, *verginella*? Are you getting soft-hearted? Watch out, that's how they try to fuck with you, by making you feel guilty. They make sheep's eyes at us and then they kill us."

Ietri isn't convinced, though. As he sees it, that was just a family of poor unfortunates. He starts a new series of crunches, even though his back pain hasn't entirely subsided. He twists his torso ninety degrees to the left, then to the right, alternately working his obliques.

"Besides, haven't you seen how they treat women?" Cederna asks.

"What does that have to do with it?"

"Keep your heels down, man! It has a lot to do with it."

"It's their culture."

"I'm fed up with that story about cultures, get it? If a culture sucks, it sucks, case closed. There's nothing more you can say. Like Japanese food."

"Japanese food?"

"Never mind. Someone needs to teach these barbarians how to be civilized, sooner or later. And if kindness doesn't work, then we'll find another way to teach them. Keep those heels down!"

Ietri can barely keep it up. He still has twelve more to go. "I don't know if that's why we're here," he persists, through clenched teeth.

"Of course that's why. Imagine if they put one of those burkas on your mother. I'm telling you, the Arabs are even worse than the Chinese. Worse than the Jews too."

They switch places. Ietri tries to picture his mother covered by a long black garment. She wouldn't look much different than she does now. A question occurs to him, but he doesn't dare ask it. Cederna blows in his face every time he raises his torso. Damn, he's strong—it's a struggle to hold his ankles down. The face of the American Indian tattooed on his abdomen crumples up and slackens. Finally Ietri spits it out: "Listen, can I ask you something?"

"Shoot, *verginella*."

"What exactly does Jew mean?"

Cederna frowns, but doesn't stop. "What the hell kind of question is that?"

Ietri immediately gets defensive. "Forget it. You mentioned Jews before, and I . . . it was just a question, that's all."

"It's a dumb-ass question. A Jew is a Jew, right?"

Now he's blushing. He knew it was better not to ask. But he's been carrying the question around for so long and for some reason, he's not sure why, he finds it natural to trust Cederna. He falls for it every time. "I know," he tries to make up for his mistake, "I mean, the whole story about Hitler and the concentration camps and all that. But . . . what I mean is . . . with a black, you can see that he's black. But if someone is a Jew, how can you tell?"

Cederna stops, panting. He leans on his forearms. He spits to the side, then stares at the sky, thinking. "There's no specific way," he says. "You just know. Some people are Jews and other people know it." Then something occurs to him; his eyes flash. "And obviously you can tell by the last name."

"By the last name?"

"Sure. That writer, for instance . . . Primo Levi. It's a Jewish name."

"That's it? The last name?"

"That's it, right. What did you think it was?"

Cederna resumes his crunches. Ietri can feel his friend's tendons lengthen in his hands and then release. "You don't know a fucking thing, *verginella*."

"Cederna?"

"Yeah."

"Could you stop calling me *verginella*? Please."

"Not a chance."

"At least not in front of the other guys."

"I'll stop when you're not a little virgin anymore, *verginella*."

Ietri chews his lip. "Speaking of which," he says.

"What?"

"Nothing."

"Now you started. Shoot."

He just can't keep his mouth shut, damn it! Where does Cederna get that power to pull the truth out of him all the time? He already messed up once, when he talked to him about girls, and now he feels like he's about to make another misstep, but he can't stop himself. "What do you think of Zampa?"

Cederna stops abruptly. "Uh-oh! Watch out! Why do you ask?"

"No reason. Just curious."

"The *verginella* has a crush on our comrade!"

"Ssshh! Come on, I'm serious."

Cederna again assumes the philosophical expression he wore when he was explaining about Jews. He really gets on Ietri's nerves when he does that.

"Zampa . . . has a nice pair of tits. But an ugly face. Plus, any female who serves in the army must have a screw loose."

"I don't know." Ietri hesitates. He feels as bashful as a little kid. "I like her a little. Being together, that's all."

"You're really an unlucky bastard, pal."

"Why?"

His friend is now sitting beside him, wiping the sweat from his armpits with his T-shirt. He has multicolored tattoos even on his biceps and a smaller one on his neck, where puncturing the skin must hurt like a bitch. Each one represents a symbol, a memory, and if you ask him, Cederna is more than happy to expound on them. He keeps Ietri on tenterhooks for a while. Then he says: "Because she's a lesbian, of course."

Ietri's head slumps. Lesbian. How can that be? Lesbians have short hair. Zampa's hair is long, golden blond. "How do you know that?"

"Come on, man, it's obvious! Besides, if she weren't a lesbian, do you think it's possible she'd be so good all the time? Twenty-four/seven thrown in with us guys without doing anything? No way. She'd be wild by now."

Ietri would like to go into it more, but they're interrupted by Vercellin, who runs up to them waving his arms like a maniac. "Guys! Hey, guys, come and see!"

"What's happening?" Cederna gets up.

For a few seconds the silhouette of his face casts a shadow over Ietri. Darkened, that's how Ietri feels, for a myriad of reasons that he can't separate from one another. And this new, shocking news.

"Come and see what Torsu found," Vercellin says. "It'll blow your minds!"

The Sardinian's hunting trophy triggers great euphoria in the Third. His platoon mates congratulate him, and Torsu stays on his feet just to enjoy the glory, despite the fact that his fever has taken a new upswing. The guys invent a courage competition: they take turns touching the dead snake—all except Mitrano, who turns out to have an atavistic terror of slithering creatures. Then a challenge is issued to see who will dare lick it. The only ones to do so are Cederna and Simoncelli; they then describe the taste, contradicting each other several times and only confirming for certain that the taste is really disgusting. Cederna wants to take the snake off the hook and wrap it around his neck like a scarf, but the others won't let him. They start dancing around the carcass, first each on his own, then in a conga line led by Pecone. Marshal René and a few others stand on the sidelines, though joining in with smiles of approval. Zampieri takes over a table and does a sensual dance. Tracing irregular circles with her pelvis, she slides her open hands from her neck to her breasts and then farther down, to her groin. Then she joins her hands above her head as if in prayer, and unwinds every joint, from her wrists to her ankles, imitating the sinuous glide of the snake. Ietri doesn't take his eyes off her for a second. Lesbian? No way—this time Cederna is dead wrong.

When their excitement dies down, the guys get on the computers to share the discovery with their girlfriends, but the women don't seem to really get it. All they do is squeal, "Eewww gross—yuck!"; they laugh but only because they hear the men laughing on the other end. Then the soldiers scatter through the base, each one in search of an audience from the other companies: Come and see, come on, we caught a snake. The pilgrimage to the Third's headquarters lasts until late in the evening. Flashlight beams flickering in the darkness converge from all over to admire the hanging reptile. Even Colonel Ballesio shows up and, contemplating the creature with his arms folded, says: "Old Mother Earth sure does produce a whole lot of disgusting things." Then he adjusts his testicles and goes away.

Lieutenant Egitto has accompanied his guest to the Wreck and is now lighting the way back to the infirmary with his flashlight. He aims the beam of light on her legs and tries to remember the shape of her bare calves, their consistency. He's pretty sure he bit them on one occasion, and that he bit down too hard, making her angry.

Inside the infirmary, Irene slips off the fleece he loaned her (she'd hinted at having had some kind of experience in the Middle East, but she wasn't equipped for the desert cold, a strange detail that renewed the lieutenant's doubts), tosses it aside without folding it, and sits on the desk. "I doubt I'll be able to sleep now that I know there are snakes roaming around loose at the FOB," she says.

The soldiers had hailed her when she entered the cement hut. They'd demanded that she photograph them as a group around the snake. Egitto had stood on the sidelines.

"We should have one of your beers to celebrate."

She'd poked around in the fridge too, evidently. "They're the colonel's. I doubt he'd be pleased."

Irene jumps down off the desk. "The colonel's, of course. I bet he won't say anything."

She bends over the refrigerator and turning around three-quarters gives him an impudent look. Egitto accepts the can of beer she hands him. When Irene pops the cap on hers, the liquid fizzes out onto her hands and she laps up the foam like a greedy cat. "Remember when we did it at Fornari's party?"

Once they'd surrendered to lust inside a friend's shower. A lightning-quick coitus, one of the transgressive highlights of Egitto's erotic life. Sure, he remembers.

"It's been a while, huh?"

Irene Sammartino is no longer anything like the impulsive, flighty girl he used to know. She's morphed into a skillful woman, one who can translate her thoughts into Dari and a moment later flirt shamelessly while sipping a can of beer.

"Yeah, a really long time," Egitto replies briefly.

Later they brush their teeth outside the tent. Neither of them feels like walking to the toilets, so they use a small bottle of mineral water. The toothpaste they spit out forms small frothy white gobs near the fence. Egitto ends up with spittle on his jacket; she wipes it off for him with the back of her hand. They laugh about it together. Brusquely, they say good night to each other and bed down on opposite sides of the canvas tarp. Egitto immediately turns off the light.

He can't get to sleep, though. He keeps seeing the guys crowded around the snake's mutilated carcass and Irene popping the tab of the can, the beer foaming over her hands. He's extremely aware that she's just a few yards away and he knows the meaning of the look she gave him just before—the word *available* comes to mind and the word *intention* is also spinning around in his head.

Skipping over several logical steps, he finds himself fantasizing about married life with Irene Sammartino. He imagines her as a woman who drags along a heap of clutter with her, fills the space with magazines and piles of paper, and leaves her clothes piled up on the couch. This doesn't bother Egitto, not too much; he observes her through the chinks of that disorder. He loses himself in a close scrutiny of her anatomical merits and defects, the way he used to back when they were together, as if attraction could be computed that way, at a desk, based on a two-column table.

Just look at what he's come to, imagining detailed little scenarios around the only woman he's shared a room with in a long time, a woman he would never, ever have wanted to meet again. Fate, or more likely someone forcing its hand, put them together and now expects to spawn the obvious consequences. But the lieutenant doesn't like the idea. He's not about to get himself in hot water, not with Irene Sammartino.

He's prepared for what happens next. Irene moves cautiously, but the silence is too absolute for Egitto not to recognize the sound of the sleeping bag's zipper inching down, then the rustle of the polyester fill, the soles of her bare feet sticking to the synthetic fabric of the floor. One step, another step. The lieutenant opens his eyes. The refrigerator's tiny LED is the only light in the tent; it looks like a distant lighthouse glimpsed from out at sea. Egitto stiffens; he considers the most effective way to get out of the spot he's in.

Now it's the zipper on his bag that's being slid open. It's not time to open fire yet, he thinks; he has to wait until the enemy gets closer. Irene lies down on top of him and starts voraciously kissing his neck, his cheeks, his mouth.

"No!"

The lieutenant's voice explodes in the silence like thunder.

She stops, but not right away, more as if she were trying to catch her breath. "Why not?"

"No," Egitto repeats. His pupils have adjusted to the dim light—they must be dilated to the maximum, as he's able to make out the contours of Irene's face above him.

"But don't you find it strange to sleep apart, you and I, just a step away?"

"Maybe. But no. I'd rather . . . not."

For a moment he wavers. His body displays an unexpected interest in that nocturnal visit; it rebels, confuses him. Egitto is no longer sure why he's steering clear of the trap. Really, why? Because he made that decision earlier, that's why. Out of a sense of responsibility to himself. To protect himself.

Meanwhile, Irene is still lying on top of him. A hand quickly slips down to the lieutenant's groin, dips into his briefs. The contact with Irene's fingers radiates pleasure throughout his body. Egitto grabs her arm firmly and pushes it away. Then he clears his throat to make sure his voice will come out sounding decisive. "Get away. Now. Good night."

She rises to her knees. That was easy, Egitto thinks, easier than he'd imagined. Irene places a foot on the floor, climbs off him. There, she's going. He's safe.

With a surprising move, the sweeping gesture of a bullfighter who makes the red cape vanish before the bull, she whips the flap of his sleeping bag open and uncovers him. A blast of cold air drifts over the lieutenant's bare legs. Egitto murmurs another no, but it's a lackluster attempt.

Still struggling with himself inwardly, he lets her have her way. In the end he closes his eyes again. All right. Okay.

When they've finished, he asks Irene if she'd like to stay and sleep with him there—the cot is narrow, but they could make do. Pure courtesy, a somewhat hypocritical and very inept offer of reparation.

"Don't do me any favors," she says. "Good night, Alessandro." Her lips lightly brush his forehead.

Walking in the dark, she bumps into something, maybe the defibrillator cart. "Shit," she exclaims.

"Did you hurt yourself?"

Irene whimpers in pain. She doesn't answer him. Egitto, under the protection of darkness, smiles.

In the pitch-black dead of night, as the lieutenant finally sinks into sleep, the two soldiers on guard duty at the main sentry tower are alerted by unusual movement in the Afghan truckers' camp. They mount the night vision binoculars to see better, but there's no need, because the headlights of a vehicle come on in the meantime. A truck, just one, sets out slowly in a southwesterly direction toward the entrance to the valley, and within a few minutes disappears.

The soldiers debate whether or not they should alert the commander, then decide it's not a serious enough reason to disturb an officer. They can just as well report the good news in the morning.

"They've decided to leave," says one.

"Yeah. About time."

Last Words from Salvatore Camporesi

From: flavia_c_magnasco@*****.it
To: salvatorecamporesi1976@*****.it
Subject: Great news!!!
Tuesday, September 28, 2010, 15:19

Great news! Remember the miniature greenhouse you gave to
Gabriele? Well, yesterday a little seedling sprouted! I think it's a
bean plant, or maybe it's tomato, I'm not sure, we got the seeds
mixed up. You should've seen Gabriele's face! He wouldn't stop
jumping up and down, he was so excited. He insisted I put the
little greenhouse on the floor, he stretched out on his stomach
and stayed there staring at it for half an hour at least, his chin
resting on his hands. He was expecting it to grow before his
very eyes, I think.

He's getting big, you know? At times some of his expressions
remind me of you, he seems like an adult. You always tell me
not to send you any photos because the connection isn't fast
enough, but one of these days I'll send you a picture anyway. I
don't give a damn about your connection. And I want you to
send me one too, I want to smother it with kisses and see how
handsome you are all tanned like that.

I love you enormously.
F.

P.S. I looked in the plant guide and I actually think the seedling is a bean plant. Wow, how tall it got! And in just a few hours.

From: salvatorecamporesi1976@*****.it
To: flavia_c_magnasco@*****.it
Subject: Re: Great news!!!
Tuesday, September 28, 2010, 23:02

Sweetheart, when I read your e-mail I started crying. The guys were around and afterwards they teased me all evening. But who cares. I can't think of anything but that seedling. You have to take care of it, teach Gabriele how to. I think there was a little hose in the kit to water it with. Or you can use a spoon. When I get back we'll plant it outside. We'll make a nice vegetable garden for the summer.

There's not much going on here. We mainly patrol the area around the base, nothing dangerous, no one comes to give us any trouble. I'm almost bored. You know, I think you'd like the desert. It gives me a strange feeling, if I stare at it too long my head starts to spin. The air seems lighter than it does elsewhere and the sky is dramatic, so blue during the day and black at night. It would be a magnificent place, if it weren't for the Taliban and all. Maybe the war will end one day and we'll be able to come here on vacation. Can you imagine? The three of us together in Gulistan. I bet Gabriele would be knocked out by the camels.

S.

From: flavia_c_magnasco@*****.it
To: salvatorecamporesi1976@*****.it
Subject: Re: Re: Great news!!!
Saturday, October 2, 2010, 19:03

I can't stand sleeping alone anymore. I'm going to get sick, Salvo, I swear. I'll get sick and you won't be able to cure me. How many more nights yet? More than a hundred. I counted them, Salvo. More than a hundred! I can't even say it. It seems impossible to me. I'd like to strangle you, really. It's starting to get cold, today there wasn't even a ray of sunshine. This weather is affecting me. I don't think I can hold up until you get your leave. Gabriele misses you too, but in his own way. I mean it, sometimes I don't understand him. Some days it seems he's almost forgotten about you and that scares me and I feel like yelling at him. I show him your photo, the one when you signed up. "Who is this gentleman?" I ask him. "Do you remember him?" He looks at me with a blank stare, as if he's never seen you. It gives me the shivers. I start talking to him about you and after a second he's distracted.

Then, just like that, the other night at dinner he points to your place. I don't get it, so he takes his plate and puts it where you usually sit. "Daddy's dish." As if you were about to come home at any moment. I ask him, "Do you know where Daddy is?" He laughs as if I'm kidding, and points to the floor. "He's downstairs?" I ask him. He shakes his head. Finally I realize that he's trying to tell me you're in the cellar. Can you believe it? I don't think I was the one who put such an idea into his head— he must have made it up. Or maybe it really was me. In the early days, after you left, I was out of my mind and said a lot of crazy things.

Anyway, now I always set a place at the table for you too in the evening. It makes us feel less alone, the two of us. I pour a bit of wine in your glass, and after I put Gabriele to bed I drink it. That's right: I DRINK YOUR WINE AT NIGHT! What's wrong with that? You have some objection? Anyway you can't do anything about it. At least by the time I get to bed I'm stupefied and I don't have to think about the fact that you're not there. Who knows how many unspeakable things you'll do down there without me. I'm losing my mind, I swear.

I love you, you silly soldier.
F.

From: salvatorecamporesi1976@*****.it
To: flavia_c_magnasco@*****.it
Subject: Re: Re: Re: Great news!!!
Sunday, October 3, 2010, 21:14

I'm feeling low today too. Last night we had a little disturbance. Nothing serious, but I didn't get any sleep. And when I got up, there was no water in the showers. It's the third time in a few days. I sponged off as best I could, but even here it's starting to get bitter cold in the early morning. I know, it seems like nothing, but it was enough to dampen my spirits. I started thinking about how rotten things are here, how everything sucks, and so on. I was so edgy that at one point I almost decked Cederna. He never knows when it's time to shut that stupid mouth of his.

I spent nearly all afternoon on the cot. I tried to rest, but I couldn't. I tried to read that book you gave me, but there was no way. Eventually I just started thinking. Especially about you and Gabriele. About all the things we could do together on a day off. Now that I'm here and can't do them, I realize that I'm often too lazy. We're both too lazy. When I get back, things will change though. We won't waste a single minute.

I should have written to you sooner. I see it makes me feel better. You're my medicine. I feel so stupid when you're not around. I'm almost ashamed to say it, but sometimes it's as if I just don't know what to do with myself if you're not with me. I thought about it lying there on the cot and I got even more worked up. Is that what you've done to me, Mrs. Camporesi? What witchcraft did you use to make me so dependent on you? You're going to pay dearly, you know . . .

S.

From: flavia_c_magnasco@*****.it
To: salvatorecamporesi1976@*****.it
Subject: Re: Re: Re: Re: Great news!!!
Tuesday, October 5, 2010, 11:38

Okay, I might as well tell you. In the end I can't hide the truth from you even if I can't see you and have to write to a stupid computer. Actually things are not going well at all with Gabriele. Yesterday they called me to the nursery because he hit a playmate. All he did was punch him actually, but it was a good solid punch and he knocked him down. The teacher was furious, she said Gabriele is manic, out of control. She used those exact words: out of control. She says that in her opinion there's no congenital problem—he simply refuses to speak, his way of manipulating us all. She said it as if he were a criminal, a monster. How dare she! She also said that if the situation doesn't improve we should consider taking him to a neuropsychiatrist. A neuropsychiatrist—you know what that means? I feel so lost, Salvo.

You want to know the whole truth? I think it's your fault. That he won't speak and that he always looks angry and that he hit that kid (though he's a snotty brat and a bully and if you ask me he deserved it). I think it's your fault, you and your damn mission. Because you should be here. It's also your fault that I feel so exhausted. And ugly. In fact, I cut my hair short. Yes, that's right! I cut off my beautiful curly hair, which you liked so much. And if you don't come back soon, I'll cut off what's left of it too. Or I'll dye it red or orange or purple. I swear. I'm so tired, Salvo. I can't take any more. Anything or anyone.

From: salvatorecamporesi1976@*****.it
To: flavia_c_magnasco@*****.it
Subject: Re: Re: Re: Re: Re: Great news!!!
Wednesday, October 6, 2010, 01:13

Sweetheart, you're always worrying about Gabriele too much. He's just a child. Don't listen to everything they tell you. The pediatrician was clear, wasn't he? He'll speak when he feels the need to. For now he's probably fine the way he is. You know what I say? Good thing he's learning to defend himself. He's always been a little fearful and too gentle. The world out there is ruthless. I would have loved to see the face of the kid he decked! When I get back I'll teach him one or two moves. And I have a few interesting ones to try out with you too . . .

You know Torsu found a snake? It was right near our tent. You'd die of fright if you saw it. That brainless Sardinian squashed its head to a pulp with a rock. He hung it up like a salami and we all started dancing around it like idiots, like some kind of tribe. It was fun. Remember that snake we found on the trail in Val Canzoi? Of course you remember. You did the rest of the walk clinging to my arm. You were terrified. You're very sexy when you're terrified, Mrs. Camporesi. As soon as I get back I'll fill our room with snakes, spiders, cockroaches, and mice—that way you'll stick to me all the time.

It's very late. I'm going to sleep. Do me a favor, call my mother and tell her everything is okay. I haven't been able to talk to her for the last several days and I wouldn't want her to worry.

S.

P.S. You can wear your hair blue, short, straight, however the hell you want. I'll still go nuts over you.

Shots in the Night

"I'm thinking of a prank," Cederna announces to Ietri as they're shaving early in the morning.

"What prank?"

"First tell me if you'll go along, then I'll tell you about it."

They rinse their razors in the same basin of warm water resting on the ground. The shaving lather floats like cream on the surface. Cederna shaves carefully, because a few pimples have broken out and he has to pay attention. He can't explain the frenzy that seizes him on certain days like today. All he knows is that he wakes up with a wild urge to do something, to pick a fight, smash things, knock people around, wreak havoc. He's been that way since he was a kid and his memories of every one of those days are partly appalling and partly glorious. If there were someone he could beat up, it would be perfect, but the enemy doesn't show its face, so he has to improvise.

"How can I tell you I'm in if I don't know what it involves?" Ietri objects.

"Don't you trust me, *verginella*?"

Ietri thinks it over. Cederna knows very well he has him in the palm of his hand. Ietri is his disciple. If he asked him to run naked toward a group of Taliban, he'd probably do it.

"Sure, I trust you," Ietri says.

"Then tell me you'll go along."

"It's not dangerous, is it?"

"Nope. You just have to keep watch."

"Okay, then. I'm in."

Cederna moves closer. He stops Ietri's hand that's holding the razor. He slides his own blade over his buddy's cheek. Ietri's eyes widen; he stiffens.

"What are you doing?"

"Ssshh . . ."

Ietri holds his breath as his eyes follow the razor's path.

"Listen," Cederna says. "Tonight, when the others are in the mess hall, we'll take the snake out of the Wreck."

"I'm not touching that thing."

"I'll do it. I told you, you're the lookout—you just have to make sure no one approaches."

"What are you going to do with the snake?"

"Put it in Mitrano's sleeping bag."

"Holy shit."

"Dead right. Wait till you see how he jumps when he finds it."

"But didn't you see how scared he was last night? He couldn't even look at it."

"Exactly."

Cederna draws the blade along his friend's jaw, carefully following the curve of the bone. Their mouths are so close that if they each pursed their lips, they'd touch. Never in a million years would Cederna ever think about kissing a man on the lips.

"What if he gets really pissed?"

"Who? Mitrano? That's just the beauty of it."

The beauty of it also has to do with getting back at Mitrano once and for all for how he made Cederna feel the night of the attack, sniveling like a woman to try to get his place back inside the bunker—but Cederna doesn't say that.

"And what if René gets mad?"

"René never gets mad. Besides, who gives a shit? If we followed his lead, we'd all commit suicide out of boredom. It'll be fun—take my word."

"I don't know. I don't think it's a good idea."

"You promised you'd do it. If you back out now you're a sleazebag. Stick out your chin."

"Okay," Ietri mutters, barely opening his mouth. "I'm in."

"The important thing is not to let anyone see us, otherwise the prank won't work. When they don't find the snake, they'll go nuts."

"Torsu is always in the tent."

"That guy's brain is fried from the computer. He won't even notice."

Cederna now focuses on his buddy's mustache, as Ietri obediently draws in his lips to stretch the skin tighter. Cederna wipes off the residual foam with his fingers. His older brother used to do that for him when he grew his first facial hair. For *him* Cederna wouldn't hesitate to run naked toward a group of Taliban and let himself be shot—you can count on that! It was his brother who taught him how easy it is to be adored by someone younger.

"Cederna?" Ietri asks.

"Shoot."

"Can you make my sideburns pointy like yours? I can't do it."

Cederna smiles at him. He's a good kid, his Ietri. He moves him. "Keep your head still, *verginella*. It's a job that requires precision."

The fact that Irene still hasn't mentioned last night's encounter is not reassuring to Lieutenant Egitto. On the contrary, it makes him more and more anxious with each passing hour. When he woke up this morning, she'd already left. He heard from the colonel that she'd gone out on patrol with the men, that she'd wanted to see the bazaar and confer with certain informants *about her own concerns*. She reappeared at lunch time, and they were sitting at the same table in the mess hall. He watched her entertain the officers with the story of a fellow soldier who, not having appreciated the report she'd made about him to command staff, had tailed her to her house and then attacked her, cracking two ribs with his fist. Everyone was amused and shocked by the story: a military man beating a woman colleague—unheard of, imagine that! That's some kind of lily-livered coward. Egitto pretended to smile. Was the episode to be believed? And why had Irene chosen that particular one? Is she perhaps trying to send him a message, let him know that he shouldn't joke around with her? After last night's accident—that's what he's calling it now, an *accident*—he perceives a certain sense of danger. He even considers the possibility of blackmail: if he won't go along with her, Irene will blow up his career simply by snapping her fingers. That's what she's telling him: from now on he'll have to obey her, become her lover, a much more elaborate strategy than a fake pregnancy. Nauseated, Egitto has left almost everything on his tray untouched, only picking at the roasted potatoes.

Ballesio invites him back to his tent for their usual afternoon talk. Actually, he doesn't even invite him—he assumes the lieutenant will follow him—but Egitto offers some muddled excuses. He goes back to the infirmary, but Irene isn't there. The lieutenant goes around the canvas divider, contemplates the portion of the space that's been usurped from him. Irene's bag is resting on the ground, unattended, a rather small backpack, appropriate for someone who needs to travel light. He looks behind him, all clear. He squats down and opens the zipper.

He sifts through the clothes, taking care not to crumple or move them around. Nearly all black tops and pants, but also a fleece sweatshirt—so she had one, then. His hands dig deeper, and he recognizes a different fabric by its feel. He takes out a nightgown, or a slip, it's not clear—a flimsy garment in any case, maybe silk, the shoulder straps trimmed with lace.

"You should see it on me. It looks spectacular."

Egitto stiffens. "Sorry," he mumbles. "I was just . . ." He doesn't have the nerve to turn around.

Irene gently removes the garment from his hands, folds it back up. Then she picks up the backpack and puts the item back inside. "You never know what might come up."

Egitto gets to his feet.

"I'm dead tired," she says. "Do you mind if I rest a while?"

"No. Of course not. Go right ahead."

But the lieutenant doesn't move. Now that they're there face-to-face, he caught in the act, they should clarify the matter left hanging between them.

"What?" Irene asks.

"Look," Egitto says. He pauses, takes a deep breath, then starts again: "About what happened last night . . ."

She looks at him, curious. "Well?"

"It happened, that's just it. But it was giving in. It can't happen again."

Irene thinks about it a moment. Then she says: "That's the worst thing a man has ever said to me."

"I'm sorry." For some reason he really does feel sorry.

"Oh, will you stop apologizing, goddamn it?" Irene's tone has suddenly changed. "You don't apologize for something like that, Alessandro. Take it as a sport, a game, a gift from an old friend, whatever you want. But *do me a favor*—don't apologize. Let's try to handle the situation like adults, okay?"

"I just wanted to make sure that—"

Irene closes her eyes. "Right. I understand perfectly. Now go. I'm tired."

Egitto beats a hasty retreat, humiliated. Everything he's done in the last forty-eight hours has turned out to be wrong. Maybe he's lost all ability to manage in life.

Corporal Mitrano has awakened many times with Simoncelli's hairy ass on his face, keeping him from breathing. It's not a good feeling. For one thing, because a two-hundred-pound brute sitting on you causes something very similar to suffocation. Then, too, it's not the type of intimacy you'd like to have with anyone, least of all with a kind of chimpanzee who has the ability to fart on demand. But worst of all is the laughter you hear all around you while you can't move—someone has handcuffed your wrists to the bars of the cot and you can't see a thing because of the buttocks pressed against your eyelids—laughter coming from your platoon mates, your fellow soldiers, your buddies. The laughing hurts even more than the sticks some of them keep lashing your bare thighs and the little toe of your left foot with.

There are endless variations on the butt joke and Mitrano has endured them all. Mouth gagged and ankles bound with packing tape. Ice down your skivvies (while you're still immobilized). Arm waxing, the classic short-sheeting, hair smeared with toothpaste, which there's no way of removing once it dries, except with scissors. The toothpaste video, in particular, made the rounds of the regiment and is now available on YouTube tagged with the keywords *wake-up call, barracks, odd shampoo, loser*. The first part is shot in the dark and the half-naked guys have green eyes like ghouls. You can clearly see Camporesi squeezing the tube and someone—probably Mattioli—egging him on: *More, more*. At that time Mitrano still bore the unfortunate nickname "Fucking Curly Locks"; the guys eagerly tore strands from his head and put them on a table, under the light, to show that they looked just like pubic hair. Thanks to the toothpaste, the matter of the nickname at least was resolved, in a certain sense: Mitrano did not let his hair grow again after he was forced to shave it all off.

None of this is important to him by now. He's gotten used to it. When he was first called up it was even worse. There they hurt him for real—they used belts, lead plates from the bulletproof vests, toilet brushes; they pissed in his backpack and on his head. That's life, of course: there are always those who dish it out and those who take it. Mitrano is one of those on the receiving end—like his father, moreover, who even catches it from his mother because he's short and puny. That's how it should be. Above all a good soldier is one who can take it.

In general, however, he prefers animals to people. Dogs especially. He likes them husky, strong and aggressive. It's not that they're kinder than men—they too live in a world of abuse, just watch them when they meet, the way they sniff each other's backsides and growl and go head-to-head—but they're more honest; they go by instinct and that's it. Mitrano knows all about dogs and he respects them. He spends much of his free time in the FOB at the engineer corps' canine unit camp with Maya, a Belgian shepherd with moist black eyes, trained to sniff out explosives. Her master, Lieutenant Sanna, lets him be with her, because Mitrano at least keeps the dog occupied and Sanna can concentrate on his own stuff, which mainly involves the meticulous scrutiny of certain auto magazines. Mitrano would give his right arm to enter Sanna's regiment, but he failed the aptitude tests miserably. School was always his weak point.

He stays and plays with Maya until supper time. He sets up an agility course in a corner of the square, with some obstacles, a tunnel made of tires and a ball. It takes him almost an hour to get her to understand the exercises, but she's an intelligent animal and eventually she learns them. The soldiers who pass by stop to watch admiringly and applaud them. Mitrano is pleased with himself. He may not be a genius—having been told that by everyone, his mother, his teachers, his trainers, and his buddies, he's accepted it—but he's truly unbeatable when it comes to training dogs. Feeling cheerful, he dishes out Maya's chow and then goes straight to the mess for his own.

In the evening he goes to the Wreck with the others, but he keeps to himself, playing on a portable game console. His companions are all worked up because the snake has disappeared. Mitrano couldn't care less—in fact he's glad, because even just seeing it from a distance gave him the creeps. He loves animals, all except reptiles. Those he really can't stand. Mattioli accuses him of having gotten rid of the snake—

naturally they'd take it out on him—but he must look so incredulous that when he says, "What do you want from me? I didn't even touch it," they're satisfied and leave him in peace.

At midnight he goes back to the tent; his head is somewhat muddled and his eyes burn from the hours spent staring at the Nintendo's tiny display. Many of the guys have already gone to bed and others are undressing. Mitrano takes off his pants and jacket and pushes his foot into his thermal long johns.

"Hey, Rovere," he says to his neighbor in the adjacent cot.

Rovere is covered nearly up to his nose. He opens his eyes, squints at him hostilely. "What do you want?"

"What do you think the Taliban are doing now?"

"What do you think they're doing? Sleeping."

"If you ask me, they're watching us."

"Knock it off, why don't you." He turns away.

Mitrano crawls into the sleeping bag. He balls up the small pillow to make it thicker and tries to find a comfortable position on his side. Sometimes his father would show up at breakfast with a black eye, or wouldn't be able to raise his coffee cup because his arm was so sore. He would keep his mouth shut. He learned that the best you can do in certain families is not ask any questions, ever, and his family is one of those.

Something is preventing him from stretching out his legs. He feels around with his foot, but the long johns hamper his sense of touch. His first thought is that some dirty article of clothing ended up down there; then the terrifying suspicion occurs to him that his buddies have once again short-sheeted him. So he slides backward to see if he can still get out. Fortunately, he can. Sitting up, he sticks a hand inside the lining to explore the bottom, grabs something. The reptile's skin has become dry, rough, and gives off a stench of rotting meat that hits the corporal an instant before he realizes what he's holding.

"AAAAAIIIIIIIIEEEEEEEE!"

He leaps up, nearly overturning the cot. He hops up and down, as if the snake were at his feet. Electric sparks are coursing through his entire body; his arms are trembling.

The soldiers wake up, ask what's going on, lights are turned on, and all this lasts just a few seconds, during which time Mitrano quickly grabs his pistol from a holster hanging on the locker handle, loads, and fires one, two, three, four, five times into the sleeping bag.

"AAAAAIIIIIIIEEEEEEE!"

He can feel the snake on him, feels it slithering over his shoulder, onto his face, feels bitten all over—the poison, my God, the poison.

"IT BIT ME! THE BASTARD BIT ME!"

His platoon mates shout at him to stop, but Mitrano isn't even aware of them. He fires more shots into the bag, causing an explosion of white feathers. The blasts make the guys' eardrums pop painfully.

René has to stop him—he's almost beside him, but Mitrano's reflexes are accelerated by adrenaline. He turns ninety degrees and aims the gun at him. The marshal halts. The soldiers fall silent.

"Calm down," René says.

Mitrano can't see his own face. He'd be frightened to see how pale he is. He'd be sure the snake had really bitten him. The blood has drained from his face, it's all rushed down to his hands, purple as they grip the Beretta. It's aimed directly at the center of the marshal's chest. You can say a lot of things about Corporal Mitrano, but not that he can't shoot. Especially at a target four or five feet away.

"Lower your weapon," René orders, but in a conciliatory tone, more like a big brother than a superior officer.

"There's a snake!" Mitrano sobs. "A snake . . . it bit me, shit!"

"All right. We'll take a look now."

"It bit me. It bit me!" Tears well up in his eyes.

"Put the gun down. Listen to me."

Instead of obeying, the corporal switches his target and points the

Beretta at Simoncelli, who freezes with one knee still bent on the cot and the other foot on the ground. Then he points it back to René.

Cederna's voice comes from a few yards away, from the shadowy back of the tent: "It's the dead snake, Mitrano."

The corporal hesitates for a second or two, confused. He takes in the news, digests it slowly. It's obvious: the snake that disappeared from the Wreck. He glances quickly at the sleeping bag to his left, as if not fully convinced. The feathers have landed on the green cover and flutter at the faintest wafts of air. Nothing is moving inside the lining.

"Was it you guys?"

René shakes his head. The others follow him.

"Was it you? *Huh?*"

"It was me, Mitrano. Now put the gun down." Cederna has stood up and moved cautiously toward his colleague, and he's now almost alongside the marshal.

"You," Mitrano says, tears still flowing profusely. "It's always you. I'll kill you, Cederna—*I'll kill you!*"

If he were to press his finger on the trigger, the top of Francesco Cederna's skull would be pierced from side to side and the bullet, once out of the tunnel, would end up embedded in Enrico Di Salvo's backpack hanging in the rear of the tent. Every man present is able to gauge the trajectory.

Mitrano is breathing through his mouth, panting. Suddenly he's overcome by a wave of exhaustion, an enormous fatigue, which subdues him and makes him sag for a moment. He lowers the pistol, and it's all René and Simoncelli need to jump him, knock him to the ground, and disarm him. Truthfully—regardless of what will later be put forth about the episode—Mitrano puts up no resistance. He simply lies there on the floor. His hand is limp and powerless when René takes the Beretta from him.

Simoncelli's butt is on his face again. Funny, isn't it? he thinks. Some dish it out and others take it; that's how it works. That's how it's always worked. As the men crowd around him, the corporal closes his eyes. He lets himself be swept away.

The gun blasts woke the sleeping soldiers and put those still awake on the alert, all throughout the base. The more zealous ones got fully dressed, then, armed from head to foot, foolishly awaited orders on what to do. The lookouts communicate via radio and can't seem to agree about the origin of the shots; they vaguely pinpoint it in the north sector of the FOB. Since no one calls for help, they soon put their minds at ease: the bursts must surely have been accidental. It happens, it can happen, that a guy may fire a shot by mistake when he's clutching his weapon in his arms at any hour of the day or night.

"What was that?" Irene asks.

"Ssshh."

The two remain silent, listening, barely loosening their grip on each other's bodies. Egitto waits for the siren to sound.

"It was nothing," he says finally. "Don't worry about it."

Thankful, she lets her hair spill over his face, then all at once tumbles down on him.

Swarms of White Flakes

It was January and it was snowing the day I lied to Marianna about her dress. I had asked my sister to sit in the backseat, but she wouldn't hear of it. As we stood arguing beside the door, tiny flakes settled on her fluffy new hairdo.

"The seat belt will crumple it," I said.

"I'm not sitting in the back like a child. That seat brings to mind bad memories. *Remember* when your father explained to us what would happen to our craniums if there was a head-on collision? Things like *that*."

Along the way she kept the seat belt loose, away from her chest so as not to crush the neckline. She rubbed her lips together and I knew she would have bitten them frantically, but she didn't want to ruin the lip gloss applied by the makeup woman shortly before. If I had offered her my bare arm at that moment, it's likely she would have sunk her teeth into it.

"A bride is supposed to feel *happy* if it snows on her wedding day."

"Why, aren't you happy?" I asked, though I immediately regretted it. Addressing Marianna's discontent was exactly what I didn't feel like doing.

She didn't notice the treacherously broad nature of the question. Looking irritatedly at the whitened tree branches, she said: "To me it's just one *more* nuisance to put up with. All those *wet* shoes. And the *mud*."

The question I'd carelessly uttered aloud, however, was enough to sink me into a bitterness that I'd felt hovering over us for some months, a growing dismay that began after the silent earthquake that had split our family in two and left me in the middle, like a chewed-up apple core. In an hour from now, Marianna would be joined in matrimony to a nice young man. She was marrying him out of gratitude, but mostly to spite our parents. She was marrying him at just twenty-five years of age and dropping everything else. She was marrying him deliberately, and that was that, and I would be the one to take her arm and walk her down the center aisle of the church, stiff and ridiculous in a role that wasn't mine, to give her away.

She flipped down the sun visor and studied her face in the small rectangular mirror. "I didn't get a *wink* of sleep last night. Naturally I was nervous, right? *All* women are, the night before. But *I* wasn't just nervous, I had *terrible* stomach cramps and they had nothing whatsoever to do with tension—they were just cramps. I took two Buscopan tablets, but they had no effect. *Of course*, if your parents hadn't stuffed us full of medicines when we were little, they might still be effective . . . Anyway, at three in the morning I couldn't find anything better to do than try on the dress again, *again*. There I was in the kitchen, in the middle of the night, dressed as a bride, like a *mad*woman. And I had those damned rollers in my hair—I don't even know why I put them in since I *hate* this stupid baby-doll hairdo. It's the same way Nini used to do my hair. Anyway, I saw my reflection in the window and I realized that this dress is horrible, it's all *wrong*."

She lifted the tulle skirt and let it plop on her thighs, like an old tattered rag. She was so disgusted with it, so unsure about the step she was about to take, that if I had said, "You're right, the dress is abominable and we're pathetic, but listen, listen to me, this whole story is abominable, it's a mistake, and the dress is only an indication of it; you don't want to marry him, you never even intended to get married, so let's turn around and go back now, everything will work out, I promise it will work out," if I had voiced the truth that loomed so shamefully clear in my head, she would have stared at me gravely for a few seconds, then burst out in that rich laugh of hers and replied, "Okay, let's get out of here, let's do what you say."

But the situation didn't seem suited to sincerity, so I said, "The dress isn't wrong at all. It looks great on you."

The white blanket on the pavement was a few inches thick and the wheels spun and froze at any abrupt movements of the steering wheel. The cars inched along slowly, cautiously. I, too, drove slowly, sticking to the tracks made by others. Feigning concentration on the driving allowed me to overlook the silence that had fallen in the car, as if it were something normal. I was aware that Marianna looked at me for several minutes, waiting for me to turn to her as well and recognize the apprehension in her eyes, finally out in the open. I knew that look, I had returned it hundreds of times, and I knew it was there waiting for me.

But I kept my eyes focused on the road, and today, whenever I think of my sister's abrupt desertion, I see swarms of white flakes that fly at us in the dark and I can still feel the enormity of her need, ignored, as she sat beside me.

When I pulled up in front of the church, a group of guests hurried inside. Only then did I look at Marianna, but she no longer expected anything from me. She was remote, absent, in the same state of passive detachment with which she endured our father's digressions.

I turned off the engine. Now I had to embrace her one last time as an unmarried woman. When I hugged her, our bodies so much alike, her chest suddenly drained of energy and she began to tremble. I held her until she calmed down.

"No idiotic jokes at the reception, you have to swear to me," she said.

"You've told me a hundred times."

"I don't want anyone yelling 'Kiss! Kiss!' or 'Here's to the bride and groom' or any other stupid toasts. I *hate* that."

"I know."

"You have to swear to me."

"I swear."

"And I don't want to make any speeches, is that clear? *Nothing*—not even a thank you. It would be . . ."

Awkward, I concluded in silence. "There won't be any speeches."

"You swore," Marianna said.

Her breathing had become shallow; she seemed to have forgotten that she could breathe through her nose, too.

"Do you feel up to going in?" I suggested. I had to suppress a note of impatience. By now we'd come this far, everyone had seen us, and a man I didn't know was in the doorway of the church, gesturing for us to enter. I had driven in a blizzard, worn a shirt that was choking me at the neck, swallowed heaps of bitterness and discomfort and spinelessness to be there that day to feign excitement for my sister's wedding: when would we decide to get out of the car and get it over with?

Marianna sighed and leaned over again to examine the intensity of the snowfall, as if that were the thing holding her back. The flakes that had accumulated on the windows since we'd stopped almost prevented us from seeing out; we were locked inside an icebox.

"Do you think they'll come?" she asked in a low voice.

"No. I don't think so. You were very clear."

"Maybe to the reception."

"They won't be there either."

She put a thumb to her mouth. She rubbed her lips innocently, absorbed in thought.

"Want me to call them?" I didn't feel like it at that point, but I asked her just the same. "I think they'd be happy to come."

Marianna's eyes widened. "I wouldn't *dream* of it. They won't take this special day away too."

Was it special? Yes, in some strange way it actually was. Marianna puffed out her cheeks like a little girl. "Nothing ever happens the way you thought it would, does it?"

"Almost never, I guess."

She checked her makeup one last time in the mirror and brushed a clump of mascara off her eyelashes. Then she threw her head back and breathed out. "What do we care? You're here to walk me down the aisle and it's much better this way. Come on, soldier, let's go get married."

She opened the door, not waiting for me to do it for her.

Death Round

_____

The Military is around, above, below, and within you. If you try to escape it, you're still part of it. If you try to deceive it, it's the one deceiving you.

The Military is faceless. No face represents the Military. Not the Chief of Staff, not the Minister, neither the generals nor their subordinates. Not you.

The Military existed before you and will continue to exist when you are no longer here, forever.

What you're seeking is already there; you just have to train your eyes to recognize it.

The Military has no feelings, but it's more friendly than hostile. If you love the Military, it will love you, in ways you don't know or can't understand.

Don't disgrace the Military, don't offend it, and above all never, ever betray it.

By loving the Military you will love yourself.

It's your duty to safeguard your life, in each and every instance and at all costs, because your life does not belong to you; it belongs to the Military.

The Military does not distinguish between body and soul; it provides for and commands both.

It's always the Military that chooses you, not you who chooses it.

The Military prefers silence to talk, a set jaw to a smile.

The glory you're after is the means the Military employs to fulfill its aims. Don't renounce glory, since it is the doorway through which the Military enters you.

You don't know the Military's aims. If you try to guess them, you'll go crazy.

The true reward of every action resides in the action itself.

Those who believe in the Military are in no danger of failing, either by suffering or by dying, because suffering and death are the ways by which it makes use of you.

So answer me: Do you believe in the Military? Do you believe in it? Then say it now. Say it!

A sputtering white clunker comes to a stop a few yards from the Afghan truckers' camp. The driver, who has the nerve to show his face uncovered, throws his personal gift to the men sitting in a circle and takes off again, hurtling back in the direction from which he came.

Before anyone gets up the courage to go get it, the truckers take time to observe the severed head of their comrade: the foolhardy soul who left two nights ago to try to reach the Ring Road. The sand-encrusted head returns their look from eyes immobilized by the last horror that it experienced. Judging by the ragged nature of the fibers sticking out of the neck, the head must have been sawed off with a small blade, probably a pocketknife. The warning is all too clear and the postman hadn't felt the need to add anything, except a scornful sneer promising the same treatment to anyone who might dare try to get away: the only fate fit for those who collaborate with the military invaders.

A few hours later the truck drivers march to the FOB in close formation, holding their friend's head high, like a white flag or a macabre safe conduct pass. Earlier, no one would have said that there were so many of them, at least thirty.

Passalacqua and Simoncelli are on guard duty at the main tower and obviously don't know what they should do. If the men marching toward them are wearing explosive charges, they're already close enough to cause quite a bit of carnage.

"I'll shoot," Simoncelli suggests.

"Shoot in the air, though."

The shot, fired into space, only rouses the Afghans further. By now they've entered the zigzagging access corridor in front of the entrance. They call out something in their language.

"What should I do? Shoot again?"

"Yeah, come on!"

Another burst, not actually in the air, just a hair away from the turbans. The dirt kicks up in about a dozen spots behind them.

"These guys aren't stopping," Simoncelli says. "I'll hurl a grenade."

"Are you nuts? You'll take them all out."

"I'll throw it a distance away."

"And if you miss?"

"You throw it, then."

"The hell I will."

As they argue, the group reaches the base of the tower. At that point, as if they had agreed beforehand, the truckers stop and politely wait for someone to come and welcome them.

"Shit," Ballesio mutters ten minutes later, when they wave the decapitated head under his nose. Then he looks at the Afghans with a curious expression of reproach, as if they were the ones who'd come up with the stunt.

The colonel, Captain Masiero, and Irene Sammartino withdraw to the command center for the rest of the morning. They don't even show up in the mess hall for lunch—three soldiers carrying trays parade by in front of Egitto. Room service, he thinks. He's offended at not being invited to the meeting and can't really make up his mind for certain whether his resentment is directed more at Irene or at Ballesio.

At two o'clock he's summoned along with the other officers and platoon commanders. The colonel has a grim look; he's sitting at the center of the long conference table, but as if he weren't involved. He avoids looking at Egitto and lets Masiero speak for him. As usual, the captain explains everything quickly, without deviating from the point or displaying a shred of emotion. The "higher circles"—the captain calls them that, with obvious contempt—believe that the truck drivers' impasse has become critical. Not only is it unacceptable that the Afghans be exposed to barbarisms such as the recent beheading of their fellow driver, but their discontent is likely to damage the company's mission's image and, among other things, constitutes a potential threat. In short, they must be escorted back to where they came from.

The captain unrolls a map where he's marked out a route in felt-tipped pen, along with several notations in his unnerving microscopic handwriting. The plan is as simple as can be: the soldiers will advance in a column along with the truck drivers, cross the valley, and reach the Ring Road just above Delaram, where they will leave the truckers on their own; they will then reverse their course and come back. The distance to be covered is about thirty miles and the estimated time is four days total, two going and two for the return. In all probability there will be IEDs waiting for them along the way and maybe some shooting, but they can count on the enemy's disorganization. The departure is scheduled for tomorrow morning before dawn. Questions?

Lieutenant Egitto has been fidgeting with the side seam of his pants as the captain speaks. He's the only one in the room who's crossed the valley: a few months earlier, in the other direction. It seems like a lifetime has passed since then. They'd found four explosive devices and endured two completely sleepless nights; on arrival his fellow battalion members were ready to drop and some were of no use for days. His earlier resentment suddenly turns into a troubled premonition. He raises his hand.

"Yes, Lieutenant."

Ballesio glares at him, as if to say he shouldn't be speaking to *him*. Egitto ignores him. "I traveled through the valley once. It's not a safe place. We should find another solution."

Masiero smoothes the sides of his goatee as his lips widen in a scornful smile. "I don't know about you, Lieutenant. But when I joined up, I had an idea that this wasn't a *safe* job."

There are some uncertain, nervous laughs, which quickly fade.

Egitto insists: "We could transport the truck drivers back to Herat with helicopters."

"Thirty truckers? Do you have any idea what that would cost us? And without their trucks. It doesn't seem like a good deal for our Afghan friends."

Ballesio squirms in his chair, as though having a colic attack.

"The valley is dangerous, Captain," Egitto says.

The quick glance between Masiero and Irene—who is sitting apart, with her back against the wall—doesn't escape him.

"Lieutenant, with all due respect, you are not being asked to concern yourself with strategies. See to the soldiers' well-being instead. Many of them seem a little run-down lately. Does anyone else have any objections? If not, preparations await us." Masiero joins his hands together like a teacher in front of his pupils. "Oh, yes, I forgot. The operation is called Mama Bear. Remember that. MB, for short. I hope you like the name—I thought it up."

Those in attendance scatter; Egitto follows the commander to his tent. Ballesio turns his back. When Egitto takes a step inside, he says: "What do you want from me, Lieutenant? I'm extremely busy."

"You have to abort the operation, Colonel."

"Have to? I *have* to? Who the hell are you to tell me what I have to do?"

Egitto is not put off. "It's a rash and risky undertaking. It won't be like the first time; the enemy is waiting for us now."

Ballesio waves his arms, exasperated. "What do you know about it?"

"The head is clearly an invitation. And besides . . ." He hesitates. "I have a sixth sense."

"I don't give a shit about your sixth sense, Lieutenant. Wars aren't fought with a sixth sense. The first five are more than enough."

Egitto takes a deep breath. He's not cut out for insubordination. He's always had a tendency to be contentious, true, a critical spirit as keen as his father's, but his intelligence is more a defensive weapon rather than an offensive one. Not this time, though; this time he's determined to assert himself. He feels light-headed, his pressure must have dropped. "I'm forced to demand that you reconsider your position, Commander."

"That's enough!" Ballesio thunders. Then, exhausted, he collapses into the chair, his arms limp. He knows endless ways to show he's worn-out. He shakes his head. "Do you seriously think that *I'm* the one who wants to go? Don't I seem to you like someone who's already had enough, Lieutenant? As far as I'm concerned, those truckers can drop dead out there under their lousy Afghan sun; pack it in along with this entire war. I'm fed up with this war, these operations, all this crap."

Warily, the lieutenant sits down as well. Now he has to adjust his tone to the unexpected shift in the conversation. "I don't understand, Colonel."

"You don't understand? You don't *understand*? Ask your little girl-friend to explain it to you."

"You mean Irene Sammartino?"

"That's right, your little kiss-ass."

Mentally Egitto revises the picture he'd formed about the morning's meeting: while earlier he'd placed Ballesio on one side, with the captain and Irene opposite him, he now puts her in the position of power. The clever girl with whom he'd had a relationship in a previous life and now shares . . . *something* with, that woman gives orders to two submissive officers. "Was it Sammartino's idea?" he asks, a little afraid of the answer.

"That woman has no *ideas*, Lieutenant. She's just a go-between, a conduit for those who rank above poor unfortunates like you and me."

Egitto can't believe that Irene would want to impose such a death sentence on all of them. He's likely to sound even more disrespectful, but he says it anyway: "I don't think Sammartino would do such a thing."

All of a sudden Ballesio places his forearms on the table and leans forward, furious. "Is it your *testicular* sixth sense again telling you that, Lieutenant? Give me a break—it's a mistake a raw recruit would make."

Egitto has no idea whether Ballesio's remarks are just guesses or whether they're certainties—he's not sure what the colonel may or may not know or who may have reported it to him. The way things stand, Irene herself could have been the one to leak it to him. Is there anyone he can trust? The insinuation, founded or not, disorients him; he feels as if he's been exposed. His nerve fails him.

The commander points a finger at him. "Listen to me. Go to confession while there's still time—you never know. You're dismissed."

The officers gather again, the various companies and individual platoons meet, and in the end everyone has a more or less confused idea of what they're supposed to do to start preparing. Morale is high, especially among those who are about to leave: although they're aware of the danger of venturing outside the security bubble in a column, it's also a chance to shake off the cobwebs after a month spent vegetating at the FOB. Besides, who'd want to be a soldier without the opportunity to do some shooting?

Cederna, who in theory at least is an enthusiast of gunfights, is the only one who doesn't share the general optimism. The phone call he has to make scares him to death. He's already put it off for hours and now twice in a row he's let two guys who were behind him go ahead.

He's bitten his knuckles to the bone and when he sucks them for the umpteenth time he can taste blood. Agnese won't take it well. His fear of her reaction only makes him more nervous. Why would he, who isn't afraid of anything, be afraid of a woman? Anger generates more fear, in a vicious circle that's driving him crazy. One thing he's sure of, though: he won't tell her anything that vaguely resembles the truth—there's no reason to. He won't tell her that his leave was canceled by that fat slob Colonel Ballesio himself because he played one prank too many and that imbecile Mitrano started shooting up his sleeping bag in the middle of the night. He won't tell her that there's a very high probability that his leave won't be granted even further on and that he's likely to be the only one in the regiment to spend six consecutive months out here. And he won't say he's sorry, never ever.

He grabs the receiver. It's still slick with the sweat of the guys who used the phone before him. Agnese answers, her voice guarded.

"It's me," Cederna says.

"You?"

"Yeah, me."

"I've missed you, soldier."

"They won't let me leave."

Why is Agnese silent for so long now? Say something, speak! "I'm sorry," Cederna adds, immediately failing to stick to his main intention.

She remains mute.

"Hey, did you hear me?"

Not a word.

"It's no use giving me the silent treatment. There's an operation that begins tomorrow. I can't tell you the details, but it's serious stuff. They need all the men and I can't get away."

"Don't you dare try that." Agnese's tone is sharp but calm, different than he expected. He was prepared to listen to her cry on the phone, to hear her rage and fume, but not this. "Don't even try to make me feel sorry for you with your operations and danger and all the rest."

"I told you. Think what you want."

"Right. I'll think what I want."

Did she hang up? Is she still there? These long silences are a dirty trick.

"Agnese . . ."

"I have nothing more to say to you."

"I'll come after you graduate, okay? We'll take a trip like I promised. The weather will be even better."

"We're not taking any trip, Francesco. We're not doing anything. Now excuse me, but I have to go."

"What the fuck does that mean?"

Agnese feigns a giggle that makes the senior corporal major shiver. "You know what? This is a wonderful graduation gift, Francesco, the best you could have given me. My girlfriends have just planned a vacation. Women only. I said I wouldn't go, because you'd be here, but I really *want* to go. I want to with all my heart and soul."

Cederna imagines that the plastic receiver is dangerously close to shattering. He loosens his grip. "You're not going on vacation with those slutty girlfriends of yours. I'll break your face if you try it!"

Agnese bursts into a loud, raucous laugh. "You really are a savage, Francesco Cederna."

It's only on a subconscious level that the soldier forms an association with a similar phrase she told him long ago in a very different context. It was one of the first times they went out together, one of the first times they ended up in bed together, and Agnese had said, "You really are a show-off, Francesco Cederna," but that time she'd gone on and added, "A show-off and also a nice guy—I swear to God no one has ever made me feel that way." He'd been, well, flattered for sure, and also surprised. Now that those earlier words echo in a peripheral part of the brain—who knows if she's aware of the connection—now that things are so much different and she has nothing more to add, Cederna feels a sense of bitterness and defeat and is unable to answer back.

It's Agnese who ends the call instead of him. "So long. Good luck with your operation."

The Third Platoon, Charlie Company, is assigned to bring up the rear, a delicate position but still better than being in the lead. Then, too, they're with the medic, which helps psychologically. On no account must the vehicles leave the track made by those who precede them, or shorten or lengthen the preestablished safety distance of fifteen yards, or take any initiative of any kind or even just dare to propose one, and blah blah blah.

Marshal René has repeated the litany a second time, identical to the first, pausing often to make sure everyone has understood. Twenty-seven voices answered, "Yes, sir," drawing the words out more each time. After which he sent the guys to take care of their final tasks. Ietri and Cederna are to disassemble, clean, lubricate, and reassemble the light artillery.

Ietri realizes that it's better to leave his friend alone; since they canceled his leave he's been irritable, he won't speak to anyone, and if you run into him with that surly look, his mouth twisted into a snarl, you get the feeling he might plant a knife in your belly just because you got in his way. He'd like to console him, but he knows that theirs is not that kind of friendship: it's more like the relationship between a teacher and his pupil, and a pupil doesn't dare ask his teacher what's wrong. He'd told him the prank was risky. At least Cederna had remained loyal and covered the fact of his complicity with their superiors. One day, when he's calmer, he'll thank him.

The two work in silence. They peer into the gun barrel with one eye shut and blow away the dust or use the compressed air pump. For the more delicate mechanisms, the sights and magazines, they switch to using a brush with soft black bristles.

Ietri hasn't yet decided how he feels about tomorrow's operation. In the locker room they said the road would be mined with explosive devices and, in fact, in the last few hours the bomb techs from the engineer corps have been going around the FOB with long faces. He'd like to ask Cederna what he thinks. It might do him good. Maybe he feels like exchanging a few words too now, to vent a little. He bites his tongue not to disturb him, but eventually he gives in. "Hey, Cederna," he says.

"Shut your trap, *verginella*."

Protect my family. Protect my mother, she especially. Protect my platoon mates, because they're good guys. Sometimes they say stupid, vulgar things, but they're decent, every one of them. Protect them from suffering. And protect me too. Protect me from Kalashnikovs, from mortars, from improvised explosive devices, from shrapnel and grenades. If I really must die, though, better a bomb, a large charge; make me blow up from a bomb without feeling any pain. Please, don't leave me wounded, without a leg or a hand. And don't let me get burned, at least not on the face. Dead, yes, but not disfigured for life. Please, I beg you.

The soldiers know how to throw a party together in record time and the circumstances demand a fitting one. During the afternoon, the FOB witnesses a fine example of cooperation among the various companies. The guys of the Third provide the Wreck and some provisions—chocolate bars, twenty-five-milliliter bottles of grappa saved up from K rations, potato chips—and the other units contribute whatever they can: the bomb techs supply two rather powerful speakers, the cooks work overtime to make some dry but tasty cakes and two pans of something that looks like pizza, others take charge of the decorations.

Headquarters, in turn, throws in plastic cups and plates, at the explicit bidding of Colonel Ballesio.

By eight o'clock the room is already full. There's not much time; muster is set for four in the morning and no one is sure when the next time he'll be able to get some sleep will be. The laughter is a bit louder than necessary, the remarks more spirited. It's clear the increased noise is essential to cover another type of din, an inner clamor common to each of them, which grows as the minutes pass. Ietri had pestered several guys to secure the role of deejay and now he's at his place behind the console. A party isn't a party without the right music and he wants Zampieri to see him at something he does well. No one tried to stop him in any case, because they all wanted to enjoy the evening, period.

Before supper he jotted down a list of bands: Nickelback, Linkin Park, Evanescence, maybe something old by the Offspring, then some serious stomping with his favorites, Slipknot, Neurosis, Dark Tranquillity. He hopes the guys feel like letting loose. On paper it had seemed like a workable playlist, but now that the party has started, he realizes that time is flying faster than he expected and he has to skip some selections to get to the meat of it sooner. Besides, no one is dancing yet, the mood is stiff. Ietri can't really say why; usually when the Spanish voice of "Pretty Fly" starts up at Tuxedo Club, he can't resist jumping into the fray. Someone, not too kindly, suggested he change the type of music, but he ignored him.

"Hey, knock it off with that noise!" Simoncelli yells from across the room.

Ietri pretends he hasn't heard him. Out of the corner of his eye he's spotted Zampieri approaching. He ducks his head to show he's busy, when actually all he has to do is select this or that number. "Pretty Fly" is coming to an end and he doesn't know what to choose next. The program he scrawled on the scrap of paper calls for Motörhead, but it doesn't seem like the right group to greet Zampieri with. He's confused, flustered. She comes up to him and he starts the first song he finds at random: "My Plague."

Zampieri sits on the table in front of him. Ietri feels tingly all over his body, as though stung by a million pinpricks. When did she start having that effect on him?

"Don't you have anything easier on the ear?"

"Why? Don't you like Slipknot?"

Zampieri makes a strange face. "I don't even know who they are."

Ietri bows his head. He again runs through the list of titles, scanning up and down. Suddenly it seems there's nothing appropriate, nothing interesting enough to make an impression on her. "Suicide, do you know them?" he asks hopefully.

"No."

"The Nevermore?"

Zampieri shakes her head.

"I'll play them for you. The Never are dynamite."

She sighs. "Don't you have Shakira?"

Ietri straightens up, indignant. "Shakira? That's not music."

"But everybody likes it."

"She only does commercial hits."

Zampieri looks around, dejected. "Well, at least people would dance. You see? No one's moving. Soon we'll be plugging up our ears."

"If you don't like it, someone else could have been the deejay. This is my music." He's angry and humiliated. If Zampieri really likes Shakira, then he's not sure how they could get along.

"Come on, don't get so upset!" she says. "You're like a little kid, taking offense so easily over music." She waves her hand scornfully. "Play whatever you want—I really don't care." Then she walks away.

Ietri stands there dumbfounded, the iPod stupidly in his hand. It takes him several seconds to rouse himself. "My Plague" ends and he doesn't have the presence of mind to put something else on. Only the guys' loud talk can now be heard in the Wreck. Zampieri has already gone back to the others, rejoined the group with Cederna, Pecone, and Vercellin and is laughing like a loon, as if she really didn't care anything about the music, or him.

"About time!" Mattioli yells out, hands cupped to his mouth like a megaphone. The others respond with applause.

What an idiot he was. He wanted to stand out and be noticed and instead he's made a fool of himself, as always. He's overcome by shame now; he'd like to disappear. Let them find their own music. Hell, they don't know a thing about it. Ietri looks at his colleagues and all of a sudden he hates them like he once hated the guys back home in Torremaggiore. They didn't understand shit about music either—all they listened to were groups chosen by the radio, wimpy Italian singers.

He crushes the plastic cup, tosses it angrily into a corner, and leaves the Wreck. The nights are getting colder and colder and he's not wearing anything over his cotton T-shirt. Who the hell cares? He walks to the phones with his hands in his pockets; there's still time to call his mother. And to think he almost didn't do it, he was so busy with that pathetic party. He passes other soldiers going in the opposite direction. Go on, go—you won't have a good time.

He finds René near the phones. The marshal is pacing back and forth, smoking. "What are you doing walking around without a flashlight?" he scolds him.

Ietri shrugs. "I can find my way around by now," he says. "You didn't stay at the party?"

"Too much confusion," the marshal replies. He looks dejected and very tense. Maybe it means that the operation won't be a cakewalk.

But at this moment Ietri has no room for fear; he's not interested, too frustrated to feel anything else. "Do you have to use the phone?" he asks.

"Me? No." René runs a hand over his razed skull. "No, I don't. See you tomorrow. Try to get some rest."

He walks away at a brisk pace; the corporal is left alone. At night, the silence at the FOB is different from others Ietri has known. It's a silence devoid of engines, of human voices, but also a silence from which nature too is absent: no birds chirping, no crickets, no streams burbling nearby, no nothing. Just silence.

His mother's voice stirs feelings in his stomach and the result is an acute spasm that makes his throat clench. "Has your intestinal problem gone away?"

"Mama, that was days ago. I'm fine."

"But you sound sad."

It's no use; she always exposes him. She has receptors that are sensitive to every crack in his voice. "I'm just tired," Ietri says.

"I miss you so much."

"Mmm-hmm."

"Don't you miss me?"

"I'm not eight years old anymore, for God's sake."

"I know, I know. Don't say that. You were such a marvel when you were eight."

And now? Now what is he? He remembers that his mother couldn't stand his music either and for a moment he's angry with her. She'd said, "It's just noise, you'll damage your ears." Once he'd called her an old fool because she said something bad about Megadeth. Only that one time, though, because the slap she gave him for it made his head spin.

"Mama, I won't be able to call you for a few days."

"Why?" She's immediately alarmed. "For how many days?"

"Four or five. At least. They have to repair the phone lines."

"But they're working. Why not leave them alone?"

"Because they can't."

"They shouldn't touch them if they're working."

"You don't know anything about these things."

His mother sighs. "It's true. I don't. But I'll be worried."

"There's no reason to be. Nothing is happening here."

"A mother who's far away is always worried."

Ietri refrains from telling her that this time, just this once, she'd have every right to be. Earlier, no, the dozens of nights when she'd stayed up waiting for him with her heart in her mouth, when she'd lost sleep for nothing. He's always been more sensible, more cautious and obedient than she imagined. He's sure she'd be disappointed to find out. Her son is nothing special; he's just like a lot of guys. "I have to go now, Mama."

"No! Not yet. Afterward you won't call me for all those days. Talk to me some more, tell me something."

Tell her what? Anything he can tell her would pain her. That the food is more disgusting than he's let her believe. That he's fallen for a woman, a soldier like him, but she calls him a kid. That tomorrow they're leaving on a mission through an area controlled by the Taliban and he's shitting himself. That this morning he saw a decapitated head and felt so sick to his stomach that he vomited his breakfast all over his boots, and that now he sees that face before him every time he closes his eyes. That at times he feels empty and sad, and old, yes, old at twenty, and he doesn't for a moment believe that he was a marvel at one time. That all the guys continue to treat him as if he were the new kid on the block and that he hasn't found anything like what he was hoping for and now he no longer even knows what he was looking for. That he loves her and misses her very much, she's what matters most to him, the only thing. He can't tell her that either, because he's an adult now, and he's a soldier.

"I really have to go, Mama."

Torsu lied to the doctor, but the lie was for a good reason. He didn't want to be the only one in the platoon to stay behind at the base, safe and sound, while the others faced the trip through the valley. They would have treated him like a slacker when they got back and he can't imagine anything more shameful. So he said he felt better, in good shape in fact, swore that for three days his stool had shown an acceptable consistency (whereas, in reality, his last bout of diarrhea had been just that morning) and signed some kind of release form. When the doc approached with the thermometer to take his temperature, Torsu said he preferred to do it himself and then read off 96.8 instead of 99.5. What's a few degrees' difference? He carried it off—the doc was distracted today and wanted the visit to be over quickly.

"So I can go?"

"If you feel up to it, I have no problem with it."

"Do you think we'll have any trouble out there?"

The doc stared at some unspecified point. You couldn't say they'd become friends, but Torsu has been in the infirmary every day (you can bet he sniffed out the dubious relationship between the lieutenant and that woman from Intelligence!) so it's as though they know each other a little by now. Egitto didn't answer; he handed him two boxes of Tylenol and sent him off.

Since he's no longer officially sick, Torsu has also let go of certain useless anxieties, like the concern about his leg, which in retrospect now seems like little more than a delirious fantasy. Still, just to be sure, he borrowed a ruler from the guys in logistics and measured his lower limbs, from heel to hip: the majority of attempts revealed a difference of less than a quarter of an inch, not so worrying after all.

What continues to bother him, however, is the silence Tersicore89 is using to punish him after the argument they had. She hasn't responded to any of his messages, not even when he wrote her that he was getting ready to go on a several-day mission in the desert, exaggerating the associated risks somewhat. He's beginning to lose hope. He's so dejected that he hasn't even set foot in the Wreck to see how the party is going. After Cederna evicted him from the tent, he came and sat outside on the ground, with his computer resting on his crossed legs. Tersicore89's profile says she's offline, but he doesn't trust that. He's almost certain she's reading his appeals. This is one of the specific times when they always chatted—or when they always *used to* chat.

THOR_SARDEGNA: can't we talk about it?

TERSICORE89:

THOR_SARDEGNA: i already wrote and said i'm sorry. many times. what more do i have to do? i was sick, it's normal to say the wrong things when you're sick, it happens to everyone

TERSICORE89:

THOR_SARDEGNA: please write something. even an insult. let me know you're there

TERSICORE89:

THOR_SARDEGNA: i'm afraid of what's going to happen tomorrow. i want to talk to you

TERSICORE89:

THOR_SARDEGNA: you're so selfish!

The monologue takes up two screens, a seesaw of apologies, pleas, and raging tirades. Torsu has about run out of imagination and hasn't added anything in the last ten minutes; he rests his chin on his fists and strikes the keyboard angrily every time the monitor goes dark.

The usual nighttime fever is burning up his forehead and muddling his thoughts—by now he no longer notices.

A soldier suddenly emerges from the darkness, startling him. "Who's there?"

"Ietri."

"Why are you wandering around like that in the dark, you idiot?"

Ietri is chilled; he rubs his bare arms with his hands. "I was taking a little walk."

"Without a flashlight? That's really dumb."

His comrade shrugs. "I'm going to sleep," he says. "The party was awful."

"You can't go in the tent."

"Why not?"

"Cederna told me not to let anyone in," Torsu says. "He's in there with Zampa."

"With Zampa? Doing what?"

Torsu raises his eyes from the screen and looks at his buddy's dark silhouette. "What do you think?"

Ietri doesn't move.

"What's with you?" Torsu asks.

"Nothing."

Then, after a while, he disappears again into the night. What an idiot! Torsu goes back to staring at the deserted monitor.

THOR_SARDEGNA: i'll wait all night if i have to

TERSICORE89:

THOR_SARDEGNA: i'm not moving from here until you answer me

TERSICORE89:

The progress bar on the computer screen runs to the end, leaving everything sadly as it was.

"No," the soldier murmurs. No one can hear him, but he repeats it: "No no no no . . . no. Please, I beg you, no."

First Corporal Major Angelo Torsu doesn't manage to stay up all night as promised, but he does hold out another half hour, enough time for Cederna and Zampieri to finish their business in the tent and about the time it takes Ietri to get lost in the FOB, in danger of nearly tripping and breaking his neck more than once. He tried to cry a little, but he couldn't even do that. He's not even capable of expressing his despair as he should. And now he's lost his sense of direction and is afraid he won't be able to find his way back to Charlie's sector; he seems to be in an area he's never been before. He lets himself be guided along by light filtering out of a tent. Approaching it, he moves the flap aside and sticks his head in.

"Ietri, my brother. Come in. Come in." Di Salvo is sprawled on a pile of colorful pillows, shirtless and barefoot. The incandescent grille of an electric heater is radiating hot air directly onto his face; he's especially purple on one side. The tent is saturated with dense smoke, hanging suspended in stagnant layers.

"Abib, this is Roberto," Di Salvo says in English. "My friend. My dear friend."

He talks like he's stoned out of his mind. Abib welcomes Ietri with a nod, then closes his eyes again. The other two interpreters don't even move.

Ietri walks forward timidly. He avoids the items scattered on the ground, sits next to Di Salvo. He automatically accepts the joint his buddy offers him, brings it to his lips.

"A nice deep breath. Good. Hold it as long as you can. You'll see how it relaxes you. Can you feel it already? This stuff is special."

The corporal inhales a second time, then again. At first nothing happens to him, except a fit of coughing. Not even the drug wants anything to do with someone like him, a *little kid*. Then an overpowering drowsiness hits him. He resists it. He wants to fill his lungs with smoke until there's no room for more. He takes a long, burning mouthful.

"Yesss," Di Salvo hisses, close to his ear.

The statue he talked about is resting on a three-legged table, along with some gutted cigarettes, tobacco remnants, and a stick of burning incense that does nothing to improve the odor. Ietri looks at the statue. It's just a piece of roughly carved wood, the hair made of dry straw. He inhales again and holds the smoke in his lungs as long as possible. In high school they competed to see who could hold it the longest; they called it the Death Round. You weren't supposed to exhale before the joint was back in your hand. Sometimes when there were ten or twelve of them, someone would deliberately slow things up and faces turned red, purple, blue. Ietri spits out air, coughs. In a flash he sees Cederna burying his face between Zampieri's legs; she spreads them for him, moans with pleasure. He inhales again, holds his breath. She's coming. Marijuana always makes his throat dry, it was like that even at school; it tastes disgusting. He used to drink gallons of iced tea to get the taste out of his mouth. Abib's statue stares at him with yellow eyes. It's just a piece of rotten wood; at the market in Torremaggiore the Moroccans sell a ton of crap like that. When his mother took him to the market, she let him buy whatever he wanted, anything, in exchange for his smiles. He'd figured it out and took advantage of it. What a marvel he was when he was eight. *"What a marvel!"* Cederna says and now he wants more, all of it. Shitty bastards, traitors. Ietri sticks his tongue out at Abib's statue, sticks his tongue out at death. Let him come for him; he doesn't give a damn. Di Salvo bursts into a gasping laugh, and he too sticks out his tongue.

"Owooooo . . . Grrrrrrrrrr! Owooooo . . ."

They're two animals and they make animal sounds. They taunt death; they split their sides laughing.

"Baaaaaaaa . . . Uh-uh uh-uh uh-uh . . . Aroooooo . . ."

Di Salvo told him that when you smoke this stuff, you feel things, everything. That was crap. All Ietri feels is increasingly depressed, increasingly sad. The tent closes in on him from all sides; the mountain outside looms over him, as does the night, all in concert—they want to squash him like a lizard. His pupils roll backward and his head sinks into the welcoming layer of cushions.

"Good boy, that's it. You see? It's special."

Part Two

THE VALLEY OF ROSES

At dawn the convoy slowly winds out, its head over a mile away from the tail. Loading operations in the square were quick, despite some last-minute snags and the somewhat obstinate Afghan truckers: all of a sudden they were uncooperative about dismantling the pitiable camp in which they'd spent the last few months. After all the hullabaloo they caused, it almost seemed like they didn't really want to abandon that pile of tents and filth. Colonel Ballesio gave a dithering speech full of hemming and hawing, which ended with his urging the soldiers to bring their hairy asses back in one piece. The men were still drowsy, but put on a bold front. They listened to the final instructions in rigorous silence, then broke ranks and set off. About fifty conveyances in all, counting both military vehicles and civilian trucks. Irene Sammartino watches them move off from the FOB.

The armored ambulance on which Egitto is traveling is recognizable by the red cross painted on the back door. Irene keeps an eye on it as long as she can as it proceeds toward the tremulous air at the horizon. She feels some longing and a strange dismay at the thought of not seeing the lieutenant again. In a couple of days she too will be leaving the outpost and there's no reason why they should meet again; circumstances have already been far too generous with them.

Last night she slipped out of her sleeping bag and went to Alessandro's cot, but before she could reach out to him, he stopped her in her tracks: "It was you, wasn't it?"

She stood stock-still in the center of the tent, in the no-man's-land between the two beds. "I don't know what you're talking about."

"You're sending people to die, Irene. I want you to realize that before it happens, because afterward there can be no excuses for you."

Coming from Alessandro, the recriminations were almost more painful than she could bear. She forced herself not to let it show. "I'm just doing my job. I'm just staff, like all the others. I've already explained it to you."

"Next you'll tell me the decision had nothing to do with you. That you only follow orders. But I know you well enough, Irene. You're a born manipulator."

"I've never manipulated anyone."

"Oh, no? Really? Odd, because I remember it differently."

"What do you remember?"

"What do I remember? *What*, Irene?"

"I did it to you, you mean?"

"When you showed up with that way of yours, months after we'd left each other—*months*—don't you remember that? You buzzed around me like a fly—you were obsessed. You popped up everywhere. Not to mention when you— Forget it. But this time it's much worse. You've outdone yourself."

Irene's feet in contact with the floor were icy; the chill rose to her ankles, her knees, and spread to the rest of her body. "I'm sorry you feel that way," she whispered. She tried to reach out toward Alessandro's head, to the spot where she imagined his head was, but his reaction was so violent that she quickly withdrew her hand. She went back to her sleeping bag and lay awake a long time.

Irene Sammartino has regrets. She should have kissed him that morning, grabbed his chin and pressed her mouth to his. She's sure that in the end he would have returned it and would be grateful to her later.

The soldiers on guard duty wave good-bye, but the men in the convoy don't look back; from this moment on all they think about is the road.

"Do you think they'll be in any danger?" Irene asks the commander.

The colonel runs his tongue along the inside of his cheeks. Irene watches that concealed worm move across his face. With his right hand Ballesio grabs his genitals and jiggles them. "Forgive the superstitious gesture," he says, "but God help them."

It's almost daytime and Lieutenant Egitto is waiting for the temperature to rise so he can remove a layer of clothing. They assigned him Senior Corporal Major Salvatore Camporesi as driver and so far the two haven't exchanged many words. Egitto has merely studied the soldier from the passenger seat, trying to deduce the salient features of his character from his physical appearance: a deeply receding hairline, well-trimmed beard, long feminine eyelashes, and bulging biceps that stick out like a couple of potatoes under his skin. A nice guy whose build makes him seem younger than he really is, a soldier like any other. Egitto knows that Camporesi would feel better being with his own men, on board one of the armored vehicles that precede and follow them, but he can't do anything about it: orders are orders, assignments are assignments, rank is rank.

Abib, the interpreter, is sitting behind them, in the compartment carrying stretchers, first aid equipment, and several bags of blood of different types that Egitto hopes he won't have to use. He doesn't feel much like talking with him either, so the silence in the vehicle is broken only by the deep rumble of the engine and the studded tires chewing up the rocks.

They proceed at a crawl, literally, because the ACRT at the head of the convoy is on foot, probing the ground inch by inch. The moment the ambulance crosses the invisible border of the security bubble—a line he's never crossed—Egitto notices a physical change, like the awakening of a myriad of nerve endings he'd thought were dead for some time. "This is where the red zone begins," he says to himself.

Camporesi smacks his lips. "I wonder if they know it too, Doc."

The map, printed on glossy paper, is resting on the dashboard; the lieutenant picks it up mainly to eliminate the sun's glare in his eyes. He studies the intricate contour lines as his gaze travels over the road on a scale of 1:50,000. They are about to cross a long uninhabited stretch with groups of structures broadly indicated as *ruins*. Farther on, when the valley's course becomes more tortuous, similar to the twists and turns of an intestine, there's a succession of other villages, a short distance from one another. From Boghal to Ghoziney there's a whole cluster of black dots. "Right there; if they're going to kick our ass, that's where they'll do it," Ballesio had said last night during their final talk, as he kept gobbling down cashews bought at the bazaar, spitting the brown skins in his fist. He'd jabbed a finger right next to Ghalarway. Under a certain slant of light, Egitto can still make out the oily mark of the colonel's fingertip.

He was wrong, though. The column makes it past the last dwelling in Ghoziney without encountering a living soul. A new expanse, wide open, appears before them. Egitto doesn't recognize any of these places. When he came through the valley in the opposite direction he must have been very unfocused, or very nervous.

At noon the convoy makes a ninety-degree turn, allowing the lieutenant to admire its extensive length. A cloud of yellow dust surrounds it, giving it a spectral look. A migration of bison, he thinks, an orderly migration. The stench of diesel is enough to make you vomit; he can still smell it but he knows that his receptors will soon decide to eliminate the perception of that odor. It won't mean that it's gone.

They advance along the dry riverbed, the river that carved the valley millennia ago and then vanished into its womb. The track follows a slight descent between two escarpments that rise higher and steeper. Since the area appears secure, they pick up speed. Camporesi does his best, but every time he touches the brake the ambulance jolts. The vehicle is weighty with its antimine chassis and doesn't have good shock absorbers. The rocking, lulling motion, the predawn wake-up, and the sudden lessening of tension cause Egitto's head to slump forward. He dozes off with his mouth open.

When he wakes up, they're stopped. A few soldiers are walking around the vehicles, within a very restricted radius. On either side, ahead, and in the rearview mirror Egitto sees nothing but velvety, reddish mountains. The map has slipped off his legs and under the seat; to retrieve it he'd have to unhook his seat belt and stick his hands down there. For the moment he decides to let it go.

He doesn't need to ask Camporesi why they've stopped. He can guess the reason, and in any case the crackling utterances transmitted by the radio quickly spell the picture out for him. The bomb techs have discovered an IED and are struggling to remove it. In and of itself, the news is not shocking—Afghanistan is mined like a pumpkin field after sowing season—but one particular detail is worrying: the explosive device was visible to the naked eye. The soil had recently been disturbed and didn't entirely cover the plate. This might mean any number of things, but among the subliminal messages the enemy may have wanted to convey, three jump out at the lieutenant: 1) we know where you've come from and where you're going; 2) this is a warning, we're offering you one last chance to turn back and let us deal with the truckers; 3) from here on out, you're in for it.

Looking back, much later, Egitto will be certain that finding the first IED was the pivotal moment when the soldiers saw the illusion of a smooth, obstacle-free mission evaporate and realized that they were in hot water. Of course, now that they've ended up there, each one keeps the thought to himself. It's one thing to suddenly lose your optimism, to realize that the operation didn't make sense from the beginning, quite another to share that foreboding. Misgivings can spread like a virus; no military contingent can afford it.

The tension, discouraged from being expressed in words, finds other avenues of release. Camporesi drums his fingers on the steering wheel in a way that irritates the lieutenant. He tries to compose complicated rhythms that he's incapable of pulling off. Listening to him, especially unwillingly, is frustrating. Egitto, for his part, is seized by a sudden hunger attack. It's strange: for months his appetite has languished—the crappy food and excess of serotonin have made him lose more than thirteen pounds since the beginning of his tour—but now there's a nitrate charge planted in the dust that was waiting just for them, waiting just for *him*, and his digestive system has issued a warning to his brain, as if his body has to prepare itself for what might follow, to store up strength to use in case of an emergency.

He looks around in search of provisions and finds the remains of a K ration on one of the stretchers, a snack belonging to one of his traveling companions.

"Is that yours?" he asks Abib. The interpreter gestures, offering it to him.

Egitto fishes out whatever is left to eat in the package: crackers, canned mackerel, condensed milk. He doesn't even spurn a leftover piece of Dutch cheese on which Abib's tooth marks are clearly visible. Not satisfied, he opens a can of meat ravioli that should be heated. He wolfs it down as is, cold and disgusting. As he's busy stuffing himself, he observes two soldiers arguing heatedly. He knows the one standing on the turret; it's Angelo Torsu, the young man who had acute intestinal flu (a few days ago Egitto had almost had him transported to Herat to make sure he hadn't caught brucellosis, or something worse). The other one is clinging to the door of the Lince up ahead; he's seen him many times, but he can't remember his name. "Who's that?" he asks Camporesi, pointing.

"Francesco Cederna. Pay no attention to him. He's a wild man."

On the few occasions he's seen him, Egitto got the impression that Cederna was an excitable, volatile type, the kind who picks fights in bars, like the guys his sister assumes populate the army's ranks. There's something disturbing about his eyes; the blinking of his eyelashes is slightly more sporadic than that of normal people.

He realizes that Cederna is teasing Torsu. The tension between the two rises, until a third soldier comes forward to calm them down. They switch positions and shortly afterward Torsu gets off the Lince. He takes off his helmet and sets it on the ground. Egitto watches him unfold a black bag and arrange it inside the helmet; then he pulls down his pants and crouches over that improvised toilet.

Now that Egitto sees the boy hunched over his helmet like an egg, his face strained, he has some misgivings about whether he acted hastily in allowing him to come. But there's nothing he can do about it now. Passengers can't be taken back at this point. The young man will just have to grit his teeth until they get where they're going.

As if called upon, Torsu looks up at him. Egitto makes a thumbs-up to ask if everything is okay and the soldier nods assuredly. There's not much chance of hiding, so he doesn't even try. Egitto, on the other hand, doesn't feel the need to look away, nor does he stop scarfing down the slop from the can, not even when the soldier stands back up and wipes himself as best he can, displaying his entire arsenal. Under normal conditions the lieutenant would have turned aside or at least pushed the food away. Not now. He watches and chews. Something in him has definitely changed since they advanced beyond the security bubble, and especially since the bomb tech found the first explosive device; where he is now, in the heart of the valley, there's no longer any trace of modesty or shame. Many of the qualities that distinguish humans from other animals have disappeared. From now on, he reflects, he himself no longer exists as a human being. He's turned into something abstract, a cluster of pure alertness, of pure reaction and endurance. Unexpectedly, he's come amazingly close to the absence of individuality that he's been pursuing by any and all means since the day his father died, the day he started taking drugs that could make him lose himself.

The lieutenant watches Torsu attend to his business, Senior Corporal Major Camporesi watches him, Cederna and the other guys watch him: all of them enjoying the scatological spectacle of their colleague Torsu, all of them without feeling any emotion.

Egitto upturns the can and swallows the congealed sauce to the last drop, then sets the can aside. An acidic belch rises from his stomach; he holds it in.

Cederna sticks his fingers in his mouth, pulls out a chewed piece of gum, and throws it at Torsu. "You're always crapping, you shitty Sardinian," he yells to him. "You're a fucking digestive tract."

The mine clearing operations go on for more than two hours. By the time they set out again the guys are bored, dazed, and all but cooked in the savage heat. The vehicles have become hotboxes. It's afternoon and any trace of their initial enthusiasm has vanished.

For Ietri things are worse than for the others, but by now he's used to believing that. It's only the first day on the road and he can't stand sitting any longer, stuck in the backseat with Di Salvo next to him, standing on the turret, kicking his thigh with his boot tip every time he changes direction with the machine gun. He always does it to him and not Pecone, as if on purpose, hundreds of little kicks in exactly the same spot, since Di Salvo is continuously swiveling.

Besides that, he has a privileged view of Zampieri and Cederna, who are sitting in the front seats, exchanging smiles, teasing glances and banter, which, as he interprets them, all refer to sex. As if they wanted to flaunt what they did to the whole world, Zampieri is sporting a livid hickey the size of a coin on her neck. Ietri has been torturing himself all these hours imagining Cederna holding her head wedged and sucking her skin. His imagination has gone so far as to picture

Zampieri's blood being suctioned to the surface to form the bruise. Did they go all the way afterward? For sure they did—Cederna isn't the type to pull back or leave things halfway. But it doesn't make much difference at this point. Ietri has decided that from now on he doesn't like any girl anymore and no longer has a best friend. It's awful to think about it. It makes him feel alone, inconsolable, and hurt.

Di Salvo lands another little kick on his nerve.

"Hey, watch it! Shit!" Ietri bursts out.

"What are you getting all worked up about back there, *verginella?*" Cederna chimes in.

What stings Ietri more than anything, though he would never admit it, is that his friend hasn't even noticed how angry he is or that he hasn't spoken to him since morning. Now he has two choices: answer him rudely and make his resentment known, or continue not speaking to him, make believe he doesn't exist. By the time he makes up his mind, however, Cederna has already forgotten about him.

Via radio, René is urging them to pick up the pace. The Third has to make up a fairly substantial gap, because in the last hour they've made two extra stops, due to Torsu's intestinal problems. The third time René denied him permission to get out of the vehicle and the soldier is now forced to perform his evacuation operations on the turret, standing, to the benefit of Mitrano and Simoncelli, whose heads are directly level with his pelvis. He drops his pants and briefs to his knees, unfolds the garbage bag, and manages as best he can.

Poor guy, Ietri thinks, seeing what's going on in the Lince behind them in the rearview mirror, but his sympathy stops there. At this moment he's too absorbed in pitying himself. He lets that insistent feeling draw him into a series of ever morbid fantasies that eventually verge on thoughts of death. It's the only way he's able to coddle himself, sinking deeper into misery.

He glances out the window, but there's nothing to see, not a tree or a house, not a color other than that of rock and sand. He's overcome by a feeling of nostalgia for the town where he grew up. When he was in middle school, and even more in high school, he hated Torremaggiore and its deserted streets. He was the only heavy metal freak within fifty miles and wore the Slayers apocalyptic T-shirts as a shout of protest. Now he'd give anything to be back there. Even just for a little while. He'd like to be dozing on the high bed with the wrought-iron headboard, in the room that was too bright in the afternoon to really sleep, listening to the rattle of his mother's pots in the kitchen, her radio set low so it wouldn't disturb him.

Why does he always want too much and always what he can't have, things in the past or, worse yet, those that will never come? At age twenty he's beginning to wish that all those desires would vanish without a trace. There certainly must be a point at which a man stops being conflicted, in which a man finds himself exactly where he wants to be.

From a dizzying height in the sky, a hawk swoops down and Ietri follows its flight. Just before touching the ground the bird soars again, picks up a current, and lets it carry him, adrift, in midair. It's a sight that the corporal finds inspiring. There, that's how he should be.

The Lince brakes suddenly, flinging him forward. Ietri's forehead hits the seat's reinforcement bar; then he bounces back. A whiplash injury to his neck that he pays no attention to, because first he has to figure out what's happened.

Di Salvo has crashed down ass-first and let out a shout; a few cases of ammunition have overturned, and there are cartridges scattered everywhere, some even between his legs. Cederna swears, then slaps the dashboard. "You guys okay?" he asks.

Automatically, Ietri replies, "Yeah." He couldn't manage to keep up his silence this time either.

At first they call it a ditch, but in all respects it's a crater, so deep that, looking into it, you can see water glimmering. A well in the middle of the desert—who would believe it? The right front wheel of the Lince has ended up in it, while the others are reared up. When Zampieri tries to step on the gas, the wheels spin around in the air, shooting clumps of earth in every direction. The real problem is that the vehicle's chassis is lodged on a rock outcropping. Towing the vehicle is risky because they might damage the gas tank and they can't leave it there because regulations prohibit it. (God only knows what the enemy would do with the Lince if they were to get hold of it!) The only solution is to try to raise it and drag it forward. But it weighs ten tons.

They have a good field of vision, so almost everyone gets out, and for the first few minutes at least they're grateful to whoever caused them to stop. They take the opportunity to stretch, bending over to grab their ankles and twisting their backs from side to side. They try decreasing the vehicle's load: after the passengers are out, the gear and ammunition are also unloaded. Cederna and Di Salvo dismount the Browning from the turret and at that point there's nothing left to remove unless they pull out the seats, as some have suggested.

It's hopeless. Even with six and then twelve pairs of strong arms trying to lift the Lince, it won't budge. René is furious and he's not the only one: Captain Masiero radioed his contempt from up ahead, shouting that he had no intention of stopping because Goldilocks isn't capable of driving. He ordered the column to be temporarily broken and René didn't have the nerve to object and say that it was an extremely risky plan. He knew the captain would lay into him and then proceed to do whatever he wanted.

Masiero, together with the bomb techs and most of the military vehicles, has continued along the track to get on with clearing the terrain. As soon as the trouble with the Lince is resolved, the rest of the convoy can catch up with them by moving more quickly. The guys of the Third and the truckers watch the vehicles that preceded them disappear behind the mountain. Now they're orphans. Their situation is as tragic as it is simple: the longer it takes them to get out of the fix they're in, the greater the distance they'll have to cover without the ACRT's protection, now in the forefront, blindfolded and barefoot in a terrain full of mines. The more time they lose, the greater the possibility that a stupid accident might turn into a much bigger disaster.

So they get busy, each however he can. They strain their biceps and cut their hands in an effort to raise the vehicle. They count one . . . two . . . lift, and only when they're out of breath do they release their grip. Even the Afghans have sensed the danger and, grouped beside the Lince, offer advice that no one understands.

Corporal Zampieri is the only one standing on the sidelines. After almost burning the clutch to drive the heap of scrap iron forward, she's now focused on vigorously resisting the tears that are choking her. What's the matter with her? Why didn't she see the hole? She thinks she must have come close to nodding off. She'd been struggling to keep her eyes open for over an hour, tempted by the urge to doze off with her face squashed against the steering wheel, and instead of spilling a bottle of water over her head, she'd let herself be lulled.

What an idiot! She feels like kicking herself. Instead she bites her right thumb and chews the skin off, since the nail has already been bitten as far down as possible. Gnawing her fingers has an immediate calming effect. During periodic visits, the doctors always make offensive comments about that habit, but she ignores them. As she moves from the battered thumb to her middle finger (which doesn't offer as much satisfaction except for the joy of ruining something intact), she reviews, one at a time, the phases she's all too familiar with, stages from similar situations in which she's fouled up: shame, the wish to disappear, fierce anger, the urge to vindicate herself.

Cederna comes over. He throws an arm around her shoulder, more comradely than affectionate. Last night Zampieri was sure he really liked her, but now she knows that his interest was just due to the general excitement and lasted only briefly. Even when they entered the tent she had the impression that Cederna wanted to have some fun with her for lack of a better alternative. Giulia Zampieri has always been the kind of girl men have a good time with. No one really wants her seriously. They do what they want with her body, sawing off her head. She knows this and by all appearances she couldn't care less.

She tried to enjoy the fun, and later, when she was having a hard time getting to sleep, she rated Cederna's performance as coolly as guys must rate their bed mates. Nothing special, hasty and repetitive. She tried to silence the insistent frustration that demanded something more, something better, and not just from a sexual point of view. She fell asleep wondering whether she'd been infatuated with him for too long, an unacceptably long time, and fearing that their little fling may have punched a hole in the sealed container that kept that feeling in check.

"It could have happened to anyone," Cederna says. "Sure, it's a fucking disaster. But it could have happened to anyone. That is, almost anyone. It wouldn't have happened to me, for instance."

Zampieri says nothing. She shrugs off his arm.

"When you can't see beyond an obstacle, you always have to go around it," he continues. "You can't know what to expect up ahead."

"Are you teaching me how to drive, asshole?"

"Hey, don't get mad. I'm just giving you a piece of advice."

"I don't need your advice. Why don't you beat it and leave me in peace?"

Cederna winks at her. He's really a blowhard. How can she like someone like that?

He leans over and whispers in her ear: "Maybe you're just a little tired. You were pretty wild on that cot."

There it is. That's what Cederna thinks of her. That she's a woman men can be brazen with, and say things like "You were pretty wild on that cot" and freely admit all the filthy acts that normally they only dare to imagine.

She gives him a shove. "I'm not the least bit tired, get it? If you really want to know, you didn't last long enough for me to even *begin* to get tired." She says it loudly so the others can hear. They turn around, curious.

Cederna grabs her arm. "What the hell's wrong with you, huh?"

"Maybe it's time we said what you're really worth, Francesco Cederna. So everyone will know."

"Shut up!" Cederna raises his right arm to smack her, but it's not clear he'd have the guts to really hit her because Ietri appears out of nowhere and comes between them.

"What's going on?"

"Get out of my way, *verginella*."

"I asked you what's going on."

Cederna stands right under his nose, Ietri a whole head taller. "Get out of here, I said."

"No, Cederna. I won't get out. You get out." Ietri's voice cracks a bit with emotion.

At the far right of Zampieri's field of vision is the wedged Lince with the guys scrambling around it, in the center the aggressive profile of Cederna, and to the left, out of focus, Ietri's. Zampieri is and isn't present. Right now her heart is blank, empty. Her arms are trembling and her cheeks burning. Men always know how to handle her, but she's learned how to handle men.

She turns slowly. She reaches out to the back of Ietri's neck, pulls him to her. The sensual kiss she plants on his mouth has no sentimental implication; it's a clear act of revenge, of self-defense, a rejection of the ferocious animal threatening her.

She breaks it off with a smack of her lips and glances sidelong at Cederna, who's turned pale. "You should ask your friend to teach you, you know. He's no *verginella*. No way! He knows what's what."

It's after five and the sun is low on the horizon when René decides to take a chance and go for broke. "We'll hook it up to the ambulance," he says.

"That way we could wreck both of them."

"We'll hook it up to the ambulance, I said."

They use a double tow hitch; then René himself gets behind the wheel. He doesn't want the responsibility for any slipup to fall on one of his men. He'd like the guys to recognize his generosity, but instead they stare at him skeptically as he gets set to start; some even think he wants to take credit for it. He tries not to pay any attention. By now he knows: the chief quality required of a commander is to be able to forsake any form of gratitude.

He steps firmly on the accelerator. The ambulance's tires spin at full speed, kicking up a dust cloud. The tachometer goes to six thousand rpm; a high-pitched screech forces the soldiers to cover their ears. The Lince rocks back and forth and seems to want to tip over on its side, but instead, with a single violent lurch, it's out of the hole. The accident leaves its mark in a silvery scar on the underside of the vehicle.

René regroups the column and they set out again, but the severed convoy doesn't get very far. By now the sun is gone. Moreover, through his binoculars René can see a village. Lartay. He can't make up his mind whether it frightens him or not. Captain Masiero got past it unscathed with his troops and is now awaiting the stragglers in an area with better visibility, beyond the group of settlements. Ending up so far apart wasn't part of the plan—the captain, completely ignoring his own error of judgment and skipping over any apology of course, had muttered into the transmitter that there was no suitable place to spend the night until they reached Buji Pass, so he'd pressed on down there, end of story. René is tempted to try to join him, but he can't run the risk of being trapped in a village in the dark.

This is the first time he's heading a mission with any real danger, the first time he has to make such a difficult decision. If he'd been handed the prospect of such an opportunity, even just that morning, he would have been dazed with excitement, but now he doesn't feel the sense of achievement he expected. He's definitely more worried than proud.

He gives the order to encamp. Although Lieutenant Egitto is the highest-ranking officer now that Masiero has left them on their own, the marshal is a more experienced strategist and the doc supports him.

René keeps the vehicles lined up in a row—in case of an ambush they could start moving more quickly—then establishes the shifts for guard duty. He feels drained. He hadn't really noticed it until the minute he turned off the ignition key and the seat under his butt stopped vibrating. His neck has tensed up, his limbs are stiff, and his back aches, especially his lower back. Not to mention he itches all over. He's not one to complain, but this time he admits: "I couldn't take it anymore."

"You're telling me, Marshal," Mattioli agrees.

But René doesn't believe the others find themselves in the same condition as he does. No one else has carried the burden of command on his shoulders.

He unfastens the seat belt, which isn't just an ordinary seat belt, but an infernal contraption composed of a metal ring on which four very taut straps converge: two of them have been squeezing his testicles the entire time. He removes his helmet, the sunglasses that made him think it was later in the evening than it was—could they have gone a little farther? hell, it's time for some rest!—and his gloves as well, then leans over the steering wheel to perform the most complicated operation: taking off his bulletproof vest. He yanks open the velcro on each side, then ducks his head like a turtle and struggles to pull it off. As soon as the vest is tugged off his body, he feels an intense burning in his abdomen, as if he'd ripped a piece of flesh off along with it. Cramps? He has no idea what's going on anymore; the pain is all one big ache. He tosses the protective vest over the steering wheel, pulls his cotton T-shirt out of his pants, and rolls it up over his belly.

When he sees the bruise he's speechless. The purplish, nearly black streak runs across his stomach from one side to the other, where the lead plate rested. It's an inch wide and in some spots vivid scrapes and clots of dried pus can be seen. Mattioli provides the audio commentary: "Holy shit, René."

The others lean forward to see, even Torsu bends his knees and sticks his head into the cab; he's white as a sheet and almost relieved that someone is as bad off as him. They all start undressing feverishly to check what's under their vests, and to anyone watching them squirm around that way, they'd look pretty comical, because it's not easy to take off that paraphernalia sitting down, squeezed in like that. They each have some redness, but no one is as skinned as René.

"You have to go see the doc," Mattioli says.

"What for?"

"You need some ointment."

"It's just a bruise."

"It's bleeding. There. And there too."

"It looks like you've had a C-section," Mitrano says.

"A C-section isn't that long, you asshole!" Simoncelli says.

"What do I know? Who's ever seen one!"

René gives in and agrees to trade places temporarily with Camporesi. Even a maneuver as trivial as that requires a degree of diligence. You can't just get out and walk the fifteen yards that separate you— there might be snipers posted right there, at eight o'clock, along the cleft in the rock face. You first need to create a security corridor with the tanks.

Finally the marshal climbs into the ambulance, in place of the driver, Camporesi. The doc has him lie down on a stretcher in the rear compartment. The medication he applies burns like pure alcohol, and maybe it is. René has crescent-shaped swellings under his armpits as well and another large one on his back. A few seconds after the doc has swabbed a wound with a cotton ball soaked in disinfectant, the burning eases, leaving a cool feeling in its place.

"Breathe, Marshal."

"Huh?"

"You're holding your breath. It's all right to breathe."

"Oh. Okay."

René closes his eyes. He's lying down. He stretches his back muscles. Relaxing his limbs triggers a kind of orgasm that spreads throughout his body.

The doc begins massaging his shoulder muscles; his hands are warm. It's certainly the most intimate contact René has ever had with a man. At first he's embarrassed, but then he relaxes. He wishes it would never end.

He's struck by the prospect of spending the night in the ambulance, stretched out, rather than cramped in the driver's seat in the overcrowded Lince, with the steering wheel preventing him from even turning on his side. However, the stretcher he's occupying belongs to Camporesi by all rights. He drove that vehicle all day; René himself assigned him that role: changing places now would be a shitty thing to do. Yet the marshal is totally wiped out. For the first time in his career, self-interest engages in a violent struggle with what's right.

It's what every one of my men would do. Not one of them would sacrifice himself for me.

That's not so, and you know it.

In the end, they're all selfish. We're all selfish. Why do I always have to act like I'm better than them? Why should I be the better man this time too, if they won't repay me later on? I worked harder than all of them. Tomorrow I have to be rested, to lead them past the village.

No, no, no! It's not right. This place belongs to Campo.

René knows that if he gives in to the stretcher's temptation, his self-esteem will be damaged forever. He'd be taking advantage of his rank to be a little more comfortable. He won't be any different from many of the higher-ups he's always despised.

Everyone takes advantage. We're all bastards, in one way or another. Besides, it's only for tonight.

He sits up. The doc objects, telling him to lie still until the pain-killer has taken effect. "Only a minute," René says.

He leans toward the radio in the front of the vehicle and contacts the Lince in front of them, asks to speak to Camporesi.

"Camporesi here, René," the soldier answers.

"We're trading places. Tonight I'm staying in the ambulance."

There's a long silence on the other end.

René presses his thumb on the button. "I'm staying in the ambulance. Over."

More silence.

"Campo, do you read me?"

"Roger that. Over and out."

When René lies back on the stretcher, however, he finds it less comfortable than before. All of a sudden he notices how rigid it is and that his arms hang down over the sides, so that he has to keep his hands clasped together on his chest like a corpse in a coffin. Maybe it wasn't worth dirtying his conscience for a little bit more space, but what's done is done. He's surprised that his remorse isn't greater after all.

Lieutenant Egitto, after cleaning his teeth with a plastic swab, without water, lies down on the adjacent stretcher. He and René are the two highest-ranking soldiers in what's left of the convoy and they will spend the night better than all the others. It's shameful and unfair, but that's how the world works. Maybe it's time René learned to come to terms with it. He inhales the stale air.

It's the evening of the first day and they've covered a little over nine miles.

———

Angelo Torsu and Enrico Di Salvo's heads stick out of the turrets of the armored vehicles, in the valley's chill, rosy dawn. The two gunners are bleary eyed and their legs are stiff. The barrels of the Browning automatics protrude oddly from the wool blankets wrapped around their necks.

"Hey," Torsu says.

"Hey."

They whisper.

"I need to go."

"You can't. You have to hold it in."

"No, I *really* need to go."

"If René catches you, you're done for."

"He's sleeping. I can see him from here. Cover me."

Torsu's head disappears for a few seconds, a duck diving under to fish in a pond. When he resurfaces he has a roll of toilet paper clamped between his teeth. He pushes himself out of the turret. He walks along the hood, keeping his balance with open arms, then places a foot on the running board and jumps down.

"Hurry up!" Di Salvo whispers.

Torsu has already picked out the right spot for his needs, a huge rock planted in the middle of the riverbed, which probably split the stream and created eddies back when the river flowed. The outcropping was illuminated by the full moon and he'd gazed longingly at it throughout the night between bouts of drowsiness that could only be likened to sleep.

As for what might hit him from above, an accurate shot in the back of his neck, for instance, he wasn't worried about that. If the enemy had wanted to shoot him, he would have done so already. He's more afraid of what might be hidden under the soil. It must be about forty steps from the Lince to the rock. Forty chances to put his foot in the wrong place and be wiped off the face of the earth. The explosion you don't hear is the one that's already killed you, Masiero had said in his course.

Torsu covers the distance with as wide a stride as he can, forcing himself to set his foot down gently (though he knows it's pointless: if there's a detonator and he steps on it, that's it—*boom*). At first he's hesitant and turns to Di Salvo every two or three steps, as if looking for reassurance. His buddy signals him to go on, move it; René might wake up at any moment and the punishment would fall on him too for keeping his mouth shut while the Sardinian committed an infraction.

Another step. It makes no difference whether he zigzags or goes straight ahead; he might as well choose the shortest path.

He's halfway there. He's gaining confidence, moving more quickly now. His gut is looking forward to the privacy and knots up even more tightly. Torsu speeds up. He runs the last few yards. Before going around the rock he bends down, picks up a stone, and throws it a little ways ahead, to scare away any poisonous snakes, scorpions, spiders, and who knows what else.

Finally he's alone. He drops his pants. The cold nips pleasantly at his bare thighs. His pecker has withdrawn, shriveled up—it looks like a filbert. Torsu waggles it with his fingers, but the little guy, recalcitrant, sputters out a miserable trickle of very dark piss.

How humiliating! He'd stood all that time on the turret, exhausted and filthy. If only he hadn't gotten it into his head to join the mission. He'd had a right to remain at the FOB. Why did he do it, then? To prove his worth, to show how great his loyalty is. Loyalty *to whom*?

Now his body has nothing left to expel, futile spasms more than anything, but it's nice to crouch there and let it go. During his illness the first corporal major got into the habit of talking to his digestive system, as if it were a creature separate from himself. He scolds it when the pain is too intense and says, "Good boy, you're behaving well," when things go better. Now he tries to calm it down: "We still have a long way to go. If you don't settle down today, Simoncelli will shoot me for real."

As he converses with his bowels, he plays marbles with the pebbles scattered on the ground and scratches the soil with his nails. To stay crouched without tearing the tendons in his heels, he rocks back and forth like a Buddhist monk. He feels like whistling, but maybe that's going too far.

Looking up, he's able to catch a glimpse of the day's first ray of light, which shines directly in his face. It's pale, tenuous, and doesn't convey any heat. The sun is clinging to the mountain so that he thinks he can see it being born. Then the fiery ball peeps out, gigantic, as if it were about to come toppling down any moment and set everything ablaze. The sky all around is veined with orange, yellow, and pink, the streaks drifting off into the extinguished blue. Torsu has never seen a sunrise so crisp and majestic, not even from the beach at Coaquaddus, when he would stay up until dawn in the summer with his friends.

"Fucking awesome!" he exclaims.

Tersicore89 should be there. Naturally, she'd find more appropriate words than his: she's a poet. But Tersicore89 doesn't want him anymore. She's angry because he doubted her. Torsu feels sad.

When his interest in the rising sun has evaporated, he attempts to clean himself off using water from the canteen.

No enemies around, or so it seems. No one has taken aim at them. If you don't count the IED found yesterday—which could very well have been there for days—if you ignore that little obstacle, there's absolutely no evidence of any hostile presence. For the first time, Torsu thinks they're making a mountain out of a molehill and that everything is likely to go smoothly the rest of the way.

"Dumb-asses," he says under his breath as he hops confidently back to the Lince, his step breezy, hands in his pockets even (but still careful to go the exact same way he came).

"What did you say?" Di Salvo whispers.

Torsu shakes his head, forget it. He's clean, feeling good, at peace. Ready to go.

By half past six they're on the move. Masiero has promised that he won't move from where he is until they reach him. Lieutenant Egitto has slept fitfully, mainly because of the cold. During the night the temperature dropped sharply and he shivered, half asleep, huddled in his waterproof poncho. Every quarter of an hour Marshal René got up from the stretcher, crept into the driving compartment, and started the engine to run the heater, then had to turn it off to conserve fuel. Finally, tired of going back and forth, he stayed behind the wheel, awake, staring out at the night. Egitto admires the marshal's remarkable tenacity. He feels a little ridiculous at deriving such reassurance from a younger man. The vacant space on the stretcher was immediately occupied by Abib, who is still snoring; even asleep he has a cocky attitude, legs spread wide, an arm behind his head.

Egitto has to manually stimulate his numb facial muscles. He has the symptoms of a cold: nose stuffed with mucus, achy bones, head like a lead balloon, maybe even a fever? Uncertain, he crunches a thousand-milligram tablet of Tylenol, then rinses his mouth. He's aware of the liver damage that can be caused by an overdose of acetaminophen, but this is no time to be overly fastidious.

René drives more smoothly than Camporesi; he knows how to deal with the holes to minimize the stress on the shock absorbers. Now that they're the third vehicle in the column, there's less dust in front of them and you can see everything. The marshal murmurs good morning, then falls silent again, as if to respect the lieutenant's slow awakening; he himself shows no signs of giving out, despite the nearly sleepless night and the wound on his stomach.

In a few minutes they're out of Lartay, all in one piece.

"One down," René says, exhaling forcefully through his mouth.

Egitto hands him an energy bar, and the marshal takes it. They celebrate like that while Abib loudly clears his nasal passages. The acetaminophen is reaching its peak effectiveness. The velvety serenity of drugs—that's one thing the lieutenant can always count on.

They leave Pusta behind them, and avoid Saydal by clambering up the slope of the mountain. These are not strategic choices made by the marshal: all they can (and must) do is follow the tracks of the vehicles that preceded them. Wherever Masiero's tire marks can be seen on the ground, they're guaranteed to find no surprises.

At half past seven they catch sight of the cluster of dwellings that make up Terikhay, which is little more than a mountain pasture, though it seemed more significant than that on the map. They climb farther and continue along the mountainside. Then they descend to the dry riverbed. They find themselves in a spot where the valley suddenly narrows like an hourglass and that's where they come upon the spectacle.

A sizable flock of reddish sheep is blocking their way, while more come rushing in from both sides. They tear down the hillside, hooves slipping and sliding: two streams of animals converge in their path, forming a whirlpool of undulating fleece. The sheep rub against each other and sniff one another's butts; occasionally one raises its head to the sky and utters a harsh, grating bleat.

Egitto is amazed at this burst of vitality. "How many can there be?" he asks.

René doesn't answer. The marshal has realized something that the lieutenant, distracted by the sheep or by the free flow of serotonin in the hippocampus, has missed. René is leaning over the wheel, biting his upper lip. "There's no shepherd," he says, then grabs the binoculars hanging on the seat. He scours the area.

It's true—there's no shepherd, there's not a soul, aside from the sheep that seem to be spewing right out of the mountain, hurtling down by the hundreds, terrified by something that the soldiers can't see.

"We have to get out of here," René says.

Egitto registers the change of color on the marshal's face. "How?" he asks. "We're boxed in."

"We'll shoot."

"Shoot the sheep?"

Torsu, standing on the Browning's turret a few yards from them, looks like he's enjoying it all. He keeps ducking in and out of the cupola, pointing at the sheep.

René grabs the radio and calls to Cederna, who is at the head of the column, but his colleague's ironic response—a bleat—is drowned out by the RPG strike that thunders behind them. The lieutenant sees the flash out of the corner of his eye through the rearview mirror. Afterward, there's just black smoke rising from one of the vehicles. Egitto holds his breath as he tries to figure out which one it is. He feels relieved when he realizes that it's one of the civilian trucks. Only much later will he be able to reflect on that momentary lack of humanity.

What follows next, until the time the Lince driven by Salvatore Camporesi blows up on twenty kilograms of explosives, blasting the passengers on board to bits—all except one, who has the good fortune to be thrown several yards away among the sheep—lasts three or four minutes at most.

Torsu, Di Salvo, Rovere, and the other gunners in the column hammer away with the Brownings. They fire at an enemy they can't see, somewhat hit or miss and mostly pointing upward.

Mattioli shoots.

Mitrano shoots.

No one has had time to figure out which direction the RPG rocket came from, so they take aim at the sheep rushing down the hill, as if they were the threat. Things become clear soon enough, however, because the enemy starts hitting them with everything they have, from all sides. Mortar shells erupt from the villages of Terikhay and Khanjak; clearly the artillerymen have had time to plan, because the strikes land a few dozen yards away. Small arms fire converges on the column from every direction, then more rockets, and shrapnel that shatters in the sky and hails down on their heads. An inferno, hell on earth.

Pecone, Passalacqua, and Simoncelli shoot.

Cederna makes out two armed shadows up above, at nine o'clock, and doesn't stop firing until he's neutralized them both. The satisfaction he feels when the first one jerks back isn't anything like what he'd imagined; it happens too quickly and from too far away—it's almost more gratifying to put a hole in the center of the silhouette at the firing range.

Ruffinatti shoots.

Ietri performs his job zealously, though it's not much: he hands Di Salvo the ammunition belts and in between dealing them out he tries to pinpoint the enemy with binoculars, so he can then give the location to Cederna. He's very calm. It's almost as if he doesn't realize what's happening. A sheep rubs up against the hot metal of the door, then looks at him intently; Ietri stands there in a daze, watching it, until Di Salvo yells: "Ammo, asshole!"

Allais, Candela, Vercellin, and Anfossi shoot.

René shouts over the radio: "Move forward—go, go, go!"

Zampieri is the one who should move because she's first in the column, but she's frozen. Her mind is a blank; all she sees is those sheep and she wonders what they're doing there, although the more pertinent question would be what is *she* doing there.

Camporesi honks the horn to rouse Zampieri. No one hears it; there's too much noise.

An RPG blows up another truck.

Egitto is blinded for a few seconds by the flash of a mortar bomb that kills a dozen sheep in one strike. The ambulance shudders.

"Move, move, move!"

The sheep are running wild. They do an about-face to clamber back up the mountain, collide with those that are racing down, and tumble along together for a few yards without ever falling.

"Move, damn it, move!"

Camporesi floors the accelerator, steers to the right to get around Zampieri's vehicle, and passes her, tires squealing. Some sheep move aside to let him through; others are ruthlessly mowed down. He makes it to the front of the column, cuts through the bleating flock, runs over a pressure plate made of two stolen graphite strips and 1.5-volt alkaline batteries with his left front wheel, sets off the charge placed under the plate, and the Lince blows up.

The charred pieces of the Lince lie scattered over the dry grass. Ietri stares at them from behind the mud-spattered window. He could rub the glass with his forearm to see better, but a part of him knows that the dirt is mostly on the outside and it wouldn't do any good. Peering more closely, he realizes that some of the burnt remains on the ground, the smaller ones, aren't mechanical but anatomical. For example, there's a boot still attached to its sole, upright, with something sticking out of it. He's not sure what the others are. So that's how a human body is blown apart, he thinks.

The blaze spreads from the vehicle to the brush, radiating a few yards.

How many sheep must have been killed by the explosion? Maybe fifty, but it might be more, a gory carpet of fleece overhung with dense smoke billowing up from the flaming chassis.

Salvatore Camporesi, Cesare Mattioli, Arturo Simoncelli, and Vincenzo Mitrano no longer exist. They've been vaporized.

Angelo Torsu, after an acrobatic flight, lies faceup thirty paces from the demolished vehicle. He lost consciousness, but came to almost immediately. He can't feel any of his limbs, he's blind, and he can barely breathe. Rather than worrying about anything more important, he's concerned that a sheep might come and lick him; he dreads the idea of a rough tongue passing over him in the dark. He's bleeding a little everywhere and he knows it.

Marshal René has completed his mental roll call. He was slower than usual, but the result he's come up with is accurate. He's missing Camporesi, Mattioli, Mitrano, and Simoncelli. Torsu is out there, unmoving, most likely to be counted among the lost, he thinks. The marshal's eyes fill with tears—something new for him.

Being heroic is not enough to be a hero.

The enemy had stopped firing, but has resumed almost immediately, seemingly only made bolder. Cederna is the only one who has the presence of mind to return the fire. He shoots, reloads, shoots, reloads, shoots, reloads, not stopping to catch his breath.

One of the last incidents that Roberto Ietri remembers about his father is the night he woke him up to take him to see the wheat stubble burning. The countryside was all in flames, the entire Daunia on fire, the hills red against the black.

Zampieri makes out bizarre shapes in the plumes of smoke: a tree, a hand, a gigantic dragon. *None of this can be real.*

Torsu's diaphragm shudders as he comes to. He also regains his sight (not entirely; his left eye is swollen and the eyelid partly shut). All

Torsu can see is a portion of sky. Wherever he is, he has to let the others know that he's alive. Assuming that there still are any others. Gathering up whatever energy he has left in his body, he directs it to his right arm and with an immense effort raises it.

"He's alive! Torsu is alive!" someone yells.

René has also noticed the raised arm. The request to take action and rescue their comrade comes to him by radio from all the vehicles. But whoever goes out there without cover is likely to stay there. Once again, he has to make a difficult decision because of Torsu. God damn that Sardinian! Marshal René, a man of sterling character, the NCO who would like to be captain, the intrepid soldier, doesn't know what to do.

"Charlie Three One to Med. Charlie Three One to Med. Request permission to retrieve the wounded man, over."

René turns to Lieutenant Egitto. He's in charge after all. "What should we do, Doc?"

Di Salvo has to let up on the Browning if he doesn't want to melt the barrel. He shoulders his rifle and goes on firing.

The whirring of the blades of an approaching helicopter. No, there are two. Two helicopters! Here they come!

Egitto replies to René: "Let's wait."

Torsu's arm drops to the ground. He starts to cry.

Recklessness is a miraculous quality of young men and Ietri is the youngest of all. He's just twenty years old. He sees Torsu's arm rise and then fall back. I'm a soldier, he tells himself. I'm a man. Zampieri's kiss is still burning on his lips and gives him courage. Shit, I'm a soldier! I'm a man! "I'm going to get him," he says. "Don't you move from there," Cederna barks. He's higher in rank, but who does he think he is, giving him orders? After what he did. Ietri opens the door and jumps out of the vehicle. He sprints, dodging the dead sheep and his companions' body parts, and in an instant is beside his buddy. "I'll get you out of here now," he promises. But then he doesn't know what to do, whether he should drag him by the hands or feet, or hoist him up and carry him on his back. But what if he has a broken spine? He's come that far and now he's uncertain. "Hang on," he says, but more than anything it's a way of telling himself: Move it!

The enemy has plenty of time to take aim. The shots come from multiple directions at once, roughly the same number of bullets in front and in back. For that reason, though jolted, the body of Roberto Ietri remains standing for an exceptionally long time. The autopsy will reveal that the fatal bullet is the one that veers improbably from his scapula and becomes lodged in his heart, in the right ventricle. In the end Ietri sags and collapses on top of Torsu.

The night the fields burned he had fallen asleep in his father's arms as they walked back to the car. He'd hardly ever stayed up so late, but in the morning he dragged himself out of bed so he could tell his mother all about it. She'd listened patiently, even the third and fourth time. Maybe this wasn't the final thought the corporal had planned on before dying, the one he'd prepared, but it's fine just the same. It wasn't so bad after all. Life hadn't been so bad.

Torsu finds it hard to breathe again, his sternum squashed by his companion. He's shivering now and he's afraid he's going to die. His face feels strange, as if someone has put ice on it. He whimpers. He didn't think this would happen, that he would die leaving everything hanging. He feels stupid for what he did, for the way he acted, in general and more particularly for the way he treated Tersicore89. What good was all that truth? What difference did it make? She loved him, she understood him. He should have been satisfied with that. Now look where he is: crushed under the dead body of a comrade with no one to miss him, no one to cry out to. Just to feel less alone, First Corporal Major Angelo Torsu hugs the lifeless body of Roberto Ietri. He holds him tight. The body still retains a little of its human warmth.

Colonel Ballesio dismissed everyone except her. When the subordinates left, he pushed his chair back with his pelvis and leaned his forehead on his folded arms. He hasn't moved again. Could he be sleeping? Is there something she should do? She could go over and rest a hand on his shoulder, for example. No, it's unthinkable. Their familiarity hasn't nearly developed to that point.

And she, Irene, how does she feel? Relieved for one thing, because Alessandro's name isn't listed among the dead. She's stunned, of course, but it's as if the real shock were slow to hit her. *You're sending people to die, Irene. I want you to realize that before it happens, because afterward there can be no excuses for you.*

A short while ago Ballesio had delivered a concise report of the battle to the soldiers assembled at the base and read the list of fallen comrades with exaggerated pauses: "Senior Corporal Major Simoncelli. Senior Corporal Major Camporesi. First Corporal Major Mattioli. Corporal Mitrano. They were on the Lince. Corporal Ietri was struck by small arms fire. The wounded man is First Corporal Major Torsu. The survivors are still under enemy fire. Now get the hell out, all of you."

Each name was greeted by sighs, moans, curses: an effective way to measure how well the victims were liked.

Irene gets up, fills a plastic cup from the water tank, and takes small sips. Then she fills one for the commander. She places it on the desk, near his head. Ballesio heaves himself up. He has a red mark on his forehead from the pressure of his arms. He gulps down the water all at once and then stops to contemplate the translucent molded plastic.

"You know what, Sammartino? I wish I had something personal to say about those guys. The men expect me to talk about their comrades tonight, to pay tribute to them, like a kind of father"; he says "father" scornfully. "Every good commander is able to. How decent he was, how brave he was, how handy he was with engines. A fucking story for each of them. And they're right. But you want to know the truth? I can't think of anything. I'm not their father. If I had kids like my soldiers, I'd spend my time kicking their asses." He crumples the sheet of paper with the names of the fallen in his hand. Then, repentant, he smoothes it out with his palm. "I don't remember the face of any one of them. Arturo Simoncelli. Who the hell is that? Vincenzo Mitrano. Him, yeah. Vaguely. I think I can picture this one too: Salvatore Camporesi. A tall guy. Does that seem to you like something I could say? 'We mourn the loss of our friend Salvatore, he was a very tall guy.' And these two? Ietri and Mattioli. I haven't the foggiest idea who they were. Maybe I never even set eyes on them. There are 190 soldiers here at the FOB, Sammartino, 190 human beings who depend on me and the mood I'm in when I get up in the morning, and I didn't bother to take the time to distinguish them from one another. What do you think of that? It's interesting, isn't it? I find it very interesting. You want to report that information to your superiors? Go right ahead and report it—I don't really give a shit."

"Commander, please."

"They're all indistinguishable. Tell them that too. Colonel Giacomo Ballesio says of his men, colon, quote, 'For me they're all indistinguishable.' This one died instead of that one, so what? It makes no difference. Tell that to your goddamn superiors. It makes no difference. They were just kids who didn't know what they were doing."

He's livid. Irene is willing to tolerate the outburst up to a certain point, as long as it isn't directed against her. She wonders what would happen if she really did decide to report the commander's words. What he's saying to her is a declaration, dictated by his grief but still a declaration, and therefore could legitimately be reported. Would she have the courage to do it? When they ask her for a detailed report on the FOB— and they will ask; after what's happened they'll want to be informed about everything—will she tell them this as well? Who would benefit from it, other than her professional integrity? She'd rather not go head-to-head with her own moral principles over such a question. The commander would be better off saying no more. She tries to interrupt, but there's no way.

"If they're dead it's because they made a mistake. They made a mistake. And I made a mistake sending them there. And you're about to make another one, writing a version in your report that won't even come close to the truth, to the complexity of the truth. Because you, Sammartino, let's be frank, don't know a damn thing about war."

Here they come, the accusations. *There can be no excuses for you.* She'll let that pass as well; then she'll turn her back and walk away.

"And then there's an infinite chain of errors that precedes you and me, but that doesn't absolve us." Ballesio's forehead is perspiring, but he holds his hands strangely still, palms down on the table, like a sphinx. "We're all guilty, Sammartino. All of us. But some of us . . . well, some of us much more so."

Viewed from above, from the perspective of a helicopter, the circle of vehicles down in the valley looks like a magic symbol, a ring to ward off evil spirits. It would be worth photographing it, but nobody does.

For the soldiers trapped in the armored vehicles the sight is less appealing: there's the carcass of the vehicle still burning in some places, the amputated, decapitated, and mangled sheep, and First Corporal Major Torsu with the corpse of Ietri on top of him.

They've arranged the vehicles in a circle, front ends pointed out, to

ensure protection to the injured soldier. A distasteful maneuver—
many of them had to crush the dead sheep with their wheels—as well
as rash, since all or nearly all of them had to go outside the track,
risking other IEDs.

As the minutes go by since the firing stopped, Lieutenant Egitto's
eyes seize on new, less conspicuous details. His window is splattered
with blood. Some of the animals, still wandering around disoriented,
have string tied around their necks. And the dead soldiers' weapons are
miraculously intact.

He'd shouted to Torsu to signal him with his arm every minute, to
show that he's alive and conscious. If he were to stop signaling, then
the lieutenant would have to come up with something, a quick rescue.
Someone would have to risk his life with him. But Torsu raises his
right hand and slaps the ground diligently. He does this seven times
in all.

I'm still alive.

I'm still alive.

I'm still alive.

I'm still alive.

I'm still alive.

I'm still alive.

I'm still alive.

It's enough time for the helicopters to scatter the last of the enemy,
make a couple of safety rounds, and attempt to land once, twice, three
times, without success. The fourth time, a Black Hawk manages to
touch down, so the others gain altitude again and continue to patrol
from above, in large spirals.

Egitto is contacted by radio from who knows where, some outpost
hundreds of miles away, in the middle of another rotten desert where
the radio operators, nevertheless, have cups of steaming coffee sitting
next to their computer keyboards. The voice gives him instructions in
the soothing tone you'd use with a child lost in the outskirts of a city,

a child who no longer recognizes his surroundings: "He's the doctor, right? Okay, it's a pleasure talking to him, everything will be all right, they'll get them out of there, they just have to follow instructions. Stay put for now, wait until they give them the go-ahead, once the area has been swept, you, Lieutenant— You're a lieutenant, right? What's your name, Lieutenant? Well, Lieutenant Egitto, choose some of your men, put them on the alert, and when we give you the signal, you'll go out there together to help the two wounded soldiers. You'll see that—"

"One of the two isn't wounded," Egitto interrupts him. "I think he's . . ." But he can't say it. Could he still be alive after the number of bullets that hit him, after the way he crumpled? No, he couldn't be.

The voice on the radio resumes, phlegmatic: "The wounded man and the deceased, then. When you've done what needs to be done to stabilize the wounded man, you'll load both of them into the helicopter."

Egitto feels a hand grab his arm. He turns to René. "The body stays with us," the marshal says.

"But . . ."

"The men would never forgive me."

Egitto does and doesn't understand René's insistence. Team spirit is something he's always observed as an outsider. Still, it's up to him to make the decision; he's in command. He's not familiar with the protocol in such a situation, but he has the impression that the marshal's request violates a series of rules. Who the hell cares?

"The body stays with us."

"That's not possible, Lieutenant," the voice on the radio replies, somewhat irritated.

"I said it stays with us. Or do you want to come and retrieve it in person?"

For a few seconds the transmitter crackles wordlessly; then the voice says: "Roger that, Lieutenant Egitto. Wait for the signal."

Judging by the way he looks, René's emotional state is not optimal. His lips are ashen, his complexion sallow, his head swaying back and forth. Egitto hands him a bottle of water and orders him to drink, and then Egitto takes a drink himself—it's important to stay hydrated, to not stop doing what's necessary.

It's up to him to plan the next steps as well. He explains to the marshal: "You and I will go out there, along with one of your men, just one. The fewer we are out there, the better for everyone. We'll take care of the bodies that are in one piece. First we'll move the body of that kid. What's his name?"

"Ietri. Roberto Ietri."

"Okay. Then we'll see about stabilizing the wounded one and put him on the helicopter stretcher. Can you stand the sight of blood, Marshal, of wounds and exposed bones?"

"Of course."

"There's nothing to be ashamed of if you don't feel up to it—a lot of people are upset by it, but if that were the case I'd have to call on someone else. I need you conscious."

"I'll hold up."

"Your man's job is to pick up the other pieces." He pauses, his throat dry again. He produces a little saliva in his mouth, swallows. How do you find the right words to say what he has to say? "Tell him to equip himself with some plastic bags."

There it is, then, the moment Lieutenant Egitto will remember more clearly than any other, the image that will first come to mind when he thinks about what happened in the valley, or when he doesn't think about it but is surprised by a vision that flashes before him: the Black Hawk lifting off the ground, kicking up a swirl of dust that engulfs the soldiers.

Torsu is already safely inside the helicopter, his head immobilized in a polyethylene collar, his body tightly secured by elastic bands, and a bottle of saline solution dripping into his forearm—the IV drip that

Egitto himself had put in. He'd swabbed the wound and wrapped it with gauze, made sure the spine hadn't suffered any injury. Torsu gnashed his teeth, kept groaning, "It hurts, Doc, it hurts—please, I can't see anything, Doc," and he'd reassured him, "You'll be okay—we're getting you out of here, you're all right." Strange, the same words that the voice on the radio had said to him a few minutes ago, which he hadn't believed at all. Why should Torsu have greater confidence? He'd managed to remove Torsu's bulletproof vest and examined his body for additional bleeding; there were only scratches. But he hadn't known what to do about the burns on his face, or the flesh torn off his cheek and eyes. He's an orthopedist. He knows how to apply casts. Hundreds of university lectures, training sessions, books, refresher courses—nothing came to his aid, not even if he concentrated; only his hands remembered what had to be done and the order in which to do it. Egitto should have injected him with morphine, but at the time he'd thought he could stand the pain. Maybe the soldier was just in shock. How do you measure the suffering of another human being? He should have given him morphine—he was burned, damn it! But it's too late now. Before disappearing from view, Torsu moves his hand one last time, to say good-bye to his buddies or as a final message for him: I'm still alive, Doc.

Torsu ascends to the heavens; René turns his back and looks out toward the mountaintops. Cederna is stepping around the charred Lince with a garbage bag in his hands, like a mushroom hunter. Shortly before, he'd angrily sent René and Egitto away and insisted on carrying Ietri's body all by himself. He'd picked him up in his arms like a child. (An awkward detail that Egitto would prefer not to think about: Ietri was too long for the stretcher, so they'd had to bend his knees; when the time comes to move him, hours later, he'll have stiffened in that position and to stretch him back out they'll have to shatter his joints. The sound of cold cartilage breaking will remain part and parcel of the memory.) Once in the ambulance, Cederna wiped Ietri's face clean with water from the canteen and spoke softly in his ear. A waste of time, which the lieutenant didn't have the heart to object to.

The valley is silent, the engines turned off. A number of minutes go by like that. Every so often Cederna stoops, picks something up, and puts it in the black bag or discards it.

Then there's Marshal René who, without turning around, says out of the blue: "I've made up my mind, Lieutenant. I'm keeping that baby. I'm not even sure it's my kid, but I'm keeping it. Whatever happens happens. No matter what, it will still be a beautiful baby."

Then there's Cederna in front of a pile of remains and shredded clothing. He covers his face with his hands and begins to sob. "How the fuck am I supposed to recognize them, huh? They're all burned, don't you see? They're all burned—shit!"

Then a sensible and monstrous guideline is established, and Egitto is the one who proposes it: "We'll make sure there's at least one whole part for each pile. It doesn't matter who it belongs to, as long as the piles bear some resemblance to the men. For the bigger guys we'll create bigger piles."

Then all the soldiers get out of the vehicles without asking permission and start helping, and meanwhile the sheep have disappeared into thin air, the living ones and the dead ones, vanished like a collective hallucination.

Then there's Egitto watching the men stare at the four piles. Cederna holds the bags open while the others fill them. When the bags are closed and tied with a knot, he writes the initials on them with a marker. Camporesi's bag is heavier than the others. Egitto could have chatted with him a little yesterday. Maybe it would have changed something, or at least he wouldn't be feeling so shitty now.

Then they travel more road, more desert, like sleepwalkers, and René sobs desperately without losing his grip on the steering wheel. The lieutenant doesn't know what to say to him, so he remains silent.

Then it's night and it's cold and there are a billion remote white stars, competing to see which is the brightest. Shut up in the vehicles, the guys stare out at them bewildered, eyes wide with shock.

People have been coming and going throughout the afternoon. They heard the news on the radio or on television, and since then they've continued to show up at her door, in twos, fours, even whole families. Until Signora Ietri went down to the cellar, spilled the contents of the toolbox on the ground, grabbed the screwdriver, removed the cover of the entry phone, and severed the electrical wires with a pair of scissors. A woman like her, who's lived without a husband for thirteen years, knows how to do certain things: she can change burned-out lightbulbs, even those in hard-to-reach places, and knows how to splice wires and therefore how to cut them as well. She lowered the roll-down shutters throughout the house, but the pests didn't give up; instead they got on the phone. They didn't quit until she answered. A siege. The last one was Colonel Ballesio, who'd seen her son alive two days ago. Was he thin? No, not too thin. Was he happy? He seemed happy, yes. Did you talk to him? I . . . well, not really, but I saw him. Signora Ietri asked all the questions she could think of. She was still unsatisfied by the time she'd finished.

But she's proud of the fact that she didn't shed a single tear. She wants to save her weeping for when she's fit to be seen. She's still a mess; she hasn't even combed her hair. The officers had arrived hat in hand when she wasn't yet ready to go out. Look at that awful hole in her pantyhose! They must have noticed it. She feels like she'll never have the energy to make herself presentable anymore. She'll have to stay like this forever, in her nightgown, with her big toe sticking out of her nylon stocking. Dear God! What did you do to him? She's widowed twice now. But the old pain isn't overshadowed by the new one. The new one climbs on the old one's shoulders and from there looks farther ahead. My poor baby. He was only twenty years old. The nail polish on the big toe is chipped at the edge. What a disgraceful impression she made! What a dishonor for the mother of a soldier. Signora Ietri bursts into uncontrollable sobs. She trails after her son, in the desert.

René's men are depleted and have lost comrades, but they have to keep going. It's the third day and they've delayed so long that they're in danger of running out of water before they reach their destination. Then they'd be in even more serious trouble.

Everyone draws on energies he didn't know he had. This time, the helicopters accompany them from above, like guardian angels, and they don't find any IEDs buried in the ground.

They rejoin the rest of the convoy and pass Buji; at Gund they are again bombarded with mortar fire, but the enemy was waiting for them on the opposite side and the offensive is ineffective. Masiero's unit returns the fire with excessive violence, while the guys of the Third are too drained even to load their rifles. They watch the clash apathetically, as if it didn't concern them. The insurgents are quickly scattered; the column moves out of the valley and finds itself on the endless plain.

Inside the ambulance Ietri's body is covered with a tarp that leaves his ankles hanging out. Abib is not at all put off by the corpse; in fact he placed his things on it while he sorted out his bag of odds and ends. Lieutenant Egitto smells a sickly sweet odor that's growing increasingly strong in the vehicle. Is it possible that the body has already begun to decompose? Logically speaking, decomposition starts the instant a man dies, but not the stench—that shouldn't come until later. It's probably just a macabre power of suggestion.

"Doc?" René says.

"Yeah?"

"Do you think they'll give us a medal of valor? For what we did."

"I don't know. Could be. If you want I can nominate you for a decoration. I saw how you acted out there."

René had refused the tranquilizers Egitto offered him. He, less courageous, had swallowed a double dose of pills along with the bottle of grappa from the K ration. The lacerated reality had reassumed its soft hazy tints.

"If anyone pins a medal to my chest, I'll use it to gouge out both his eyes, Doc."

"Better not to, then."

"Right. Better not to."

They're moving along more quickly now. The cloud of dust that envelops the column is dense again, and for all Egitto can see, they might very well be traveling alone. A drugged lieutenant, a distraught marshal, a cunning Afghan, and a dead man, in the midst of a swirl of yellow haze. "Were you serious about the baby?" he asks.

René pulls a cigarette out of the open pack on the dashboard. He lights it between his grimy fingers. "I want to teach him to ride a motorbike." René is overcome by emotion again; Egitto watches him struggle to contain it. "They killed five of my men. Five out of twenty-seven. Do you realize?" The cigarette ash falls in the space between the two seats. The inside of the ambulance is a pigsty by now. "Maybe it'll be a girl instead. I want so much for it to be a girl."

At three in the afternoon they reach the Ring Road and clear the way for the Afghans' trucks to move on. They're thanked by a trumpeting of horns and that's all the gratitude they'll bring home. Go to hell.

The military convoy continues along the paved road to the base at Delaram. Colonel Ballesio has arranged for the men to be guests of the marines for a few days, enough time to get back in shape.

In a huge hangar, a Latino guy with a pitted face gives the soldiers a briefing in English. Then he distributes forms to fill out and copies of the base's internal regulations. No alcohol. No shouting. No shooting. No photographs. The guys crumple the sheets of paper and stick them in their pockets.

Although the mess hall stays open an hour later than usual just for them and offers delicacies they're no longer used to—an abundance of sugary drinks and cakes inches high topped with multicolored icing— few take advantage of it. For the most part the guys withdraw to the hot showers, in solitude. Lieutenant Egitto does the same. He lets the jet suffuse his face, then rubs himself hard, all over, with his nails. Dry skin, along with grime, slides down his legs, eddies around a couple of times, and finally disappears down the drain.

A helicopter flies Ietri's body out and in exchange drops off a military psychologist, who shakes hands with everyone on the runway and smiles as if he's arrived late at a party. His name is Finizio, he's a lieutenant commander in the navy, and he gives the impression of being too young to delve into anyone's mind, including his own. He has a slightly crooked eye, which gives him a spaced-out look, and he appears flabby to the touch. Although the newcomer is higher in rank, Captain Masiero makes sure his remark reaches his ears loud and clear: "Just what the fuck are we supposed to do with this guy?"

The marines' offices are all occupied, so space for the psychologist to work is set up in a corner of the mess hall, near the hot beverage machines and a power generator that works intermittently, making it necessary to speak loudly when it turns on. The psychologist is available to receive the men starting an hour after meals until an hour before. Going tent to tent, he distributes a handwritten sheet with the sequence he's established. To avoid any chance of misunderstanding, he makes it clear to the soldiers who promptly tear it up before his eyes that the psychological interview is not an optional opportunity but the order of a superior.

Marshal René volunteers to go first. He wants to set a good example, but it's not only that. He needs to pour it all out—he feels like a poisonous gas has spread through him, filling his head, his stomach, even settling under his nails. Three or four different thoughts are haunting him. He'd wanted to confess to an American cleric, and he'd followed him through the base to the entrance of the chapel, but the language barrier and a reluctance of a technical nature—wouldn't it be a further sin to confess to a Protestant minister?—kept him from doing so. A psychologist won't cleanse him of his guilt—that's for sure—but at least it will give him a chance to unburden himself a little.

"I should let you know up front, sir, that I don't believe in these methods," he starts out after shaking Lieutenant Commander Finizio's small hand for the second time.

"Don't worry about it, Marshal. Have a seat. Make yourself at home."

René sits down in the exact center of the bench, back straight and head sternly rigid.

"Get *more* comfortable, Marshal. As if you were alone. If you feel the need to, you can even lie down. You can close your eyes, put your feet up on the table, whatever you like. Whatever comes naturally."

René has no intention of lying down or closing his eyes. He shifts his rear end back, just to show compliance, then resumes his earlier position. Put his feet up on the table in front of a superior—not a chance!

"I'm comfortable like this."

Finizio, who, unlike him, has a proper chair, relaxes against the seat back. "I want you to know that this is a place where you can be free, Marshal. It's just you and me here. No one else. No camera, no microphone. I won't take notes, either now or later. Everything we say will remain confined to this space. So I'd like you to speak openly, without omitting or censoring anything." He joins his small hands, tilting his head and staring at René fixedly. The psychologist remains silent for quite a few seconds.

"Do I have to start?" the marshal finally offers.

"Only if you feel the need."

"Meaning?"

"Meaning that if you feel like saying something, you can say it. But you're not obliged to speak."

What the hell does that mean? Are they supposed to sit there and look at each other? "Couldn't you ask me questions?" René says.

"I'd rather follow your flow without influencing it."

"What if I can't?"

"We can wait."

"In silence?"

"Even in silence. Why not? There's nothing wrong with silence."

They stay that way for another minute. Anxiety rises in the marshal's chest. He mistakes it for the uneasiness of being silent with a man he doesn't know, the sensation of having been caught red-handed at some offense. His brain nervously runs through the topics he could start with. There was something he wanted to say, something that was more important to him than anything else: how he stole Camporesi's place in the ambulance and how a few hours later Camporesi was blown up along with his other men. He can't manage to get that merciless association out of his head, but now that he should talk about it he can't imagine a way to start that won't put him in a bad light with this superior.

Most of all he'd like to make him understand that his intention was good, that there was a *strategic plan* behind his decision and that it wasn't pure selfishness—that is, well, maybe he had been selfish, just a little, like any of them would have been, damn it! Besides, he hadn't slept in two days—have you ever tried not sleeping for two days and driving nonstop on a road full of rocks and bombs with the lives of all those men on your shoulders? No, I bet you've never experienced it, no one has ever experienced it, and he had that gash on his stomach, burning as if the devil himself were blowing on it, burning like a muriatic acid compress. It wasn't selfishness, believe me, not at all; it was just for a few hours and if he'd only known, if he could have predicted what would later happen, he would have gone back to the Lince himself, you can be sure of that, he would have sacrificed himself for Camporesi and he wouldn't be there blabbering in front of him now, he'd be a pile of ash and remains now, or maybe he would have avoided the disaster. Of course he would have avoided it, because he's a good leader who knows what he's doing and he loves his men and would sacrifice himself for them; you can swear to it, I've always been willing to sacrifice myself for the other guy. It's the only thing I know for sure about myself, that's right, but then why am I here, now, why am I still alive, me, why me?

"You see? Have you noticed?" Finizio says.

"Noticed what?"

"Your breathing has changed. You're using your diaphragm—it's going much better."

René isn't aware of any difference in his breathing. Instead, he has the feeling that his neck is shrinking, that his head is slowly sinking into his chest.

"Marshal, are you all right? You're a little pale. Would you like some water?"

"No. No, thank you. No water."

The longer he waits to say something, the more twisted his thoughts become. Now he feels that the hand that's crushing him has to do with Finizio, that he's the one controlling it, like a transparent extension of himself. The man is stealing his oxygen, sucking it all up for himself. And he won't stop staring at him; maybe he's trying to hypnotize him. René ducks his head to avoid his gaze. "Lieutenant, couldn't you ask me some questions? It would help me."

The psychologist smiles again, a forced smile with that irritating condescension. "We're doing just fine," he says.

"Just fine? But we haven't even begun!"

Finizio opens his arms. Some of his gestures really make him seem like a priest. Someone once said to René, "You should talk to the chaplain about it." It seems like such a long time ago.

"I'm expecting a baby." Clearly it was his gut that expelled air in the form of words without him suggesting it; it was his diaphragm.

The psychologist nods, his smile firmly in place. Is it René's imagination or did he already know what he was about to say?

"That's good news. When's the baby due?"

Due? He doesn't know. He hasn't yet done the calculation. "In six months," he throws out. "More or less."

"Good. You'll be back in time, then."

"Yeah."

They fall silent again.

"I hope it's a girl," René adds.

"Why is that?"

"Because girls . . . well, they don't get themselves in certain situations."

"Are you alluding to the accident the other morning?"

René clenches his fists. "No. I mean, maybe."

He's not getting any benefit from the interview, only renewed frustration. The psychologist addresses him in an excessively even tone of voice. He seems to want to accuse him of something. And when he remains silent, like now, it's even worse. The idea of offering moral support is a trap, probably. But what is he suspected of? Treason? Abuse of power? Homicide? He won't fall for it.

"Marshal, are you familiar with the term 'post-traumatic stress syndrome'?"

"Yes, they talked about it in the training course."

"And do you think post-traumatic stress may have something to do with you, at this moment?"

"No."

"Are you sure?"

"Yes, I told you. I don't have tremors or hallucinations. Last night I slept and I didn't have nightmares."

"So you're not experiencing a phase of post-traumatic stress."

"Tremors, hallucinations, nightmares. Those are the symptoms I remember."

"Are they the only symptoms?"

"Yes. That's what they taught us in the course. And I don't have them."

"So what did you dream about instead, Marshal?"

"I never dream, sir."

"Never?"

"Never."

Cederna, when his turn comes, is even less cooperative. His companions' long faces have put him in a bad mood; he thinks it's ridiculous for them to be competing to see who can display the most grief over what happened. They should have thought of it before. It's sad, in fact, goddamned sad, and he's hurting too, but he certainly has no intention of showing it. Besides they're at war—what did they think, that people don't die in war? He's a realist and sometimes reality is hard to face, because existence is raw and it bites you, but if you want to be smart, you have to keep your eyes wide open, at all times. Instead they're making him meet with a psychologist. A navy guy, besides. Of all the bullshit the army has subjected him to, this is undoubtedly the worst.

". . . so I'd like you to speak freely, without omitting or censoring anything." Finizio completes his introduction and sits there waiting, but Cederna is quick to throw him a curve.

"With all due respect, Lieutenant, there's nothing I want to talk to you about."

"Forget the formalities, Cederna. In fact, let's do this. From this moment on I am no longer a captain. Look, I'll even take off my stripes. Now I'm just Andrea. And you? May I call you Francesco?"

"Cederna is fine, Lieutenant. Senior Corporal Major Cederna is even better. Or soldier, if you're more comfortable with that. Francesco is only for my friends."

"And you think I'm not a friend?"

"I think it's unlikely I would have a friend like you, Lieutenant."

The psychologist flinches. Cederna has to contain a grin of satisfaction. He has him right where he wants him.

"And why is that?"

He shrugs. "I choose my friends by instinct. I sniff them out. I'm a wolf—didn't they tell you?"

"No, they didn't tell me. And what did you sniff in me?"

"No censoring?"

"Like I said."

"The stench of compromise. And piss."

"Piss? Really?"

"You're pissing your pants being here, Lieutenant. You'd rather be nice and comfortable behind a desk, far away from these god-awful places. Instead look where they've sent you."

Finizio nods. Cederna enjoys seeing him disconcerted.

"That's interesting. I'll give it some thought. Do you want to tell me about some god-awful place I haven't yet seen, then? Maybe the valley you came through."

"Why should I?"

"Because I haven't been there."

"Do a search on Google. Just enter the name. Try 'fucking hell.' That way you can get a taste of it from behind your desk."

"I'd rather you told me about it."

"I don't feel like it."

"Okay, Cederna. I understand how difficult it is to communicate at this time. To externalize emotions other than anger. It's all still very raw and grief silences us. You're afraid that if you open the floodgate a river of pain will pour out that you won't be able to stand, but I'm here to help you."

"Grief doesn't shut me up in the least. I can talk as much as I want. Blah blah blah blah. See? Even more, blah blah blah blah. I just have nothing to say to *you*, Mr. Lieutenant Commander." Now the psychologist will dismiss him and this idiocy, too, will be over. Let him go ahead and write his venomous report afterward. Cederna has a résumé that would make any commission's eyes pop. To get into the special forces, they certainly won't be looking at that psychological shit.

Finizio looks up, his expression less conciliatory. "I see that you were the one who gathered up your friends," he says point-blank. "It must have been a very painful task."

"Who said they were my friends?"

"They weren't allowed to call you Francesco either?"

"It's none of your business what they called me."

"Did they smell of piss too?"

"Shut your mouth!"

Finizio consults a folder. "I think they were your friends. One in particular. I must have noted his name somewhere . . . Here it is. Corporal Roberto Ietri. You two were—"

"Leave him out of it."

"It says here that you—"

"I TOLD YOU TO SHUT UP, ASSHOLE!"

The psychologist remains expressionless. "Do you want to talk about this one? About Corporal Ietri?"

The blood is pounding in his ears. It's the first time Cederna has let himself think about Ietri since he whispered to his corpse. His friend's forehead had already been cold when he touched it, the shape of the sideburns still visible, though somewhat botched; Ietri wasn't practiced enough to keep them perfectly trimmed. He hadn't had time to learn.

Without realizing it Cederna stands up. Now his massive bulk is looming over the navy officer. "Can I tell you what's really going through my head, Lieutenant?"

"Please do."

"What's going through my head is that you are a disgusting piece of shit. You come here and tell me that grief silences us. *Us* who? You weren't there. You were somewhere else. On one of those ships, reading your fucking psychology manuals. I know guys like you, *Lieutenant Commander*, you hear? The ones who've gone to university. You think you know everything. But you don't know squat. NOT A THING! You like to get into other people's heads, don't you? Stir up the shit. You'd enjoy hearing me tell you all about my private affairs. You'd like that, right? You'd be all aroused there under the table. Ugly cross-eyed fucking pervert. Don't you ever dare mention Corporal Ietri in front of me again, you hear me? He was a real man. You knocked on the wrong door, Mr. *Psychologist*. There are plenty of faggots here—go look for them outside. Unfortunately for you, I'm not one of them. I don't talk about my goddamn business with just anybody. This interview is over."

When he leaves the mess hall, slamming the door behind him, he feels like beating someone up, banging heads, bashing, shooting, killing. Instead he rushes over to the tavern, where he orders the closest thing to an alcoholic drink—a can of Red Bull. It's not enough to rinse out his mind. Ietri plunks himself back in his head again, dead and then alive. Was he really a friend? He certainly was the nearest thing to a friend he'd found in a long time. As an adult, you no longer have any real friends, that's the awful truth. You leave the best years behind and you settle for scraps. Ietri was better than scraps, though. What the hell is happening to him? He's becoming a crybaby. The *verginella* is gone. That's it, finished. It's time to face reality, toughen up.

As he tries unsuccessfully to calm down, he listens to a conversation between two marines. He doesn't understand all the words, but he hears them mention a masseuse who practices at the base. For Cederna, a masseuse in a military camp means only one thing, and in fact the marines are enthusiastic as they talk about her, making unmistakable gestures with their hands. That's just what he needs to get rid of all the rage in his body: sex. Then for sure he'd be able to wipe it all out of his head: the bloody sheep, Ietri's hair matted with sand, the ambush, Agnese treating him like a loser, and that psychologist's face asking to be smacked. He'd sweep it all away.

He interrupts the soldiers and asks them how to find the woman.

He goes there after supper. The directions lead him to a set of sheet metal buildings near the prison, in an area off the beaten track. A sign that says "Wellness Center" is Scotch-taped to the door. The hours of operation aren't listed.

Cederna knocks, but no one answers. He pushes the door open. A woman sprawled out in a plastic chair is smoking a cigarette. The white apron she's wearing over her fleece sweatshirt makes her look like a cook. Her facial features are neither Western nor Asian. Under the pullover her arms must be fleshy and flabby.

"Massage?" Cederna asks.

The woman nods behind the pall of smoke. She gestures to him to wait. Then she gets up, stubs the cigarette out in an overflowing ashtray, and moves aside a curtain dividing the room into two parts. On the other side there's a cot with folded towels on it, and a bowl of water on the floor with four flower petals floating on the surface.

"Ten dollars for thirty minutes," she says in English.

"Huh?"

"Ten dollars. Thirty minutes." The woman enunciates clearly.

Cederna is unfamiliar with the hourly rates for a masseuse and has only a vague idea of those of prostitutes, but it seems like highway robbery to him. Ten dollars! Nothing at the military bases is that outrageously expensive. But he has a desperate desire to have her hands on him. "Okay," he says, and starts for the cot.

The woman stops him. "First you pay."

Greedy bitch! Cederna flips through his wallet. He shows the woman a bill. "Five euros. Like ten dollars."

She shakes her head sternly. "Ten dollars, ten euros."

"Okay, okay. Fuck." He slaps a creased ten-euro bill in her hand, as if she were stealing from him.

The woman doesn't turn a hair. She invites him to lie down. "Undress," she orders him.

"What?"

"Undress, you. You naked," she explains by gesturing, then pulls the curtain and leaves him to himself.

It's just the kind of place where what he needs to happen happens. He holds a towel up against the light—it's very threadbare in some spots, almost see-through—and he brings it to his face to sniff it. He feels a vague sense of uneasiness. If Ietri were still alive they would have come here together. For the corporal it would have been just the right time; he could have dumped that nickname, *verginella*. Or maybe not. Cederna would have gone on calling him that even afterward. They would have had a few drinks together and he would have grilled him for details. He feels dizzy; he has to lean on the cot to keep from falling over. Why does his mind keep going back to him? He has no intention of saddling himself with a ghost. He has to banish it right now.

He unbuckles his belt. He undresses quickly, though he takes the trouble to fold his clothes. He has to think about himself; there's no other way to get ahead in life. He's paid ten euros and he might as well get everything he can for it. He strips off his underwear as well. He stands there naked, unsure what to do. Maybe he wasn't supposed to undress completely—the masseuse wasn't clear about the underwear. Suddenly he feels embarrassed. He puts his boxers back on and lies down on the cot like that, but immediately has second thoughts. He hops down, pulls them back off, and stretches out on his stomach again, with the towel over his butt.

"Ready?" the voice on the other side asks.

The massage starts at the extremities. Cederna is surprised by the woman's strength. She pokes her fingers one by one into the tight spaces between his toes and then tugs as if wanting to yank his bones out. With her thumb she presses on a point at the center of the sole, causing a shiver to spread out and race up to his head. Then she moves on to the calves. Her palms, slick with scented oil, slide over Cederna's muscles.

He stares at the floating rose petals, motionless in the bowl.

From the thighs, she ventures under the worn towel and strokes his buttocks. On the way down, her fingertips graze his groin, then pull back right away, leaving him unsatisfied. His body is full of tension that he's having trouble letting go of.

Don't think, don't think. Stop it. Don't think.

The woman kneads his back; it hurts but he grits his teeth. She works on the cramped nerves at length, torturing them with her thumbs. When she sticks an elbow between his shoulder blades, Cederna lets out a groan and shrugs her off.

"Massage too strong?" she asks, not at all frightened.

His pride prevents him from telling the truth. "No, not too strong. Keep going."

It relieves the pressure, in any case. Cederna likes it when she gets to the back of his neck and his scalp. He struggles not to fall asleep, until the woman brusquely orders him to turn over on his back, then starts again. Back of the foot. Ankles. Quadriceps. Now she's more perfunctory. When she's done with his legs she gets rid of the towel, tossing it aside. Cederna's prodigious erection is right under her nose, in plain sight.

There. Now we're getting somewhere.

He opens his eyes for a moment, takes a peek at the woman's face. She doesn't seem unsettled and he feels a little affronted by this. She massages his abdomen distractedly.

Cederna has never had sex with a foreign woman. He could easily pick up an illness from someone like her—AIDS, gonorrhea, or something hideous and unknown, one of those infections that disfigure the genitals. Never mind; he'll worry about it later. He'll wash himself off thoroughly. Right now he just wants to get rid of Ietri's ashen face that has suddenly appeared before him.

The woman has turned off the neon ceiling light and in its place switched on a lamp with a red-tinted bulb. The squalor of the small room is softened, though not entirely. As she keeps prodding around his groin, teasing him, a dark infinite sadness overcomes the senior corporal major. He suddenly feels a longing for Agnese, for Ietri, and for something indistinct and his alone, like a secret he knew a long time ago and has forgotten.

"Baby massage?"

"Huh?"

"You want a massage for your baby?"

Cederna flounders in his sadness. The masseuse explains, making the same gesture used by the marines. Seen from below, in the reddish light, she's not very attractive. It doesn't matter. Cederna tries to pull her to him by the arm. She twists free, again displaying her strength. "No! No sex!" she shrieks. "Only massage."

Bewildered, he lets go. "No sex? But I gave you ten euros!"

"No sex," the woman insists and takes a step back, folding her arms.

Cederna punches the side of the cot with his fist.

"Baby massage? Yes or no?"

He gives in. Okay, baby massage, whatever. As long as it takes him away from where he is. He lets his arms drop along the sides.

"You want music?" the woman asks.

"No. Please. No music."

At the American base, garbage of all kinds has piled up alongside the wooden walkways and in the drainage ditches. A population of feral cats moves cautiously through the trash; occasionally the cats stop, spot something, then pounce forward. René doesn't see even a single rat, but clearly they're around, and in abundance.

He enters the phone center, which compared to the makeshift arrangement at the FOB looks like the command center of a space agency. He searches his phone directory for Rosanna's number and dials it without giving himself time to hesitate any further—he's already wavered too long. The phone rings four times, but finally she picks up.

"It's me. René."

"Oh, my God."

The lag in the signal allows time for one last, weak-willed uncertainty. Is it really what he wants? He's about to tie himself down to a woman he barely knows, a woman who's much older than he is; he made love with her a handful of times and they watched old movies together. He's setting himself up for serious consequences, difficulties he can't even imagine, unhappiness maybe. The conflicting pros and cons rise up in his mind again, but this time René rejects them. He knows what the right thing to do is. He has a clear picture of himself and the child lying on a green stretch of grass and, at the end of the day, that's the best fantasy he's come close to in a long time.

"How are you? Are you wounded?"

"No. No, I'm fine."

"I heard all about it on the news. They mentioned your name. What a horror, René. What a terrible atrocity. Those poor boys."

"Rosanna, listen to me. I had a lot of doubts, I thought and thought about it. I didn't think I could do it, that you were— Well, we barely know each other, right? And we have a lot of differences. But life here has opened my eyes. God chose for me not to die. He decided that I should look after our baby, so he can grow up with a father. I thought I still had too much to do for myself and instead there's nothing more I have to do for me—it doesn't matter to me. I want the baby. I'm ready. I am, believe me."

"René, listen . . ."

"I've already thought of everything. Last night I sat on the cot with the flashlight in my mouth and I took notes, I wrote up a list. There are a lot of things to arrange, but we'll make it. You can move in with me—the house isn't huge, but it's big enough. I'll have to clear out my study, but there's just a bunch of crap in there. It's not even a real study, I just call it that. I can throw everything out and make room. I'll be a good father, Rosanna, I swear to you. I've been a bad leader. I let five of my men die, but I'll make it up, I'll be a perfect father. I'll keep him with me always. I'll teach him to ride a bike and play soccer and . . . everything. Even if it's a girl. I'd like so much for it to be a girl. Have they told you yet? Is it a boy or a girl, Rosanna? Tell me, please—I want to know."

He hears her breathing on the other end. She's crying. He wishes she were there with him; he'd hold her close and wipe her tears. It's right for her to cry, because this is their tragic and joyous moment, the beginning of their life together and many years from now they will remember it.

"You're a fool, René."

"No, Rosanna. I'll do everything right, I swear. The two of us . . . we'll find a way."

"Shut up! Don't you get it?"

"What?"

"It's too late now."

René's mouth is dry. He's talked a lot and is in a rush. The Americans' voices are loud—they're shouting into the phones, barking; they're not very considerate. The racket is making his head spin. "What did you do?" René says.

"It's too late."

"Rosanna, what the fuck did you do?"

The sheep hurtle down the slope and falter on their glabrous hooves, their faces contracted in terror. Something is wrong, there's no shepherd. They want to screw us. Fire, fire, fire with everything you've got. The truck explodes with a roar that leaves their ears ringing. They must be ready, they must be on their guard. The baby isn't yet a baby, it's a mosquito. They suck it out with a tube and in five minutes it's all over.

"Good-bye, René," Rosanna says. "Take care of yourself."

The masseuse's name is Oxana; she's thirty-eight years old, but she looks older. She comes from Turkmenistan, which in Cederna's imagination is just another abominable place somewhere in the north, another place not worth knowing. There's not much more she'll allow him to know: when the soldier tries to start a conversation, the woman cuts him short, pointing to the cot, or if they've finished, the door. She answers his questions in monosyllables, and never asks him anything about himself. To get back at her, Cederna forces her to reduce the time she spends on the massage, grabbing her hand immediately and placing it where he wants it. She's not happy about it; the preliminaries allow her to feel less disgust for herself—Cederna is not so insensitive as to not realize it. His way, everything is over in a few minutes. Then he finds himself out the door again, at loose ends there at the U.S. base, having to deal with a tension that instead of abating keeps growing and growing. In the time it takes him to reach the tent where his companions continue to remain silent and remorseful, he's horny again. He craves Oxana. He can't think of anything else.

In a single day he's gone to the masseuse five times. The hand job is demeaning, it doesn't fully satisfy him, but what else can he do? She shoves him away if he tries to get more. When he happens to find the door at the compound locked, he kicks and punches it. "Come out of there!" he yells. He walks around the base aimlessly and goes back less than half an hour later. She's there. He beleaguers her with questions—can he possibly be jealous of a prostitute? She'd simply gone out to go to the toilet. He struggles to calm down.

Before the third evening in Delaram he runs out of money. He tries to persuade Oxana to give him a free session. She won't even let him get near the cot. Cederna hurls a load of insults at her. It doesn't do any good.

He goes back to the tent even more frantic. He asks Di Salvo to lend him some money. He's the best friend he has left.

"I wouldn't even lend you a dime, you asshole."

"Please."

"Beat it, Cederna. Go beg from someone else."

He turns to Pecone, to Rovere, to Passalacqua, even to Abib. They all tell him they don't have any money or just flatly say no, with a rudeness he doesn't feel he deserves. Finally he tries Zampieri.

"What do you need it for?"

"I can't tell you."

Zampieri's eyes are lined with dark circles. "I wouldn't give it to you anyway," she says.

"It's an emergency."

"No. It's not. We've already had an emergency. Now there's no emergency anymore."

"Come on, Zampa, help me out."

"Do you know how many hours it's been since I've slept? Eighty-four. I counted them. Eighty-four. I don't think I'll ever be able to sleep again."

He walks away. He hasn't scraped together even one euro. He doesn't know what he'll do if he doesn't come up with the money.

Before supper he's back in front of Oxana's compound. He'll give her something in exchange. He has a very nice knife—it's worth much more than ten euros. A knife with a rubber handle and antireflective coating on the blade. It will cost him to part with it, but he'll buy another one just like it back in Italy.

He bursts into the small room and this time she's on the other side of the curtain with someone. She chases him out, swearing at him in her own language. Cederna sits outside on the ground. It grows dark as he imagines what the woman is doing with the other soldier. He's sure she must allow him to go further, of course, because he's an American. When the man comes out, he shines his flashlight on him briefly. A black guy. Oxana has just been with a black man! He rushes in like a fury, slamming the door behind him. He wants to catch her still half naked. Instead Oxana is wearing her usual apron and is placing clean towels on the cot.

"Were you with that guy?"

She gives him a scornful look. She shrugs. She doesn't understand.

"Tell me. Do you perform these little services for blacks too?"

"Do you have the money?" she asks him, not turning around.

"No," Cederna says.

"No money, no massage."

She's ready to send him away again. He has to calm down. Cederna pulls the knife out of his belt. "I have this," he says.

Oxana jumps back. She presses against the wall. "Put it away!" she cries. She tries to reach out a hand to the drawer of a wheeled cart.

She's misunderstood him. Cederna didn't mean to hurt her. He bursts out laughing. "See how fast you've changed your tune now?"

"Put it away!" the woman repeats.

What does she take him for? A badass? "Okay," Cederna says. "If that's what you think, then let's have some fun."

He moves close and rolls the cart away with his foot. She doesn't take her eyes off the black blade.

Cederna brandishes the knife in his hand (he can twirl it 360 degrees between his fingers, one of the many little tricks that make him the envy of a lot of people). "Oh oh oh," he says. "No money, no massage? And that guy who was here before, did he have money?"

Oxana huddles on the floor. "Please," she begs.

It's at this point that Cederna fully realizes the possibility that is being offered to him by the six-and-a-half-inch blackened steel blade.

His money has run out. Oxana is alone. Who's going to go and report it? Officially she doesn't exist—there are no prostitutes inside a military base. And in a few hours he'll climb aboard a helicopter and return to the FOB. Even if the masseuse enjoyed internal protection, which seems likely, her buddies wouldn't have time to get organized and come looking for him.

Only a few seconds go by between reflection and action. The army trained him to react quickly.

He helps her get up, gently. He pushes her toward the cot, makes her turn her back. Oxana obeys the knife point as if it were a magic wand. She's strong, but not strong enough to prevent him from securing both her hands with his left. He uses his right hand to undress her and undress himself, the bare minimum, then he grabs the knife that he's been clenching in his teeth and places it under her chin. He sinks it into the flesh of her neck a little, without cutting her. He doesn't want to hurt her.

You really are a savage, Francesco Cederna.

I'm a wolf—didn't they tell you?

Oxana is no longer screaming; her moans might also be cries of encouragement. She stiffens when he bites her shoulder and Cederna feels driven to do it again. He wants to rip her to shreds, chew her up. He's drooling on her neck, her hair. There, the thoughts are fading, finally. The ghosts are evaporating. That's all he needed; it wasn't much. He's a soldier; he knows how to get what's denied him.

Afterward, he won't remember much. Only his last look at the masseuse before he flees the compound: the pullover rolled halfway up her back, the apron on the ground, slacks and panties scrunched up around her ankles, and a pair of shapely legs, pale in the reddish light. One of them is shaken by a slight tremor. Cederna, sated, lumbering, disbelieving, charges out, swallowed up by the night.

Giulia Zampieri has been wandering through the American base for hours, in a darkness that unlike the absolute darkness of the FOB is interrupted by neon lights over the entrances to the barracks. Her mind is blank, as if someone had sprayed it down with a hose. She turns a corner behind a tent and comes across a makeshift swing: a truck tire hanging by two chains from a metal tripod. What are the marines doing with a swing? It sounds like some kind of a joke: What does an American soldier do on a swing? The only thing he can do, Zampieri thinks: He swings.

She sits on the rubber ring and leans back into the opening. She gives a push with her legs. The chain screeches. She touches the ground again with her toes, then begins moving the way she was taught a century ago, in a previous life: bend and stretch, bend and stretch . . . She flexes her torso to accelerate the swinging. The swing lulls her, back and forth in the warm, dark, stagnant air.

By the time the soldiers return to FOB Ice, the weather has changed. It's been raining nonstop for three days, a fine, debilitating rain. In a very short time the region reaches the average annual precipitation level, then doubles it, triples it. The dust on the ground becomes muddy sludge, then liquefies completely. Wherever there's a slope, however slight, the slime oozes down. The rivulets converge into a torrent that runs through the base from north to south and spills out the main entrance. One by one, weak points in the tents' impermeability begin to appear and the infinite imprecisions with which they were erected become evident. The men are forced to dig ditches around each perimeter, patch holes, spread tarps. For them it's a cruel, cynical lesson on how life goes on: some have died, but those who've survived have to roll up their sleeves, make sure they stay dry.

Lieutenant Egitto placed a bucket under a tear in the roof. The drops plunk down at regular intervals, like the ticking of a clock. He's also spread some rags on the ground, at the entrance, so the soldiers can scrape their boots when they come in. Only a few show up, however. A new sense of reserve has spread through the base in the aftermath of the mission: who has the nerve to seek treatment for conjunctivitis, the flu, or a harmless hernia when five companions died under enemy fire and another is virtually out of commission? Egitto himself takes part in that unprecedented version of personal neglect. He's stopped shaving, he hardly eats, and he washes sparingly, even his teeth.

Irene is gone. He found a note from her rolled up inside one of the bottles of antidepressants, which she replaced with a handful of jelly beans. An affectionate gesture, though also meant to chide. The note simply has her initials and phone number, no greetings or comments. Why did she leave her number? And what is he supposed to do with it? He's put it away among his personal effects, certain that he won't use it.

He doesn't feel sad, either about her departure or—on a much more serious level—about the men's deaths. Maybe it's the pills that hold him back, or else he's no longer capable of feeling. Though the second hypothesis troubles him, the first is not much consolation. He's experiencing something he already knew: that all grief, suffering, and compassion toward other human beings can be reduced to pure biochemistry—hormones and neurotransmitters, inhibited or released. When he realizes this, what he finds himself feeling, unexpectedly, is indignation.

Since he's unable to come up with anything better, he decides he'll force himself to do it: it will be his own personal form of atonement for the horrors he witnessed and took part in. Abruptly, one Friday night, he stops taking the medication. He unscrews the cap and empties the powdery contents in the trash basket. In its place he chews a raspberry jelly bean. He suspends the treatment cold turkey after eight months, violating the recommendations of the pharmaceutical company with surreptitious glee.

He expects some kind of aftereffect as a result of not taking the drug, but for days nothing happens, if you don't count insomnia and a few brief hallucinatory episodes. His mood is a level plain. The grief remains frozen, someplace else. The lieutenant starts to doubt it exists at all. He remains unmoved during the funeral service performed in the mess hall by a visiting chaplain. He's unmoved when he talks—mumbles—on the phone with First Corporal Major Torsu, in Italy, where he's about to undergo his third maxillofacial reconstructive surgery. He's unmoved by the fragile, absent sound of Nini's voice, or when the first sun in days breaks through the veil of clouds and restores the mountain to its golden splendor.

After meals he still goes to talk with Ballesio. At first the colonel seems uncertain as to what attitude to adopt with respect to the general mourning. Then, evidently, he decides it's best to follow his instinct—that is, carry on as if nothing has happened. He has his own way of trying to raise Egitto's spirits, which is not very effective. More and more often they remain silent, Ballesio concentrating on the pipe he's recently taken up, Egitto watching the smoke rings formed by the colonel's lips, which dissolve as they float upward.

Egitto's body is first to react. He gets a fever, a high one: at night it hovers around 104 degrees. His body temperature hasn't risen that high since he was a child, when Ernesto would examine him, listening through his stethoscope, his mouth and nose well protected by a mask. Huddled in his sleeping bag, Egitto perspires profusely, racked by shivers. He stays in bed for two days in a row, but doesn't ask for help. He has them bring him a basin of water, enough so he doesn't have to leave the tent. Ballesio comes to see him once, but he's too sick to remember, afterward, what he said to him and what he replied. All he remembers is that the colonel didn't stop talking and waving his arms around as he loomed over him with that big round moon face of his.

Then, as suddenly as it had come, the fever goes away, leaving him dreamy and strangely energetic, determined about an action that he hasn't yet begun and isn't even aware of. Egitto feels like walking, moving; he treks from one end of the base to the other several times a day. If only he could leave the FOB, he'd set off and run for miles without tiring.

The only available means to get away is the phone, however. After ten days of putting it off, he decides to dial Marianna's number.

"I've written you eight e-mails—*eight* of them. I called every damned ministry office to find you and you didn't *bother* to return my

call. Do you have any idea how *upset* I was? It was *awful*. Didn't you
think about how worried I'd be?"

"I'm sorry," Egitto says, but the apology is automatic.

"I hope they'll send you home now. *Right away*."

"The tour lasts another four months."

"Yes, but you've suffered a *trauma*."

"Like a lot of others here."

Marianna exhales loudly. "I don't *feel like* having this discussion
with you anymore. I'm . . . worn-out. Have you called Nini, at least?"

It's the first time in many years that Marianna has expressed interest in their mother, concerned about the fact that Nini might also be
worried about him. Egitto is astounded.

Obviously he's mistaken.

"Have you spoken to her about the house?" his sister adds.

"No."

"Alessandro, I asked you to please take care of it. This is the right
time to sell—in fact, we're *already* late. With the crisis in the real estate market, that place is depreciating every day."

Only now does he get it: the stopper that's bottling up his emotions
and is now pushed out by pressure is not due to compassion or pity; it's
not due to grief. It's due to pure anger, and it erupts from his stomach,
flooding his spinal cord and spreading through the nerves to their
peripheral endings.

"You could have spoken to her," Egitto says.

"Are you crazy, Alessandro? I *don't speak* to her."

"You're the one who's interested in selling the house. You could
have spoken to her."

"Look, what you've been through can't have been pleasant. I realize
that. But that doesn't give you the right to take it out on me."

"I love that house."

"You *don't love* that house. *We* don't love that house, remember?
Remember how it was to live there?"

"It was all a long time ago."

"That doesn't change *any*thing, Alessandro. Not a thing. They didn't even come to my wedding. They didn't give a damn."

"You've never asked me what this place is like."

"What are you talking about?"

"You've never asked me what it's like. Here."

"I think I can imagine what Afghanistan is like."

"No, you can't. You can't imagine it. There's a huge mountain, without a single tree or a tuft of grass. Right now the summit is covered with snow and the boundary between the snow and the rock is sharp, like you wouldn't believe. And there are other mountains, much more distant. At sunset each of them takes on a different nuance—they seem like theater curtains."

"Alessandro, you're not well."

"It's a magnificent place." The scaly patches on his skin are throbbing in unison, they're about to burst. Perhaps there's new skin underneath, an intact epidermis. Or maybe there's only bloody, gory flesh. "And another thing, Marianna. On your wedding day, as we walked down the aisle, we weren't invincible. We just told ourselves we were. We told ourselves it was just fine that way, better even, that everyone would see that we were . . . free and independent. But it wasn't true. Only two crazy people believed it. Everyone else felt sorry for us."

Marianna is silent now, as the lieutenant experiences the sour taste of having gone too far, crossing a line he hadn't even dared consider before.

"Talk to you soon, Marianna," he says.

He has time to make out his sister's final, muffled protest: "So you're on her side now?" A stab in the back. There's nothing he can do about it. He hangs up.

No, he's not on Nini's side. He doesn't know whose side he's on anymore.

Part Three

M E N

The Innocent Life of Nutrias

In the final days Ernesto would leave the house in the late afternoon to take the same invariable walk along the riverbank. He bundled up more than necessary, layering woolen sweaters and pullovers, as if to restore volume to a body that was losing it. He walked with his gaze turned upward, his expression skeptical, until he came to the bend where the waters widened into a stagnant cove. There he would sit on a lacquered metal bench not far from the river's edge. He would catch his breath, measuring his jugular heart rate with the help of a wristwatch. When the levels returned to normal, he took a paper bag out of his pocket with some dry bread, which he crumbled slowly between his fingers, clearing his throat. Sometimes, instead of bread, he brought apple slices.

The nutrias he fed were filthy animals: a kind of large rat with a rheumy snout, long white whiskers, and glittering wet fur. They lived between the backwater and the muddy shore, piled on top of one another. "You see?" he said to me one day. "They're like children. Ready to step over each other for a little something to eat. They're so innocent. And needy. Shameful opportunists."

As the rodents crowded around the food, Ernesto spoke about Marianna, about when she was a little girl. He repeated the same secret word games I'd heard dozens of times, somewhat worn-out by now in the telling. He couldn't manage to reconcile them with the retaliation his daughter had inflicted on him; maybe he wasn't even able to recognize it as such. Retaliation for what? he would have asked. But he'd never been very inclined to question the matter. He preferred to settle for a collection of fantasies. As for the daughter who still existed somewhere, he didn't mention her. As the crow flies she must not have been too far away from the nutrias' pond, but she was certainly light-years away from his heart. In retrospect, the astounding transformation in the last days I spent with my father was precisely that: I had always believed he didn't have a heart. Only now was I able to see that it was hopelessly broken.

When his condition suddenly worsened, I took three weeks' leave and moved home. I was Nini and Ernesto's guest, a guest in the room where I'd grown up. Lying on the bed, I could see the door to Marianna's room, the same door I'd stared at countless times trying to guess what was happening on the other side, full of apprehension when she'd lock herself in with her friends on afternoons when our parents weren't home.

I had my own personal set of towels and a toothbrush in my toiletry kit. Each time, after using them, I put them back in my suitcase. I didn't feel like leaving something that belonged to me in the bathroom or anywhere else. Every surface of every piece of furniture was so imbued with the past that it would certainly have swallowed my item up instantly, transporting it to another temporal dimension, no longer reachable. At night, when I studied my face in the mirror, my gaze fell on the giraffe and elephant decals. *Here's my toothpaste, here's my brush, I won't hurry, I won't rush. Working hard to keep teeth clean, front and back and in between.* I recited their nursery rhymes silently to myself, feeling neither rancor nor nostalgia.

Nini's discreet, inflexible order still governed the apartment. A few weeks later, on the very day my father died, she would leave with a small suitcase, move in with her sister (widowed before her), and never return. Only then would I realize how slight her attachment had been to the house where we'd all lived together. If she'd ever really loved it, at some point she'd stopped, and none of us had noticed it. I might have picked up some signals, might have noticed, for example, that household chores tired her out more and more (she'd given in and hired a foreign woman who helped out every other day, violating three or four articles of her Fundamental Charter of Sobriety at once), but it had been some time since I paid attention to Nini's decline.

After Marianna's mutiny she'd begun failing, day after day, in mind and body. She still reacted to stimuli as you'd expect she would or, more precisely, as you'd expect an automaton resembling a small, sixty-year-old woman would do. When she smiled, rarely, her smile was vacant and reminded me that I, in any case, would never be sufficient motivation to rekindle joy in her. Not even Ernesto could anymore; Nini witnessed the rapid course of his illness as if it were the manifestation of a divine retribution that concerned them both. At one time she would have voiced that unspoken feeling with words like: "Well, we *certainly* deserved this!"

Mornings were taken up by Ernesto's hospital visits and by the vast, daunting bureaucracy that went with them. He had worked in the same hospital for thirty-one years, in a ward scarcely forty yards and two flights of stairs away from the urology department where he was now being treated. He'd been a step away from being appointed department head, yet he enjoyed few privileges. He waited his turn like any other patient, on the row of blue plastic chairs in the corridor, fidgety, talking nonstop. At that time he was obsessed with chemical solvents found in the pigments used to paint the walls of that hallway and others, with electromagnetic pollution, and with the abundance of phthaleins in the plastic packaging of the hospital meals, which, in fact, caused prostate cancer. He estimated having ingested more than eight thousand pounds of contaminated food. As if knowing it now made any difference.

From time to time a younger colleague recognized him and would stop to exchange a few words. Ernesto took advantage of it to corner the doctor and criticize the treatment he was being subjected to. He expounded on alternative therapies he'd come up with overnight, citing exotic and somewhat dubious sources from recent oncological literature. He could never trust a specialist as much as he did himself and his own insights, not even in an area that was not within his province. In those impromptu medical lessons, which often strayed into general didactics, he was still persuasive enough often to win me to his side. But clearly he had a hold over me by then and that's all there was to it. The man in the white coat would nod impatiently, only seemingly caught up. And if he were to pass by again in the course of the day, he wouldn't stop a second time.

"Life doesn't give back much," I said to him one morning, since I was sure a similar thought was haunting him. Ernesto shrugged. He didn't feel like answering. Age had chipped away at various aspects of his persona, but not his respect for reasoning, which always had to be logical, deductive. He wouldn't tolerate ranting about what reality was or wasn't, unless there was tangible evidence. Besides, he seemed to answer me with his silence: it's *clear* life doesn't give back what you deserve.

One night in February he had a respiratory attack. The ambulance came for him and took him to the hospital. He was admitted to intensive care, intubated, and put on a drip. They were considerate enough to give him a single room, with a window that afforded a view of snowy mountains that turned pink at dawn. When it was evident that he didn't have very long, Nini, fairly composed, told me: "Go call her. Please."

I left the building. I had forgotten to put on my heavy jacket and the cold surprised me. I walked over to a bare birch tree and laid my hand on its trunk; inside the sap flowed slowly and persistently. I thought about the silent struggle of plants and all of a sudden I was seized by anger. Is this the way it was to end, then? Two individuals declare war for the rest of their lives, consuming everything around them, and eventually death brings them together again in a hospital room, as if nothing had happened. What became of the threats, the long faces, the intransigence of everything *I* had gone through?

Marianna replied groggily: "It's six fifteen, Alessandro. What do you want?"

"They admitted Papa."

"Are you talking about Ernesto?"

"About Papa, yes."

I heard my sister reassuring her husband—"Go back to sleep; it's nothing"—then the rustling of sheets, a few steps. She resumed speaking in a louder voice: "And what am I supposed to do about it?"

"He's dying. He might not have long. He has an effusion of blood in his—"

"I don't care *what* he has. Don't tell me. Did he ask you to phone me?"

"He's sedated. He can't talk."

"He talked enough when he was conscious."

"Marianna, this is no time for—"

"For *what*? Give me a break, Alessandro. The alarm clock goes off in an hour and I don't want to look like a *total* wreck when I get to work."

"Are you serious?"

"Does it seem to you that I'm joking? You know full well how hard it is for me to get back to sleep, so I guess at this point I'll just lie in bed with my eyes *wide open* until seven o'clock."

I kicked the tree trunk. A spiral of white outer bark broke away and fell to the ground. The inner bark beneath it was smooth and clean. I bent down to run my hand over it. The anger vanished as abruptly as it had come. It gave way to a great anguish, something like a last hope for salvation, which you'd forgotten about until a moment ago and which suddenly appears before you. Marianna had to join me, right away—it was essential. If she didn't jump into the first taxi as quickly as possible, if she didn't make it to Ernesto's room in time to see him still breathing, if tears didn't flow from her eyes, if she didn't hug Nini and hold her close, if none of this happened, then there would be no redemption for us. We'd survived an overdose of pain and might endure still more, but we wouldn't make it through the realization that there was no sense to all that travail.

"Please come," I begged her. "Our father is dying."

For a moment Marianna was silent. I listened intently for a sign of tears that would finally save us, all of us.

"For me, he doesn't exist."

Eight years earlier another phone call, equally grave though more submissive in tone, had marked the culmination of my sister's dark period and confirmed her conclusive severance from Nini and Ernesto's asphyxiating universe. Looking back on it now, it seems to me that the decisive chapters in the family life of us Egittos were all brought to a close in the same way: on the telephone. Only miles and miles of cables, buried deep in the ground, made it possible to confront subjects that, face-to-face, were too intense even to be mentioned.

After Marianna had racked up an impressive series of As and A-pluses on her report cards, which Nini kept in a folder in the top drawer of her dresser, after she'd garnered wide-ranging merit citations, Marianna's scholastic career had come to an abrupt standstill. Not that there hadn't been any warning signs. In high school Marianna had gone through months of languid, unwholesome indolence during which her average lagged, but each time she'd made up for those periods in which she'd slacked off with tremendous effort, regaining her preeminence. The decline was almost imperceptible. Still, if Ernesto had applied the same strictly quantitative methods to her performance that he used to assess the rest of the world, if he had plotted a graph of her final exam results from first grade to the brink of graduation, he would immediately have noticed that they formed a descending curve.

For my part, I noticed that slight, continuing transformation by the way Marianna's freckles seemed less apparent each time summer rolled around. I had always thought that the pigmented spots on her cheeks were responsible for my sister's miraculous powers: after all, weren't they what differentiated her from the rest of us mediocre beings? But each spring they appeared less distinguishable. Since she'd gotten into the habit of getting a head start on her summer tan by resorting to tanning beds, afterward they were barely visible. By the time she reached her fourth year of university, nearly graduating with a degree in art history—a subject that didn't interest her much, but that complied with the creative bent that we liked to attribute to her—the freckles had disappeared entirely, like stars above a polluted city. And she herself simply stopped.

The exam wasn't even the most challenging, a paper on William Blake. On the first attempt she got a C and decided to retake the test. She made a brief fuss about it, but her despair and fierce railing against the teaching assistant who had questioned her obscure interpretation of the *Great Red Dragon and the Woman Clothed in Sun* seemed like a pose, aimed at masking a more serious, fundamental indifference. When she tried again, a month later, she was rejected by the professor herself. We sat at the table dumbfounded while she described the professor as an incompetent bitch, a frigid old hag who needed a good you know what; Nini clutched the silverware fretfully meanwhile, not daring to contest those views.

I was rooting for Marianna, as always, but it didn't help much. There was a third failure, then a fourth, in circumstances that were never very clear. The fifth time Marianna showed up for the exam without her blue book, sat down in front of the professor and her teaching assistant, and remained silent, staring at them until they grew impatient and dismissed her.

After the exam she came looking for me, wanting me to come home that night at all costs—yes, it was *essential*. The year before I had allowed the deadline for deferring the draft to pass, defying the family's general opposition and initiating the first of my unspoken getaways. I now resided in the barracks, but, in exchange for a favor to a superior, I was able to satisfy her.

At dinner, between sobs and hysterical tears, Marianna announced that she was dropping her studies. No one went to her; no one caressed her distraught, tearstained face. We watched her writhe like an animal caught in a trap. Her pain resonated in me with equal intensity, but I could do nothing to mitigate it. Nini expected me to say something. Ernesto went on eating, taking small bites. Finally, at the end of what he must have considered to be a childish display typical of his daughter, he said: "In the morning you're coming to the hospital. With me."

I didn't catch on at first, yet it was quite simple. For a professional like Ernesto Egitto, a respected physician who had always denied the existence of anything in man other than the workings of the body and the mental will that allows him to use it, there could be only one diagnosis: he had watched Marianna sitting at her desk for entire afternoons; therefore, if her determination wasn't at fault, it necessarily had to be something in her body. Hadn't his little girl always been tops in her class? The most persevering, the only infallible one? *Oh, but I have to go to school!* she used to say to Musona. Something in her ability to function had to be jammed and he would find out what.

I have only indirect knowledge of what took place in the various hospital wards over the following months, reports that Ernesto delivered for my benefit on the infrequent occasions when I spent my leaves at home. He would reel off the tests he'd subjected Marianna to and summarize her medical record, which grew more and more sizable, as if he were gathering experimental data for a scientific publication or wanted to present me with real-life examples of what I was meanwhile studying in my college textbooks. Marianna did not participate, did not comment; it was as if she were transparent, absent. Once in a while she would nod or smile briefly, without feeling.

To start with, Ernesto had an X-ray taken of her head. For several days we listened to him comment on the merits and limitations of my sister's cranial structure. The electrocardiogram revealed a slight extra-systole and Ernesto insisted on repeating the EKG under stress. Having ruled out skeletal and vascular abnormalities, he conjectured a malfunction of the lymphatic system and that avenue as well was pursued to the most improbable consequences, then proven to be fruitless. Based on blood and urine analyses he excluded a number of common ailments, although the high level of bilirubin led him to consider some serious pathology related to the liver. He accused Marianna of drinking too much alcohol, but it was such a ridiculous supposition—she hardly ever drank—that not even Nini, always very attentive to the developments of the testing, gave it any credence. So he settled for labeling my sister with Gilbert's syndrome, another possible concomitant cause of her recent collapse (that's what he called it now: her *collapse*).

Another deciliter of blood was drawn from Marianna's occluded veins, looking for evidence of rare diseases or autoimmune disorders. By the second month spent following Ernesto around from one outpatient department to another, Marianna looked anemic more than anything else, although her red blood cell count indicated the contrary. Her case was now in the public domain and we'd almost forgotten the symptom that had sparked the search: a university exam gone awry. By now we saw her as ill, in danger. She was simply too weak and tired to object. Or, as I figured out later on—and as I should have intuited by certain spirited glances she occasionally threw me—she wanted to see how far Ernesto would go to show the entire world how grave his insanity was, even at the cost of wrecking her own body.

It was after the gastroscopy report came back negative that Nini unexpectedly said, That's enough, they couldn't torture her any further. She'd known long before that there was nothing wrong with her daughter's constitution, but found it too arduous to oppose her husband's intentions. Now, however, he had to stop. An argument broke

out. On the rare occasions when Nini countered him, Ernesto routinely
withdrew into unremitting silence. He spent hours and hours in the
dark and Nini sometimes found him lying supine on the bath mat, his
arms crossed over his chest like a dead pharaoh. One evening he didn't
come home. That's when Nini ordered Marianna to do what some time
later she would ask me to do. "Go call him. Apologize. Tell him to
come home."

"Me, apologize to him?"

"Yes, you."

"Why should I?"

"That's how he is."

Nini said no more. In the Egitto family you had to know what was
necessary without someone having to explain it to you. Marianna
didn't have to be asked twice. As though considering for the first time
the bizarre, predictable evolution of what she herself had triggered, but
through a bulletproof glass, she walked resolutely to the phone, dialed
Ernesto's number, and in a monotone said, "I apologize. Come home."

University, meanwhile, was a problem of the past, which no one
dared bring up again, just like the senseless interlude of the medical
tests: swallowed up forever by silence. Marianna barricaded herself in
her room for the rest of the academic year. It was a kind of quarantine.
When I saw her, I thought she seemed happier and more carefree than
she'd been for a long time.

When summer came we left on a trip, she and I together with some
friends. The final destination was the bleak coast of the Baltic Sea, but
when we'd crossed the border between Austria and the Czech Repub-
lic, Marianna said she wanted to go back and asked to be taken to the
nearest station, where she would take the first available train. "I don't
feel *comfortable*, okay? I don't like these places—they make me feel
anxious."

She forced the group to stop for a day in a small, nondescript village
near Brno; in the end the others continued on, annoyed by the delay and

by the fact that they would now have to crowd into the remaining cars. "I don't understand why you didn't go *with them*," Marianna protested, but it was clear she was grateful to me and, in a sense, considered it appropriate. I convinced her not to ruin the vacation entirely: we'd gone that far, we could at least visit Vienna. "Vienna won't make you feel anxious," I promised.

I have a confused, fragmented recollection of those last days together, the patchy memory you might have of a hurricane that catches you asleep. Marianna was intractable, seemed constantly on the verge of tears. She ate little, almost nothing. At restaurants or the small kiosks where we stopped for lunch, she stared at the food as if questioning it, until she pushed it aside, bored.

After a few days I gave up eating too. The feeling of hunger is the only unifying element of the otherwise disjointed episodes of that trip. I was hungry as Marianna, her expression fierce, viewed the tormented female bodies in Egon Schiele's watercolors and then declared, "Let's get out of here, right now. I *hate* this museum." I was hungry as we lay awake, lying on the double bed we shared with some embarrassment, dredging up a series of old anecdotes that left us smiling or feeling really bad. I was faint from hunger, and nauseous, during our silent ride on the Ferris wheel, when Marianna turned to me, her eyes devoid of everything I knew of her, and said, "I'll never have anything to do with them, ever again." And I was hungry during the interminable trip back, under a rain that was incessant from start to finish. Without realizing it, we had resorted to the most fundamental form of purification that Ernesto had taught us: keeping the stomach empty for the greatest number of consecutive hours we were able to endure.

After our return Marianna became inscrutable to everyone. She carried out the strategy she had in mind with the meticulous style that I had always admired in her. She went back to the young man she'd been seeing halfheartedly until a few months earlier, a dull, adoring type whom Nini disapproved of with all the silent force of her demeanor;

she moved in with him, and a year later married him. She rejected any invasive attempts by our parents and any mediation on my part. She was successful in the virtuoso endeavor of never saying another word to Nini and Ernesto, not even by mistake, not even to say, Leave me alone. She performed her descending scale once and for all, at a dizzying tempo and without a false note, down to the lowest notes on the keyboard.

That's how it had all ended up: Ernesto's invectives, the celebratory rituals, the love lavished and withdrawn, Nini's admonitions, the cautions, the fierce, unflagging study, the math Olympics where she finished second, the endearments, the music drills, the pounded chords that traveled down through the five floors of the building to the garage and from there sank underground, the syntactically perfect, glacial high school compositions—each element had played a part in winding Marianna up like a spring. A million turns of the key behind the back of the tin soldier she'd been. When fully wound, she'd started marching swiftly toward a finish line. It didn't much matter if that finish line coincided with the edge of the table: in our family, we all had a certain familiarity with going over the brink.

After the wedding we hardly ever talked about our parents anymore, or about our friends, about anything we had in common. When I went to see her, Marianna was always with her husband. I didn't understand how a vendetta could be carried out so coldly and kept up with the same dogged persistence. She had decided on everything long before. A little maneuver had triggered a disastrous course. There hadn't even been a real battle; everyone remained motionless in his trench, watching. On the other hand, I must have learned at least one lesson from the study of bones: the worst fractures are the kind that occur while standing still, when the body decides to go to pieces and does so in a fraction of a second, splintering into so many fragments that reassembling it afterward is unthinkable.

At Ernesto's funeral not many people asked me about Marianna.

Some avoided asking out of a natural tendency to be wary, but over the years most had formed an idea of the situation that was bewildering and shocking enough to make them keep their mouths shut. Apparently rumors could even leak out of a house as well sealed up as that of the Egitto family.

A few days after the burial I turned to a psychiatrist colleague at the military hospital. I asked him for a prescription without allowing him to examine me first or explaining any of the reasons that had brought me there. I just said that I had never felt so weary in my entire life, and that an equally great agitation, combined with the incredible fatigue, kept me from sleeping. It was up to him—any substance capable of knocking me out for a while was fine; all I wanted was to rest, to disappear. "If you won't do it, I'll ask someone else. Or I'll sign it myself," I threatened.

The colleague reluctantly wrote out the prescription, urging me to see him again in a month. I did not go back. I found it more convenient to order a supply of the drug for the army, a sufficient number of boxes to get by for a long time. One pill a day, each to erase a single question to which over time I had found no answer: Why do wars break out? How does one become a soldier? What is a family?

Grass Keeps Growing

The soldiers' return home from the mission in Gulistan coincides with the arrival of spring. This is unfortunate for them: the season is too heartrending. The days never end and they convey a sense of insatiable frenzy, while the air laden with scents brings only painful memories to the surface. Marshal René is fighting it with everything he's got. He knows that with a little discipline you can survive any degree of pain; you just have to plan, you just have to keep busy.

He turned down his leave and the week after their return he was at his post in the barracks. His relatives in Senigallia were offended, but having to face their sympathetic faces was right at the top of his list of things to avoid. He wakes up at six thirty with his running clothes ready on the bedroom chair, at work he fills his days even if it means performing the same tasks twice, and at the end of his shift he stays at the gym as long as he can. Monday evenings he plays squash with Pecone, on Thursdays he has his aikido class, on Fridays he finds someone to go out with or else goes out alone. For the weekends, which are also the hardest time, he plans long motorcycle rides, or schedules time to clean out the garage, or any other unnecessary chore that comes to mind. Thanks to video games, he's also managed to fill the smaller, more insidious holes in his days. He follows the schedule with discipline and makes no significant variations, day after day, week after week. A man like him could go on like that forever.

A hardly pleasant activity that has occupied him, among others, consists of the round of visits to relatives of the deceased, which he's tackled systematically and which is about to conclude, today, in his meeting with Salvatore Camporesi's wife. The fact that he's kept her until last, that he's procrastinated for so long, is undoubtedly significant; it would merit reflection, but the marshal has no intention of examining the subject too closely.

They've been sitting together in the shade of the porch, in front of the Camporesi home, for almost two hours, while the child Gabriele plays quietly, crouched on the steps. From the outset Flavia has been determined not to do anything to make the conversation less difficult than it is. The fruit juice she offered him was warm and the bag of cookies she placed in front of him was an unfamiliar, worrisome brand that he didn't dare touch. It's clear that, at this moment, she's not prepared to pay much attention to formalities.

They've smoked more than they've talked, nonstop. After asking permission for the first few cigarettes, Flavia has gone on helping herself to the packet without asking. There are only three left and when they run out, the marshal imagines, it will be time to end the visit. Despite his discomfort, he's not looking forward to saying good-bye: Flavia Camporesi is the youngest and certainly the prettiest widow he's come across. The word itself, *widow*, seems to clash with her figure.

"Look—what a mess," she says suddenly, pointing to the garden, as if to distract his insistent gaze away from her.

René pretends to be surprised, although, walking the few feet between the outside gate and the house, he'd already noticed the neglected state of the yard. The grass comes halfway up their legs, green spikes have shot up here and there along with some wild poppies that look lethal, and the hedge that runs along the fence is overrun with wild, unruly new growth.

"I told him we shouldn't get a house like this. But for him it was like an obsession. His parents live in a place like this. Salvo always wanted to replicate his earlier life—he drove me out of my mind. By summer it will be a jungle here."

"There's no one to help you?"

Although they'd made an appointment, Flavia hasn't bothered to put on makeup and her curly hair, tied back with a rubber band, could maybe use a washing. None of this is enough to detract from her face.

"For a while his father came. He took care of it. But after the accident he always wanted to talk about Salvo. He kept me in the kitchen for hours—it was exhausting. I told him to let it go." She pauses. "I'm sure he mostly wanted to check up on me. He has no right."

"I could help you myself. Cut the lawn, I mean." He says it impulsively and is immediately afraid he's made a mistake, like stepping into quicksand.

Flavia looks into his eyes for a split second, with a mixture of tenderness and pity. The cigarette burns down between her fingers. "Never mind, René. Thanks just the same."

"I'll gladly do it."

"You'd do it because you feel sorry."

"That's not true. And besides, there's nothing wrong with that even if it were true."

"If you mow the lawn this time, in a month the yard will be in the same condition and I'll find myself back at square one. Then I won't know who to call and I'll call you, and you won't dare say no to a desperate widow, even though you won't feel much like doing it anymore. And so on, every month, until you get sick and tired of it and come up with an excuse not to come. You'll feel guilty and I'll feel abandoned. Let's not get into a predicament like that, René. Unfortunately, grass keeps growing. There's nothing we can do about it." She pauses a moment, then adds: "It's not your fault that Salvo is dead."

The marshal feels a twinge in his chest. If she only knew! If she knew how mistaken she was and how many miles of lawn he'd have to mow to make amends for what he took from her. He'd have to fell a forest with a penknife. "And if I don't mind?" he insists.

Flavia flicks a bit of ash off her sweater. "Do you at least know how to use a mower?"

"Tell me where it is. I'll show you right now."

She blows smoke upward. "No, not now. Today isn't lawn day."

"When would it be, then?"

"Saturday, in the morning." She crushes the partially smoked cigarette in the ashtray and stands up, as if it were suddenly late and she wanted to end the visit. "You have time to change your mind, though. You don't have to let me know. And please don't do it."

But René is not one to back out. He keeps his promise—in fact, in the days leading up to it he thinks of nothing but that. On Saturday he shows up early at the Camporesi house. Flavia is still in her robe. She'd forgotten about their appointment, and he registers her failure to remember with unexpected regret.

He lied to her: he's never done any yard work before—he's always lived in an apartment. In any case, it doesn't seem all that difficult. Relying on certain amateur videos he's studied on the Internet, he gets to work.

He runs the lawn mower over the grass, in one direction and then the other. He imagined it would leave strips in different shades, like on soccer fields, but something isn't right. There must be a special technique that he's not aware of. He notices Flavia watching him from the porch with a faraway look, as if seeing someone else in him as he moves about. She's now wearing a low-necked T-shirt, without a bra. She's standing in the exact spot where the sunlight shines directly on her face. "You've never done this before, right?" she says.

René looks over the portion of the yard he's already mowed. "Is it that obvious?"

Flavia smiles. "It's still better than before."

He ends up staying for lunch and for a good part of the afternoon.

Then, like the first time, Flavia's mood suddenly changes and she sends him away abruptly, without warning. She promises to call him if she needs further help, but from the way she says it, it doesn't seem like she means it.

As he drives home, René is unsettled. The day has taken an unexpected turn. He's left with a chunk of the afternoon to fill; *Halo 8* is waiting for him at home, but he doesn't think he'll be able to lose himself in the game. He has the feeling that all he'll be able to do is indulge in the disgraceful, perilous longing that has overwhelmed him since he shut the gate behind him: longing for the garden of one of his fallen soldiers and for his unapproachable wife, standing on the porch.

Two days later, he gives up his squash date with Pecone so he can station himself in his car outside Flavia Camporesi's house. He stays there until it gets dark, staring at the lights that turn on and off and wondering whether the months in the valley haven't really turned him into a wack job after all.

He goes back the next night and the one after that. Soon enough his evening watches outside Flavia's house become a routine finale to his days in the barracks, so that, at a certain point, he plans for it by bringing his supper along. He parks close enough to see everything, and far enough away to not be spotted. He doesn't know what he's watching for. All he has to do is glimpse Flavia, or her son, behind a curtain, steal a moment of their shattered family life, to feel better and at the same time to renew the apprehension that keeps him riveted there. As if he needs to continually make sure that nothing bad has happened to those two defenseless creatures. As for the physical thrill he feels toward the widow Camporesi, it has nothing to do with the kind of infatuation for certain girls he'd experienced a long time ago, as a teenager. It's a more complicated feeling that he can't—or doesn't want—to decipher.

Sitting in the car with the radio turned off, his thoughts don't dwell on anything for long, but are always more or less the same: the phone call from Delaram base camp, too late, to Rosanna Vitale; the garbage bags with the men inside; little Gabriele who finally decides to imitate him, getting down on his knees like him to pick up the dead leaves under the hedge, but one at a time, because his small hands can't grasp more.

The marshal's routine falls completely apart and he doesn't give a damn. He just wants to keep watch, period. He's considered the fact that sooner or later a police car could pull up alongside and ask him why he's been parked there for so long, but there's not a chance he'll give up being near the purple house that Salvatore once bought to prolong his life as a child. There's still a very long time yet—too long—before he'll have to mow the lawn, and meanwhile there's nothing else he can do to keep his anxiety at bay. Grass keeps growing, but not fast enough.

He receives a phone call from an old acquaintance, Valeria S., a client from the days when he used to supplement his income. No one has called him before her. They must have found a replacement during the months he was gone, or they heard about what happened and decided to stay away. He agrees to an appointment out of his usual impeccable courtesy and also because he wants to have sex (the last time was in a previous incarnation, with a woman who was pregnant by him).

In front of the door he begins to think he splashed on too much cologne, a sign of insecurity, an obvious clue that he's now out of practice. It doesn't matter; much of the scent will disappear along with his clothes. Valeria S. gets right down to business. They jump each other's bones while they're still in the living room. Both seem ravenous and desperate. The woman has a nice lithe body and after shrugging off her blouse she arches her back over his forearm and offers her taut breasts to his mouth. Not one wrong move, not a single wasted glance, gets in the way of their hasty migration toward the bedroom. They yank and kiss and rouse and stroke each other, not letting go for an instant. Not even the nuisance of putting on protection ruins the synchronization; René quickly takes care of the job with one hand while keeping her distracted with the other.

He's playacting, but it's such a familiar act that it doesn't require any effort. He pins Valeria beneath him. Her eyes are closed and her face has a vague expression. She demands a little pain and he gives it to her. He squeezes a nipple between his front teeth until she cries out. He even slaps her on the face.

When the coupling settles into the repetitive rhythm of penetration, though, he realizes that something is wrong. He seems to see Valeria shrinking, slipping away from him. But it could also be the opposite: he could be the one slipping away. The girl, a few inches from his eyes, becomes an indistinct object and the sounds in the room are cushioned as well.

A distasteful clot forms in the marshal's chest and rises to his throat. Nothing like this has ever happened to him before today, yet his body seems to have a primal knowledge of what is happening. All of a sudden he's sure he won't climax, that in a few seconds it will even be intolerable for him to continue. And the very instant he thinks it, the premonition comes true down in his groin.

Later, Valeria insists that he accept the money anyway: "Even though you didn't come, I did, so the service is valid just the same."

René is hesitant, crushed, not so much by shame, but by the vestiges of the anxiety that gripped him a little earlier in the bedroom. They agree on half the amount: half pay for half a fuck. It seems fair. Before sending him off, the girl tosses him one last consolation: "It's normal, René. After what happened to you. You'll go back to being the man you were. You'll see."

But that's just the point, René thinks as he rushes down the stairs to at least spare himself the awkwardness of waiting there for the elevator: Does he really want to go back to being the man he was before? And who the hell was the man he was before?

He stops running in the morning, stops lifting weights in the gym, stops roaming around on his motorcycle. Now all he does is keep watch over Flavia Camporesi and her son. He realizes how risky it is, but he can't resist the powerful, burning need to keep that amputed family in his sight. The rolling shutters raised in the morning and lowered in the evening, the unfailing way Flavia takes Gabriele's hand as soon as they pass through the gate, her extreme caution when she drives the car out of the garage, then immediately glances into the mirror to check her face—all this is soothing and at the same time fuels his anxiety.

Occasionally, more and more often, he ventures out and rings the doorbell. Flavia welcomes him, though sometimes she goes back to sit on the couch and forgets about him. She still conveys the sultry negligence of the first day. Since the muggy heat settled over Belluno, she hasn't worn anything but a cotton nightdress, always the same one, very short on her thighs and with a wayward shoulder strap that stubbornly slips down to her elbow, partially revealing her breasts. Most of the time she doesn't even notice. Flavia's nudity attracts René with a power that he can't deny. If he gazes at her for long, he's forced to get up, find some manual task, or rinse his face with cold water.

What is he thinking of? How did he end up in that house? She's the wife of one of his men, forbidden fruit, the red zone. He was used to managing erotic urges, to utilizing them just as he did his limbs, his weapons, the leather steering wheel of his German car, but now they're muddled up with a sense of guilt and shame that intensifies and confuses them. He feels out of control. Then, too, his failure with Valeria S. has challenged the very foundation of his masculinity. He's afraid that crossing the valley has transformed him into one of those slimy individuals who spy on carnal acts from a distance without having the guts to act—a voyeur, an impotent observer. He despises men like that—he's never understood them. Anyway, it's already been three months since he spoke with Flavia on the porch and since then there have been no developments between them.

Inexplicably, despite all of the precautions, word about his visits leaks out. One day, in the mess hall, Zampieri plunks down in front of him. "Hey, Marshal. They're saying you're having an affair with Campo's wife. Is it true?"

"No."

"Still, that's what they're saying."

"I give her a hand with the yard. She's all alone."

Zampieri taps her lower lip with a fork. "Do you seriously think that's a decent thing to do?"

"You're on the wrong track, Zampa."

"I once saw a movie where something like that happened. It ended badly."

He can't be certain, but it seems that since that day the guys have tended to avoid him. He tries not to think about it. He hasn't done anything wrong; he's only offered to help a mother in need. As for the reasons driving him to be so conscientious, no one can possibly guess them, much less understand them; they're his business.

The guys might well be upset for other reasons. Replacements from other companies have arrived and so far René's efforts haven't been enough to create a climate of cooperation. He himself was cool toward them in the beginning; he struggled to memorize their names, continually asking them to repeat them, and this must not have made them feel very welcome. The veteran troops eat on one side, the new ones on the other. The veterans train on one side, the new ones on the other. The veterans think the new guys can't understand a damn thing about what they've been through—and they're probably right—while the new ones don't consider that a good reason to be mistreated, and find creative ways to express the fact that the exasperation is mutual. The overall picture is frustrating. The marshal had big plans for his platoon, certain that its skills and glory would grow, yet here they are in a state of total disarray.

Maybe it's Zampieri's gall that gives him the push he needed, that makes him a little more daring. One afternoon he suggests to Flavia an idea he's been thinking about for weeks, but says it as though it has just occurred to him: "How about getting dinner out sometime, the two of us?"

She emerges from the depths of one of her absent interludes. She looks at René as if he were a stranger who'd snuck in, a hint of disgust tugs at her mouth, then she leaves the room without a word. When it's time to say good-bye, she coldly orders him not to come back again.

Every year in late July, the barracks in Belluno organizes sports tournaments. The six hundred soldiers who participate don't do it because they're forced to, but they don't do it for fun either: the fact is that extracurricular activities allow them to rack up points useful to career advancement. The competitions attract journalists from the local papers and various sponsors, quick to offer tempting prizes just to have their logo printed in large letters on the bibs. There is also a substantial round of betting prompted by the events; Ballesio is aware of it and does nothing to hinder the illegal activity because he considers gambling, like other male vices, part of every good soldier's pedigree.

Rumor has it that this year the colonel has put twenty euros on Masiero for the summer biathlon. The bookies, including Enrico Di Salvo, give the captain three-to-one odds, making him the odds-on favorite, while René, who had always been a worthy rival, is barely given nine. The assessment of the marshal is symptomatic of the condition he's in: he's visibly heavier, out of shape, nervous. None of his men has bet a dime on him winning, and he knows it.

For this reason, his comeback in the second half of the event astounds him. With no particular effort, René finds himself outdistancing Masiero by a few dozen yards and racks up a higher score than the captain in target shooting, hitting four cardboard silhouettes right in the heart. It's the first time he's won that stupid competition and the first time he couldn't care less.

On the podium, however, he relishes the satisfaction of standing over the captain's bald head. The soldiers applaud from the stands and his group of men is easily recognizable because they seem to have gone bonkers. Even from a distance, the marshal has the impression that it's the first source of shared pride for his newly reconstituted platoon.

"Congratulations, Marshal," Masiero snarls.

René realizes that his hand is sweaty. "Congratulations to you, Captain."

Ballesio awards the third-place winner a clock radio that projects the time on the wall. Masiero, in addition to the medal, receives a steel Suunto wristwatch, an underwater model with a large dial and a wide array of functions. It must cost three hundred euros at least. His prize, René figures, must be worth even more.

He bows his head and lets the commander place the gold-plated medal around his neck. Then he unwraps the package. He feels Masiero's cold eyes on him and from his top spot pities the man for still being obsessed by their futile match.

The marshal, the first-place winner, also gets a watch: a measly plastic Swatch with a green-and-black camouflage band. Incredulous, René's eyes question Ballesio, who pretends he doesn't understand. Then the marshal turns to Masiero and the captain smiles at him: there's always something new to learn about command.

He doesn't have to wait long for his consolation prize, however. It's a stifling night, already past one, and René is stationed in the street because the light is still on in Flavia's room. He's almost dozing off—it wouldn't be the first time he fell asleep in the car and then woke up at dawn, aching and stiff—when the interior lights up with an electric blue gleam. An instant later his cell phone wiggles on the empty pas-senger seat, next to the leftovers of his take-out supper. Flavia's name appears on the display.

The marshal listens intently for the sound of approaching police sirens, but doesn't hear anything. "Hello?"

"Are you still out there?"

René the strategist, René the sharp-witted man who less than a year ago set off on a mission destined to turn into a bloodbath, would have said no, then would have moved cautiously from the incriminating spot to a more secure hiding place. Instead, this new screwed-up ver-sion of himself can't help telling the truth: "Yeah, but I'll go if you want me to."

"No. Stay a little longer."

"Can't you sleep?"

"I can hardly ever. Last fall I lived as if I were in Afghanistan too; now I think I'm just a little unhinged. Do you know what time zone the dead are in?"

"No."

"I'm sorry. That was a bad joke."

"You don't have to apologize."

"You were good in Sunday's competition."

"Who told you that?"

"I was there. Gabriele pointed at you while you were being awarded the medal. I think he recognized the lawn mower man."

"It must be time to mow again."

Flavia ignores him. "A neighbor complained about the pile of ciga-rette butts he finds each morning at the curb. You should use the ashtray."

"Okay. I'll remember that."

"Salvo used to say that some days your clothes smelled of smoke so bad that it was impossible to be around you."

"I guess he was right."

"Do you still go with cougars?"

The question is fired at him point-blank. René struggles to contain his shock. "I don't know what you mean."

"Look, Salvo told me about your second job. So, do you still see them?"

"No. Anyway, they weren't cougars. Just friends."

"How much do you charge?"

"I don't want to talk about it."

"Come on, I'm curious—tell me how much."

"It depends."

"On what?"

"On how well-off they are."

Flavia laughs loudly. René holds the phone a few inches away from his ear.

"How altruistic! And if I were to hire you?"

"Don't kid around."

"A young mother with her dead husband's survivor benefits. You should be generous."

"Stop it!"

"Fifty? A hundred? I can manage up to a hundred."

"I wouldn't go to bed with you."

"Why not?" Her tone has suddenly changed. "So it's true then, that I'm used goods, ready for the scrap heap."

"It's not that."

"Oh, no?"

"You're . . ." He begins, but can't find a way to finish.

"Salvo's wife? A widow? A bizarre sense of moral ethics. Anyhow, forget it." Suddenly she's aggressive. She takes a breath, as if to compose herself. "I'm going to sleep."

Can her intentions be serious? Does she really want to invite him in? Not long ago she kicked him out for daring to talk about having dinner together and now she's longing to have sex with him? Maybe she's just teasing him, but René doesn't hesitate to explore the possibility: "However, if you . . ." he throws out.

"A hundred euros is a lot for me right now," Flavia responds quickly.

"We don't have to discuss money."

"Yes, we do."

His head is spinning. He's negotiating a fee to service the wife of the man he let die. "Thirty is fine," he says without thinking.

"I'm not asking for charity."

"Fifty, then."

And so, still incredulous, he finds himself usurping the bed of one of his soldiers. They're in complete darkness, in a sweltering room that René has never seen in daylight. Flavia is lying on her stomach, naked, her legs clamped tight, as if awaiting a punishment. René has never found himself trembling before approaching a woman. Is he afraid of failing again? Or is it the unusual circumstances that terrify him? He's fantasized about this moment for so long that now, caught off guard, he's slow to get aroused.

He's having second thoughts. Flavia doesn't move, doesn't encourage him. Lying motionless like that, she might even be asleep, if it weren't for the fact that she's plainly on her guard. When René kisses her neck, she jerks her head violently, resisting. Then he lightly traces her back along the curving line of her spine, playing for time, but Flavia rejects any kind of foreplay. She stops his hand, pulls him to her by the hips. She wants to be just a body, not a person; she wants to be any other anonymous client from his second career. René feels overwhelmingly sad. Get on with it, Marshal, that's all they want from you.

But no, the woman he's now slipping into is Flavia Camporesi. And nothing about their coupling resembles the identical, restrained services performed for Valeria S. and Rosanna Vitale and Cristina M. and Dora and Beatrice T. and the dozens of other women whose names he has forgotten. For the first time in his life, René is making love with all of his muscles, not just his pelvis, and his head isn't able to formulate coherent thoughts.

He closes his eyes to regain control, but he's struck by a burst of blinding red flashes, gunfire and explosions everywhere. Then he's back in the room, without slowing down for a second. This isn't how you do it; this isn't what the clients want; this isn't what they pay him for. His orgasm is ready to explode and he can't stop it. Flavia's face is pressed against the mattress. She's breathing heavily or crying, René can't tell, but he pushes her head farther down, as if he could make her sink into the sheets. In less than a minute he comes, while the red of the explosions pours from his eyelids and floods the room.

Only later, when they're still lying down, with no bodily contact between them, does Flavia begin talking again. She doesn't waste a single word to label what has just happened, to consider its implications or justify herself. Instead, she wants to hear about the desert, what their days were like and how long their guard duty shifts lasted, what they ate, and who led them to commit the ill-considered act of leaving the base, as if she were asking Salvatore those questions on any ordinary night. She wants to know if her husband still kept his closely trimmed beard or if he sometimes shaved it off, if he mentioned her, and how often, and in what context.

René fills her in, patiently. He feels a miraculous absence of embarrassment in talking about the senior corporal major, lying there on his half of the bed after another performance that should be judged awful according to his old criteria but that, on the contrary, has satisfied every nerve in his body. He is equally surprised to find that he doesn't feel guilty about having once again stolen Salvatore Camporesi's place to sleep.

The next night, in the BMW's air-conditioned bubble, he awaits a signal. Everything is repeated in the same order: they have sex like strangers, hypnotized and rank with sweat, and when their bodies are drained of grief they start talking. It goes on like that for the rest of the summer.

On August 6, Flavia grills him about the details of Operation Mama Bear and when she meets with his resistance, she becomes angry and accuses him of being a slave to stupid rules, like all the others. On August 9, she tells him about all the anxiety Salvo kept bottled up inside him, and how he released it only at night after falling asleep, through violent muscle spasms. Had he noticed? No, not really. On August 28, she hammers him about a leather bracelet, which, naturally, René doesn't remember at all. Still, he swears he saw it on Salvatore's wrist every single day spent at the FOB, of course, every day, he never took it off. He's forced to lie to her frequently, especially when she keeps asking (August 31, September 7, 9) about the appearance of the body, which they didn't allow her to see. But what can he tell her, that they weren't even sure the remains were Salvatore's and that in any case there was no trace of his hands or his eyes? That her husband had been blended together with the others? On September 13, Flavia gives him a lesson on responsibility and on the consequences that the affection of the people around us have on each of us, whether we care to recognize it or not. René only pretends to understand. On September 26, she screams at him to get out and threatens to call the police—what does he want from her anyway? There's nothing for him here, only misery. He should turn his goddamn car around and go find someone sunny and cheerful, forget these damaged goods. René swallows the outburst with bitter sorrow, but for the first time he considers the possibility that their seeing each other may have to do with something more than loneliness and grief.

On September 30, the marshal stays until morning, because Gabriele has a high fever and Flavia is anxious. In the middle of the night the boy wakes up wailing. He's wet the bed. René holds him in his arms while Flavia cleans up. The child's body is smooth and limp, as though lifeless. On October 5, he has to make an extreme effort to talk

Flavia out of believing that Zampieri and her driving are completely to blame for what happened. Who knows where she got such an idea—he himself probably suggested it, when he presented his own version of the days in the valley. Other nights he just listens to her cry and when that happens he doesn't try to stop her.

On November 18 they're still awake, listening to the howl of a blizzard outside. René feels that something has changed. He's told her everything—everything he could—and there isn't a single corner of the FOB left unexplored for Flavia. He could kiss her good-bye and leave for good; he knows she wouldn't try to hold him back. Instead, he finds the nerve to invite her to dinner again. She replies after a long silence: "Do you know what we're in for?"

"I think so."

"No, you don't know. I'm not alone, René. I have a child, if you haven't noticed."

"I like Gabriele."

"The problem isn't whether you like him, but whether he likes you. You see? You already got it wrong."

"I can make it right."

"You don't know anything about it."

"I know all I need to know."

"René, let's not get into a mess like that."

A pellet of ice hits the window. "And if I want to get into it?"

Flavia hesitates. "If you want to come into my house, you have to leave the barracks first."

"You know I can't do that."

"Then I can't either. I don't want to have anything to do with war anymore."

"Flavia . . ."

"Either you promise me right now or leave, and starting tomorrow don't come back."

Marshal René is about to put up an argument. The army is his whole life; he's sacrificed for years to get where he is. He opens his mouth to object, but suddenly all his aspirations seem to have lost their importance. The unwavering stars that guided him since his youth and led him here, to the room of a woman who doesn't belong to him and her silent child, all those stars are now topsy-turvy, unrecognizable. René is ready to let them go in a second.

You'll go back to being the man you were. What happened to that man? He's evaporated, or he's taken a long leave of absence. He's definitely not there with him now. The marshal sees a blank slate before him, a future waiting to be filled in.

"All right," he says. "I'll make the arrangements."

The Evolution of the Species

—————————

"Because, look, you're young and you're new here, you don't know how things work in the platoon and not only that—now it all seems perfectly clear to you, you have a plan, you say I'll do this and I'll do that and I'll go straight to where I want to be, maybe you think you'll end up a marshal or a lieutenant, right? How much do you lift at the gym?—two hundred is pretty good, it's not exactly the greatest, but it's good enough for your size. And how do you do on the rifle range?— I watched you, yeah, you have a tendency to ease off the supporting foot and lean backward, you always hit too high, but it's a fault that can be corrected, you just have to learn a few tricks—however, there are two or three much more important things you don't know and the first is that you'll never become what you want to become, get that into your head. It's tough to swallow, but you have to accept it sooner or later, better you should know it, it's like aiming too far afield, you follow me? If you're not going to finish that chicken give it to me, plop it right here. Every weapon has its range, see, and you have to know what yours is, you have to aim at the right target, so at least you won't waste any shots and you'll know when the asshole who wants to hassle you is close enough to fire at. Keeping your feet steady is certainly a big advantage—I can give you a hand if you want, stay and watch me—do you have a girl? That's important, it keeps you anchored, there was a guy here before you, you remind me of him a little—well, this guy looked like you, he too had a long, long head like an eggplant and his eyes—I don't know, you have something in common, who knows what, but the point is that he was a complete washout when it came to girls, too timid, and his timidity screwed him. I mean, he never really tasted the things in life that are the most delectable, as we two know, so I'm glad to hear you have a girl, it's a good start—if you need any advice in that regard just ask yours truly, the Cederna information desk is open twenty-four/seven, I know all about it—hey, we could go have a beer some night, I know a place that's not bad, they have five hundred different types, well-known brands, imported from Belgium and Germany—well, maybe it's because you haven't yet found one that's right for you, in that place you'll find one for sure, they also have British ales—anyway you can drink something else, they don't only serve beer, what the hell, that way we can shoot the breeze a little, I'll give you some tips—are you fucking kidding me? And who is she? Does she handle your calendar? You're still too young to be tied down, give yourself some time, man, explore a little, believe me, you need someone who can teach you how to deal with women, if you give them too much leeway you're done for—go get me another dessert, would you—the same, yeah—so let me tell you, last night I was with my girl, we had just finished . . . Well, you know—what the hell do you care what her name is?—Agnese, her name is Agnese, happy now?—so as I was saying we'd finished and I don't know what came over me, you know how it is with us guys, those times when you don't feel like staying there and cuddling and shit, when you just can't stand being in that room a minute longer or you might suffocate, you know, right?— you have no idea what I'm talking about, I can tell from your eyes—no, you don't know, but it didn't used to happen to me before either, I was always . . . well, never mind—no, it has nothing to do with not being able to get it up, are you listening to me, damn it? This happens later, *afterward*, when she expects you to hug her and whisper sweet nothings to her, well, so there comes a point when you can't stand being stuck to another body anymore, because what she's demanding of you is too much, it seems ridiculous, I know, but it happens, it's natural evolution, a physical thing, you need some peace and quiet—I left, simple, I put on my shoes and shirt and beat it, cleared out of there to get some air, to breathe the scent of the night a little, at this time of year it's fantastic, you should go out and smell it these nights, it charges you up—some time ago I rented a cabin in the upland valley, it was a time when I didn't feel like seeing anyone, I'd even taken a break from Agnese and I stayed up there all by myself, recharging my batteries, only there was no heat and when winter came, well, with all the damn snow I couldn't even get to the barracks—yeah, the pipes even froze, a friggin' disaster—so anyway, I go to spend the night there, minding my own business, and this morning when I get home I find her sitting on the couch, in a snit—the lunatic has been sitting there the whole time, can you imagine?, on the couch, waiting, her eyes red from crying so hard—she tells me, 'If it happens again I'm the one who's leaving, got it?,' and I say, 'No, I don't get it, shut your mouth'—that's how you deal with them—we're getting married next year—what? You say that because you're young and you don't know anything yet, how old did you say you are?—exactly, wait till you hit thirty, you'll see how things change, it's the thirties that back you against the wall and put a gun to your forehead, like this—sorry, I didn't mean to hurt you, you sure are delicate—I could call you that, *delicatezza*, what do you think?, Delicate Flower, or maybe Eggplant Head—let's get out of here, do you have any change for coffee? I'm broke—anyway, age thirty is the most fucked-up time of your life, because you already have some real . . . responsibilities, that's the word, responsibilities that you don't really want but that you can't just shrug off, it's time to start a family and get going with everything else, kids and so on, otherwise it'll be too late and you'll have disobeyed the demands of the species—the human species, kid, you have to be prepared when you get to thirty, you have to be—on the mark—and realistic, you know what realistic means? It means, I don't swallow anybody's stories, that I don't buy into the fantasy about how everything is dandy, I see things as they are and decide my own version—in the end it's all about having balls, those who don't have them don't survive, it's evolution, Darwin said it—get me one of those too, the chocolate one, I'll pay you back later—there's a whole slew of people who go bonkers after thirty, you can't even imagine, take the commander of our old platoon—no, you didn't meet him, it was before you got here—I told you, you didn't meet him, damn it, his name is René, Marshal René, happy now? Listen to what he did, he went and saddled himself with a family that wasn't his, he took a woman with a kid—a kid who isn't *his*, Eggplant Head—I mean, it isn't natural, it seems obvious to me, spend a night, okay, but to get hitched—that bastard took someone else's family, the family of a dead soldier, and now he makes believe it's his—he never shows his face around here anymore, the crummy opportunist—he's a waiter in a restaurant, a dive, I'd never set foot in there, I guarantee you—where was I? I was explaining something important—give me a cigarette— right, age thirty, well, the point is that it's not easy by any means and it's not what you expected, you follow me?, and though it all seems crystal clear to you now, as if you could control each piece and say, Hey, guys, lookie here, look how great I am, and tell yourself that everything will turn out just fine, well, we'll talk about it again in ten years, champ, and we'll see if I haven't told you the god-awful truth, we'll meet again right here and you'll tell me, You know what, Senior Corporal Major Cederna? You were right on all counts, goddamn it! Life gave me a good kick in the ass and landed me where I never thought I'd go—no, she has nothing to do with it, otherwise why would I be getting married?—anyhow, if you need any advice you can come to me, I won't hold back, I can give you a hand, maybe we'll go have that beer we've been talking about—tonight, what do you say?—what about tomorrow?—well, whenever you like, I'm always ready—no, it's that I don't have much to do at night—because a lot of things lose their appeal, that's why, and you can't do anything about it, even though before you liked going out and meeting a million imbeciles like yourself, and every time you went on leave all you thought about was getting as drunk as possible, later on you don't feel like it anymore—it's not *you*, it's your body that's changed, it's evolution, shit, it orders you to quit doing all that crap, you know how much I lifted on the bench at your age?, shoot—no, sir, 130 per arm, 260 total, two sets of ten, and if you ask me I could still do it, but I don't feel like it, you know?—anyway, there are too many nights, one after the other, one after the other, non-stop, you don't know how to fill them anymore—you're gonna see a lot of things, kid, things you won't be able to get out of your head anymore, you're young, you're just getting started."

Other Mountains

The disciplinary committee, as it is pompously referred to in the summons, is composed of three members. Two are external: a major and another officer who isn't wearing stripes, both with southern Italian accents—Egitto doesn't know them. The chairman seated in the center is Colonel Matteo Caracciolo, with whom the lieutenant has an association that goes so far back it can easily be mistaken for friendship, though it's characterized by a certain impenetrable distance. In words, at least, Caracciolo is on his side. If Egitto leaves it all to him—the colonel told him yesterday in private—everything will all work out, the incident will soon be reabsorbed (he used that very term, *reabsorbed*, as if he were talking about a brain trauma). Afterward, however, he refused to clarify the exact nature of the allegations, as if he were embarrassed—but of course Egitto could sleep peacefully! According to Caracciolo, it would be all a bunch of nonsense, the usual minutiae typical of the army.

The colonel continues addressing him familiarly in front of the other committee members, even though they give the impression they don't appreciate the lack of formality. He opened the hearing by making it clear that he finds it completely pointless to rehash circumstances dating back more than a year, when they're already talking about a new mission for his brigade. But what can you do? The bureaucracy's pace does not necessarily coincide with that of human beings—in fact, the two almost never coincide.

An oppressive pall hangs over the overheated room, whose space is almost entirely taken up by a rectangular dark wood table. Egitto longs to close his eyes. Despite Caracciolo's reassurances, he didn't sleep at all last night and now he feels sapped, exhausted, irritable. He's afraid this is not the right morning for an investigation into his actions—being tired always makes him disinclined to cooperate. Moreover, he now realizes that he's drawn to the freedom sometimes granted when life is suddenly turned upside down. He's sure he'll find a way of screwing everything up before they even get into the discussion.

The dossier that's been opened on him concerns his actions at FOB Ice during his second tour of duty there and the way in which his conduct may have in part—Caracciolo stresses "in part"—contributed to events in October. For a moment Egitto, distracted, lets his mind pursue that expression. So that's how they decided to dissociate themselves from the men who died in the valley: "events in October," as if equally significant events existed for December, April, June, August . . . He wonders what this month's events will be. For sure, they won't have anything to do with the current investigation.

Caracciolo is careful to list the lieutenant's commendable actions before moving on to the more—here he pauses a moment, searching for the most appropriate adjective, and, after finding it—"controversial"— looks at the other members for approval, which they withhold. He moves on, *as he was saying*, to the more *controversial* aspects. He cites an episode of a child zonked out on opium whom Egitto miraculously saved, along with three other less exemplary actions that he's forced to fictionalize a bit. Egitto is not particularly grateful for the favor.

The major, charged with taking minutes, is making very few notes. Egitto is only half listening—they haven't gathered at ten in the morning on this milky gray day to compliment him. He's roused suddenly, though, when Caracciolo mentions First Corporal Major Angelo Torsu being wounded in battle. It's clear to Egitto that they've reached the crux of the discussion.

The soldier's family—which consists only of his father and a host of more distant relatives (first, second, and third aunts, uncles, and cousins) since Signora Torsu recently passed away—has filed charges against the lieutenant. With the gathering of testimonies from Torsu's fellow soldiers, it came to light that at the time of the convoy's departure the first corporal major was recovering from a severe case of food poisoning caused by eating local meat, in blatant violation of the health regulations, among other things (an irresponsible act for which the doctor in charge should be held accountable, although, Caracciolo is quick to point out, that charge is not the specific focus of the interview; everyone present understands that demands in the field of operations can't be judged a posteriori, since each of them has been there—they all know that, right?).

But First Corporal Major Torsu . . . that's a hell of a problem. Especially given the condition he's now in. It's understandable that the family is looking for someone to blame—let's admit it, a scapegoat. (The major doesn't say those last words, in all likelihood deeming them to be biased.)

"The situation," Caracciolo continues, "is complicated by a report drafted by a neutral observer who was visiting the FOB during the period in question."

Egitto's arms jerk involuntarily, just the kind of somatic reaction that should be avoided in such circumstances. He grips his knees to keep himself anchored. The observer Caracciolo has so mysteriously referred to is actually a *she*, but Egitto has the distinct impression that he's the only one in the room who knows it. He decides to keep that little detail to himself.

In Irene Sammartino's report the lieutenant is described as being—and here the colonel quotes verbatim—"in an evident state of lethargy, fatigued, not very lucid," which would explain his "injudicious assessment" of First Corporal Major Torsu's physical condition. Caracciolo adds, on a personal note, that a little exhaustion seems to him the least you could expect after months and months spent in that hell; again the major taking minutes stops writing, leaving out the justification.

Lastly, the colonel reminds Egitto that this is a friendly interview. He invites him to take the floor, but Egitto is still absorbed by the image of Irene, sitting at a desk in a darkened room, tapping swiftly on her keyboard and then printing her document. She'd complained that her computer was continually being requisitioned: they must have given it back to her. *I'm just staff, Alessandro, like all the others.*

"Lieutenant?" the colonel prompts him.

Why did she do it? Was it because he didn't call her? No, that's absurd. She did it because that's her job; she had no choice. She was assigned to submit a report and she wrote it. Irene Sammartino is not the type of professional who shirks her responsibilities. She treats the system's infirmities with a determination that keeps her from having any regard for anyone.

The lieutenant has a sudden feeling of tenderness toward her, for the solitude life has forced on her: transferred from base to base, among strangers, compiling reports for which she is then hated—a stateless individual hopelessly on the outside. Was it because of this similarity of theirs that they clung so tightly to each other in the darkness of the tent? He can imagine the regret his friend must have felt as she reread the report. Maybe she walked into the kitchen, poured a glass of wine, and swallowed it down in one gulp. He can still clearly picture the ceremonious way she has of tossing her head back when she has a drink, but he can't say he misses her, not really. Not all forms of attachment correspond to longing.

"Do you recognize these?"

The officer to the left of Caracciolo had been silent until now, as if waiting for the right moment to enter the scene. His voice is higher than one might imagine from his imposing physique. Egitto turns to look at him.

He's holding up a transparent plastic bag, the body of proof. It contains a handful of yellow-and-blue capsules: by the looks of it, enough for a month's treatment. Jumbled up in the bag like that they look innocuous, even cheerful.

"Are they yours, Lieutenant?"

"They were mine. Yes, sir."

The officer puts the evidence back on the table, satisfied. The capsules' gentle clatter sounds like a drizzle. The major is feverishly taking notes.

Caracciolo is now studying him with a look of consternation. He shakes his head. "I'm forced to ask you, Alessandro. How long has this situation with the psychotropic drugs been going on?"

Egitto grips his knees even tighter. He sits up straighter. "Please, Colonel, don't you call them that too."

"Why, what should I call them?"

"Anything but that. *Antidepressants. Medication.* Even *tablets* is fine. But not *psychotropic drugs*. It confers a rather hasty moral judgment."

"And don't you think a moral judgment is called for?"

"Why?"

"Because of the fact that you take those . . . those things."

"Drugs," the officer to his left suggests. The major records it: *drugs*.

Egitto replies slowly: "If you feel the need to formulate a moral judgment about it, you're free to do so."

Suddenly he's out of patience. Not because of the way they're grilling him, not because of the hostility shown by the external members, which they make no attempt to hide, and not because they've waved a bag in front of him containing irrefutable proof of his weakness. The problem is something else. Irene Sammartino, the disciplinary committee, the distant relatives of First Corporal Major Torsu, avid for justice and also for money . . . they're all right, and the realization hits him like a resounding slap. He shouldn't have let him go. He'd left it up to the soldier to decide, believing that Angelo Torsu's body belonged to Angelo Torsu, period, whereas he was his appointed guardian. He'd found it more convenient to look the other way instead, wallowing in a pall of indolence and self-pity. *Fatigued, not very lucid. An evident state of lethargy.*

It seems that, in the end, his innate inclination to not intervene has had its consequences—the worst possible. Caracciolo said it well earlier: a moral judgment is called for, and theirs can only testify against him. Why, then, does he suddenly feel so alert, refreshed almost, as if things were finally falling into place?

He takes a deep breath, then another. Then he turns to the colonel: "I take full responsibility for what happened."

Caracciolo grabs the major's arm. "Don't write that! It shouldn't be recorded . . . you can clearly see that we're still framing the situation." The major is skeptical, but indulges him. "Alessandro, please don't be rash. I'm sure there must have been some circumstantial reasons why you chose to act one way rather than another. You probably need to take your time and reconstruct them calmly."

"First Corporal Major Torsu was not in any condition to confront a mission of that kind, Colonel."

"Yes, but that has nothing to do with the explosion and all the rest! And if it hadn't been Mr. Torsu on board that Lince, on the turret, but someone else—" He stops, perhaps realizing that his line of reasoning is about to exceed an acceptable level of cynicism. He tries another approach: "If we always used the utmost caution in war . . . well, it would be a disaster—we'd be defeated in the blink of an eye . . . At one time they didn't send soldiers back from the front even if they had pneumonia, let alone a little diarrhea."

The colonel is doing his best to defend him. *The incident will be reabsorbed*, he'd promised him. But for Egitto it's too late: the hemorrhaging coagulated some time ago. Torsu was flung out of the Lince, among the stunned sheep, his cheeks raked over the rocks.

"It was my duty to safeguard the corporal's health."

"Two hundred men!" Caracciolo talks over him, as if he hasn't even heard him. "Imagine worrying about *two hundred men* day and night.

The probability of an oversight is huge. And we're not talking about a normal place, we're talking about—"

Egitto raises the volume of his voice slightly: "I made a mistake, Colonel. The responsibility is mine."

He reasserts it so firmly that this time Caracciolo can't prevent the major from recording it. Speechless, he stares at Egitto: Why is he doing it? Why does he want to cause problems for himself, unnecessarily? You don't get anywhere by being a hero, by being conscientious— hasn't he figured that out yet?

But it's not a matter between them, nor an issue of loyalty to a principle. For Egitto, it's much simpler than that: it's purely about understanding what concerns you and what doesn't. The bodies of the soldiers at FOB Ice were his concern. He responds to the colonel in silence: *Go ahead, do what you're supposed to do and get it over with.*

Caracciolo sighs. Then, in a tone that is no longer quite so amiable, he says: "It would be best for us to resume this conversation later on. The lieutenant has the right to have some time to develop his defense strategy." He straightens the packet of papers, evening out the pages.

"What about these?" the officer without stripes asks, shaking the bag of pills.

"Oh, for God's sake! Do me a favor!" Caracciolo explodes. "Throw them away!" Then, turning to Egitto: "Alessandro, you should know that we are considering a suspension of two to four months, plus a penalty that we'll discuss later. Pending a resolution, I am obliged to relieve you of your duties. I realize that you reside in the barracks, but you will have to find a temporary accommodation. I will do my best to see that the room is returned to you when you return to service."

"It's not necessary, Colonel." Egitto says it without having planned to. There it is, then, a new opportunity to change his life.

Caracciolo is visibly disappointed. "What do you mean?"

"I accept the maximum suspension. And you don't have to worry about the room. In fact, Colonel, there's something I'd like to talk to you about."

He manages with very little baggage: two crammed duffel bags and a backpack—living in the barracks has trained him to travel light. He'll decide later what to do about the furnishings he paid for out of his own pocket; for now they'll be stored in a warehouse in the outskirts.

Marianna came running at the news of his imminent departure. She's wearing a very long black sweater and heavy makeup that coarsens her pale complexion.

"They *can't* kick you out like this. It's crazy."

"They're not kicking me out. They're reassigning me. It's pretty normal, you know."

"Yeah, sure, *too bad* they didn't even give you the chance to choose. Retaliation, plain and simple. To send you to such an abominable place. Belluno, who's ever heard of it? I didn't even remember where it *was*, until today."

He didn't tell her the real truth. In fact, what he told her is his own rather sketchy version, full of omissions. All the energy he feels charged with isn't enough to make him admit to Marianna that it was he who decided to leave, to give it all up, as she'd said earlier on the phone. "They make excellent knödel up there," he jokes. "You know what that is?"

Marianna shakes her head. "Who cares."

She's sitting on the bed, her back against the wall, her shoes disrespectfully resting on the soft white mattress stripped of its sheets. Her chin tucked into her chest makes her look kind of sulky. Egitto isn't really sure why, but his sister still has an adolescent way of curling up into a fetal position. Maybe it's just that in his eyes she will remain eternally young, a little girl, even when she has gray hair and wrinkles. It occurs to him that this is only the second time she's set foot in his room: the day he'd arrived and now, when he's about to leave the barracks.

"I'm telling you that if we put it in the hands of an attorney, for sure—"

"No lawyers. Drop it."

Marianna toys with her fingers, trying to touch them together one by one. She's capable of supernatural concentration; her motor coordination is as perfect as it used to be. Even after all the battles she's involved him in, the affection that Egitto feels for her remains intact.

"Anyway, it's not fair that you're going so far away. And I don't understand the reason for all the rush, given that at the moment you're *suspended*."

"I have to look for a place to live. Get myself settled. You can come up as soon as I get squared away."

She jumps off the bed and casts a cold eye on the stripped mattress. "You *know* I don't drive on the highway. And since he's had back problems, Carlo can't handle long trips. He had an operation, in case you don't remember."

"That's right. I'd forgotten that."

All Egitto needs to do now is make yet another promise, fabricate the first nagging thought that will disturb the future that awaits him. "Then I'll come back here," he says. Though he adds: "As soon as I'm able to."

Marianna gives him a quick peck on the cheek. They've never been comfortable with effusive shows of affection, and they both remember the few fleeting ones they've exchanged, which marked events of extraordinary import. She starts toward the door. "I really have to go. It's *late*. She rummages absently in her handbag, then turns to look at him, knitting her brows. "Keep in mind, Alessandro, you've never been able to look after yourself very well."

On the contrary, at least judging from the way things start out, that doesn't seem to be the case. In Belluno, Egitto quickly finds an apartment to rent: not much bigger than four hundred square feet, but charming in its own way. It's the best he can afford with his pay cut.

He's surrounded by furnishings that he chose more for functionality than for aesthetics. They don't remind him of anything. In time, perhaps, each piece will acquire some meaning.

Before now he had never considered the idea of setting up house. Living in the barracks made him feel transitory and he took it for granted that it was his optimal state, the only one possible. He struggles to let go of that view of himself, but if he were to judge only by how he feels now—at peace, free, moderately serene, except for certain ups and downs—he'd begin to wonder whether he'd been wrong for a long time. It may be that Alessandro Egitto really is made to exist in the world like other human beings: at ease, buoyant.

Meanwhile, people are starting to know him in the neighborhood. When he reveals a piece of himself—to a guy at the café, the two lone clerks at the local bank, the woman in the laundry with a bandaged wrist following her recent surgery for carpal tunnel—he's repaid with an added grain of trust. It's a slow process, a meticulous labor of reclamation from suspicion: the construction of a security bubble whose only hypothetical perimeter is the white-rimmed circle of the Dolomites.

In his free time after getting the apartment fixed up, he serves as a volunteer with the local blood donor association. The mobile unit is parked in a different place each day, and from the open back door the lieutenant watches various forms of communal life unfold, lives far removed from combat, yet each related to a specific embodiment of the war. Not many people climb the metal steps to offer their arm to his needle; overall, the elderly appear more generous than their grandchildren, but it's only because they're wiser, he thinks—it's just that young people don't yet know how forcefully blood is pumped through the arteries, and how it gushes out when one of them is cut.

Every now and then he goes out to dinner with the male nurses he works with. They are quiet evenings, at least until alcohol loosens them up enough. The men don't feel the need to know about Egitto's past, or why he moved away without having a permanent job. For a short time there's even a girl. Egitto visits her apartment and she his, a couple of nights each. But she's still young, just twenty-one; a river of experience lies between them and they both know it. They stop seeing each other without shedding any tears.

Sometimes he wonders where he'd be now, if what actually happened hadn't happened there in the valley, if on a night like any other an Afghan driver, a man he didn't know, hadn't decided to drive off in a diesel truck, if Angelo Torsu hadn't been pitched out of a blown-up jeep, and if Irene Sammartino hadn't considered him responsible for all that. But they're idle questions, and he quickly decides to put them to rest.

He's drug-free. When he wakes up short of breath in the middle of the night and can't get back to sleep, he takes to pacing through the house, trying to control his breathing. If in the morning he's weak and listless and feels like he's in terra incognita, in another world, he falls back on these measures, waiting for it to pass. It may take days, but eventually it happens. Staying off drugs is neither a struggle nor an achievement. He doesn't rule out the fact that he might use them again, might entrust his well-being to disinterested science—somewhere there's a room with no exit, always waiting for him—but not now.

One weekend in March, without telling anyone, he takes a plane and flies to Cagliari. To get to Angelo Torsu's house he has to rent a car and travel west from the capital city. He goes the long way just to enjoy the coastal route. He drives slowly, drawn by the scenic views and the water roiling against the rocks.

On duty at the housing paid for by the city where Torsu has been living since he was discharged from the various rehab centers, he finds a young man with thick, unkempt black hair and heavy-lidded eyes. "I'm from the parish," he explains. "I come two afternoons a week, on

Thursdays and Saturdays. With Angelo there's not much to do anyhow. I can study almost the whole time."

Egitto has appeared in civilian clothes and said he was a friend (with the legal case pending with the soldier's family, he suspects his presence around there wouldn't be appreciated). Maybe that's why the volunteer feels at liberty to add, "This shitty war. I'm a pacifist, of course." He checks the clock, one of the few touches adorning the walls. "It's still not time for his nap to be over, but I can wake him. Angelo will be happy to have company. No one ever comes here."

"I'm in no hurry. I'll wait." Egitto pulls a chair out from the table, sits down.

"The same thing happens with the elderly," the volunteer continues. "Those of us in the parish also go to nursing homes, you know. After the first few months, people lose interest. There's only one girl who keeps coming. Fairly often, I mean. Her name is Elena, do you know her?"

"I'm afraid not."

"She's a pretty girl. A little chubby." He waits for Egitto to shake his head no again. "Anyway, she sits with Angelo and reads him books. She doesn't care whether he understands or not, she goes on reading." He toys with a strand of hair falling over his forehead, leaving it sticking straight up on his head for a second. "How long has it been since you've seen him?"

"More than a year."

Since October two years ago, to be precise, since Torsu's body, wrapped in a silver thermal blanket, was taken up into the sky and on board a Black Hawk with machine guns on both sides. But he can't bring himself to admit that to the pacifist.

"Then you'll find he's changed a lot, Mr. . . . ?"

"Egitto. Alessandro."

The young man's face darkens. He studies him for a few seconds, as if he's made a connection. Maybe he knows all about it. Egitto prepares himself for his reaction. "Are you a soldier too?"

"I'm a doctor."

"And those burns, how did you get them?"

So, a misunderstanding. Egitto smiles at him, anticipating the apologies he imagines will soon be delivered. He touches his face. "No, these have nothing to do with it."

The young man is visibly curious, but too polite to insist. "Tell me one thing, Doctor," he asks instead. "How did Angelo manage to disappear like that?"

"Disappear?"

"He . . . went away. As if he had made up his mind to. At least that's what I think. He's hiding away somewhere and doesn't want to come out anymore. How can that be, Doctor?"

All of a sudden Egitto feels tired, exhausted from the trip. "I don't know," he says.

The volunteer shakes his head. People expect a doctor to provide all the answers. "Anyway, the Lord knows where he is."

Then they go on waiting, in silence, until the hands of the clock mark four on the dot. The young man snaps his fingers. "It's time. I'll go wake him."

He returns after a few minutes, holding Angelo Torsu by the elbow, not as if he had to support him, more as if to guide him. Egitto wonders if the slight movement of the soldier's lips is an attempt to welcome him, a smile maybe, but he realizes that he keeps doing it. The lieutenant stands up, straightening his jacket, and takes Torsu's hand to shake it.

"Bring him near the window," the volunteer suggests. "He likes to look out. Right, Angelo?"

Egitto isn't capable of conversing with someone who doesn't respond; he feels too awkward. The same thing happens to him at gravesides, especially Ernesto's; it also happens with newborns and even with patients groggy from anesthesia. And though no one is observing him with Angelo Torsu now in the bare living room—the volunteer has withdrawn to the kitchen to leave them alone—he's unable to utter a word. So they remain silent. They simply stand there, side by side, in front of the window.

An army badge is pinned to the corporal major's robe. A fellow soldier must have brought it to him who knows how long ago; then no one bothered to take it off. Egitto wonders if he likes it. More likely he's completely indifferent to it. We take it for granted that a person who doesn't say otherwise is grateful for any tie with his past life, and for our attention, that he wants to go over to the window just because we decide to take him there, but we don't really know that. Maybe Torsu just wants to sit in his room in peace, by himself.

He can still see. Or at least his pupils contract when the light grows more intense. It's the overly smooth skin of his cheeks and neck that make his face incongruous. They took a flap of skin from his backside and grafted it onto his face. A miracle of modern surgery—an abomination. Torsu's body functions, but as if it were uninhabited now. He incessantly chews something between his teeth that isn't there, like a piece of tough meat: the words that for months he hasn't been able to pronounce. Other than that he seems tranquil, watching the street where cars rarely pass by. *The Lord knows where he is.* Someone has to know.

Egitto stays for what seems like an appropriate amount of time. He has the impression that his breathing and Torsu's are now in sync. He doesn't know if one of them has followed the other or if they reached that synchronicity together. When the absurdity of being in that house becomes unbearable, Egitto picks up the bag he brought with him. He takes out a wrapped rectangular box and hands it to the soldier. When he doesn't take it, Egitto balances it on the windowsill. "They're jelly beans," he says. "There was a period when they were all I could eat. I hope you like them too." He studies Torsu's face, looking for a sign.

The soldier ruminates, absent. Maybe he should tear off the paper, take a jelly bean, and make him taste it. Better to let the volunteer do it, though. "I'll take you back to your room. You must be tired."

He won't come back a second time. What he'll do, for a few years, will be to send the corporal major a box of candy identical to this one for Christmas, along with a brief note of greeting, until they're returned to him with a nondelivery notice from the post office; then he won't attempt to find out the new address. That, along with a portion of his salary, will be the only remaining bond with the man he sentenced to death, the man whose life he saved. He'll let time act on his remorse, slowly wearing it down.

After the four-month suspension the day comes for him to resume service. He's a little nervous as he takes the street leading uphill to the barracks of the Seventh Alpine Regiment. The first day of high school, his thesis defense before graduation, the Hippocratic oath: it's that kind of agitation, which bewilders and revitalizes him. *Emotion* would be a more fitting term than *agitation*, but he still uses that word with restraint.

He stops for a moment, just before his armpits start to perspire. He looks up at the gray massif of the Schiara. The clouds are huddled around the peak, as if they were conferring. Whereas in Torino the mountains were a distant border that emerged and vanished depending on the smog, whereas in Gulistan they were a forbidding wall, here in Belluno he could reach out and touch them.

The soldier at the guardhouse raises his hand in salute and remains stock-still as the lieutenant walks by him. Egitto is escorted to his new office on the first floor of the main building. Someone in the room next door is talking on the phone with a marked Trentino accent, laughing often. Egitto goes to the window overlooking the parade ground, which is surrounded by poplars. It's a good location; he'll like it here.

"Lieutenant?"

An NCO stands in the doorway uncertainly, looking like he's about to knock. Who knows why he hasn't and why he's called to him instead. "Yes, Corporal?"

"Welcome, sir. The commander has asked for you. Would you please follow me?"

Egitto picks up his hat, which he'd placed on the table, and adjusts it slantwise on his head. They go up two floors, then halfway down a hall. Here the corporal stops in front of an open door. "He's in here," he says, motioning for Egitto to enter.

Colonel Giacomo Ballesio puts down the sandwich that he was clenching with both hands. He wipes his mouth with the back of his hand, then leaps up, bumping the edge of the desk with his belt buckle—the lamp teeters and a pen rolls to the floor. Ballesio pays no attention to that little mishap. He throws his arms open, joyfully. "Lieutenant Egitto, finally! Come in, come in. Sit down. Let's talk."

Translator's Note

The military rankings used in the novel are English translations of the Italian ranks, which differ from NATO equivalents. For example, many of the soldiers bear the rank of *caporalmaggiore*, corporal major or simply corporal, as opposed to NATO's private first class or simply private. Other examples are marshal (*maresciallo*) versus NATO's master sergeant, or first corporal major (*primo caporalmaggiore*) versus NATO's lance corporal.

The *genio* is the Corps of Engineers, the unit responsible for military civil engineering projects (fortifications, trenches, etc.) as well as explosives detection. The bomb disposal unit is part of the *genio*.

Little Trees or Arbre Magique are disposable air fresheners in the shape of a stylized evergreen tree, marketed for use in cars. They are made of a material very similar to beer coasters and are produced in a variety of colors and scents.

The Lince is an armored four-wheel drive tactical vehicle produced by Iveco and adopted by the Italian Army. It is similar to a Humvee.

When Second Lieutenant Puglisi provokes a fight at the latrines by trying to get ahead of Corporal Major Di Salvo, he warns the corporal not to mess with him because he's from Catania. Di Salvo, undaunted, retorts that he's from Lamezia. Catania is in Sicily, Lamezia Terme in Calabria.

The third of Franz Liszt's Three Concert Études is usually known as *Un sospiro*, Italian for "A sigh."

The Croma, the car Egitto's family affectionately nicknamed *La Musona*, is a sedan produced by Fiat. The first model appeared in 1985.

The expression *luna mendax* (lying moon) is a counterintuitive Latin mnemonic for remembering whether the moon is waxing or waning: When the moon looks like a D (fuller on the right), it's growing, *luna crescens* (you'd logically expect it to look like a C); when it looks like a C (fuller on the left), it's diminishing, *luna decrescens* (you'd expect it to look like a D).

Dari is the variety of Persian spoken in Afghanistan, where, along with Pashto, it is one of two official languages. Also known as Afghan Persian, Dari is mutually intelligible with Persian (Farsi) of Iran.

The Red Zone, outside the security bubble, is a term loosely applied to all unsecured areas beyond the range of a military post.

A hecatomb describes any immense slaughter. In ancient Greece and Rome, it referred to a public sacrifice offered to the gods, consisting of a hundred oxen.

The Schiara is a mountain in the Dolomites in northern Italy, near the town of Belluno.